THE SLAB

by
Jeff Mariotte

THE SLAB

Written by
Jeff Mariotte

Illustrations by
Tommy Lee Edwards

IDW Publishing
San Diego
www.idwpublishing.com

The Slab

Book design by Cindy Chapman
Edited by Kris Oprisko

Published by
Idea + Design Works, LLC
2645 Financial Court, Suite E
San Diego, CA 92117

www.idwpublishing.com

ISBN: 1-932382-07-0

06 05 04 03   5 4 3 2 1

Printed in Canada

A book of this scope owes much to many people. Trying to prioritize them is hopeless,
but thanks to Ted Adams, Robbie Robbins, Cindy Chapman and the IDW gang; Tara O'Shea;
Chris and Scott and Jack and Nancy and John and Mel; Wallace Stegner, Charles Bowden,
Edward Abbey and other chroniclers of America's desert lands; everyone who's braved
those deserts with me; my fellow booksellers everywhere; Tommy Lee Edwards; Howard
Morhaim; and of course my family, near and far, especially Maryelizabeth, Holly, and David.

For Maryelizabeth
-JM

part 1
kenneth butler

The raven's wing feathers gleamed, black and wet looking in the morning sun, like ink freshly spilled from the bottle. The bird walked with a stiff-legged gait, wings held to its sides as if pinned there. To maintain equilibrium, just before thrusting its pointed beak into the warm, oozing mass at the side of the roadway, it raised one wing like a high-wire artist's balancing arm and jabbed downward with its head.

The raven had no way of knowing—and its tiny brain would not have been able to comprehend, even had it witnessed the event—how this morning meal had come to be here at the edge of the desert road that ran north-south, skirting the eastern shore of the Salton Sea. The raven hadn't seen the jackrabbit waiting patiently on the side of the highway at dawn, hadn't seen the red 1974 Camaro that came barreling up the road twenty miles an hour faster than the posted speed limit, certainly hadn't seen the driver of the Camaro spot the jackrabbit and swerve, aiming for the creature instead of trying to dodge it. The raven hadn't seen the jackrabbit twist mid-stride, with a vain hope of avoiding the onrushing fender. The raven hadn't even heard the whine of the Camaro's engine as it disappeared up the road or the laughter of the driver and his passengers as the jackrabbit twitched and died in the sun's first light.

The raven was only pleased to have found the meal. A bit of intestine clamped firmly in its beak, the raven hopped backward two steps, cocked its head both ways to look for predators, and then, catching sight of an approaching vehicle, took flight.

Below, the jackrabbit's warm corpse waited for other scavengers—insect, avian, and mammal—to clean its bones. Death at the edge of the Salton Sea was nothing new, and certainly it was nothing that rabbits or ravens contemplated in any way. It simply was.

Carter Haynes had an office in a high-rise building in San Diego with windows overlooking the harbor, the bay, and the Coronado bridge. His receptionist was hot and wore skirts that showed most of her thigh, he drove a Lincoln Town Car, his condo had an even better view than his office, and his bank account was healthy. The national economy was taking a nose-dive and terrorists had attacked American shores, but Carter was, so far, insulated from those events. And the President was talking about cutting capital gains taxes. Life was good.

Today, Carter was far from that office and that condo and the wife who shared it with him. He had, a short while ago, driven past a water tower on which a line was painted to delineate sea level, and that line was far above the highway. His Town Car's

A/C kept the valley's heat at bay but the day would unquestionably be a scorcher. Vivaldi on CD isolated him from the outside world; the Four Seasons, moving through their progressive stages, formed a protective bubble around him as he buzzed through the unfriendly landscape. Here, in Southern California's agricultural heart, Carter felt supremely out of place. He was city folk personified. He was a real estate developer.

The only sense that needed to extend out of the car and into the farmland was sight. He watched fields of alfalfa and lettuce and sugar beets whipping by, saw tractors churning earth, giant stacks of hay under green or blue tarpaulins, insects spinning crazily around the car in the wake of its passing.

At El Centro he pulled off the interstate and onto the 111, which would lead him up through Brawley and Calipatria, up along the western edge of the Salton Sea to his final destination for today, Salton Estates. This was not his first trip to Salton Estates, and it would not be his last, not by a long shot. Carter Haynes was about to become a regular visitor to Salton Estates. That was the bad news, as far as he was concerned. The good news was that the visits would, ultimately, pad his bank account even more, putting him in a position to buy the building his condo he was located in, if that was what he chose to do with his wealth.

Carter knew it was probably shallow, but hey, somebody had to be the richest man in San Diego. Currently it was probably someone in the computer business, or maybe biotech. It had been real estate in the past, though, and he wanted to see that it was again. Once he'd achieved that goal then he'd see about having kids, raising a family, all that other stuff that just got in the way of getting up a good head of greed.

Anyway, a man had to have priorities.

Through a finger-sized part in dusty Venetian blinds, Lieutenant Kenneth Butler of the Imperial County Sheriff's Office, Salton Estates substation, watched Billy Cobb climb out of his squad car, hitch up his Sam Browne belt, and stride into the office. Deputy Cobb was tall, six-five, if his employment physical was to be believed, and watching him get out of a car always reminded Ken of a small piece of paper unfolding into a large one. This was only one of the ways that Billy Cobb amused Ken. Most of the others, though, Ken understood, had to do with what he considered to be Billy's somewhat slow mental processes, and the fact that the ICSO had given Billy a gun and a badge sort of put a damper on how much entertainment value he could derive from that.

But, he reflected, in Salton Estates, with a budget roughly the size of the average high school sophomore's allowance, you had to work with the tools you got. This substation was by far the smallest in the county, but Ken Butler had needed a Deputy and Billy Cobb was willing to work for him. And—so far, at least—he hadn't killed anybody.

Ken tapped on his desk as he sat down in his swivel chair. Knock wood.

The front door opened and Billy Cobb let himself in. His uniform was clean and crisp, but Ken could smell the cloud of cologne Billy inhabited as soon as the Deputy was inside the door.

"What's up, Boss?" he asked. The greeting was either ritual or the only greeting Billy had ever mastered. Ken hadn't decided which.

"You need to get up to the Slab," Ken told him. "Carrie Provost called, says she found a skull up there this morning."

Billy Cobb angled his head, the way tall people did sometimes. He'd have been a good-looking kid if he weren't so damn stupid, Ken thought. Stupid people, it shows in the eyes. No spark there, no gleam of intelligence. Billy's eyes were practically cobalt blue, but empty.

"A human skull?"

"What she says. Of course, would she recognize the difference if she was looking at a human skull or a monkey skull, that's the question."

"Or a bobcat or a fucking bighorn sheep," Billy added.

"Just check it out," Ken instructed. "Try to calm Carrie down, she's a little freaked out. And if it is human, tag it, bag it and bring it here."

Billy Cobb saluted lazily and turned on his heel. Ken Butler watched him go, then hoisted himself out of his chair and crossed to the door, opening it to get some air in and chase the smell of Paco Rabane out. He stood in front of the Sheriff's office and watched Billy's squad car roar off into the morning sun.

It would be another hot one, he knew. They always were, this time of year. September in California's Imperial Valley. The mercury would push past the ninety degree mark by mid-morning and rest in the low hundreds the remainder of the afternoon. That was a relief, though—in dead of summer the temperature could climb to a hundred and twenty, and passed the century mark an average of a hundred and ten days a year. The air outside held a lingering scent of dead fish from the nearby Salton Sea, mixed with the agricultural smells of the neighboring communities. The rich, fecund organic stink made even Billy's cologne seem like a reasonable choice.

Ken raised a hand to a passing van that he didn't recognize–a Dodge Ram 250, the bronze paint of which had oxidized to a reddish mud color–turned, and went back inside his office. Time to switch on the fan, try to get a jump on the heat before his mid-morning visitor showed up.

The van passed through the rather magnanimously-titled Salton Estates in a heartbeat. Penny Rice barely noticed the collection of dusty, sun-bleached single-story buildings. The overall color scheme was monochromatic; except for the blue of the sky reflected in the sea, almost the entire landscape—mud and rocks and bushes and buildings—was the same flat ocher color.

One minute the van rumbled through desert scenery, the Chocolate Mountains hunkering on the right, a low muddy slope dropping to the gentle lap of the Salton Sea on the left, to the west as they drove up the north/south highway. They'd already dropped off Larry Melton, down toward the south end of the range, and Dieter Holtz near Niland. Now it was Penny's turn.

Mick Beachum had the wheel, and the passenger seat next to him was empty. Penny used the back seat to spread out and do a final triple-check of her pack and everything she'd be carrying in with her, but she also avoided the front for another, more personal, reason. Mick had been getting more aggressive in his attentions lately—had, she was sure, arranged the drop points specifically so that the two of them would drive this last leg alone. She wanted the bulk of the seat back between them; a symbolic shield if not much of an actual one.

"You sure you're okay about this?" he asked, craning his head to look at her in the back seat instead of watching the road. He had pulled off pavement a few minutes before, and they bounced over a rutted washboard track heading past the Slab and toward the Chocolates. "Not nervous?"

"Of course I'm a little nervous," Penny replied. "You know, trespassing on military land and all. Not so much about getting bombed or anything—I've had bombs thrown at me before. It's no fun, but I'm still here, right?"

"Can't argue with that," Mick said. He turned back to the front just in time to keep the van from lurching off the road. "You got your cell, your CB, and your GPS, so we can get to you in a hurry if we need to?"

"I'm locked and loaded."

He was quiet for a few minutes, paying attention to the topo map unfolded on the passenger seat, comparing the lines on it with the jeep roads and washes that intersected the dirt path they drove on. He must have made the right choices, Penny reflected, because in a few minutes he had crossed the cement-banked Coachella Canal at one of the siphons and stopped before an invisible line marked only by signs on tall wooden posts. Here there was no wire fence, like the ones they'd found farther south when they dropped off Dieter and Larry. Penny read the signs, letters in stark black and red on a white background:

DANGER
LIVE BOMBING AREA
UNEXPLODED ORDNANCE
KEEP OUT

in English and Spanish, which did nothing to calm her nerves. She'd been vaguely jittery since they'd passed through Salton Estates, and more so since they crossed the side-road that led up to the Slab. Her destination lay on the other side of the imaginary line, inside the LIVE BOMBING AREA, and while it was true that she had a certain amount of experience with being shot at and having, as she put it, bombs thrown at her, thanks to the U.S. Army and, in particular, President George H. W. Bush and what she still believed was his deference to the gigadollars the petroleum business had put toward his election, it wasn't an experience she was especially anxious to repeat. Now, of course, the man's idiot son was in the same office, put there by the same petrodollar interests. And damned if there wasn't another war in the offing, though this one far more vague and uncertain, against an enemy who just might be the guy next door.

Climbing from the van, she realized that her uniform hadn't changed that much—she was wearing olive greens and tans, shorts and a tank-top with an off-white long-sleeved cotton shirt pulled over it and tied at the waist, thick olive socks under tan hiking boots. She'd packed her backpack much as she'd learned in Basic. She carried, as she had in the Gulf, plenty of water.

The big difference—besides who signed her paycheck—was that, in the Gulf, when she'd been blown up, it had been by a mine the enemy had planted. Now, she was crossing the line intentionally, leaving behind everyone she knew to venture, illegally, into a bombing range operated by her own government, during a time of high alert and roaring tension.

She settled her backpack on her back, tapped the canteens clipped to her belt. Full. She was ready.

And Mick had, of course, scrambled out of the van instead of just driving off. Typical, she thought. One thing you could say about him, he was persistent.

"You know where you're going?" he asked.

She gestured straight ahead, where the road they'd come up on continued, but more primitively, overgrown with desert brush. "Right up there. Into the hills, and then I look for a good place to make camp."

He nodded, his blond dreadlocks swaying with the motion of his head. "That's it, then," he said. "Hug for luck."

Hug for luck my ass, she thought. But to piss off the guy who was supposed to come and get her if she ran into trouble seemed, at the very least, counterproductive. Once the project was finished, she'd talk to him, set him straight. For the tenth time. She moved toward his outspread arms.

He pulled her close, enjoying, she guessed, the swell of her breasts against his chest. He smelled like sweat and garlic, and his unshaven cheek scraped her face like sandpaper.

"You take care in there, Pen," he said with what seemed like genuine sincerity. "Don't take any stupid chances."

"We didn't take stupid chances, we'd have to cancel the whole project, Mick," she said. "Don't worry about me. I'll be fine."

Which, she knew, was nothing but the worst sort of wishful thinking. She'd taken the steps necessary to ensure that she would be fine, inasmuch as they were under her control. But the bigger questions, of course, were not at all within her sphere of influence. As she walked away from Mick, across the unseen line and up the primitive jeep road toward the darker-brown hills ahead, she felt Mick's gaze on her ass, like an unwelcome hand, until he was finally out of sight.

Billy Cobb hated the way the washboard road juddered the squad car. The road up from town was mostly paved, but once you got back into the maze of concrete slabs that made up the area folks just called the Slab, the road wasn't maintained, and then even that primitive paved road petered out and became nothing but dirt and rock. A man needed a sport-ute out here, and that was a fact. Butler, of course, had his old Bronco, which he seemed to love like the wife he didn't have. And, Billy thought as he pulled the car onto the Slab, it really should have been the Lieutenant checking out something like a human skull being discovered, not a Deputy, even though he knew that Ken was supposed to be meeting with that real estate guy today.

Man had a fine brain, and he was fair. But he was shy, Billy knew, not hide-in-a-closet shy but it was trouble just the same. It got in the way of doing his job sometimes.

The good part of it was that there would come a day when he would step down, and then Billy would be there, next in line, logical choice. From there it was only a few steps up to a job down in El Centro, maybe eventually Imperial County Sheriff. Sheriff Cobb had a natural ring to it, and when he was Sheriff he could requisition funds from the County to buy himself a new Expedition every year if he wanted it.

And Carrie Provost! Jesus God, why did she have to be the one to find it? If ever there was a reason that humans should be muzzled, she was it—the woman could talk all morning about the texture of her Corn Flakes. Give her something genuinely interesting, like finding a skull, and Billy figured there was a good possibility that he'd still be here come nightfall listening to her jaw about her discovery.

He slowed down as he wove his way among the mobile homes, trailers, buses, broken down cars and camper shells that made up the Slab. There were only a few locals out this morning, it seemed. Old Hal Shipp sat outside of his RV in a busted-up lawn chair, the kind with the ribbons of contrasting colors woven together, but half the ribbons on this one seemed to be sprung and trailing on the ground. Billy raised a hand to the old man, but got no response. Shipp's wife, Virginia, stepped out of their ancient Minnie Winnie—wheels gone, rust-covered cinderblocks propping it up—with two tumblers of lemonade on a plastic tray in her hands. She smiled and nodded her head at Billy. She was a good woman—a saint, the way she put up with Hal, whose memory was shot and who, half the time, thought he was back fighting Nazis in World War Two. Billy touched the brim of his Smokey hat at her and kept going.

The Slab was a weird place, there was no getting around that. It was, literally, a series of vast slabs of cement poured on a flat stretch between the Chocolate Mountains and the Salton Sea. At the beginning of Hal Shipp's war, the military had decided that the best place to train troops to fight the Nazis in North Africa was in one of America's hottest and driest deserts. Imperial County fit that bill, and besides, this was California's ass end, where the waste-brown Colorado dribbled down into Mexico, so there'd been a few farmers in the Valley but mostly empty land, and no one to complain about the noise. They'd built a camp up here, then abandoned it right after the war. There was nothing left of it but the slabs now.

Flat and level, the slabs were a perfect parking place for recreational vehicles. So that's what they had become. But not primarily for tourists, although its population exploded during the winter months, with as many as two thousand snowbirds moving in and parking their mobile homes on any unclaimed stretch of cement or dirt. But during the hot months, most of the RVs here were, like the Shipps', permanent fixtures. People lived on the Slab year round–even though there were no services like water or plumbing or electricity and they had to drive into Niland to pick up their mail–most of them, because it was cheap. As in, free. No one taxed them, no one came around to collect rent or mortgage payments. Anyone who could afford a broken-down motor home and a generator to power it and some food at the market in Salton Estates or Niland could live there. The Slab attracted society's outcasts, retired folks, nudists, survivalists. A few drug dealers had set up shop there but they tended to be frowned upon, even ostracized. This was a white, conservative, blue-collar bunch, mostly, people tired of paying taxes and living by society's rules. Imperial County's only real concession to their existence was to send a school bus up, during the school year, to pick up the dozen or so young kids and haul them off to become educated.

One thing that had always struck Billy Cobb as strange, which he noticed again as he threaded between the RVs, was the yard sales. People hauled the most bizarre crap out of their homes and put it up for sale, and their neighbors bought it, putting their own crap up for sale to make room for it. This formed the basis, as far as Billy could see, of most of the cash economy of Slab society. Outside the Hudsons' Winnebago was a folded ping pong table with a sign taped to it offering it for sale for five dollars. Never mind that there wasn't a double-wide on the Slab with room inside it for a ping pong table. By the weekend, somebody would have bought it, and they'd set it up under the shade they made by jamming poles into the dirt a dozen feet from their trailer and stretching a sheet between them, and they'd drink beer and play ping pong for a couple of weeks until it got old, at which point they'd sell it to some other neighbor for the same five bucks.

In the past few days, Billy noted, patriotism had flourished like a fast-growing fungus among these people who had willingly turned their backs on governments large and small. Flags, those printed in the newspapers and taped to windows, small plastic ones hung on foot-long sticks, and even a few full-sized cloth ones, were everywhere in evidence, competing for space with animal skulls, faded Christmas lights that had never been plugged in, random graffiti and other attempts at personalizing the mass-produced housing these people lived in.

Carrie Provost's mobile home was the same as most of the others, in that it looked like it had been decorated by a coalition of the blind and the insane. An army of ceramic beings defended its ramparts: gnomes, trolls, elves, deer, sheep, geese, ducks, rabbits, and a single pig, on the side that Billy could see on his approach. Most of them were cracked or broken in some way—a good number of them having suffered bullet wounds somewhere along the way—but the pig looked brand new, pink and shiny in the morning sun.

Aluminum foil coated every window, which was not all that unusual in the desert. It deflected the heat that would otherwise be magnified by the window glass. In Carrie's case, though, Billy thought it might serve the secondary purpose of blocking the radio transmissions of invading aliens. He had heard that she'd covered the whole roof of the trailer with the stuff too, but had never cared enough to climb up and check.

On rusting wire hangers, she had hung a wide and bizarre variety of found items from the edge of her roof. Anything discovered in the desert seemed to be fair game. The hollowed-out shell of an ocotillo branch hung next to the skeleton of a small bird, next to the carcass of a television set with its picture tube blown out, next to a shredded tire. The overall effect was strangely disturbing, a kind of museum of litter and cast-offs that meant nothing to anyone but its curator. Billy was a little surprised that Carrie had made the effort to find a phone so she could report the skull, rather than simply hanging it from yet another coat hanger.

He parked the Crown Victoria in front of her place, got out, and sauntered up to the door. It had taken him a couple of months, once he'd decided on law enforcement as a career, to perfect the walk he wanted to use. He'd adapted it from a John Wayne walk he'd seen. He kept his legs somewhat stiff, moving at the hips, arms swinging freely. He felt that this walk gave the impression of a coiled jungle beast, ready to run or strike at any moment, and emphasized the spread of his shoulders and the depth of his chest, two features of which he was especially proud. The chest, in particular, was the result of many hours on a weight bench in the back yard of his parents' home in Brawley. He didn't know if Carrie Provost was watching, or anyone else for that matter, but he didn't care. The walk was second nature by now.

Carrie had a screen door pulled closed, with an open interior door. Billy tapped on the screen. "Carrie!" he called. "Ms. Provost! You here?"

"Coming!" Carrie Provost called from inside the mobile home. There was a clattering noise, like sheet metal hitting a concrete floor, and then she appeared in the doorway a moment later. "Sorry about the racket," she said. "I don't have room to turn around in here."

"We can talk outside if you'd rather, ma'am. It's Deputy Cobb." Truth to tell, he'd rather she came out than to set foot inside her place.

"Oh, you're here about that skeleton head?"

"The skull you found, yes ma'am."

She stepped down from inside, pushing open the screen. Carrie Provost was in her fifties, and she looked like she'd lived in the desert the entire time. Her skin was dark and leathered, muscles stringy, hair bleached and limp. She had big stained teeth and her eyes had that perpetual smoker's squint, as if there was always smoke drifting into them even when she didn't have a cigarette going. She wore a baggy T-shirt with a Marlboro logo on it, a giveaway at some long ago county fair or supermarket promotion, and her thin legs protruded from cut-off jeans. Rubber flip-flops on her scarred and wrinkled feet completed the ensemble.

"Can I see it, ma'am? The skull?"

"Oh, sure, just a minute," Carrie answered. She climbed the two steps back into the trailer. Every time the screen door flopped open the cloying stench of cigarettes wafted out, as if someone had emptied an ashtray into Billy's mouth. He hated cigarette smoke.

Inside, there was another loud metallic rattling and then a muffled "Sorry!" from Carrie. A moment later, she reappeared with a plastic supermarket bag in her hands.

"Here you go. I put it in this Vons bag to keep it clean." The skull's outline could clearly be seen imprinting the hanging bag. She handed it to Billy, and he carefully set the bag down on the cement slab and opened it.

He was no forensic pathologist, but even through the scorch marks and black smudges of ash, the skull definitely looked human to him. A gold tooth shining up at

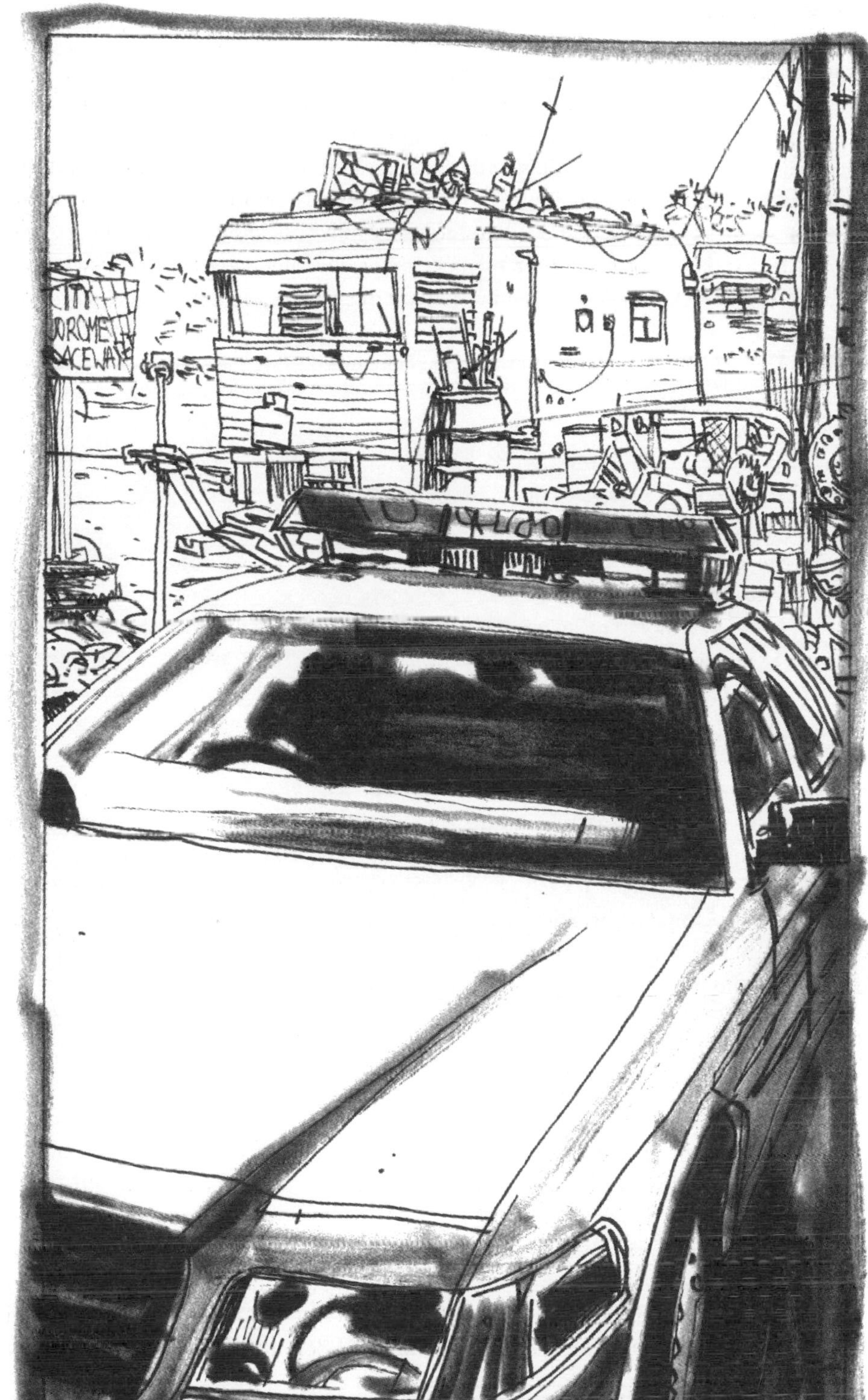
CITY
DROME
ACEWAY

him from the lower jaw clinched it. And the neat circular hole in the forehead, in combination with the larger, jagged one at the back of the skull, pointed to a cause of death. Billy felt his stomach flop like one of the Salton's dying fish. This had just become a murder case, and he was the first officer on the scene.

"Looks like somebody punched his ticket, don't it, Billy?" Carrie said. "That's a bullet hole, right? I seen that on TV before. Exit wound out the back."

"I'll have to take it to the lab to be sure, ma'am," Billy said, not wanting her amateur deduction to cloud his own professional judgment. "But it does look that way at a glance, yes."

"Well, I'm no expert," Carrie went on. "Just know what I see and hear, if you know what I mean."

"Yes, ma'am. Can you tell me how you happened to find it?"

"Well, you know the fire pit, right?"

The fire pit was where, most nights, residents of the Slab gathered around a roaring bonfire to talk, drink beer, sometimes watch the "fireworks," which is how they referred to military bombing runs in the Chocolates, and generally enjoy their freedom from both taxation and representation. "Yes ma'am."

"Well, I was over there last night, at the fire pit. Just talking and, you know, hanging out with the neighbors, having a couple of beers, I guess. Anyways, I got close to the fire once to poke a stick in it, shove some logs around and all. And that's when I thought I seen it, or something anyway that didn't look quite right. It was hot and all, though, so I just left it until this morning. Then I went back and poked through the ashes a little, and there it was. That gold tooth just about glowed at me. I pulled it out of there and took it home and then went down to the Lippincotts' because they have a cell phone, and I called the Sheriff. You don't suppose it was Arabs put it there, do you? You know, like in New York?"

It took Billy a moment to make the connection, since he didn't recall any Arabs putting a skull into a fire pit anywhere in New York. But then he decided that she must have meant the Islamic terrorists who had attacked the World Trade Center.

"No, ma'am," he assured her. "I don't believe it was. Do you remember who was at the fire pit when you found it?"

"I didn't say anything at the time, because, like I said, I wasn't sure what I seen, entirely. But the usual group was there, I guess, the Hudsons and the Lippincotts, Jim Trainor, the Shipps, Rusty Martin, Lettie Bosworth, Hank Dunn...I guess the McNultys were there for a bit." She stopped, chewed her lower lip for a second. "But wouldn't it make more sense to make a list of who wasn't there? I mean, if you put somebody's head in a fire pit, you probably wouldn't want to be there when it was found, would you?"

"That depends on when it was put there, I guess," Billy replied. "You don't know that, do you? Unless you check it every morning?"

Carrie Provost hesitated before answering, as if considering whether or not to give away a secret. "You find some great things in there once in a while," she said finally.

She pointed to a metal lunchbox suspended on one of the coat hangers. It was fire-blackened and the plastic handle had melted, but it was probably from the 1960s, and the cast of Gilligan's Island was still recognizable on the side. "I found that in the fire pit once. And money, now and again, coins, you know, not bills."

Billy found himself oddly moved by this side of the woman. A little frightened, but moved just the same. "Yes, ma'am," he said. "I'll tell you what. If you can write me out two lists—one of the people you know were there last night, and one of the people you know who weren't there last night, why then, I'll check them out and maybe we'll get someplace."

"I guess I can do that," she agreed.

"I can pick them up at the meeting tonight, if that's all right."

"Oh, the big meeting." She nodded. "At the fire pit, yeah, I'll be there."

I'll just bet you will, Billy thought. As he headed back to his squad car, he shook his head slowly. The Slab, he thought. What a weird fucking place.

"Who was that?" Harold Shipp asked his wife. The world called him Hal, but she invariably went with Harold.

"Who was what?" Virginia countered.

"Who you just waved to."

It took Virginia a minute to realize what he meant. That deputy, Billy Cobb, had driven past almost fifteen minutes before, and she'd "waved" as best she could with a tray of cold lemonades in her hands. He'd responded by tipping his hat, as best he could while driving a car. She had thought the whole exchange had slipped by Harold unnoticed, but apparently he had seen it.

"Oh, that was the Sheriff's Deputy, Billy Cobb," she said once she'd puzzled out what he was asking about.

"Cobb?" Harold repeated. "He's from Georgia, isn't he?"

"No, I don't think so. I think he's from El Centro or someplace. He's a local boy."

"Ty Cobb's from Georgia. The Georgia Peach."

"The baseball player?"

"That's right," Harold said, chuckling at some private memory. "And I knew a Cobb in the service, James Cobb, I think. He wasn't from Georgia, though. Minnesota or Wisconsin, somewhere cold. He loved it when it was cold out, and damp. Sweated like a pig when the sun came out and warmed things up."

"He wouldn't like the weather here," Virginia observed.

Harold looked around, as if he needed to visually catalog the air temperature, which was already in the high eighties. After a moment of that, he looked back at Virginia, and she could tell by his blank expression that he'd lost the thread of the conversation. He covered by lifting his lemonade to his lips and taking a long drink. She didn't push it. She had learned by now that pushing it would only result in anger or an argument, and she didn't want that. It was heartbreaking enough to see his memory go, bit by bit, as if, at eighty-one, his brain had decided to shut down cell by cell. She had grown tired of compounding the hurt by pointing it out when he couldn't remember something or follow a conversation. All she wanted to do now, and until the day he died, was to protect him from harm or pain. So she shrugged off his lapses, and she took care of him as best she could.

"Lemonade tastes funny," Harold said. He moved the cup away and a little trail of lemonade ran down from his mouth to his chin. She dabbed it with her finger, and his hand caught hers, his touch impossibly gentle, his workingman's hands restored with age almost to the softness they must have had in his infancy. He held her hand to his lips and he kissed it. For the hundredth time that day—and it wasn't even noon yet— Virginia Shipp's heart skipped and swelled and broke all at the same time.

Chapter 02

Ken Butler had poured himself a second cup of coffee, but it had tasted funny and he'd opened the back door and poured it out into the little weed-choked lot behind his office. The Salton Estates substation was in what had once been a bait-and-tackle shop right on the main highway, and the bait shop owner had tried to grow a garden out back. When the Sheriff's Office took over, they'd gutted the place except for a walk-in cooler that had been converted to a holding cell, and brought in a couple of desks and a teletype machine. Now Ken had a computer, a fax machine, and a couple of telephones to call his own as well. It was no high-tech wonderland but it did the job.

As he shook the coffee out of his mug he looked down the slope toward the cocoa brown waters of the Salton Sea, two hundred and some feet below sea level. After the little weed patch, there was nothing between here and the lake's edge but mud. Even from here, he could see the glint of dead fish on the surface of the mud, and their smell was ever-present. He was used to that stink, though, and it wasn't as bad as when the algae bloomed and decomposed or selenium and other chemicals in the water killed off birds by the thousands, so it wasn't the Sea's odor that had made the coffee taste funny. It was only now, thinking it through, that he realized it was a coppery taste in the back of his throat that had been with him unnoticed since he woke up this morning.

The taste was at once familiar and rare, like a species that a birdwatcher has seen pictures of many times but only glimpsed once in the wild. Rare, because it had only come to him four or five times—five, he corrected, because he could still enumerate them—over the course of his fifty-two years on God's green Earth. The first time had been on that day in Vietnam, the day he still thought of as the day in the tunnel, though he'd been a tunnel rat and had spent a good many days in tunnels.

Ken also thought of that day in a different way—as the day the magic came. And when he'd tasted this peculiar flavor since, like fresh pennies caught inside his throat, those too had been on days when the magic had come back.

Which made today suddenly crystallize for him. Something would happen today, something strange and miraculous. It might be good or bad, but it was on the way, and there was no dodging it. Just over a week ago bad magic had struck in New York and Arlington, Virginia, but that hadn't been his magic. He was sure there was no relation to the strange taste in his mouth now.

He started to look back over everything that had happened since he'd rolled off his rack, just in case it had already taken place and he'd missed it. But he didn't get far at that before the front door opened behind him.

Glancing at his watch, he realized that it had to be his eleven o'clock appointment, right on time. He turned away from the Sea, closed the back door, and faced his visitor.

"Mr. Haynes," he said.

"Sheriff Butler."

"Lieutenant," Ken corrected. "There's only one Sheriff, and he doesn't leave El Centro all that often."

"Sorry, Lieutenant." Carter Haynes stepped forward, hand out like a politician looking for a baby to kiss or a wad of cash to grab. Haynes dressed like a politician, too. His charcoal gray, pin-striped suit must have cost more than a thousand dollars—Ken knew that he, a man who tended toward boot-cut Wranglers when out of uniform, had a tendency to underestimate the cost of fine clothes—and the mere fact that Haynes wore a suit out here in the middle of the desert marked him for a fraud or a fool, in Ken Butler's eyes. His thick black hair was carefully cut and combed off his face. He had intelligent brown eyes, widely spaced, and a fixed smile that looked genuine at the same time that it looked like a permanent feature. There was something a little unsettling in his skin, though, which was extraordinarily sallow, kind of unhealthy-looking beneath a layer of tan that looked so uniform is must have come from a salon rather than from being outside, and lips that were naturally as red as if they'd been lipsticked. An interesting study in contradictions, Ken thought. Carter Haynes came across as a man to be reckoned with.

But not one to be trusted.

He pointed to the guest chair across from his desk, a wooden schoolteacher's chair. "Have a seat, Mr. Haynes. You have a good drive out? San Diego, isn't it?"

"That's right. It was very pleasant, thanks. Nice to get out of town occasionally." Carter sat down in the guest chair, his lean frame making it look comfortable somehow. Ken sat behind his own desk, suddenly conscious of his own boots, worn at the heel and toe-scuffed, in the presence of this expensively-dressed visitor.

"Guess I'm just a country man at heart," he said. "City living didn't agree with me."

"It's certainly different than life out here."

"But you want to build out here."

"That's right," Carter said. "And I can tell you why. It's because I know what life's like in the city. I know there are plenty of people, people like me in San Diego and Los Angeles and Orange County. People with plenty of money, but who are tired of the rat race, tired of the traffic and congestion and noise and crime. We want a place where we can get away from that, a place where there's quiet and natural beauty and peace of mind. We could afford Palm Springs or Palm Desert, but those places are getting overbuilt. What we want is a place like Salton Estates. Especially now, when those who can afford to might be looking for a place they can go that's out of harm's way. Nasty business back east, right?"

"Sure is," Ken answered. People who knew he was a Vietnam vet kept wanting to talk to him about the nation's war plans. He was tired of it, so he steered the conversation back to the matter at hand and away from the terrorist attacks that had dominated the national conversation since that awful Tuesday morning.

"You're planning to build on the Slab."

"Exactly."

"You've managed to purchase that land?"

"That's right," Haynes said. "The government's been doing a lot of unloading lately. Closing military bases, selling off land they don't need or want. I happened to own some land they did want, near Yellowstone. We made a deal."

It wasn't Ken's place to criticize business decisions, but he knew that developers had come into the area before, hungry to make a killing, and they usually were lucky to get away with the clothes on their backs. Salton Estates had, in fact, been named for one of those would-be resort developments. Roads had been graded and paved, lots carefully marked off, a marina and a couple of model houses built—but not enough people had wanted to buy into a beachfront resort where the sea might rise up and flood your home, dead fish would wash up onto your property every morning, and the chemical stink would keep you inside half the time. The developers had run out of money and interest. The marina was flooded now, the model houses stripped for parts, and the streets and lots mostly vacant.

"You know other people have tried to build resorts out here, right? Without notable success."

Carter Haynes rubbed his hands together like a hungry man sitting down to big meal. "I can't give away all my trade secrets, Lieutenant Butler," he replied. "But I can tell you that one of the major stumbling blocks those earlier investors had is about to go away. Another one already has."

"Stumbling blocks."

"That's right. The first one is money—those developers paid a premium for land right on the lake, with a nice view of the mountains behind. A beautiful spot, and worth premium prices. If the lake was healthier. But it's not, not so far. The Slab, though, is back away from the lake. You can see it but you can't smell it. And it's closer to the mountains, so those views are better."

"And what's the other stumbling block?"

"That's the one I can't tell you about yet," Carter said. "That's my secret weapon."

Ken steepled his fingers, resting his upper lip and his salt-and-pepper mustache on their tips. "Fair enough," he said. "So tell me about what you expect from this meeting tonight."

"I'm prepared to make these people a generous offer," Carter said. "I own title to the Slab now, all legal and above-board, and I could just evict everyone. But I don't want to play the game that way. Those people are living there under a certain set of expectations, and it's time for those expectations to change. But that doesn't mean they should be screwed."

"I won't argue with that."

"So I hope to get everyone, or as close to everyone as will come out, to gather around so I can tell them all at once what the offer's going to be. Of course, over the next few weeks we'll be visiting each one separately, signing releases and turning over checks."

"They'll like to hear that, I expect," Ken suggested. "But you might want to keep in mind the kind of people you're dealing with. This is a very independent-minded bunch. They tend to make Libertarians look like Socialists. You might be offering them something they can use, which is money, but you're asking them to give up the one thing money can't buy, which is freedom."

"Do you think they're likely to get vocal?" Carter asked, a note of concern in his voice.

"I imagine you'll hear some raised voices."

"Anything else?"

"I'm assuming—and I know what happens when you assume, but I do it anyway—that you're expecting some dissent, and that's why you want us there."

Carter nodded. "I figure it can't hurt."

"I don't have any doubt that they'd let you down off the Slab alive, even if we weren't there to keep an eye on things. But we'll be there, just the same."

"That would be good," Carter said, his tongue running across his unnaturally red lips. "That would be really good."

Ken was about to say something else when a screech of brakes outside the office interrupted him. He glanced out the window, and saw only a cloud of dust hanging on the still air, then the tall shape of Billy Cobb loomed into view, heading for the door.

When he burst through it he held a stained plastic Vons bag in his right hand.

"That it?" Ken asked him.

"It's human, Ken," Billy said. "And look. It's—" He stopped himself, noticing Carter Haynes for the first time. "Sorry, I didn't mean to interrupt your meeting. It's just—"

Ken pushed himself up from the desk and crossed the office. He gestured to the bag. "Let me see."

Billy held the bag open so Ken could look inside. He did so, lips pressed together, silently analyzing the bag's grim contents. He felt a sudden tug of urgency. Haynes was just a rich guy, a roadblock in the path of him doing his real job, and he wanted the guy out of his office.

When Ken had seen enough he looked up at Billy. "Get it down to El Centro, to the Coroner's office."

Billy paused, looking at Carter Haynes and back at Ken as if waiting for an introduction.

"Today," Ken added.

Billy tossed off his standard salute and left.

Returning to his desk, Ken said, "Sorry about that."

"Don't worry about it," Carter said graciously. "Everything okay?"

"There might be a bit of a snag to your meeting tonight, after all," Ken warned him. "Looks as if we may have an ongoing homicide investigation up at the Slab."

Carter's eyes widened. It was barely perceptible, but it was the first indication Ken had seen that the man could be made to lose his cool. When Carter Haynes spoke again, there was new tension in his voice.

"Do you think that's absolutely necessary?"

Ken just looked at him for a moment. "It's a homicide investigation," he said. "It isn't something I can just sweep under the rug."

Carter looked around the office, waving a hand to indicate the surroundings. "You have a nice little set-up here, in a Mayberry kind of way," he said. "Just imagine what you could do if you had an actual tax base here in Salton Estates. Luxury homes, real property taxes. You and Deputy Fife could buy some new trucks, upgrade that PC, maybe hire someone to answer the phones, you know?"

"And I wouldn't object to that," Ken countered. "But that doesn't mean I'm going to stall this investigation, if it turns out to be warranted."

"There's a chance it won't?" Carter's tone was hopeful.

"There will have to be some questions answered," Ken replied. "I don't know that it will turn out to be a full-fledged murder case. That'll depend on the lab results."

"I'll keep my fingers crossed," Carter said.

"Somehow," Ken observed, "you don't strike me as a man who relies a lot on luck."

Four of them had made the annual Dove Hunt for all thirteen years. Vic Bradford had joined two years in. One of them, Ray Dixon, was a relative newcomer, with only seven years. And this was the second year without Hal Shipp, who was still missed by everyone.

Vic Bradford took mental stock as they cruised the towns of southern Riverside County. By now, it was all ritualized, done the same way every September. The first day, they said goodbye to their wives and families and piled into someone's car, this time Cam Hensley's Navigator. They drove up to the cabin they kept in a remote valley outside Blythe, unloaded their gear and groceries, and got down to some heavy drinking. The booze and storytelling went on most of the night, and finally they crashed for a few hours. The next day, bleary-eyed and hung over, the Dove Hunt began in earnest.

When they'd first invited him to take part, Vic had felt a tangle of conflicting emotions. He had just turned thirty-two, still young but starting to think, now and again, about thirty-five and then the inevitable slide into the forties and beyond. He was past that now, of course, and he realized that the forties weren't as bad as he'd feared back then. Now, though, it was his fifties that loomed, and that really scared him.

He had felt honored to be asked. He'd heard that the other guys were going out hunting, of course. Then once he learned what it was really all about, he was appalled and intrigued and excited all at once.

He was only peripherally a part of their crowd, he thought, until he realized that not having obvious social ties was part of the whole idea. Cam Hensley looked like an accountant, with his balding, graying hair and thick black glasses, but he was one of the wealthiest men in the Valley, owning tens of thousands of acres of prime farmland. The thing that bugged Vic about him was his forehead: bulbous, as if he had extra brains inside there trying to get out. And while his hairline had receded almost to the point of nonexistence, right at the top and center of that huge forehead was this patch of black hair, an island of hair, unconnected to the rest, that Cam refused to shave. He kept it trimmed, which was new—until a couple of years ago, he'd grown it out and tried to connect it to his other remnants of hair by creative combing. But still, it looked like an aberration and Vic wished he'd just shave it already.

Silver-haired, tanned, and fit, Kerry Williams owned a Caterpillar dealership in El Centro. Kerry maintained an air of mystery about himself, though he occasionally talked about intelligence work in Central America during the eighties. Vic was never sure how much of that talk was true and how much of it was self-aggrandizing bullshit. He had no real reason to doubt Kerry's word, but the self-aggrandizing part was undeniable. Kerry Williams considered himself a leader of men, and if this group was any indication then maybe he was.

Terrance Berkley and R.J. Rocknowski were closer to Vic's social status and income level. Vic and Rock actually lived right on the Slab, while Terrance had a mobile home in a park in Niland, almost on that town's border with Salton Estates. He paid for his berth, but at least he had plumbing and power, and since he lived with his wife and her twelve-year-old son from her first marriage, things like phones and an address were more important to him. With his Marine-length haircut and broad shoulders, Ray Dixon looked like the soldier Kerry had once been, even though he'd never been in the military at all. Ray worked at the sugar plant in Brawley and lived down there, in a second floor apartment, with his wife. They had come together at their kids' Little League games—Cam and Terrance both had boys—at church functions or political fund raisers, at planning board meetings, at boat rental docks on the Salton, at the liquor store buying suds. There hadn't been any master plan, any grand design. They were just a group of men who ran into one another around the area, found that they had common interests, and decided to put together a hunting trip.

But that first one had not gone according to plan. No one could say, or would say, whose idea it was, though Vic suspected Kerry Williams. Kerry was the one, after all, with the special ops experience. In his shadowy Latin American days, he implied, he had developed certain tastes that were hard to satisfy in *El Norte*. And he had the strongest personality; he could talk the other guys into nearly anything.

Strike the "nearly," Vic thought. He had already proven that, thirteen times over.

They told stories about the various Hunts, usually the same stories every year. But the guys who had been there that first year wouldn't talk about it except in the vaguest possible terms. They wouldn't describe exactly how it had gone down, and that secrecy carried over from year to year. People who heard about the Hunt asked questions and made a variety of assumptions—that the men spent the week in Nevada, gambling and visiting brothels, that they went down to Mexico for the same thing but without so much of the gambling. Those who went on the trip were sworn to secrecy, though, and their close-mouthed satisfaction just made the speculation that much wilder. Vic was able to make some guesses about that first time, based on how the ritual had played out since he'd joined, but they would only be speculation.

As they always did, the second day after the hard night of drinking and shouting and laughing and, this year, bitching about the Muslims—the bonding time that was required if any of them were to get through this—they cruised the back roads of Riverside County, heartened by the sight of American flags fluttering in yards and from businesses and plastered to windows everywhere. Dove season was over, legally— it ran from September first to the fifteenth, then kicked in for another forty-five days in November. But they didn't want real dove hunters to be out while they were, so they habitually waited a week or two after the season closed. The delay just made the anticipation sweeter, and they didn't really give a damn if they brought home any birds.

Somewhere out there was their Dove.

This year, it was Ray Dixon who spotted her. It happened in Mecca, a few miles above the north shore of the Salton Sea.

"There!" Ray shouted anxiously. "Right there!" He pointed toward a *mercado* called Leon's. Its brown stucco wall was striped by the shadows of three date palms. Signs in Spanish filled its windows, completely obscuring any view in or out.

Stepping out of the door, oblivious to her fate, their Dove had a six-pack of Corona in one hand. A plastic bag with various dry groceries in it dangled from her other wrist. A thick tangle of rich black hair framed a pretty face, with huge brown eyes, smooth olive skin and a button nose. Her full lips were pulled into a private smile, as if she'd just shared a joke with the shopkeeper inside. Heavy breasts stretched a form-fitting striped black and white tank top that tucked into tight brown jeans. Her sandals had thick wedge soles—too high for walking around town in, Vic thought, but they made her look taller than her five-six or so. All in all, she was a lovely girl, the prettiest one he could remember.

Cam, behind the wheel, slowed down as he passed her.

"Not bad," he said, appraising her as he drove by.

"What are you doing?" Ray demanded. "You'll miss her! Go back!"

"Patience, my son," Cam said. He made a hard right at the next intersection. Heading around the block. "If it was too easy, it wouldn't be a Hunt."

"I'd just hate to miss her," Ray insisted. "I mean, she was hot."

"I got to agree with you there," Rock said. "That body, she could do porn." The ability to do porn was, Vic had learned, the highest compliment Rock could pay a woman. Angelina Jolie, Nikki Cox, Ashley Judd, Dolly Parton, they were all tops in Rock's book because they could do porn. Not that they would, but they could. Janet Reno, Laura Bush, Margaret Thatcher, and Bea Arthur all shared a less elevated status, as women who could not do porn. It was, in its fashion, refreshingly non-ideological. Rock would vote for a woman for President, as long as the woman was built like Pam Anderson and her running mate carried the moral authority of Ron Jeremy.

Cam kept quiet, hanging another right, and then another. The woman had crossed the street and covered most of a block in the time it had taken them to circle around. The houses here were tiny stucco constructions on small lots, jammed right up next to one another. Cam gunned the engine a little and pulled up behind her. "See?" he said. "Put a little sport into it."

"Look at that ass," Ray Dixon said.

Vic had already done so, and found it exceptional.

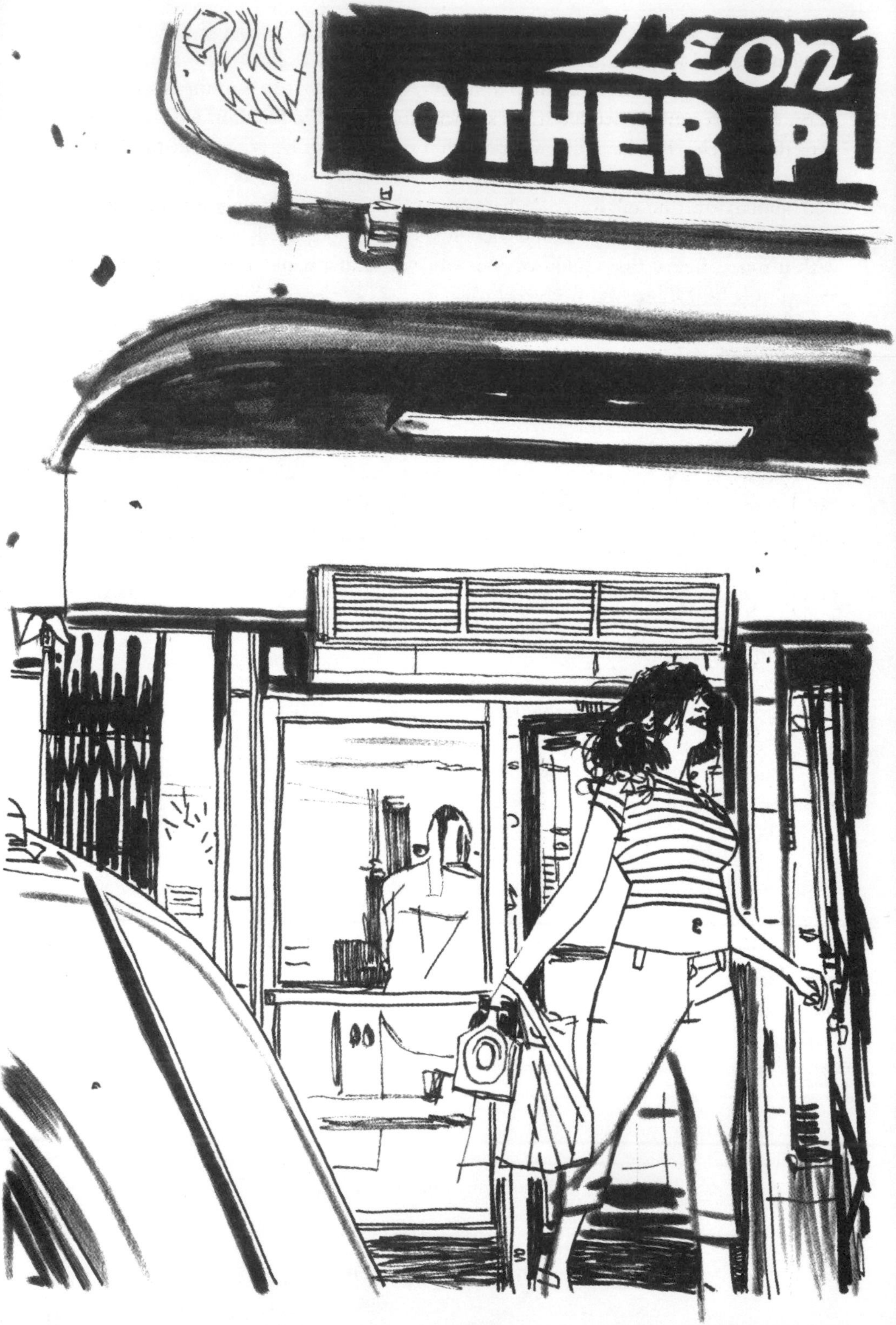
Leon
OTHER PL

"Oh yeah," Rock said. "She could be a star."

"Lookouts?" Cam had always been a practical man.

"Clear on my side," Terrance Berkley called from the front passenger seat. Terrance pretty much needed a bucket seat to himself or his bulk would spread all over the bench—he was a big, sloppy side of beef of a man with wild red hair that looked like he styled it with a blender.

"Nobody over here," Kerry Williams reported from the driver's side rear. Just the sound of Kerry's voice intimidated Vic—it was low and gravelly and he always spoke with a tone of supreme authority. He was glad that he and Ray Dixon sat in the second row buckets, while Rock rode on the rear bench with Kerry. Rock's muscular arms were crossed, his ponytailed head whipping from side to side as he watched for witnesses.

With the street clear of visible onlookers, Cam gunned the Navigator again and pulled up ahead of the girl. She was aware of the SUV's presence now, and became even more so when Cam cut in front of her, one wheel jouncing up onto the sidewalk. Doors opened and men spilled out in a practiced move.

"Excuse me?" the girl said. She started to say more, but Rock slipped behind her and clapped a strong hand over her mouth. Cam grabbed her ankles and upended them. Within seconds, a gag had been tied across her mouth, her wrists had been bound with plastic handcuff strips, and she'd been dropped in the Navigator's luggage compartment. Cam hopped back behind the wheel and squealed away. No one had shown up on the street during the process.

Vic turned back to look at her, writhing on her side, eyes wide with terror, a film of tears and sweat sheening her cheeks.

The Dove Hunt was on.

Chapter 03

Darren Cook slept well into the afternoon, waking only when the heat building up inside his Fleetwood Jamboree finally got to be too much, and then he clawed his way out of sleep, slick with sweat. His dreams had been troubled and convoluted, filled with images of carnage. Bodies piled upon bodies as in a concentration camp or a natural disaster of some kind, blood everywhere, blood and brains and raw, ragged flesh as far as he could see, a smell like spoiled meat clogging his nostrils.

His thrashings had torn apart the bedding and he woke with his face pressed against the thin, bare mattress. He pushed himself off the bed, and headed into the tiny, cramped head where he took a loud, lengthy piss. He alternated between scratching his ever-expanding gut and finger-combing long blond hair that had encountered neither water nor shampoo in several days. Finished at last, he made his way through the empty camper to the kitchen. The coffeepot was cold and empty.

"Maryjane!" he shouted, surprising even himself at the fury in his voice. "Why the fuck isn't there any coffee?"

A moment later the screen door opened and Maryjane leaned inside, a glistening green bottle in her hand. Already at the brew, Darren thought.

"It's like a thousand degrees in there," Maryjane pointed out. "I didn't think you'd want a hot drink, for God's sake."

"Give me a beer, then," Darren growled, determined to keep his mad on.

"You're standing right in front of the fridge, Darren."

Darren started to answer, but stopped himself and opened the refrigerator. Inside he found an old half-carton of milk, some eggs, a moldy square of cheese, part of a loaf of bread, and some lettuce so brown it looked like ancient parchment. No beer.

"Oh, yeah," Maryjane said, and he could hear the pleasure in her tone. "This is the last one."

He lunged for her but she dodged him easily, ducking back out of the RV. He followed her onto the slab outside, unmindful of his nakedness. Maryjane laughed at him and handed him the beer. "For fuck's sake, put some clothes on," she said. "Nobody wants to see that."

He ignored her. "Why'd you let me sleep so late for?" he demanded.

"What's the difference? Not like you have a job to go to or anything. You did, maybe we'd have some groceries in that icebox."

She was right about that, he knew. He sometimes worked as a mule, carrying dope across the Mexican border for some dealers he knew down in Calexico. More often, it was Maryjane, though, since women could usually cross with more ease than men. And when there was no money there, she could go to San Diego or up to Vegas, work shaking her moneymakers in a strip club for a week or so and earn some cash that way. But it had been a while since either of them had brought home so much as a dollar. It was looking like time to get back to it.

He took a long pull off the beer, finishing the bottle and hoping she didn't spit in it before she turned it over. Then he turned, still naked, and hurled the bottle off into the desert, listening to it crash against unseen rocks with a certain satisfaction.

That reminded him of another image from his dreams, one that he'd forgotten about until now. Maryjane herself, lifeless on a cement floor someplace, with a neat round hole between her wide-open eyes. The image, he knew, was horrible, and he was chilled to realize the distinct pleasure he got from seeing it.

He noticed that Maryjane was watching him, a strange expression on her face that he could only read as flirtatious. "You'd better get inside," she said, gesturing toward his crotch. "I don't know what's got you so revved up, but maybe we should go use that thing instead of letting it go to waste."

Penny Rice hiked for a couple of hours, enjoying the sunshine on her face and arms, the clear sky, the surprisingly lush foliage around her, standing in stark contrast to what could be found on the public side of the line. The creosote bush on this side grew tall and thick. Spiky green wands of ocotillo towered over her, and the sides of the hills were coated with dense cholla forests, their thousands of needles glowing in the afternoon sun. In just an hour of hiking she had seen the tracks of various critters: rabbits and snakes and kangaroo rats and coyote. Ravens, turkey vultures, starlings, the occasional dove, and assorted little gray birds she always thought of as LGBs flitted around her, hopping from plant to plant or catching afternoon thermals. For a brief while, a tiny gray lizard dogged her steps, keeping to the shadows underneath the lowest fringe of bushes. She was glad to have some time alone, far from telephones and televisions, the constant psychic scream of the internet, the righteous indignation of talk radio's insane ideologues.

The thought of finding herself in a war zone again unnerved her a little. She had volunteered for the Army during a period of relative peace, planning, in the aftermath of her mother's long hospitalization and then death, to serve her hitch and then use the G.I. benefits to fund her education. But then Iraq invaded Kuwait and she found herself on a troop transport headed for the Persian Gulf. They'd landed at night, and she remembered stepping out of her temporary barracks the next morning—she had been born and raised in the moist, fertile American Southeast, and had never seen a desert except on TV—and thinking that she had never imagined a place where everything was the color of sand. Now, however, she knew that not all deserts were like that—that, in fact, her first impression of the Gulf's deserts had been mistaken, too. Life was there—you just had to look a little harder for it.

Hiking had always been one of life's pleasures, as far as she was concerned. It was the most egalitarian pursuit she could imagine, beyond class—the poor could do it as well as the wealthy. The physically challenged, she supposed, those in wheelchairs, or with infirmities that made walking difficult, probably couldn't take the enjoyment that she did from it. But even they could find pleasure in being outside, rolling in a chair or slowly perambulating down a city sidewalk or a park's pathway.

Penny had been raised in southern Virginia and in South Carolina's low country. She had grown up hiking through swampy forests of cypress and pine, or on Appalachian hillsides in Virginia and West Virginia. She hadn't, in those days, thought of being outside as a political activity. It wasn't even something she talked about much, especially after her father died when she was thirteen. He'd been the one who had introduced her to hiking. Her, and her two brothers. His wife, Penny's mom, had never been strong, never been the outdoorsy type at all, and that was a special bond she and the boys had with their father. After he was gone, she alone kept it up. He'd never politicized it, though; to him, it was about being outside, being alone, finding peace in the simple physical act of planting one foot in front of the other in some wild setting.

War had ultimately caused her to re-think that. The massive devastation of pristine desert landscape she saw during Desert Storm had politicized the outdoors for her, made her come to think of wild places as treasures that needed to be saved—as islands of peace in an increasingly violent world. Returning to civilian life after serving in the Army there, her newfound political beliefs had resulted in a quest, finally bringing her to the Washington, D.C. headquarters of the Wilderness Peace Initiative.

And that association had proved, she believed, to be the most meaningful of her life, finally leading her to this action in California's Chocolate Mountains. Which could, she knew, turn out to be the most dangerous thing she'd involved herself in since the Gulf War. But she believed in the cause, and that made a little danger worthwhile.

Besides, she had yet to see any signs of bombing. No craters, none of the unexploded ordnance she'd been warned about. Instead, she was finding that, at a glance, at least, the theory they were working with seemed to be true: that instead of being destroyed by the military's bombing activities here, the landscape—except for specific places where bombs had fallen—was protected from the day in, day out damage caused by civilians. She hiked along a dirt road presumably used by military personnel when they needed to come into the range for some reason, but unlike the dirt roads in the public lands outside the range, this one wasn't intersected by other roads every couple of miles. There was no litter in sight. No bulletholes marred the tall stalks of agave or the occasional golden barrel cactus. This was like seeing what the southern California desert must have resembled sixty years before—before World War Two, before the postwar boom that had fueled the paving over of much of the state.

She stopped at the top of a rise, glancing back at the ground she'd already covered and ahead at the taller hills she had yet to cover. She wanted to get deep inside the range before setting up camp and addressing her actual purpose for being here. Dry-mouthed, she uncapped a canteen and took a deep pull.

The water tasted sour to her. She swished it around in her mouth and spat it into the red dirt. She held the canteen up, sniffing from its mouth. Smelled okay. She took another sip, swished, swallowed.

The taste seemed somehow familiar, but she couldn't place it.

She screwed the cap back on the canteen, clipped it to her belt, and resumed walking.

Billy Cobb always felt a little uneasy when he went down to El Centro, a little intimidated. Sharp-uniformed officers, their cars clean and polished, their boots shining, populated the Coroner's office. El Centro was quiet, compared to those human cesspools of Los Angeles and San Diego to the west, but compared to Salton Estates it was a bustling metropolis. Sheriff's officers here saw genuine action. Drugs, murder, grand theft auto. Real police work was done here.

By contrast, Billy often felt like a glorified messenger boy.

Leaving the Coroner's office—he had been summarily dismissed after dropping off the skull—he tried to soothe himself by enjoying his favorite aspect of the job, the feeling of his gun against his hip. He had never fired it in the course of duty except on the range, but it pleased him to know it was there. Not many people, in these modern times, got to walk around with a gun strapped to their belt.

He had met a deputy in a bar down in Brawley who had been in an actual firefight a few years back. Half a dozen punks with semi-automatic weapons had been cornered after trying to rob a farm equipment dealer's payroll. Six squad cars had responded, and the resulting gunplay had destroyed a good chunk of the dealership's inventory. Billy had listened with rapt fascination to the man's story, seeing in his mind's eye each bullet spanging off metal, shattering glass, driving through flesh and bone.

That was the story that had inspired Billy to apply for a job, to become a Sheriff's deputy. Of course, being assigned to sleepy little Salton Estates wasn't part of his original plan. But it would work out all right, Billy figured. He was an optimist. There would come a time when he would see some real action. He had even considered enlisting, in the days following the attack on the World Trade Center. There were terrorists to kill, and an experienced law enforcement officer might be just the guy to go and kill them. But that would mean giving up his place in line to take over the Salton Estates substation. He'd just stay where he was, he decided, and God help any terrorist who showed his face in Imperial County. Billy could wait—there was no big hurry.

And there was no hurry to get back to Salton Estates now, he decided as he unlocked the squad car. Lieutenant Butler would need him for the meeting on the Slab tonight, but if he took an extra hour or so to get back, no harm done. He knew a street corner where a man in Sheriff's tans could get his knob polished for free, just about any time of day, or at least that's what the local guys claimed. Billy had never tried it. He thought it was about time he did.

Ken Butler ate his lunch out of a brown paper bag, sitting at his desk. He was working his way through Wallace Stegner's novel "Angle of Repose," reading whenever he had a few spare minutes in the office, so he pulled it from his desk drawer and flipped to his bookmark. He knew he should be out in the community, having lunch at Mary's, maybe, a shop on the shore that sold bait and beer and burgers. But the burgers at Mary's always tasted fishy to him, and the fish in the Salton were poisonous, like eating straight mercury right out of the thermometer, as far as he was concerned. The trade-off was that he could socialize with the locals. The downside was that he'd have to socialize with the locals, listening to their war talk. If he heard one more overweight fifty-year-old man threaten to pick up his twelve-gauge and buy a ticket to Afghanistan, he thought he'd go berserk.

All things considered, he was just as happy to sit in his office with a book and a turkey sandwich. The turkey tasted off, but he'd known that it would. Just one of those things you had to put up with, days like this one.

He'd only managed a few pages when the phone rang.

"Sheriff's office," he answered, somewhat grudgingly, replacing the bookmark between the pages.

"Ken, it's Henry."

Henry was Henry Rios, Ken knew, up in Riverside County, at the Thermal substation. He sounded tense. "What's shakin', Henry?"

"Hard to say for sure, man," Henry replied. "There's been a reported abduction of a young woman, Mexican, down in Mecca. Eyewitness saw it from inside his living room, looking out the window during his afternoon talk shows. But he's not a very reliable eyewitness—reason he's home during the day is because he drinks too much to hold a steady job. Anyway, no one has reported a missing person yet, so I don't know how seriously to take it."

"Could be no one would notice she was gone until later tonight, when she doesn't come home."

"That's true," Henry agreed. "That's why I'm calling around. Just want people to be on the lookout for a dark Lincoln Navigator with several white males and a Mexican girl in it. Just in case."

"You have a description of her?"

"Of ninety-nine percent of Mexican women everywhere," Henry said. "Late teens, early twenties. Black hair, olive skin. Wearing dark jeans and a tight top. Healthy build."

"By healthy, you mean lean and toned, or stacked?"

"Way the witness reports it, a regular brick shithouse."

"Got it. I'll take a look around," Ken assured him. "I find anything I'll let you know."

He shoved the remains of his sandwich back into the paper bag and tossed it into the office's mini-fridge. Glancing at his watch, he swore. Almost three, and no sign of Billy since he'd been sent down to El Centro. The boy had better be back before I have to go up to the Slab for that meeting, he thought, or there'll be hell to pay.

He cast a sad eye toward the little refrigerator that contained his lunch and headed out the door. The Bronco waited outside, parked in what little shade a spindly cottonwood provided, with a windshield screen on top of the dash for a little extra insurance. Even so, it was hot inside, metal parts searing like a branding iron when he touched them. The wheel was covered with a leather strap that kept it cool enough to touch, but drawing the seatbelt across his chest was like walking into a flaming branch. He cranked up the air and backed out of the short driveway.

There wasn't much town to Salton Estates, but there were hundreds of square miles of desert around. Thousands, if the abductors—if there had, in fact, been an abduction—had time to get out of the area. If he had taken a pretty young Chicana, Ken figured, he'd head for the Mojave Desert. It'd take a military operation to find someone out there who didn't want to be found. And from Mecca, it'd be a short trip, up the 111 through Palm Desert and Palm Springs to the 10, then east a ways. The last thing you'd do would be to head south down the 111, which would trap you between the Salton Sea and the bombing range, eventually dropping you on Interstate 8 or skipping that and continuing on to the border towns of Calexico and Mexicali.

That would be the only reason he could imagine they'd come his way—if their final destination was Mexico. But that made no sense either—why snatch a Mexican girl in the States just to take her into Mexico? The idea of a bunch of white guys in a high-end SUV trying to hide anonymously on that side of the border was laughable, anyway.

As he pulled out of his reserved parking space in front of the office, catching a glimpse of the Salton shimmering in the pounding sun, he thought again about the real estate developer, Haynes. Maybe the guy could make his plan work. But then again, maybe not. This whole region had been, since the first white man came through looking for the Seven Cities of Gold, beset by people trying to turn empty desert into profit.

The Salton Sea itself was a corporate accident, an inadvertent sea formed by the California Development Corporation when greedy developers tried to turn the desert into farmland—which they would control, of course—by diverting the flow of the mighty Colorado River and irrigating the wastelands of the Imperial Valley. But they didn't reckon with the massive loads of silt the Colorado carried, filling up their waterway far too soon. In a misguided attempt to direct the water where they wanted it, they cut a new channel around the silt-blocked area. Heavy flooding in the winter of 1905 broke through their canal, diverting the river's entire flow into their little valley, flooding homes and Indian settlements and the very land they were trying to farm, filling the bed of the ancient Lake Cahuilla, and creating the largest lake in California. Birds liked it, when it didn't kill them. Since the same philosophy—basically, Ken thought, "It's our water, so fuck you"—had resulted in the damming and diverting of so much Colorado River water that Mexico barely got its legal allotment and the river's Delta had pretty much dried up, the birds on the Pacific Flyway needed someplace to go. The Salton was what they got, poison or no.

It was poison because the Salton was a lake without an adequate means of water exchange. Water flowed in from the Alamo River and the New River that came up from Mexico, bringing with it untreated or barely treated sewage, industrial wastes, and who knew what else. Once a truck had fallen into the river and its paint had been stripped by the New River's toxic sludge by the next day. The truck's cargo—human waste—hadn't even added enough toxins to the water to be considered a problem.

Locally, run-off from irrigated Imperial Valley farmlands trickled in, carrying with it large amounts of fertilizer that could poison the Sea even more. With nowhere to flow to, the water in the Sea evaporated, leaving behind massive amounts of salt and concentrating the other chemicals in the lake. The Valley provided a third to a half of all the winter vegetables consumed in the country, so there was probably some merit to irrigating the place, but the cost to the Salton was high.

In addition to those who tried to profit by controlling the flow of water, there were others trying to pull gold from the ground. At the southern end of the Chocolate Mountains, below the military Impact Area, a foreign gold mining operation took millions of dollars out of the earth while paying only a tiny fraction in lease fees and nothing in royalties. Farther east, near the Arizona border, another company was trying to start a gold mining operation on land sacred to the Quechan Indians—the only stretch of earth on which windows existed, or so they claimed, which enabled them to walk to other worlds, or ten thousand years into their own past. But in spite of those ten thousand years of history, a century ago the Bureau of Land Management had taken away the part of their reservation that included that sacred ground. In its final days, the Clinton administration had denied the mining company's application, but now it was being reconsidered—and since the new Interior Secretary had hired members of the gold company's law firm for her staff, chances were good that the short-term profit of the powerful would win out over the religious beliefs of the Quechans.

Ken hoped that Carter Haynes had carefully considered the difficulties that the Valley often threw at those who would profit from it. As the California Development Company had learned in the twentieth century's first decade, the desert had a way of subverting the will of mere humans.

He drove for an hour, covering the main road and the side streets, but there was no Navigator to be seen, no crew of white guys in any SUV with a Hispanic hostage. Finally giving up, he turned around in the parking lot of the Corvina Café, just below the Riverside County line, and headed for the office, hoping that Billy had made it back.

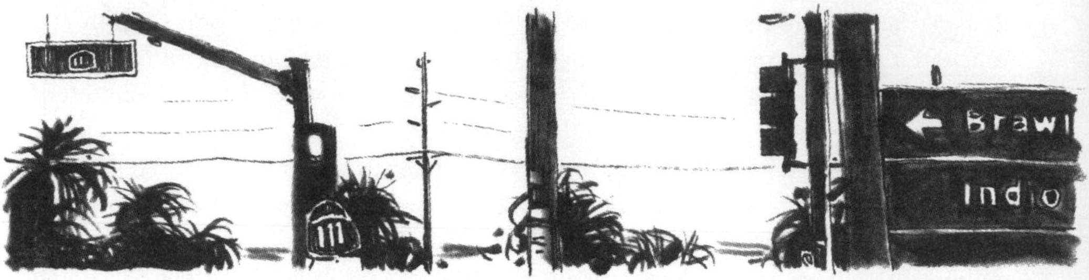
111
Brawl
Indio

Billy found the corner that had been described to him, and standing on the corner—just back from it, actually, leaning against the wall of a liquor store, windows plastered with signs advertising ICE COLD BEER and CHEAP CIGS and GOD BLES AMERICA, he found the woman. He assumed she was the one, anyway, or that there were more than one but they'd all provide the same service. All that he'd been told was the where, not the who.

But she looked the part. She could have had more meat on her bones and she could have been better looking and she for damn sure could have been younger, he supposed. She was stick thin, a meth-head, he guessed, or a heroin addict. Her wispy hair looked like limp straw, and her skin was dried-out from the sun. She wore a miniskirt that showed off scrawny legs that could have been attached to a chair, and a tube-top over breasts that barely dented it. He thought streetwalkers usually wore high heels, but this one had on faded red sneakers, so he figured maybe that only applied to city girls.

Well, he thought, no promises had been made about quality. Just price.

Making sure that no one was watching, he pulled the squad car over, opened the passenger window, and beckoned to her. She eyed him for a moment, spat once onto the hot sidewalk, and then ambled over to the cruiser, taking her time. Billy's fingers drummed on the back of the seat. The longer he sat here the more likely someone would come down the road. El Centro in September was pretty quiet because when the heat raged, people stayed inside as much as possible. But all it would take to bust him was one car.

Finally, she reached the street, leaned into the window.

"I don't know you," she said.

"You don't need to. Get in."

"You arresting me, officer?"

"Should I? Is that the way you like it?"

She laughed, a cackle that turned into a hacking cough.

"Just get in, for God's sake," he said, agitated. He leaned over and tugged on the door handle.

She pulled the door open and climbed in, sitting down and wiping her mouth with the back of her hand. Before she was even settled, Billy hit the gas and lurched away from the curb.

"Jesus," the woman said. "You in a hurry or something?"

"You ask a lot of questions for a whore."

"Who said whores ain't curious?" she replied. "Anyway, if you're not arresting me, where you taking me?"

"You tell me," Billy said. "Where's a good place?"

"Oh…" she said, as if just now catching on. She was a tease. Billy kind of liked that—teasing was fine as long as the payoff was there at the end. And it didn't take a detective to figure out that this woman knew all about the payoff. "Well then, make a right at the corner."

Billy made the right. "Where we going? Your place?"

She made a huffing noise that he figured was probably a laugh. "There's a carport in that alley up ahead," she said, pointing to a rutted dirt track behind a faded brown apartment complex. "It's usually quiet back there. Nobody's going to bother us, and your car's invisible from the street."

"You sure?" He was still nervous about this whole thing. His heart hammered in his chest and he could feel sweat running down his ribs. He'd never done anything like this, but he had to admit that there was a thrill to it. The lure of the forbidden or some shit, he thought. He turned into the alley. She was right; the carport was deserted, the dozen or so apartments above it silent. And it wasn't like he was planning to take a long time.

He pulled into the shade of one of the carport slots and killed the engine. "This good?"

"This is fine," she said. "Cash first. Forty unless you want something more complicated than head."

"Head's fine, but…in case you didn't notice, I'm a Sheriff's Deputy."

"I noticed," she said.

"So I was thinking you'd do me for nothing."

"You thought wrong, stud. Girl's got to earn a living."

"I could run you in right now. You solicited me."

"You could. Of course, I could talk about how you made me get in your car and drove me here. Look, I don't want no trouble, handsome, I just want to make some bank."

Billy felt himself filling with an unexpected—and unfamiliar—rage. His face felt hot. "I don't pay for it," he snapped. "Ever."

"Then you should get it the same place you usually do," the woman replied. "Your right hand, probably." She pulled on the door handle, opened the door, and left the car.

"Hey!" Billy shouted. "Get back in here!"

Instead, she broke into a run. Billy scrambled from the car, nearly slamming the cruiser door into the stucco carport wall as he did. Squeezing between car and wall, he dashed into the alley. She was already out of sight. Her footsteps still echoed in the silent town, though. Billy ran into the street and spotted her rounding a corner. She'd lost one of her red sneakers but was making still remarkably good time for a woman, much less a woman with one foot bare on pavement that was at least a hundred degrees, probably more like one-fifteen or twenty.

He sprinted down the middle of the street toward the corner. Besides the apartment building there were small single-family homes here, all stucco, all dark and quiet. It was like he'd wandered into some kind of ghost town. The only thing he could hear now was a distant air conditioner humming and the buzz of a fly that strafed him. In sequence, he realized three things: he'd lost the hooker, he was very exposed out here in the street, and he had his service weapon in his hand.

That last was particularly troubling.

He holstered it and jogged back to the alley. How had a simple urge to put his cock in somebody's mouth ended with his Glock 22 drawn? He knew that he'd have shot her if he'd seen her there on the street—the mental image of her flying forward, a spray of blood and skull spewing out ahead of her, came to him, and he shivered.

Back in the squad car, he sat for a minute with his hands gripping the wheel, shaking uncontrollably. As soon as he felt like he could control the vehicle, he backed out of the alley and headed for home.

Sitting in his favorite chair, windows on both sides of the RV open to catch a breeze that was more wish than expectation, Harold Shipp had fallen asleep. He awoke an hour later, alert and clear-headed. He rose and went to the window, looking out at the gray slab under its coating of sand and debris. A tiny bird hopped around, then took wing for the brush surrounding the slab.

Harold turned around and saw Virginia watching him. "It's September," he said.

"That's right. All month."

"They're out there. The boys." He looked back out the window, as if trying to see beyond the brush, as if trying to grow wings so he could rise up into the air where he could see over the miles. Behind him, Virginia said something. He could hear her voice but not her words. It didn't matter, though. He had only been making an observation, not really seeking confirmation. After this many years, he knew what the Dove Hunt schedule was.

What he didn't know—couldn't know—was how much Virginia was aware of. Harold knew about his own condition, knew he suffered Alzheimer's, even had a vague idea that it meant that plaque deposits had built up on his brain that made him forgetful, confused, lost. Times like these, when he could remember and process information, were rare and getting more so. But after he had his spells—could they still be called "spells" when they had become the norm? he wondered—he retained none of what had happened while he was gone. He could have told Virginia everything, or nothing. To ask her would only mean opening a door he didn't want to go through, and since the possibility remained that he had told her nothing, he wanted to leave that door shut as long as he possibly could.

He had sworn to secrecy, as they all had. If it was within his power, he'd keep that vow.

He found that he was suddenly excruciatingly thirsty. He hoped Virginia had some iced tea or lemonade made, but if not, a tall glass of water would do. It would taste funny—and he was clear-headed enough to know what that meant—but right now that didn't matter as much as getting some liquid into him.

He turned back to the kitchen, where Virginia waited.

Desert Storm had taught her a thing or two about desert camouflage, so by the time Penny had finished setting up her camp, she was convinced that it would be all but invisible from the air or from the ground, unless someone happened to come right up to it. A large camo groundcloth, in uneven browns and tans with a scattering of green, was spread on the ground, anchored with rocks and a couple of stakes. All her gear was stowed on the groundcloth. Above that, and overhanging by several feet in all directions, she'd raised camo netting, through which she had twined bits of local vegetation. The netting would, she believed, prevent people flying overhead from seeing her even when she sat at the low, flat boulder before her groundcloth that she had determined would be her kitchen. A series of big rocks shielded her from the rear, and she'd made camp on the west side of a rise above a wash, out of flash flood danger. From here, she could keep an eye on the wash. If anyone came in that way, she'd see them long before they saw her. She had cut cross-country away from the jeep road for almost a mile, and put two hills between it and her base camp.

She was brewing a celebratory cup of herbal tea—which she suspected would taste just as wrong as her water had—when she heard the crunch of a footfall, not far away. She instantly shut off the propane burner and listened for it to repeat. To be caught before she even started would just suck too much to be believed.

Hearing another footstep, Penny left her cooking gear where it was and slipped into the wall of rock at her back, standing between two of the biggest boulders and watching her own back trail. From the sound of it, someone was dogging her path. She'd already scouted the rocks and knew that, if it came to it, she could duck between these two big chunks of sandstone and go up and over the ridgeline behind her. That would give her a head start back out of the gunnery area.

After another couple of minutes she saw a head come into view, and then the rest of the body. She was already leaving her hiding place among the rocks, though, because she recognized him as soon as his long yellow dreadlocks appeared. His broad, simple features were arranged in a strange smile, like a kid who thinks he's putting something over on Mom. His tie-dyed shirt was about the farthest thing from camouflage a human could choose to wear.

Mick Beachum.

Who was supposed to be, at that moment, setting up a command center in a motel in Salton Estates or Niland.

"The fuck are you doing here, Mick?" she demanded loudly.

He stopped in his tracks, startled for a moment, and the oddly juvenile grin vanished. Mick was a big man with long, gangly arms and legs, ending in huge hands and feet. His face was almost totally without guile, every thought or emotion etching itself there with utter transparency. Penny wouldn't have described him as handsome, but there was an innocent, puppyish quality to him that she supposed some people might find kind of endearing.

If only, she thought, he could keep his mouth shut. And make some better decisions. And learn to take no for an answer.

"Looking for you," he said. "I followed your trail. You didn't exactly hide it."

"I didn't realize I needed to. No one's going to know where I came into the range except you."

"Yeah, that's what I figured."

"Which still doesn't answer the real question," she reminded him. "Why did you follow me?"

"I got to thinking," he began. Anytime that happened, trouble wasn't far behind, she knew from long experience. "I realized that I didn't need to be in a motel." He shrugged his shoulders, hefting his backpack. "Everything I need is in here. We can have a mobile command center, right out here, and I can be around to help out if you need it."

"If I'd needed help we'd have planned for that from the beginnin'," Penny said. When she was upset or anxious, the Southern accent she had otherwise squashed after the Gulf War crept back into her voice. Her "I'd" became "Ah'd," she dropped ending sounds, even the rhythm changed to one with more of a musical lilt. Just now, she was plenty upset. One thing about puppies—you could talk to them and talk to them, but that didn't mean they learned until you rubbed their noses in it and gave them a swat. "What if there's an emergency? You're supposed to be someplace central so y'all can cover all of us if somethin' happens."

"I'm only an hour from the van, if I hustle," he said, trying his hardest to be reassuring but not quite pulling it off. "And here, I'm closer to you and to Dieter."

"But without wheels. And on the wrong side of the line. You'd best go back."

"I just hauled all this crap in here, Penny." His tone edged dangerously close to whining. He seemed to realize it, and dialed back the drama a couple of notches. "I thought you'd be glad. It seemed like a really good idea to me."

"Yeah," Penny sighed. "The thing about a plan, though, is that it's best to stick to it unless there's an overwhelmingly good reason to change it. 'Because I felt like it' doesn't count."

"Look, I can go back, Penny, if you want." Mick looked up at the sky and Penny followed his gaze. The sun perched above the hills to the west, ready to slide behind them. It would be dark before he made it halfway.

"No, don't try to do it tonight," Penny finally said. "Crash here, then tomorrow morning you can help me set up before you go back."

His face broke into that big, goofy smile, revealing an array of uneven teeth. "Okay," he said. "Anyway, the view here is a lot better than…well, anywhere else."

She chose to ignore the comment, tossing him an icy glance but nothing else. He was, in his own awkward way, trying to compliment her looks. She'd heard it before, from him, but it did nothing for her.

Penny had always been realistic about her own looks. She wasn't willing to put much effort into appearance, but she did have a thick mane of light brown hair that was usually pulled back into a ponytail and tied with a rubber band or scrunchy. It was unruly, though, and tended to strike out on its own with no notice. Her face was okay, she thought. It worked, its parts were in the right places and there was nothing misshapen about any of them. Her eyes were an unusually light green that contrasted nicely with the brown hair. She had always kept fit, more through being outdoors than in a gym, so her body was as toned as it was going to get: strong legs, probably too muscular in the calves to be really shapely, firm ass, breasts a little on the large side but enhanced by strong pecs. And with a shirt on, no one could see the five-inch scar across her abdomen, her permanent souvenir of the Persian Gulf.

On the Slab, Lettie Bosworth made dinner for her husband Will.

She worked over a propane stove in their mobile home, making a casserole out of various leftovers and canned meat. With a very few exceptions for restaurants or visits to friends' homes, she had made dinner for Will every night for the past thirty-four years. He never cooked, not even barbecue. He never skipped a meal. She had heard about men who traveled for business, but when Will had been in business he'd been a barber. There was no travel involved, and he was home in time for dinner every night. Since he'd retired six years before, he'd been home for every meal.

She supposed there were women who would appreciate such a faithful record. He didn't go out with other women or carouse with buddies from the barber shop. He went to work, and then he came home. In the morning he did it again. Retirement had only changed the part where he went to work. There was talk of war, but she didn't think she could count on men in their seventies being drafted.

She had had to drive a borrowed truck all the way to Brawley to find rat poison. Even when she had, she wasn't sure what it would do. She'd heard about it in movies and TV shows, but that was fiction. She didn't know if it would kill him instantly, or just make him sick. Depended on the dose, she figured, but there was no handy little chart inside that detailed its possible effects on a human being.

But that was okay. Either result would be fine. She didn't wish Will dead, necessarily. She was just looking for a change in the routine.

She poured a little more in, replaced the cap, and put the rat poison back under the sink.

Lettie figured the casserole would disguise the flavor pretty well.

Lucy Alvarez bounced in the back of the Navigator like a kernel of corn in a popcorn popper, each bump or jolt the SUV took throwing her against one of the walls or tossing her up to slam back down against the cargo area floor. With her hands and ankles bound tightly and a gag across her mouth, all she could do was kick and make muffled screams. But the men in the front ignored her, for the most part, only turning around when she tried to raise herself up high enough to be seen from outside the vehicle. Then one of the guys would turn around and push her back down.

The ride took hours. Much of the trip, she was sure, was off-road. The whole time, none of them spoke to her, though they spoke of her quite a bit, appraising every part of her body they'd been privileged to see, and many they hadn't.

"You think she'll bruise back there?" one of them asked after a particularly brutal jounce.

"You care?" another had answered. "What is she, a piece of fruit?" They had all laughed at that one.

Lucy's emotions hopscotched from terror to rage to self-pity; every time she tried to pray, for deliverance from these men, for protection, for a boulder to fall from the sky and crush their car or a cop to stop them for speeding, to be transported away with a wish, her thoughts became so jumbled that she lost track of where she was. There was no telling what they wanted with her, but there was no way it would be good. Men didn't kidnap someone just to shower her with gifts and crown her a princess. At the least, she figured she was looking at being gang-raped. At worst, she would die in some awful fashion.

There was, of course, one other possibility—they might have kidnapped her for ransom money. If that was the case, they were going to be seriously disappointed.

By the time they stopped she was parched and nauseous. Her arms, cuffed behind her, had gone numb but they had ached for a long time before that and would again, she knew, when sensation came back into them. Her back and neck felt like they were on fire, and her legs were as sore as if she had run a marathon.

She thought she'd never get the taste of the gag out of her mouth. But then, there was a good chance that she'd die with it there. Who knew what these men had in mind for her?

When the SUV's back was opened, she looked up from her position on the floor, wide-eyed and fearful. She knew she probably looked like a scared doe, and she hated that. At the moment it was the best she could muster.

The car had parked somewhere out in the desert near an old shack, mud-walled with a simple tarpapered roof, dark in the long shadows cast by the sun dropping behind a nearby hill. Two of the guys pulled her from the vehicle, one muscular with curly gray hair in a yellow polo shirt and khakis, the other smaller, furtive-looking, with straight brown hair and a drooping mustache that gave him a dour expression. He wore a T-shirt with a silhouette of a deer in cross-hairs and a gun shop logo on it, over camouflage fatigue pants. That one said, "There you go," as they stood her on her feet. But when they let go of her, her legs couldn't support her weight and she collapsed into the dirt. She felt tears spring to her eyes, though she fought to hold them in.

"Come on, get her," the curly-haired guy said. The tone in his voice, and the speed with which the mustached guy and a couple of others jumped to obey, indicated to Lucy who was in charge here. The man had spoken with the confidence that his command would be carried out swiftly and efficiently. She wondered if he had been a military man in his younger days.

She had, on the ride here, determined to remember as many details about all of them as she possibly could. If she did manage to get out of this alive, she wanted to be able to put all these men in jail.

The mustached guy held the cabin door open while two of the others held her arms and helped/dragged her inside. The curly guy that she took to be their leader, or at least their Alpha dog, had gone in first, carrying an armful of rifles. The man on her right was older than the others, with thinning black hair turning to wiry silver on his temples. His prescription glasses had clip-on sunglasses attached. He wore a white guayabera shirt, though he was no Mexican, and black slacks. On her left was a younger guy, muscular in an orange tank top and jeans, with long blond hair pulled back in a ponytail. She thought about trying to pull free from their grip, but realized that she wouldn't be able to take two steps without falling down until her legs recovered from the cramped ride.

The cabin, once they had her inside and a couple of lanterns lit, turned out to be nicer than she'd expected. The furnishings in the main room were primitive but adequate—a couple of old couches and some thrift-store chairs arranged around a stone fireplace, all atop an ancient wooden floor. Sleeping bags were rolled neatly and stacked near one of the couches. The guns were leaned against one of the bare adobe walls, less than twenty feet from her but far out of reach. A kitchen area held no modern appliances, but there was a camp stove and several coolers on the counters. Certainly there would be no indoor plumbing, but she hadn't seen an outhouse, so that was still a mystery.

The curly guy had taken a beer from one of the coolers and sat in the most comfortable-looking of the various old chairs. Lucy's escorts led her to one of the couches and shoved her down onto it. Springs stabbed at her butt, which was still an improvement over the past few hours. She rolled her head from side to side, trying to work out the kinks in her neck and shoulders.

Now she could see the last two guys. At first glance she'd thought they were all Anglos, though a couple were deeply tanned. But now she saw that one of them was black. He was extremely short, not much more than five-five, she guessed, but heavily muscled. His hair was cut short, in an almost military trim, and his small brown eyes bored into her like an oilman's drill into the earth. He wore a dark blue T-shirt and dark shorts, like gym shorts, with expensive athletic shoes. The last man was the heaviest one of the bunch, with a big gut and a big build overall. She figured he must have topped two hundred pounds, probably more, and he wasn't more than six feet tall. His hair was bright red and unkempt, as if he didn't own a brush or a comb. His T-shirt, white except for the stains and a couple of torn places where pasty skin showed through, had to be an XXXL, and still when he sat down it rose up over the rolls of his belly. Like the guayabera guy, this one wore glasses, but in contrast to the older man's heavy black plastic, this guy's frames were wire. He looked like a computer programmer, Lucy thought, who had accidentally found himself far from his keyboard.

When they were all settled and those who wanted beer had some—except Lucy, who would have given anything for any liquid at that point—the curly-haired man, who sat with his bottle and examined her dispassionately, like a man looking at a used car, finally spoke. She'd guessed it would be him.

"Why do women have tits?" he asked, without preamble. Without waiting for an answer—not that any was forthcoming, certainly not from Lucy, who wouldn't have dignified the question with a response even if she hadn't been gagged—he went on. "So men will talk to them." A couple of the other guys chuckled, mostly nervous laughter. It sounded like they'd heard the joke before. The speaker unfolded a long buck knife and began using it to pare his fingernails as he spoke, flicking them into the cold fireplace as he finished each one. "You belong to us now. We'll take good care of you."

Lucy shrugged, tried to indicate her bound arms by shaking her head at them. He seemed to understand.

"For tonight, your hands will stay tied. We'll take the gag off to let you drink in a few minutes, but then it goes back on, and stays there. By tomorrow you'll understand how far we are from any living soul, and how little good it would do you to scream or make a fuss of any kind.

"Today and tonight, no one will touch you. We'll take the cuffs off your ankles so you can stand, walk around in the cabin, stretch a little. If you need to use the facilities, let one of us know and we'll take you to the head.

"In the morning, you'll be given more to drink and a little to eat. Then you'll be untied, and allowed to go.

"You'll have a twenty-minute head start. Then we'll come after you. If you get away, get back to civilization, whatever, then you're free. If we catch you, then you're really ours and we'll do whatever we want with you.

"Let me emphasize that last part. Whatever we want. No rules, no laws, no boundaries."

He closed his eyes for a moment, as if enjoying some inner vision, and then took a swig of beer.

"I suppose I should tell you that no Dove has ever gotten away from us. And some of them genuinely came to enjoy our attentions. Maybe they were women who like that kind of thing anyway, who were into some group action. Is that one of your fantasies, little Dove? Being taken over and used by a group of strange men?"

She wouldn't give him the satisfaction of agreeing or shaking her head. She stared at him, fire in her eyes.

"Ah, it doesn't look like it," he continued, closing the knife and shoving it back into its case on his belt. "Doesn't really matter to us, I assure you.

"Oh, and you noticed that I called you a Dove? That's what this is, little Dove. This is our Dove Hunt. You're the Dove. And we're very good hunters."

As the afternoon wore on and night fell, Lupe Alvarez's concern had turned to genuine worry. Lucia had simply gone out to the store for some beer and chips for her brothers, who had been working hard building a new room on the house. The mercado was less than a mile from home, and the whole trip should have taken twenty minutes, at the most. But she had been gone for hours now.

Jorge recognized the anxious look on her face as she stared at the phone, saying a silent prayer that it would ring and Lucia would be on the other end. "Mama," he said. "We got to call the police."

She had resisted that all afternoon, not only because Mexicans, even legal ones, didn't tend to think of the authorities as their friends, but also because calling them would mean admitting that something terrible had happened. But they'd tried everything else—Jorge and Diego, Lucia's brothers, and Raul and Oscar, Lupe's husband and father, respectively, had gone out in the boys' truck, combing the streets for hours while Lupe had waited at home by the phone, worrying her rosary until her fingers ached. She had lit candles, she had prayed to the Virgin and the Saints. Diego had even called Dagoberto Morales, Lucia's ex-husband, the one who had been so cruel to her that she'd been forced to leave him and move back home.

It broke Lupe's heart that her daughter would be divorced before she was even twenty-two. She hadn't wanted the girl to marry him in the first place—there had been something shady about him, something that didn't sit right with Lupe, from the very beginning. But when Lucia set her mind to something, she usually did it. This was a girl who had never owned so much as a tricycle, or training wheels, but the day she decided she wanted to ride Jorge's big two-wheeler, she had climbed up onto the seat and, by the end of the afternoon, was an accomplished rider. Lupe thought that Lucia had inherited her own stubborn streak, and then had improved upon it.

So Lucia got married when she wanted to get married, and when it became clear to her that Dagoberto was no good, she made up her mind to get a divorce. And Lupe had to admit, with all the men in the house, it was nice to have another woman at home again, even if only for a little while.

But nothing was worse than this—not knowing where she was, feeling certain that something so horrible she couldn't even put a name to it had happened.

"He's right," Oscar said. "It's time."

Lupe looked at her father. He was usually the last to want anything to do with the authorities. He'd been illegal when he'd moved to the *Estados Unidos*, and had remained here, with that status, for more than a decade. Dodging the law had become second nature to him, and continued to be even though he and the rest of the family had been citizens for several years now.

"If you think so…" she began.

"I do," he said. He sat in his chair, feet up on the ottoman, arms crossed resolutely. The circulation in his legs was bad and he had to keep his feet up when he wasn't working or they swelled and ached. Anyway, he was in his early seventies, and had earned the right to relax in the evenings. But he didn't look very relaxed right now—with his silver-rimmed glasses perched on his nose, he looked every inch the strict schoolteacher he had been back in Veracruz. Only the bad legs and the stringy, tanned arms and the pale circle on his head where his hat kept the sun off during the day revealed that he'd spent the last fifteen years working outdoors instead of in a classroom.

"They'll just tell us to wait twenty-four hours," Diego said. "It's on every TV show."

Diego was the bigger of the boys, practically a giant compared to his parents Lupe and Raul, neither of whom were taller than five-six. Construction work had put muscles on both boys, but on the smaller Jorge they looked somehow unnatural. Diego just looked like an Aztec prince.

"If that's what they say, then that's what they say," Oscar insisted. "Still, you must try."

Lupe wasn't quite sure how making the call had become her responsibility, but she didn't question it. Keeping the family whole was a woman's job, she supposed, and this fell into that category somehow. Since Mecca was an unincorporated community, there was no local police force. Instead, she found the phone number of the nearest Sheriff's substation and called.

When she was finally connected to Henry Rios, what he said chilled her to the bone.

"I'm glad you called, Lupe. We had a report earlier today, about a possible abduction. But it was just from one eyewitness, and not a very reliable one at that. He didn't know who was taken, or by exactly who, or in what kind of vehicle. It was all really vague."

"So you think it's my Lucia?" she asked, fighting back tears.

"I don't know. But it's a possibility we'll have to look at. Don't you worry, Lupe, we'll get your girl back if she's really been taken. It's kidnapping if someone snatched her, and that's Federal—we'll bring the FBI in. They don't screw around with this stuff."

"But why—why would they kidnap Lucia? She has no money for a ransom, no—"

"We're not in a position to answer that yet," Rios said. "We don't even know for sure that's what happened. But we'll have every law enforcement officer in Riverside County looking for her, and like I said, the FBI will be involved if it turns out to be a kidnapping. Meantime, you let me know if you hear from anybody, even if they tell you not to call the authorities. Especially if they tell you that. You understand, Lupe? This is your daughter's life we're talking about, so we don't want to take any chances. Let the people who do this for a living take care of it."

His words were terrifying, as if he were already certain of what had happened to Lucia. By the time she hung up, tears were flowing and Raul was beside her, wrapping his arms around her.

She let her husband hold her as she said another silent prayer for her daughter's safety.

Carter Haynes had hired a crew to set up a wooden stage on one of the slabs, with a podium on it and electric lights beaming down on him from tall poles. A microphone installed on the podium broadcast over a p.a. system so he could be heard over the rumble of the generators powering everything. He'd picked the best spot available for his address, but "best" was, he had learned, loosely defined here. It was across a broken, fragmented cement slab from a fire pit around which the locals congregated in the evenings, though, which meant there was a built-in audience, many of whom already had lawn chairs. In addition, a couple of rows of chairs that looked as if they'd been ripped right out of an auditorium sat at one edge of the slab, and they were mostly full. Notices had been posted about this meeting for a couple of weeks on the Slab's bulletin board, near the old cement guardhouse that stood on the road leading up from Salton Estates.

Carter stayed off the stage while people gathered, shooting the breeze with Colonel Franklin Wardlaw, USMC, from the Marine Corps Air Station Yuma. Butler, the hick Lieutenant, and his doofus Deputy, Billy Cobb, whom Carter had already begun calling, in his own mind, "Corn," stood off to the side, trying to look official and useful.

Wardlaw was just here as window-dressing, to demonstrate that the deal had the military's support, but Carter had welcomed him with a big smile and a friendly handshake when he'd arrived. He was everything one would expect from a Marine colonel—tall and beefy and white, with short hair and the jutting jaw of an American hero. The good Colonel believed he owned the Chocolate Mountains, and in many respects he might as well have. The range butted almost right up against the Slab— separated from it only by a thin ribbon of canal—and the bombing missions Wardlaw's people ran in those mountains were one of the major sources of free entertainment for the Slab dwellers.

"You know," Carter said, "it's very important to the people who'll be buying homes here to know that they won't be hit by any flying shrapnel or anything."

Wardlaw smiled at that, and his teeth were every bit as straight and white as if they'd been specially constructed by a Marine dentist. "They don't need to worry about that. We keep a wide berth from the civilian population. Sometimes they can see the drops, but they can't feel them."

"There's kind of a safety zone, right?" Carter asked.

"That's right," Wardlaw assured him.

As they spoke, Carter led Wardlaw off to the side, away from his aide, a tall African-American marine Wardlaw had introduced as Jenkins. "Would you be willing to travel a little? Attend sales presentations, from time to time, in L.A. or San Diego?

Some of these people might need a bit of convincing, and it sure sounds good coming from you. Of course," he added, before the Colonel could object, "your expenses would be covered, you'd be put up in first class accommodations, and we'd arrange a generous stipend for you."

"A stipend, you say."

"That's right. We don't need to talk numbers right here, but I'm sure you'd be happy with it. This is a very crucial aspect of the sales pitch, and not one I want to take any chances with."

Wardlaw didn't look at him, but worried with the toe of his dress shoe at a strange-looking mushroom that had grown up in a crack in the cement slab. "I'm a busy man, as I'm sure you understand," he said. "But I've always believed that the military and private enterprise have to be fair and helpful with one another. I'm sure we can make some sort of mutually satisfactory arrangement."

They shook hands again, and Carter excused himself to head back to the platform. Used to urban functions, he had visited Eddie Bauer before this trip and wore a new yellow cotton duck shirt with khaki slacks and deck shoes. He was surprised to see the locals showing up in rags, virtually—torn T-shirts, overalls, ancient stretch pants, filthy, grease-stained jeans. These people, he realized suddenly, were poor. He had known that, but had not really processed what it meant. Now, faced with the reality of it, he understood.

What he was offering them would seem like a fortune.

Lieutenant Butler gave him a heads up. "Reckon that's all you're gonna get," he said. "Most folks are here, and the ones that aren't probably aren't coming."

"I guess I'll get to it, then," Carter said. He nodded to Butler and Corn and mounted the stage, feeling the warmth as the lights bathed him. Crossing to the podium, he switched on the microphone and pulled it from its stand. Better to hold it like a rock star or an evangelist, he thought, than like a CEO at a sales conference. This would be, he knew, his one opportunity to get these people on his side.

He looked out at the crowd of about seventy with a solemn expression and waited for them to quiet.

"Good evening," he began. "And thanks for coming out tonight."

"Didn't have to go far," someone in the back mouthed off. The rest laughed. Carter allowed himself to crack a smile.

"Yes, that's true," he continued. "Nevertheless, I appreciate it. I know that you people, like all Americans, were stunned and horrified by the cowardly attacks on New York and Washington nine days ago. Life isn't back to normal yet—I don't know, frankly, if it'll ever be back to what we consider normal. But life has to go on. Progress continues. Our economy is strong and it can take a few hits. The American people aren't as soft and weak as those terrorists believe."

He paused for applause, and there was scattered clapping but no outburst. The Lieutenant had warned him that these people had a strong independent streak. The Slab was, some said, practically a country to itself, where the laws of California and the U.S. barely applied.

"Let me get one of those rag-heads in my sights!" someone shouted. There were whoops and hollers at that one.

"We'd all like to get our hands on those terrorists," Carter said. "And in our audience we have a distinguished military guest who some of you know: Colonel Wardlaw from the Yuma Air Station. Colonel, maybe you can nail a few terrorists for all of us!" Another burst of applause and whoops met this comment. Wardlaw nodded and smiled politely.

"But before you get the wrong idea, I'm no politician and I'm not here to talk about the attacks. What I am is a businessman. Business, capitalism, the profit motive, that's what made America great. That's what the terrorists are fighting against, but capitalism is stronger than whatever they would replace it with. And tonight, I'm here to share the proceeds of capitalism with all of you."

He paused to let that sink in. The crowd was quiet now, waiting for an explanation.

"I know you all love living out here, on the Slab. Free of rules, maybe free of taxation, able to do your own thing without making mortgage or rent payments. Sounds good to me too, let me tell you." He tossed in a chuckle there, and had it returned by his audience. But he knew he was on thin ice here. "But things change, and we have to roll with those changes. So here's the deal. My company has purchased the land we're all on—the whole Slab—from its previous owners, the federal government. Our intent is to build a real Salton Estates—not the one that failed, down along the shore, but a workable one right here in one of the loveliest spots in the world. We'll be putting up luxury homes with one of the best views in the best state in the union, of our own Salton Sea, backed by the Chocolate Mountains."

From the crowd he heard definite grumbling now, so he pressed on quickly. "Now, legally, I could just have each and every one of you evicted from the premises. But that's not why I'm here. I'm sure Lieutenant Butler doesn't have any interest in enforcing something like that, either, even though it would be his job to do so. No, I think you'll like my idea a whole lot better."

"You sayin' my Jayco ain't a luxury home?" someone shouted.

Carter ignored him and went back to the podium, replacing the microphone in its stand and letting the suspense build for a moment. Before he spoke, he gripped the podium's sides. "We're expecting to make a profit from this deal, or we wouldn't do it. So, in the interests of fairness, we're going to share that profit with you, up front, out of our own pockets, before we even see a dime."

This drew some approval from the crowd—a few claps, a couple of shouts.

"That's right," he went on. "Because I know you'll have to move somewhere, pick up stakes, as it were, I will be coming to visit each of you personally over the next several days. And I'll be bringing two thousand dollars to every household on the Slab."

More applause at that. He'd been right—to these people, two grand was a significant amount of change. His sources told him there were fewer than seventy separate permanent households on the Slab, so the payoff wouldn't be too expensive. And it'd save money over the long run—if he'd gone the eviction route, there would be legal costs, security costs, the risk that some disgruntled ex-Slabber would come back and torch or vandalize the houses after he'd put some real money into them. Everyone would have to sign a release to get their money, agreeing not to badmouth the new Salton Estates Corporation and to move at least ten miles away from the Slab—to make sure they didn't just set up a new camp right next to the planned resort—but when he was dangling cash in front of them, he thought that process would go smoothly.

On a high note, Carter wrapped up quickly and got off the stage, promising to answer questions individually when he visited each home. The lights were killed, the generators shut down, and Sheriff Butler walked him to his Town Car. A hotel room waited in Palm Desert, and he couldn't wait to get there and shower the grit of this place off him.

This had gone more smoothly than he'd expected, but he still hated the Slab.

Ken's house—a wood-framed bungalow at the edge of Westmorland, on a corner lot framed by scraggly oleander but also sporting some particularly healthy, jagged-leafed ocotillo that bloomed flame red in spring—was quiet that night. The smell of the steak he'd broiled still hung heavy in the kitchen. But in the bedroom he'd converted into a kind of den, he had a window open and a fan going so the air just carried the rich, fertile odor common to most of the Imperial Valley.

The fan was the only sound Ken could hear, drowning out even the insistent buzz of insects from outside. He'd had the TV on for a while but couldn't take it any more. Either there were entertainment programs that didn't seem to have any connection to the world as he now knew it, or there was bad news. The President had addressed Congress and made demands that were unlikely to be met. Planes and ships had been deployed to the Persian Gulf; Afghanistan's ruling religious zealots, the Taliban, had so far refused to turn over Osama bin Laden; and Ken had the distinct impression that the world was slipping toward a war that could never really be won.

As much as he was opposed to the idea of declaring a war that could ultimately result in the deaths of millions, he thought that part of what bothered him was just the knowledge that the world had been changed, permanently, and no one, including him, had any idea what the new world would look like.

Ken's job was keeping the people of Salton Estates safe. He took it very seriously. At night, emergency calls went to the main Sheriff's office in El Centro, but Ken was on call twenty-four/seven. Suddenly, though, Americans everywhere were faced with a threat he couldn't do anything about.

He logged on and checked out some of the chat on the internet for a while, but every room he went into was the same. People talked about the war, about the attacks, about their anger and feelings of helplessness. Frustrated, he signed off after just a few minutes and sat in the dark den. Bookshelves surrounded him, mostly containing the Western history books that were his only real hobby, but somehow he didn't think he could focus on reading right now.

Carter Haynes, the real estate developer, had compared his office to Mayberry. Ken was old enough to remember having watched Andy Griffith as a boy, and he had always been fond of Andy's basic approach to law enforcement. He'd been the Sheriff who refused to carry a gun, and yet he managed to keep the peace in Mayberry. Ken knew that had been fictional, though with some basis in reality, and a very different time and place. He carried a gun because he had to, and he would use it if necessary to keep the peace in Salton Estates. So far he hadn't needed to. He hoped that would continue to be the case.

But not only was there terror in the skies, he now knew there was a killer in his own territory. Shortly before leaving to meet Haynes up at the Slab, he'd had two disturbing phone calls. One was from Henry Rios up in Mecca, confirming that there had now been a missing persons report filed—a young lady named Lucia Alvarez, who went by Lucy, was missing, and she matched the description of the victim in the snatch job Henry's eyewitness had reported. The other call was from Risa Emerson in the Coroner's office. She had confirmed that the skull Billy had taken down had come from a female human, and certainly the victim of a homicide. The skull had taken a .45 slug in the forehead at short range. She would keep working on it, she promised him, and she'd let him know more when she could. But she wanted him to know right away that he had a murder on his hands.

Tomorrow, the fire pit would become a crime scene. He could have done it tonight, but to what purpose he didn't know—by the time Risa had called, it was already burning. By morning it would be cool enough to look at.

He switched on a floor lamp and picked up the Stegner novel again. He knew he'd have a hard time sleeping tonight. Nights like this were the worst, the kind that made him feel Shannon's loss like a man sometimes feels pain in a long-since amputated arm. That was the first thought that struck him on that Tuesday morning when he watched the planes slamming into the World Trade Center again and again—that the people who had loved ones in the twin towers were the ones who were truly going to suffer, going to sleep alone and waking up alone and always, always, remembering what it had been like to lay in bed listening to the one you love breathing beside you.

The day he lost Shannon had been a magic day, too. He'd tasted it as soon as he'd awakened, thick as a mouthful of blood, charged like an electric current in his brain.

It was in 1989, in the spring. The kind of April day when the locals in San Diego try to skip work and go to the beach, because they know that when the tourists come in June, the beaches will not only be overcrowded but socked in with low clouds, overcast for most of the day. He was a cop then, getting up in years but still able to buckle his Sam Browne belt on every day, able to keep up with all but the fittest of the young breed. A Montana native, he'd settled in San Diego after Vietnam and had met his wife there.

Shannon taught fifth grade in a public school in Chula Vista, but now it was spring break and Ken worked a night shift so they were spending time together running errands. On this sunny morning, they had gone to a suburban supermarket and bought bulging bags of groceries for a barbecue later in the day. Ken carried several rustling plastic bags to the car, but Shannon had stopped to chat with one of the cashiers. He had known all day that something strange would happen, something close to miraculous, because that's what it meant when he could taste the magic. He waited for it with a mixture of anticipation and apprehension—more the former than the latter, because generally when the magic came it proved helpful, a positive thing.

On this occasion—and all these years later, he remembered it as clearly as if it had just happened moments before, the pictures as sharp in his mind as HDTV—he had stopped at the trunk and turned back to see where Shannon was, and he saw her, just stepping off the curb with a grocery bag cradled in her arms, still laughing at something the checker had said.

He saw Shannon there, and he saw the truck, an eighteen-wheeler with the logo of the supermarket on its side, engine roaring as it picked up speed, bearing down on Shannon.

The bags fell from his hands and he turned to run toward his wife. But then the truck sped past her and he saw Shannon emerge on the other side, bag still in her hand, a funny half-smile on her face, as if she was saying, "That was a little close, wasn't it?" the way she would.

But a moment later, he realized that the magic was showing him things that weren't there, because the truck hadn't passed by. It was still closing on her, and now he saw it all in slow motion—the driver, face a rictus of terror, fighting the wheel and the brakes but with no results; Shannon, looking up finally at the truck and realizing that it was coming straight at her, faster than she could move. Ken ran, but the magic slowed him down, held him back, as if running through deep water or peanut butter. His arms and legs couldn't get any speed up and he was still a dozen feet away when the truck clipped her—Shannon diving backward to dodge it, but a fender still catching her in mid-air, and that was enough, she was picked up and thrown into the air, and by the time Ken's muscles worked right again Shannon was hitting the ground twenty feet away and sliding, hard pavement scraping the flesh off her cheek down to the bone.

Sixty-seven bones were broken, the doctors told Ken. Death was almost instantaneous. No one wanted him to think that she'd been alive the whole time she'd flown through the air, seeing the supermarket and the parking lot and her husband whipping around in dizzying circles as she tumbled to her death. She didn't suffer, they told him, though they couldn't have known.

And that didn't even begin to speak to his own suffering.

The magic had failed him—worse, it had betrayed him, this time. It had taken the woman he loved from him—the only woman he had ever loved. This had been no freak accident. The truck driver said afterwards that his truck seemed to have a mind of its own, that his foot had been nowhere near the accelerator, but the brake hadn't responded to him, the wheel wouldn't turn, there was nothing he could do to avoid hitting Shannon. Ken believed him. The magic had come back, and the magic had attacked that which was most precious in the world.

Ken didn't respond well. He'd started drinking heavily, even on duty. He'd volunteered for dangerous assignments. He found himself tempting fate, leaving the squad car and walking around, alone, in San Diego's toughest neighborhoods. The magic hadn't protected him then, but something else had. Fate, or pure dumb, luck had kept him alive long enough to get fired.

That was, finally, the event that had sent him into the desert. He couldn't stay in San Diego. Its streets and beaches and palm trees and parks reminded him of Shannon and what they'd had together. He couldn't get a job, and for a long time he'd just stayed in his house, in the dark, drinking and avoiding the world. Finally, though, when it seemed that he could sink no lower, when the depression threatened to rob him of every ounce of humanity, the magic came back again, for the last time until today.

This time it was barely noticeable—he couldn't even tell for sure if it was a magic day or something else entirely, maybe a summer cold that left a slight metallic taste in his mouth. But on this July day, three years later, the world had seemed somehow bright and new and inviting, so he'd gone for a walk around his neighborhood. He'd been inside so much that some of his neighbors probably thought he was a hermit or a myth, a story to scare kids with. This day, this glorious summer day, though, he felt renewed. He walked and walked, and didn't stop until a sudden breeze plastered a sheet of paper to his leg. Ken reached down and peeled it off, and glanced at it before he threw it away.

It was a flyer announcing a job opening in the Imperial County Sheriff's Office.

He went home and started packing.

As annoying as she frequently found Mick—and that was annoying indeed—Penny couldn't help being a little glad that he'd thrown the plan out and joined her in the bombing range. The theory was that, with a big chunk of America's warplanes in or on their way to the Afghanistan, no one would waste ammunition by dropping bombs in the range tonight. But that was just theory, and theory sometimes had an unpleasant way of disproving itself. By tomorrow, the pilots would know there were people on the range, and any bombing activity would cease until they were found and removed. But for tonight there was always the possibility that she had made camp right on top of an intended target area. And if she was going to be blown up, she thought, some company might not be a bad thing. Even Mick's.

They didn't dare risk an actual fire, and Penny turned down Mick's repeated suggestions that they huddle together for warmth when the night turned cool. So instead they sat up for a while wrapped in their own sleeping bags, talking under an enormous canopy of stars.

"They don't give a damn about Christ's admonishment to turn the other cheek," Mick said, repeating his theme for the evening. "They just want to go all Old Testament on someone's ass, and I don't think they really care who."

"I don't agree with it," Penny countered. "But you can sort of understand the impulse."

"To kill?"

"To try to persuade other would-be terrorists that they can't get away with it."

"But they were willing to die in the first place," Mick argued. "So how does killing them teach them a lesson?"

"Like I said, I don't agree with it."

"I know, Penny," Mick said, his tone softening. "You wouldn't be here if you did. Days like this I just feel like I'm arguing with the whole world. Like I'm the only one who sees the light and everyone else is ready to spill blood just to have something to do with their hands."

"And you're a voice crying in the wilderness?"

Mick laughed, craning his neck to survey the empty dark around them. "Literally," he said.

"Listen, Mick, no offense, but I'm kind of glad we're out here where there's no talk radio and no cable news. Do you think we can just be silent for a while, maybe get some sleep?"

"Sure," Mick agreed. "Sure, that's a good idea. Plenty of time to talk tomorrow, right?"

She didn't answer, because it sounded like he'd already forgotten his promise to leave after they were set up. She didn't want to get into another argument, though. What she really did want was silence. She wanted to commune with the wilderness, to be at peace with the velvet touch of night and the eternal flow of the natural world around her.

Ten minutes later she heard Mick's steady breathing and knew he was asleep. She stretched out and shut her own eyes, happy to join him in that.

True to their word, her captors had given Lucy a bottle of water and taken off her gag long enough for her to drink it, though they'd made it clear they weren't going to engage in conversation and would answer no questions. Then two of them had escorted her, weapons in hand, to an ancient outhouse down a short trail away from the cabin, where her hands had been uncuffed so that she could clean herself when she was finished. She had stayed in there longer than they'd wanted, exulting in finally being able to move her arms again. Finally, they had pounded on the walls, threatening to come in after her, and she had emerged. They'd cuffed her again, hands still behind her back, and they'd all gone back into the cabin.

At bedtime, she was allowed to choose whether to be face up or face down. She chose down—feeling slightly more vulnerable but at the same time not wanting to have to look at her captors. Her cuffs were removed again and she was bound, arms extended, legs spread, to four D-rings bolted to the floor, so her limbs made a big X in the center of the living room. If there had been any uncertainty as to the fate that awaited her with these men, this arrangement erased it. She'd be a prisoner, a slave to their pleasures. Then, most likely, dead, since she couldn't imagine that they'd let her walk away after they'd finished with her.

The men took shifts guarding her, beginning with the guy in the muscle shirt, who sat in the curly guy's chair, rifle across his legs. If anyone had asked her, she'd have sworn that it would be impossible to sleep in such circumstances. But that turned out not to be the case. Sleep was a mercy, a blessing, taking her out of her situation and back into a world where things made sense, where people didn't snatch others off the street and call them doves. She felt it coming, felt her mind begin to drift in unexpected directions, and welcomed it.

Harold found that he didn't sleep much these days, a fact that filled Virginia with dread. She kept the trailer door locked at night, in case he forgot where he was and wandered off, he figured. Of course, he'd also have to forget how to open a locked door from the inside, and so far, though his memory was often bad, it hadn't become that bad.

Still, he didn't want to frighten her, so most nights—most nights that he remembered, anyway—he simply sat up late watching old movies or sitcoms on TV. They had a VCR and solar panels and had all the power they needed for simple things, and he hadn't lost the ability to change channels.

For some reason that he couldn't quite put his finger on, tonight he very much wanted to watch a war movie. One of those classics about World War II. He didn't care from what era, or what part of the war it dealt with—Casablanca would be fine, as would *Tora, Tora, Tora* or *In Harm's Way* or *The Bridge at Remagen* or *The Guns of Navarone*. He wanted to see the camaraderie of men in combat, and preferably those fighting for what he considered a noble cause.

He loved Virginia more than he could ever express, not being very handy with words. She was the best thing that had ever happened to him, and his fifty years of marriage to her had been satisfying in so many ways he couldn't begin to enumerate them. But she was all he had, and that was a lot of weight to put on one person's shoulders.

Somewhere out there in the desert—surely at the cabin now, sleeping off the night's drunk—were the last men he'd faced combat with. Combat of a different kind, for a cause that was anything but noble. But still, they were men and they had carried arms together. They shared secrets and they shared history and they had placed their lives in one another's hands, and not a one of them had betrayed that trust.

Harold knew why he couldn't be with them—who would trust a man with a gun who couldn't even remember his own name half the time? Knowing the reason didn't mean he didn't miss it, though. He tried to remind himself that it was wrong, inhuman, what they had done together for so many years. That was not, he thought, the kind of man he was. His was the "Greatest Generation," they were saying now, people who had willingly risked everything to go to a foreign land and fight for justice. People like that wouldn't—couldn't—do the things he had done. There was some kind of gap, an empty spot, in his brain or his heart or his soul, to let him willingly go along with such acts.

That, he decided, was the real reason he couldn't sleep at night. Not just that he had gotten old and required less sleep, not even that his most strenuous physical activity these days was walking out to a lawn chair and lifting a glass of lemonade to his lips. It was the memory of the things he had done coming back to haunt him. His brain tried to shield him from it by shutting down, by turning off the memory banks, but that was only so effective. There were nights that it worked, but there were too many others, when it failed to protect him from the memory of his own crimes.

He snatched up the remote and pointed it at the TV, jamming his finger down on the CHANNEL button again and again, trying to find something, anything, that would shut off the torture his memory inflicted on him. Nothing worked, and he knew this would be a long, difficult night.

Chapter 07

Penny and Dieter and Larry had made a big deal of synchronizing the new digital alarm watches they'd purchased in San Diego before driving into the desert. When it beeped her awake in the morning, an hour before sunrise, she knew that Dieter and Larry were also waking up at their own campsites. She shook Mick awake—he had been expected to be encamped in a motel, so he didn't get one of the spiffy watches—and started a pot of coffee. While the water boiled she went off into the desert to fulfill her toilet needs, and when she got back he was up and preparing breakfast for them both.

They ate quickly and headed out to get their first task accomplished before the sun came up. Using satellite photos they'd purchased on the web, they had identified what looked like reasonably flat, bare spots in three different areas in the mountains. Penny and Mick hiked quickly to the one nearest their camp. The aerial view had been fairly accurate, it turned out. To be exactly the blank slate they wanted they'd had to clear away some stray rocks, but for the most part, it was a wide stretch of brown earth with no plants, flat as a city street.

"This is perfect," Mick said.

"Not perfect, but close enough," Penny replied.

"Close enough." They set to work.

Within thirty minutes they were done. With light-colored rocks, to show against the brown dirt, they had spelled out NO MORE BOMBS in letters big enough to be seen from hundreds, maybe thousands of feet up. Dieter would be writing WAGE PEACE, while Larry's slogan was WAR NO MORE. This kind of stone art, geoglyphs or intaglios, was actually very traditional in this part of the world, with a string of images, maybe thousands of years old, still visible from the air from Blythe all the way down to the Yuha desert near the Mexican border.

Every day until they were caught, they would either change their messages slightly or make new marks upon the land, so that fly-overs would reveal that there was still someone alive within the Impact Area. Their continued presence would ensure that the bombs wouldn't fall. At least, that was the theory.

As they walked back to camp, Penny touched Mick's arm. "Hey, I'm sorry I shut you down last night when you wanted to talk, Mick."

He looked at her and smiled. "No problem," he said. "I'm getting kind of used to it."

She didn't know exactly how to respond to that—it was true, but not something she wanted to get into just now. Instead, she veered in a slightly different direction, focusing it on herself in a desperate attempt to keep him from thinking there might ever be a them. "It's just something I do, you know? I kind of keep people at a distance, I guess. Keep walls up."

"You have to let them down sometime, Pen."

"That's what they tell me. I guess I just haven't found my time yet."

"Have you tried?"

"Now and again," she said. "I don't know if it's a defense mechanism, or what. I just don't seem to be comfortable letting people get too close."

Penny began to wish she'd initiated this conversation last night, in the dark. She kept her head down, picking out a path in the early morning light. But she felt the heat of his gaze on her, studying her.

"Maybe you should give it another shot, Penny. You might find that you like it."

"I…I don't know," she said. "I like sex. I like physical contact. I like having people to talk to…except when I don't. I know it doesn't make sense."

"Not a lot," Mick agreed.

"And it's not that I don't want a relationship," she went on. "But even if I'd found the right guy, which I haven't, that takes a lot of…you know, time and energy. And I've just been too busy for that." Which is true, she thought. But maybe a bit of a dodge all the same. And I don't think I could get much more pointed without cutting his throat.

"So," Penny said, changing the subject completely. Another wall, another defense. When it gets too personal, step aside. "So, you think this will work? Really?"

They had all agreed that it would—they wouldn't have come if they didn't think there was a reason to be out here, she knew. But thinking that on the floor of someone's Connecticut Avenue apartment and thinking it on the ground in the middle of a live bombing range were two very different things.

"No," Mick said. His honesty surprised her, but that was often the case with Mick. "Do I think it'll end war for all time? Absolutely not. Do I think it'll at least make them stop bombing one of the most beautiful spots in the American West? Maybe, at least for a little while. Maybe we'll get enough publicity to make people pay attention to the Chocolates. Chances are if you went more than fifty miles in any direction you'd have a hard time finding anyone who had ever heard of this place. If we can capture some eyeballs, then the battle's half done, right?"

"I suppose."

"We want a world at peace," Mick went on. "A world where the military doesn't need bombs—better yet, a world where we don't need a military. But that's not going to happen any time soon, especially now. Especially with Bush and his friends firing up the war machine again. That just makes our job that much harder to do—but also, that much more vital. If we can get people to think about peace—to consider the idea that peace is a viable alternative—then we've done more than we could have hoped for.

"So I guess that's the answer, Pen. Will this do what we want it to? Not a chance. But can it do things we haven't even dared to consider? Absolutely it can. That's why we're here, why you and Larry and Dieter are risking having your heads blown off."

"And you, now," Penny pointed out.

Mick shrugged. "I guess so."

She stopped and smiled. There had been a time when she might have given him a hug at that moment. But not any more. Now it would just confuse him, make him hope for things that weren't going to happen. She kept her hands, somewhat uncomfortably, at her sides. He wasn't the man for her but that didn't mean he wasn't—disregarding his awkward social skills—a good man.

"Thanks, Mick," she said, meaning it.

Ken knew that crime scene investigators could discover amazing things from careful examination of a scene where a crime had taken place or evidence had been abandoned. But he was no trained forensic technician, and the fire pit at the Slab was hardly pristine. It had burned the night before, as it did every night. It stank now, like old ash and burnt garbage and urine, as if the locals pissed on it at night to put it out. Likely they did, once they'd tucked away a few beers.

Oddly, the metallic taste remained in his mouth, and nothing that had happened the day before seemed to fit the previous pattern the magic had established. He'd never had it last more than a day, but it seemed to be hanging on. He wished it could do something about the smell of the ashes before him.

Carrie Provost stood nearby, watching him work. He sifted through the ash with a screened tray, much like panning for gold. Anything he found big enough not to fall through the screen went into one of a series of plastic evidence bags. So far mostly what he'd found were charred beer cans, melted lumps of plastic, nails and screws, and one pair of pliers. He'd also come across two unknown chunks of something that might have been bone fragments. Of course, they could have been from a steak as easily as from a person.

"You think you're going to find a fingerprint or somethin' in there, Kenneth?" Carrie asked. "Because most people, they won't touch that with their hands. When it's not hot it's filthy, if you know what I mean. All that dirt and muck and ash. People put their hands in there, they leave fingerprints all right—on everything they touch for the rest of the day."

"Then it ought to be pretty easy to find out who put that skull in, right, Carrie? I just follow the prints around the Slab."

"I don't think that'll—ohh, you're teasin' me, ain't you, Ken?"

"I'm teasing you, Carrie. Tell you the truth, I'm not sure I'll find much in here of value to anyone, especially me. But I have to look."

"I did the right thing, didn't I? Calling you when I found it?"

"You did the right thing, Carrie."

"And you don't think it was me, do you?"

"I don't think so, Carrie. I'm pretty sure if you'd put it in the fire pit, you'd have let someone else dig it out."

"That's the way I see it. Unless of course I was trying to fool you into thinkin' that."

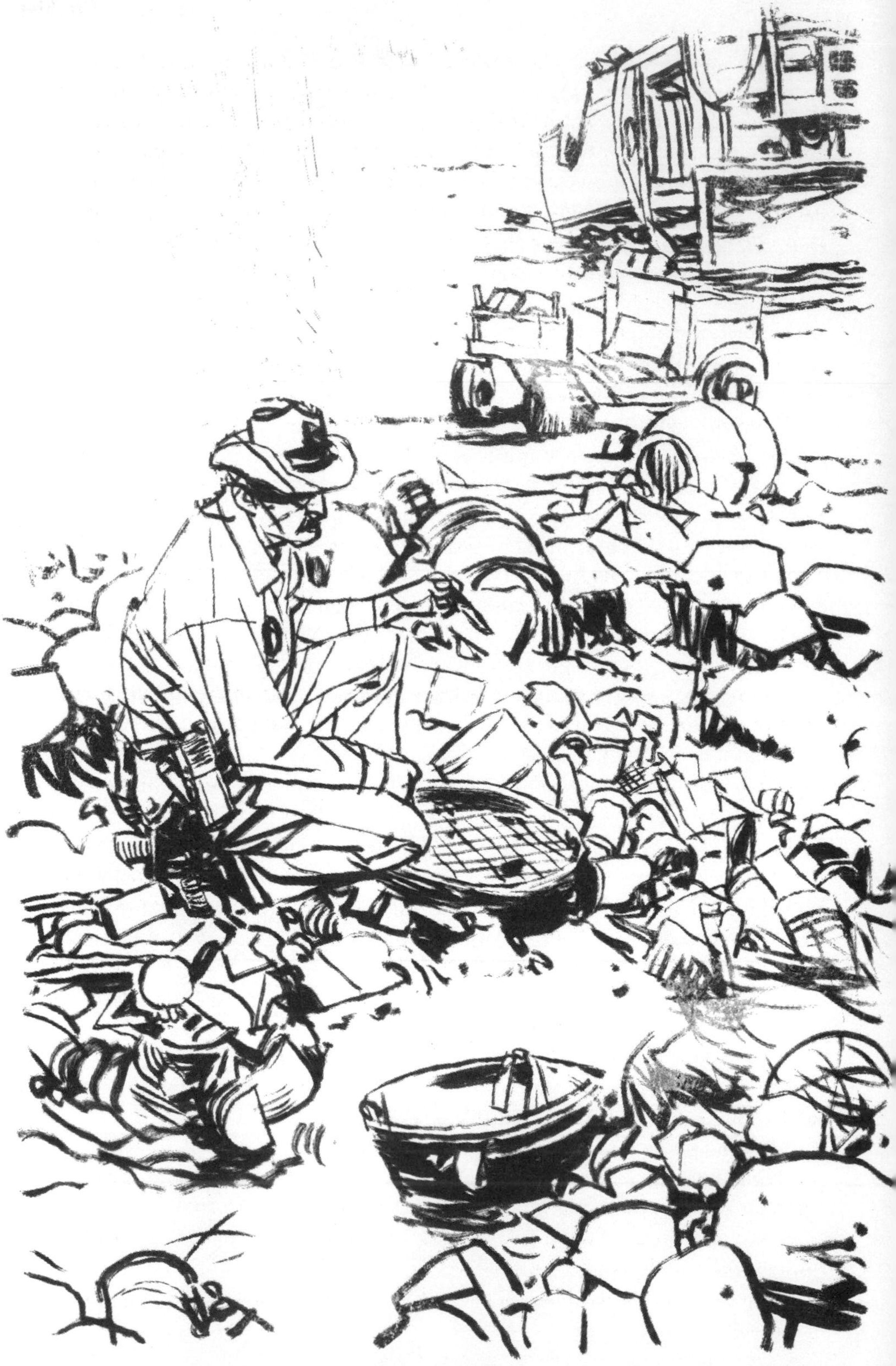

"Well, you might have a point there," Ken said, shaking his tray. A rock stayed in it, so he picked the rock up with tongs and dropped it into yet another plastic bag, which he carefully sealed. With a permanent marker he wrote the day's date, the location, and "rock" on the bag's label. It suddenly occurred to him that there were probably firefighters and rescue workers performing this exact same process in Manhattan—sifting through the ash, looking for body parts. Except the Carrie Provosts they had to deal with were mothers and brothers and spouses, driven half-mad by tension and fear and hope. Goddamnit, Ken thought as tears welled in his eyes. He couldn't even wipe his own face with his hands, encased as they were in latex gloves caked thick with ash and muck from the pit.

"You okay, Sheriff?" Carrie asked. Her concern sounded real and he didn't bother to correct her nomenclature.

"Yeah, just got some grit in my eye."

By the time he'd finished—"finished" being a relative term, which in this case meant that he had sifted as much crap as he was going to and was pretty sure he hadn't found anything at all helpful—a small crowd had gathered to watch. He recognized Clyde Wills, a tattoo artist whose body was his own best calling card, old Hal and Virginia Shipp, Maryjane Peters, who lived with a loser named Darren Cook, Jaye and Jim Gretsch, and there were a couple of others who he couldn't place. Peeling the gloves off his sweaty hands, he dropped them into a larger plastic bag and loaded up the evidence bags into it, then rose and turned to face the spectators.

"I'm here to investigate a possible crime," he said. "A human skull was found in this fire pit. Do any of you know anything about how it came to be there?"

A murmur of negatives.

"Well, if you think of anything, or hear anything, let me know. I'll probably be coming around to visit each of you privately, too. Only unlike Mr. Haynes, I won't be bringing a couple of grand with me when I come, just a lot of annoying questions."

That, at least, got some smiles. The entertainment apparently over, the people started to drift away. The Shipps, having wandered by after showering in the natural hot spring tank, were the last to go. Virginia hovered almost as if she had something to say, but maybe it was just her way of letting Hal get some air, Ken speculated. There was a blank look on Hal's face as he watched the proceedings, and when Ken looked at him, the old man stepped forward, his hand extended.

"Pleased to meet you," Hal said. "My sister said you were a Sheriff."

Ken caught Virginia's gaze over Hal's shoulder. Sister? The two had been married for decades, Ken knew. And Hal had known Ken for years.

"Pleasure," Ken replied, reaching for the hand.

"Harold's been like this all day," Virginia said. "Exhausted, probably. Sat up all night, far as I can tell. When I found him this morning he was just lost."

Ken got closer to Hal, and their fingers touched, and then they clasped hands firmly and Ken felt like he was holding a live wire. A shock went through his entire body, leaving his arm numb and shaking. Hal reacted with surprise too, and dropped Ken's hand.

"Boy, we got a little static electricity going that time, didn't we, Ken?" he asked.

"I guess so," Ken said. Wherever Hal had been, he was back now.

"What brings you back to the Slab?" Hal continued. "Following up on that real estate guy's pitch?"

"Oh, no," Ken said. "He'll follow up on that without my help. I'm actually doing real police work, Hal. You know anything about a skull that ended up in the fire pit?"

Hal looked like he was thinking it over. "No, no, I can't say that I do. How long do you suppose it's been there?"

"Well, that I don't know," Ken replied. "A little while, at least."

"I sure hope you find whoever put it there, Ken. Best of luck to you."

"Thanks, Hal. Appreciate it. You folks take care." Ken gathered up his bag and equipment, touched the rim of his Smokey hat, and carried everything to his Bronco. His arm still tingled from the unexpected shock of touching Hal Shipp.

The men untied her for breakfast, allowing Lucy to eat a plate of scrambled eggs and a few pieces of steak they had cut for her, standing at the kitchen counter with only a fork. When the gag came off, the curly-haired guy who had done most of the talking so far did some more of it.

"None of what we talked about last night was negotiable, doll, so don't waste any effort trying to talk us out of anything. Just use it to eat. You'll need your strength, believe me."

The other guys laughed at that. Lucy took his advice and downed the food as fast as she could, in case they changed their minds again. Someone put a cup of black coffee in front of her and she swallowed that too.

"Here's the thing," the curly guy continued. "We're lousy hunters. We're shitty hunters, if you want the technical word for what we are. But what we're doing here, it's not really hunting, you see? We're sportsmen. It's something entirely different. Hunting's when you track something down so you can kill it. We have no interest in killing you—although we would if we had to. No, our interest is in tracking you, for the sport of it, and then using you. For the sport of that."

Lucy nodded her understanding, shoveling in her last forkful of eggs. She ate fast, not knowing if they might at any moment decide she'd had enough time. She didn't want to upset her stomach but she figured she would need the fuel. When she had downed the last of the coffee, she realized she still had the fork in her hand.

"Can I keep this?" she asked.

"A fork?" the guayabera man asked with a chuckle. Today he wore a military-style olive drab T-shirt and camouflage pants, though, as did all the others, so she knew she'd have to come up with a different name for him. She noticed they'd been careful not to use their names in front of her. She took that as a positive sign—maybe they intended to let her live, after all. "You want to keep a fork?"

"You guys have the guns, so it seems only fair," she said.

"Sure, darlin'," the curly guy said. He was definitely the decision maker of the bunch, and the first one she'd plunge the fork into if she ever got the chance. "You can keep the fork. Enjoy it. You need to use the can before you get going?"

"Sure," Lucy said, willing to delay the start any way she could. A few minutes sitting around in the shade while they stood outside in the sun, getting more and more anxious and disturbed—she would take that. She knew it wasn't much of an advantage—it wouldn't compensate, for instance, for the fact that her wedge sandals were just about impossible to run in. But it was something, and she had decided during the night that she would cling to any positives she could. Negative thinking was just going to get her dead.

When she got inside the outhouse, she realized, too late, that she should have asked for water instead of coffee for breakfast. Water would do her more good and stay with her longer. But it wasn't like they'd offered her the choice—the coffee had just been put in front of her. If she hadn't accepted it, she might well have gone thirsty.

Once again, she sat inside until they banged on the walls and insisted she come out. When she emerged, she was still cool, but the two guys who had escorted her out had already sweated through their T-shirts.

"Let's go, bitch," one of them snarled. He was the one with the drooping mustache that made him look perpetually miserable. Probably he is, she thought, or why would he participate in something like this?

She just gave him a smile. "Show some respect," she said. "You don't own me yet. Maybe you never will."

"Oh, we own you, bitch," he said. "Just like you were bought and paid for. You just don't know it yet."

"We'll see." Lucy said, trying to maintain a pleasant demeanor. It was fun to see just how much it pissed this guy off when she was nice to him.

The other escort, the muscular one with the ponytail, seemed to understand her psychological warfare, though, because he grabbed the mustached guy's arm. "Let it go," he said. "She'll find out soon enough."

"There's thirteen graves around here full of bitches didn't think we owned them either," the mustached guy said, ignoring his friend's advice.

"Shut up, man," the ponytailed guy said. "You too," he said, directed at Lucy. "You just keep quiet."

She nodded and smiled as they walked her back to the house.

The other men were scattered around the couches and chairs of the cabin's main room, looking like they were ready to get going. "You know the rules," the curly guy said. "You get away, you get away. You don't, you're ours. You get a twenty-minute head start. Any questions? Too bad. It's really very simple."

She had questions, but none that she would bother to ask. What the mustached one had let slip answered the most important one. If they brought her back here, not only would they use her but then they'd kill her. So she wasn't coming back to this cabin, ever. Curly was right. It was very simple.

"I'm ready," she said.

"Nobody's stopping you. Clock starts now."

Lucy turned without a second look back and ran out the door. As soon as she was outside, she took off the sandals and looped them over her wrists. It would hurt to run on the dirt and sharp rocks, but she'd make far better time barefoot. At the same time, she didn't want to let go of the sandals, because they might come in handy later on.

She still had the fork, tucked into the rear pocket of her jeans.

Bare feet slapping the hot stones and fallen twigs and raw earth, Lucia Alvarez ran for her life.

Carter Haynes wasn't foolish enough to think that most people on the Slab would have checking accounts, or would know what to do with a check if they were given one. But he also wasn't stupid enough to bring cash to a place like this without protection. The bodyguard he'd hired was a walking mountain of a man named Nick Postak. At six-five, he towered over Carter, and he looked like he was probably double Carter's weight, too. He had a big beefy face with small eyes under a heavy brow, a thin line for a mouth, and a wicked-looking red scar that ran from the outer corner of his left eye all the way down his cheek, past his ear. He wore jeans and a polo shirt stretched to its absolute limit by muscular upper arms and wide shoulders. Its tail was left untucked to hide the pistol Postak carried in a holster at the small of his back. Carter carried the cash in a briefcase. With Nick Postak at his side, no one would be crazy enough to try to take more than their share.

Also in the briefcase were contracts. They were simple, two pages each, no fine print. The head of each household—and he used that term loosely, in a place where a "household" might live in the back of a broken-down van—had to sign before he or she got the green.

The first four stops went as planned. A little finessing and the contracts got signed. It didn't even hurt to hand out the eight grand, because he knew it'd be coming back to him in spades. A small price to pay.

Those four stops had taken about ninety minutes, which meant the sun was getting high and hot by the time he and Postak exited the fourth hovel. But there was something different outside this time, besides blinding light and the smell of baking aluminum siding.

This time, there were five men watching them as they made their exit. The five men were big men—not Postak's size, but big nonetheless. One of them was tattooed from head to foot, with a shaved head and bulging muscles. Another looked like a Viking or a Hell's Angel or some unholy combination of both, with a thick red beard and a long mane of red hair and a build like a refrigerator with legs. The other three weren't quite as imposing, but since most of the Slab's residents tended to be retirees and their grandparents, these five looked like the youngest and most dangerous of the lot.

They started across the slab toward Carter and Postak. Postak stopped, hands held casually behind his back, except that Carter knew he was going for his gun, that in fact his intent was anything but casual. For the first time, he wondered if bringing this much cash with him to this godforsaken Slab was a bad idea. Carter held up one hand over his eyes, blinking against the sun at their backs.

The Viking twitched a thumb toward a broken-down RV, the next disaster of a home in line for Carter to visit. "You coming to see me?" the man asked.

"If that's where you live," Carter replied, keeping his voice steady. He could sense Postak's tension. The big man had made himself still, barely breathing, but ready to move.

"It is," the Viking said. "But you ain't invited in." He didn't sound like he was kidding.

"You do understand that I just want to get your signature on a document, assuming you're the head of the household, and then I'll pay you two thousand dollars?"

"And then I'll have to move off the Slab," the Viking said. He spat into the dirt. "And how far is two grand going to get me out in the world? Pay first and last month's rent and a security deposit on someplace and it's gone. What good is that?"

"It's better than nothing, which is what you'll get if you don't accept the offer. The land is legally mine, and everyone needs to get off it."

The Viking looked around at his friends. They didn't look like they'd be easy to move. "You can try," he said.

"I know you may not like to admit it," Carter reminded him. "But the law does apply out here, just like it does everywhere else."

"That's what they say. I'll believe it when I see it."

"You'll see it, soon enough," Carter said. He raised his voice. "Do the rest of you men feel the same way?"

All four of the others nodded or grunted what must have been affirmatives.

"Show me where you live, then, and I won't bother calling on you. And you'll get no money. But those who will go along with the law will still get paid, so don't try to stop me from delivering their payments."

The Viking smiled broadly, revealing uneven yellow teeth flecked with gold. "Wouldn't dream of it," he said.

Imperial County contained more miles of dirt road than paved road, probably by a factor of two to one. Off-roaders, hunters, farmers, drug and illegal alien smugglers up from Mexico, and the Border Patrol tracking them all kept the dirt roads busy year-round, though traffic fell off somewhat during the hottest parts of summer.

For this duty, Billy Cobb had borrowed Lieutenant Butler's Bronco. Even so, he complained at every stretch of washboard, every jounce or drop that slammed his butt against the seat or his head into the roof. The Bronco was ancient and its suspension's best days had been long ago. It beat the hell out of the Crown-Vic but still, Billy figured a more contemporary SUV would be a good use of Sheriff's Office funds. What if it was Arab terrorists I was looking for out here, instead of possible kidnappers, he thought. They'd be driving around in a Humvee or a Cadillac Escalade or a Mercedes goddamn Unimog and here I'd be, shaking my spine out my asshole in this old burner.

But he was out anyway, and so were deputies from every substation in Imperial and Riverside Counties, checking every road, every barn, every empty canyon accessible by four wheel drive. They'd been told to look for a black or dark blue Lincoln

Navigator. But so far there was no clear determination if a kidnapping had in fact happened, or if the Navigator even existed. The FBI hadn't even been called in, because the evidence that a crime had been committed was so flimsy.

All in all, Billy thought he'd be more help up on the Slab, helping the Sheriff investigate the very real murder they'd found evidence of there. Or down in El Centro, tracking down that hooker who'd run away on him. The more he thought about her, the more steamed he became.

The old jeep road he was on now snaked alongside the Chocolate Mountains, just outside the aerial gunnery range the Marines operated there, following the course of the Coachella Canal. The road was long and narrow in spots—once, when he met some four-wheelers out in an old Dodge Raider, he'd had to back up an eighth of a mile to find a pull-out wide enough to let them pass. It wound through a deep canyon, the rocky sides of which were so close that he was afraid he'd scrape the Lieutenant's vehicle.

But at least there was shade inside the canyon—pulling out on the other end he was back in bright, direct sunlight, bearing down on the Bronco as if someone had covered it with a thick blanket. Billy swore and cranked the air conditioner another notch. The desert was still out here—if there were birds, they stayed in the shelter of bushes or cacti. Mammals hid underground, snakes and lizards probably sunned themselves on flat rocks away from the roads. No one moved around more than they had to.

But cutting across the road was another, even less-traveled dirt trail, with unmistakably new tire tracks on it. Billy had planned to skip that road—he wasn't even sure where it ended up, but it cut across the canal and then up to the north, so maybe out of the county altogether, and almost no one ever used it.

Which just made it more intriguing now.

He made the turn and headed north, rear wheels sliding a bit in the dirt as he did. But they caught again, and he followed the narrower track. If he could find the girl and bring her home safe, he could move up his mental timeframe for becoming Sheriff, he knew. He might even get Butler's job right away.

After a quarter mile or so, the tire tracks made another turn, this time into a dry, dusty wash. Billy followed suit. The Bronco's wheels spun a little as they hit the sand, then bit in and the vehicle moved forward. But something bothered Billy as he straddled the tire marks in the sand. After a moment, he determined what it was, and he braked to a full, sudden stop, kicking up a cloud of dust that enveloped the SUV.

There was no way that a Navigator had a narrower wheelbase than Ken's old Bronco, he decided. So the very fact that he was straddling these tire tracks meant that they hadn't come from a Navigator or probably any other luxury SUV. This was more likely something little, a Rav-4 or a Chevy Tracker or something. Maybe even an old Suzuki Samurai.

But it was not the vehicle he was looking for. Not even close.

Shit, he thought, pushing the door open and getting out. He kicked at the sand. This is a dead end. They're not out here, if they even exist. He couldn't believe how angry he was, and once again, his service piece was in his hand before he even realized it. He took aim at a ball of teddy bear cholla cactus clinging to the end of a branch twenty yards away and let fly.

His first two shots missed, zinging off into empty desert somewhere behind the cactus. But his next one connected and the cholla ball disintegrated. He moved his aim down the branch, shooting off chunks of it with each squeeze of his trigger. Finally, he emptied the clip into the tiny plant's trunk, chopping it down completely.

And the whole time he shot at it, instead of seeing the cactus, in his mind's eye he was looking at that streetwalker down in El Centro.

At Kerry's signal, each man grabbed his own gun or guns and headed out the door. Vic carried an Ithaca 12-gauge shotgun that had been Cam Hensley's. Hunting had never been a hobby or even a real interest of his, except for these once-a-year excursions, so he'd never bothered to get one of his own.

Besides, what they were really doing out here had very little to do with guns.

Their Dove had been given a twenty minute head start, as Kerry had promised her. It took less than a minute for Rock to find one of her footprints in the sand—she'd already taken her sandals off—so they knew which direction she'd gone. East, into the rising sun. And into the deepest part of the Mojave desert. It'd be a long time before she found human population in that direction. Maybe in a few days she'd find herself at the Grand Canyon, if she survived that long. Vic didn't think she would.

"Fucking hot," Ray Dixon said. He had sidled up next to Vic, his gun held like a baby in the cradle of his powerful arms.

"Yeah it is," Vic agreed. "Must be that global warming shit."

"I heard global warming makes the winters colder," Ray said. "How's that supposed to work?"

"It's all bullshit anyway," Vic said, brushing at his mustache. Sometimes on hot days he regretted letting it grow so long, as his upper lip sweated like a bitch.

The world is a big freaking place, he thought. Just look around at the miles of unbroken desert, dotted with Joshua trees, populated only by lizards and snakes and a few hardy beetles. How could people make it hotter, and what was the problem if they did?

They followed Rock and Kerry in a kind of loose column, Cam walking alone a dozen paces or so behind the leaders, he and Ray about the same distance behind Cam.

"Where's Terrance?" Vic asked.

"Kerry told him to hang back here, make a few loops around the property and then wait inside," Ray explained. "He doesn't trust this one, thinks she just might be hiding out to double back and steal the truck or something."

"Wouldn't put it past her," Vic agreed. "Got a mouth on her, that's for sure."

"That ain't all she got," Ray observed.

"So is he just waiting there till we get back? He misses out on the whole hunt?"

"She does double back, then he'll be the only one who gets to hunt," Ray said.

Vic thought about that for a moment. It was true. Anyway, it wasn't the hunting that he found most entertaining, though he thought it was Kerry's favorite part. For him, it was what came after—having the girl available to him and his friends, whenever they wanted, any way they wanted. The hunting just seemed like a necessary step to break her down, get her to the point where she'd submit to that without putting up a fight.

Or at least that's what Kerry claimed was the purpose. Vic wasn't so sure…secretly, he thought Kerry just enjoyed this part of it.

"You ever think about the morality of this?" he asked Ray. "What we're doing?"

Ray shrugged. They humped a small hill and started down the other side. Rock and Kerry were farther out in front now, Cam still in the middle but dropping back. The girl's trail cut cross-country rather than sticking to any established path, so they walked through brush, past Joshua trees and low, furry cholla. "Fuck morality," he said. "Six thousand Americans died last week in New York. Was that moral?"

Vic didn't know exactly what that had to do with their present activity, but he answered anyway. "No, of course not."

"So what's one Mex girl up against that many Americans? No more important than a drop of piss in the ocean."

"Yeah, I guess so."

"You better just never let Kerry hear you talking that shit. He's got stories about stuff he saw down in Colombia and Nicaragua'll curl your fucking hair. He don't think those people are even human."

"But this girl's not Nicaraguan or Colombian, is she?"

"Who knows? Who cares? Far as Kerry's concerned, man, they're all the same. Me, I think he's killing the same girl over and over again, in his mind anyway."

Ahead, Rock and Kerry had stopped and waited for the others to catch up. When they did, Kerry pointed to a flat slab of gray rock half-buried in drifting sand. On the rock was a reddish-brown stain shaped like the ball of a foot.

"Why does a woman have legs?" Kerry asked them.

So she doesn't leave a snail trail, Vic thought, having heard the same gag every year he'd been going out on the Hunt. But he didn't bother to say it. Kerry's jokes weren't meant to be funny, he'd determined, but somehow instructive. Although what lesson Kerry wanted to teach wasn't always clear.

"So she doesn't leave snail trails," Kerry said after a moment. "Look, she took her sandals off right out of the gate," Kerry pointed out. "So she's already bleeding. I thought this one was going to challenge us, but she'll be crippled by mid-afternoon. We'll probably find her parked on her ass begging us to take her back to the cabin."

"That's okay with me," Cam said, clutching his own groin. "I like it when they beg."

Mindy Sesno cashiered in the Shop-R Mart, two miles up the 111 from Ken Butler's office. He stopped in to pick up a pre-made turkey and cheese sandwich on French bread and a bottle of Lipton, sweet, no lemon, the way God intended it, a bag of Ruffles and a Hershey bar.

"Lunch of champions," Mindy said when he put it and a twenty down on her little conveyor belt and she had conveyed it up to the register. Mindy was thin and remarkably pale for someone who lived in the middle of the desert, and Ken had never seen her when her light brown eyes weren't sparkling as if she's just heard, or told, a joke that was both funny and just the littlest bit dirty. Her dark brown hair was almost the same shade that Shannon's had been, and Ken wasn't sure how he felt about that because Mindy was the first woman with whom Ken had wanted to sleep, and who he thought might be willing to sleep with him, since Shannon had died, and he didn't want to see her hair spread on a pillowcase beneath him and forget who he was with.

"Brain food," he replied with a smile. "Keeps me thinking."

"You looking for that girl that's disappeared?" Mindy asked. Her tone was one of concern, not idle curiosity, Ken thought.

"This minute, I'm looking for some change from my twenty," he said. "But yeah, Billy's out beating the bushes for her now. I've had some other things on my plate, but I've been out when I could be."

"Hope you find her."

"I hope she's not really out there to be found."

Mindy put a hand over her mouth—a schoolgirl's gesture that somehow looked perfectly natural on her. "Do you think that's possible?" she asked with surprise.

Ken shrugged once. "Lots of young ladies disappear every year," he said. "Most of them are runaways, leaving an abusive relationship, or following the stars, seeking their fortunes. Lucia Alvarez might be one of those. Maybe she just plain got tired of living in Mecca."

"Hey, I live in Salton Estates, and do you hear me complaining?" Mindy asked with a laugh like a bell's chime. "But I heard there was a witness."

"There was a man inside his house with the shutters closed working on a forty-eight hour drinking binge," Ken corrected her. "He thinks he looked out the window once and maybe saw something. Then again, when drunks used to see pink elephants they didn't bother calling the cops about it. I think I liked those days better."

Mindy blushed a little as she put his purchases into a paper bag.

"Don't get me wrong," he said. "If she's out there, in trouble, I want her found and we will find her. But if she doesn't want to be found, chances are she won't be."

"Well, if she knew you I'm sure she'd feel comforted by the fact that you're on the case, Ken." Mindy handed him the sack. "I would, anyway."

He took the bag from her, his fingers grazing hers as he did so. He held her gaze a moment, considering whether this would be a good time to ask her to dinner or maybe a movie up in Palm Desert. But the moment stretched too long, and he broke the connection. Probably talking about a potential kidnapping is not the best prelude to asking for a date, he thought. He'd try again soon, leading into it with some kind of more upbeat conversation.

"Thanks, Mindy." He shook the bag, as if to demonstrate what he was thanking her for. "I'll see you later."

"Stay out of trouble, Ken," she said behind him.

"I'll try. You do that too."

He pushed the glass door open with his free hand and stepped out into the blasting heat, feeling Mindy's gaze on his back all the way out the door. As he did he examined his own hands, creased and calloused, black grime worked so far into the lines and under the nails from working on his own car and house that soap and water could never completely clean them. He wondered if Mindy would even want those rough hands on her; he imagined they would shred her supple skin, like silk caught on a nail.

He was always surprised by how fast news raced around the valley, even though he'd lived here for long enough to have experienced it many times by now. At least she'd wanted to talk about Lucy Alvarez—even that was a relief after the days and days of everyone wanting to yack about the terrorist attacks. Mindy had the now-obligatory red, white, and blue ribbon pinned to her pink blouse, and an American flag flew outside the Shop-R Mart that had never been there before, but it looked like she might be capable of shifting her attention to other things, and Ken considered that a good sign.

As he walked to the squad car—since he'd loaned his Bronco to Billy Cobb, he was reduced to driving Billy's cruiser—he saw a an orange Ford Pinto, its paint so sun-blasted it was hard to tell where the rust stopped, backing out of a parking space as another car passed right behind it. He flinched, waiting for the crunch of metal on metal, but instead there was only the long wail of a horn as the passing car rushed by.

Across the Pinto's rear window, blocking most of the glass, was one of those American flags that newspapers had printed up. Ken walked up to the driver's side of the car. The driver was a man he'd seen around but didn't know, not a resident of Salton Estates but maybe Niland or Calipatria or someplace, a skinny guy with a brand new FDNY ball cap pulled down over stringy hair, wearing a flag T-shirt and sucking on a cigarette. Ken figured someone somewhere was raking in a hefty profit on phony FDNY hats. That and charity scams and car companies advertising deals—like interest free loans for those who needed them least—implying that it was un-American not to buy a new car pissed Ken off no end.

"I got nothing against the American flag," Ken began. "But your rear window is no place to put one. You nearly backed into that car. You do that in your Pinto, the whole thing is likely to explode."

"You ain't a patriot, Sheriff?" the guy asked him. His tone was angry.

"I think I'm as patriotic as the next guy, son. But my job is public safety, and you're not a safe driver with your rear view blocked by a sheet of newspaper. Please move the flag."

"Or what? You going to arrest me for showing pride in my country?" He flipped his cigarette out onto the road. Skin cancer was the number one medical problem in the Valley, Ken knew—no one but the most diligent could avoid the sun beating down day in and day out, most of the year. But lung cancer was up there, as was cirrhosis of the liver: the illnesses of those with little money and less hope. Following those self-inflicted plagues were a variety of others, most of which were possibly tied to the massive amounts of fertilizers and pesticides needed to grow crops in the middle of a desert, seeping into the groundwater.

"I can't arrest you for talking back or for being an asshole," Ken said. "But I can arrest you for reckless driving, and take your car."

"I'd like to see how long you kept your job after the newspapers heard about that."

"I'd like to see how long you have to walk if you lose your driver's license for threatening a law enforcement officer's livelihood," Ken replied. "Please get out of the car."

"You ain't serious," the guy said, hands gripping the wheel as if afraid Ken might drag him out bodily. "Arab terrorists are attacking New York City and you're hassling me over a flag?"

"No, sir, I'm hassling you over your demonstrated inability to drive safely with a large portion of your rear window covered. Get out of the car."

Ken backed away from the door as the man got out. He was tall, and even thinner than Ken had believed at first. His black Levi's were baggy and torn and flapped loosely around his thin legs. He couldn't stand still, but bobbed and twitched and wriggled as he waited in the sunlight. Drug addict, Ken thought. He couldn't tell what the guy was using—crack or crystal meth seemed more likely than heroin, unless he was jonesing for a dose, because of his irritability and tension. Heroin would have calmed him down, not hyped him up.

"Let me see your driver's license," Ken said.

The guy gave Ken a fuck-off-and-die look but fished his wallet from his jeans and passed it over. Ken studied the license for a moment. Barton Vander Tuin, with an address in Brawley. Brawley and El Centro, Ken knew, had far more than their legitimate share of drug addicts. With a largely seasonal work force, long hot summers, nothing much to do, and an impoverished tax base that couldn't provide much in the way of social services, too many people turned to drugs to get through the days and nights.

Ken scribbled the name into a wire-bound notebook he carried and handed the wallet back. As Barton was replacing it in his pocket, Ken leaned into his car, reaching into the back and peeling the flag from the rear window. He folded it neatly along its original fold and handed it to the man.

"Here's your flag," he said. "Put it someplace safe. I don't want to see you driving in this town with your vision obstructed again, and I don't want to see you driving under the influence either. Get home safely and clean up, or we're going to have a problem."

"Hey," Barton started to protest.

Ken cut him off. "Save it."

He turned away and went to his car. Behind him he could hear the patriotic junkie getting back into the Pinto and gunning the engine.

What a world we live in, Ken thought as he watched the orange car drive off. What a world.

Ken knew he should have arrested the guy once he'd realized he was under the influence, but he hadn't trusted his own self-control by that point. Having his patriotism questioned pissed Ken off no end. He had served his country when it was his time to, and done it without complaint. Since then, he'd worked in law enforcement, which he considered service of another, equally valuable kind. It was damn sure no one did it for the money.

Most of his time in the Nam was a blur of sweat and mosquitoes and fear now, the details, after so many years, mercifully indistinct. Except for one day—the first day he'd experienced the magic—which still remained as fresh in his mind as Mindy Sesno's peach-flavored scent.

It was January of 1967, and the 1st Infantry Brigade, 173rd Airborne, was involved in Operation Cedar Falls. The stated purpose of the operation was to clear out the area called the Iron Triangle. About twenty miles outside of Saigon, the VC used the area as to stage repeated attacks on the city, and the brass wanted it to stop. The challenge was, it turned out, that the VC were operating from an incredibly complex system of tunnels under the Triangle, so most of the time the G.I.s sent after them couldn't even find the enemy.

Which meant that volunteers were needed for a special mission. Since the year before, the name of this type of volunteer had changed, from Tunnel Runner to Ferret, before finally settling on Tunnel Rat. Unlike most Tunnel Rats, Ken was six feet tall, but he was just eighteen, wiry and limber, so he could scoot around the tunnels the VC had dug years ago, when fighting the French, and expanded upon more recently.

This particular day, Ken had awakened around dawn, as usual. The day was sticky already, not dry and hot like the desert he'd become accustomed to in later years. This kind of heat sapped your strength, and while he hated to fall asleep because you never knew what waited out there in the dark, the fact was that he found himself sleeping a lot, whenever there were a few minutes of down time, simply because of the climate. Upon awakening, he'd felt the strange metallic taste in his mouth, but he didn't know what it was. He purified some water to brush his teeth, then swished some around in his mouth and spat it out, but the taste didn't go away.

Then there was no more time to worry about it, because he had a job to do. With a small patrol, he hiked through the jungle to a spot where they had previously identified a hatchway into one of the tunnels, covered with mud and hidden in a trench. Ken stripped off his shirt, because that just got in the way down there. He was supposed to wear a cap with a headlamp and a microphone attached to it, with a communication wire spool on his belt. The wire would run all the way back to the surface. But Ken hated the whole contraption, which rarely seemed to work like it was supposed to, and which he was always afraid he'd get tangled up in. Besides, talking down in the tunnels, even quietly, seemed like the nearest thing to suicide he could imagine. So he scrapped that. He'd be down there with just a knife, a Smith & Wesson .38 revolver, smaller and more reliable than the Colt .45 he usually wore as a sidearm on the surface, and a flashlight. Once he had the lay of the land he'd go back down with a satchel charge or a bunker bomb to blow up the occupants, if any.

Fully outfitted, Ken lowered himself down the hole. He hated this part most of all—going down feet-first, completely blind. Anything could be waiting down there. Mines, feces-smeared punji stakes, scorpions, enemy soldiers—the variety of ways someone could die in the tunnels was just about endless.

On this occasion, though, none of those things waited right at the entrance. Finding himself completely inside the tunnel, Ken began to inch his way forward. He didn't turn his light on yet because he didn't want to make himself a target prematurely. So he moved in the dark, on his belly, probing with his fingers at the hard earth below, around, and above him. A wire hidden among the roots of a tree could, he knew, trigger a mine. Bamboo covered with leaves and mud on the floor could be a pitfall onto sharp punji stakes.

The doorways were the worst part, though. Sometimes they used sealed hatchways, almost submarine-style, so that if part of the tunnel was flooded or fragged the rest of it wouldn't be affected. Going through those doors was always terrifying. Charlie could be on the other side with a garrote, waiting for a U.S. head to poke through. Or soldiers might be waiting with rifles. Or any of the other traps could be duplicated. These guys took no chances with their tunnels.

Ken had been inside for more than an hour, and he hadn't seen a living soul. After passing through two interior hatchways, he'd found what seemed to be living quarters for several people, with folded clothes and tiny cook stoves—smoke was carefully piped away from the tunnels themselves, and other pipes, barely wider than a stick of bamboo, provided circulation. All this and a few boxes of ammo indicated that there had been people here recently. Which could mean they knew he was in here, and were moving toward another exit—or setting a trap.

Still, he kept going.

Another hatchway.

Heart pounding in his throat, he cracked it, listened. No sounds. He pushed through, reached ahead with one hand and touched the floor, then the ceiling. The floor was kind of far down, as if the tunnel on the other side of the hatch was a couple of feet lower than this one. Maybe it's an older section, from the French days, he thought.

He went through the hatch, reaching down for the floor with both hands. Because of the angle, he hit the floor with more of his weight, and he was off balance as his legs came through the hatch, and the floor gave way beneath his fingers.

He tumbled down, thinking, shit, I'm dead.

Bamboo strips tore at his skin as he plunged through the false floor. But when he hit bottom, he felt solid ground. No stakes. No mines. He didn't understand.

And then he felt the skin of the cobra as it writhed against his bare skin.

He lurched away from it, flicking on his light at the same time. There were three snakes, two banded kraits and a cobra. The kraits were small snakes, only about two feet long, but their venom was deadly. So was the cobra's, for that matter, and this one looked to be about six feet long, though it was coiled up so Ken couldn't tell for sure.

He needed to get out of the pit, which was only about four feet deep. But he was afraid that any sudden motion would attract more attention from the snakes. Slowly, he tried to bring his .38 into firing position.

The first krait didn't wait for him. It darted toward him, mouth opening, fangs gleaming in the glow from his flashlight. Before the thing could reach him, though, the cobra struck—not at Ken, but at the krait. It caught the smaller snake in its mouth, fangs sinking in right behind the thing's head, and whipped its own head back once, flinging the dead krait to the side.

The second krait almost seemed to understand what the cobra had done. It began to slither away, heading for the shelter provided by broken bamboo that had fallen in with Ken. The cobra didn't give it a chance to get there, though. It lunged, killing the second krait as easily as it had the first.

Ken watched all this in rapt fascination, but when the cobra turned its gaze on him, he realized he should have used the opportunity to get away. The snake eyed him almost as if it had intelligence. Ribs on the sides of its head flared out, forming the hood for which cobras are famous. He knew these snakes could spit venom, though he couldn't remember in his panic if that was as poisonous as being bitten.

Still keeping its gaze locked on Ken, the cobra stretched its length up, and up, like a snake charmer's accomplice impersonating a rope. When it was high enough, it set its head down on the shelf that was the tunnel's real floor, and the rest of it followed. Ken held his fire—shooting the gun would announce his presence up and down the tunnel, and if he could, in fact, survive this trap he'd have a good chance of getting the drop on anyone in its depths.

He stood, watching the snake, and putting his hands on the sides of the pit in order to hoist himself out if the snake actually went away. But the cobra only slithered a couple of feet down the tunnel before it stopped and looked back at Ken.

"Follow me," it said.

In retrospect, Ken realized that an important aspect of the whole magic thing was the ability to believe in it. He would have sworn, before that second, that there was no such thing as a talking snake, that anyone who said there were talking snakes was a liar, and that if you said Ken Butler believed in talking snakes then that made you a damn liar.

But in that moment, without even thinking about it, Ken believed. That was how powerful the magic was. It erased doubt.

He followed the snake.

The cobra took him on a grand tour. They never did find any Viet Cong—the tunnel had, it seemed, been cleared out shortly before he'd arrived. But it showed him where other booby traps were, it led him through the ammo dumps and barracks, it pointed out the best places to put bombs when he came back down.

Finally, several hours later, the cobra showed him to the exit, a different one than the entrance he'd used that morning. Ken had opened the hatch and stood blinking in the sudden sunlight, letting his eyes acclimate. When he could see again, he looked around for the cobra, but it was gone.

Ken shrugged, the magic still working its mojo on him, keeping skepticism at bay. A talking cobra tour guide. It wasn't like the thing had carried on a running conversation or anything—since that one phrase, "follow me," it hadn't said a word until the very end. As Ken had checked out the exit, looking for any final booby traps, the snake had whispered to him. "Didi mao," it said, "didi mao." Vietnamese this time, instead of English, but every grunt learned those words almost as soon as he arrived in country. Get the fuck away from here.

Ken got. Once clear of the tunnel, he went looking for his patrol.

And he found them, near the hatchway he'd used to go inside.

Every one of them was dead. Small arms fire, a couple of grenades, maybe. They'd certainly returned some fire but they must have been seriously outnumbered. Parched, Ken picked up the canteen of a PFC named Friedman, but when he shook it he heard shrapnel rattling around in it. He tilted it, and blood poured out with the last few drops of water.

Gradually, Ken understood that if he'd been out here with them, he'd be dead too. As it was, the VC who had done this must have known there was someone in the tunnel, must have gone in looking for him. Only the cobra, leading him through the underground maze, had saved him.

He ran all the way back to camp, working out a story the whole time to explain how he had come to be spared. The next day he'd accompanied a mission back to the tunnel to retrieve the bodies and kill the VC who had slaughtered his friends.

After that mission, he'd never volunteered for tunnel duty again.

But he never forgot that taste in his mouth. He never forgot his first magic day.

part 2
harold shipp

"You know, even when they bombed us at Pearl," Hal Shipp said, "there were still those who didn't want to go to war. You remember?"

"Barely," Virginia replied.

Hal laughed. They sat on a settee in their motor home, watching a tiny black and white TV, powered by solar panels Hal had installed up on the roof. The rabbit ears had a hard time bringing in a signal here, but they could get a couple of the networks okay if you didn't mind some snow. The news had included coverage of peace marches on college campuses, which had prompted Hal's comment. "Well, you were young," he said. "I remember. Not many agreed with them, but they were there. Conscientious objectors. Nothing wrong with speaking your mind, even if you're wrong. I thought they had every right to believe what they wanted, I remember."

She pressed more firmly against him, her shoulder pushing into the yielding flesh just above his ribs. "I'm glad you remember."

"I remember a lot," he told her. "I enlisted on a Friday. It was raining in the morning, but it had cleared up by afternoon. It was about three weeks after Pearl Harbor, and we all knew we were going to war. I wanted the Pacific Theater but I ended up in France anyway."

He knew he had problems with his memory—at least, he remembered Virginia telling him that he did, though he couldn't remember those specific times when his memory had failed him. He was willing to take her word for it, though—she wouldn't lie about something like that, and anyway there were those times he just couldn't account for any other way. More of them than ever, lately.

Not today, though. He'd been a little foggy when he'd first awakened, but not since he touched Ken Butler's hand and got a jolt like the time when he was a boy and had jammed the rifles of two metal toy soldiers into the holes of an electrical outlet to see what would happen, and what happened was he'd been knocked off his feet onto his ten-year-old butt and the metal gun barrels had melted into small black blobs. The shock had been a lot like that; it was nothing like the static electricity he'd blamed and he'd be damned if Ken hadn't known that too, but he and Ken had both been willing to laugh it off because there were other people around, people who didn't know what it might really be about, and if there was ever a time to tell them that wasn't it.

Because today was a magic day, Hal was sure, as yesterday had been. And the other thing he was equally sure of, as sure as he'd ever been about anything, was that Ken Butler knew it.

And that could only mean that Ken had them too.

Hal shook off the thought of that. There was nowhere to go with it, not right now.

"You know I was with the 30th Division, right?" he continued. He didn't give Virginia a chance to respond. "Old Hickory, we were called, because they were mostly Southern boys in the Division, originally. 119th Infantry, 2nd Battalion. We moved to Florida, then Tennessee, then Indiana, before we shipped out to England. After that…well, you've heard my Omaha Beach stories."

Virginia shuddered. "Yes, and I don't care to hear them again."

"That's good," Hal said. "Because I'm not inclined to talk about them. We landed there on D-Day plus four, to replace those poor boys from the 29th who'd been chewed up by the Germans there. But what I want to talk about came weeks after D-Day, the first week of July, in fact, and I'm pretty sure it's a story I've never told you. Never told anyone, for that matter, not even the day it happened."

Virginia straightened up on the couch, planted both of her feet firmly on the floor. "Are you sure you want to talk about this, Harold?"

He considered her for a moment. She had shrunk, over the years. She'd never been tall but now she seemed almost doll-like, skin like fine porcelain, smooth to the touch, a faint network of veins visible just beneath the surface. Her hands and feet seemed too tiny to be real. Looking at her rubber flip-flops, he wished he'd made the kind of money that could have kept her in fine leather shoes and a decent house. But that kind of thinking did nobody any good, he knew. What's done is done and there's no undoing it. And anyway, not all the decisions that had brought them here had been in his hands, not by a long shot.

"It's not that, Gin," he replied. "Not that I want to talk about it. But I have to, and I think it has to be today. I suppose you don't have to listen if you don't want, but I wish you would."

"Of course, darling," she said. "Let me just get us some lemonade or iced tea."

Harold shook his head. "Just water for me," he told her. "It'll taste awful, and I'd hate to waste anything."

She cocked her head and looked at him quizzically. "I'll explain in due time," he said. "Just hurry back."

She went into the galley area and rummaged in the icebox for a few minutes, returning with a glass of lemonade and one of water over ice on a plastic tray, and a couple of cookies on a saucer. She set the tray down on a white plastic parson's table within easy reach, and returned to her position beside Harold on the sofa.

"We were trying to liberate the French city of St. Lo," Harold continued. He took a sip from his water and made a sour face. "Yep, still tastes horrible. Anyway, I'm not going to give you the full play by play of the military operation. The 29th gets most of the credit for taking St. Lo, and as far as I'm concerned they can have it. But they wouldn't have done it, or at least not as easily, if it wasn't for the 30th. We took Hill 30, which the Germans had used as a vantage point to see the whole city. After that, we opened up France for Patton. Wasn't for us, the war still would have been won but it would have taken several months longer to win it. But that's taking the story in a different way—I start going there and it'll take months to finish it.

"So we're outside St. Lo, and we're supposed to cross the Vire river and get up the hill and take it. The Germans have fortified the top of the hill, they've got 88s and 105s up there, and Panzers. We have artillery too, and air support, but still and all, it's a bloody fight. Bloody and wet."

He remembered the stink, the smells of sweat and bodies and gunpowder and fire and the river and the flooded farm fields, all mixed in the July air like a noxious cocktail mixed by Hell's own bartender. The sharp stench when a man is blown open, so different from the butcher shop smell of a body that's been hanging upright, wedged into a hedgerow and shot a couple of dozen times because from a distance, through the fog, you couldn't tell whether it was alive or dead. Until you were over there you wouldn't think death had so many different scents. But he didn't want to share that with Virginia. Some things a man had to protect his wife from.

"We were coming in from the south, through a tiny town called St. Fromond-Eglise. This was farm country, and the village wasn't much more than a handful of stone buildings and of course a beautiful church on the town square. The Nazis had owned this area and most of the men were dead, the women and kids mostly stayed indoors and tried to keep away from the Germans. Most of the people lived outside the village itself, in big farmhouses that had been in their families for generations. They were happy to see us coming, I can tell you that. You never saw such joy on people's faces as when American G.I.s came into town.

"But on this day—" Harold stopped short, suddenly unable to put his finger on just what it was he'd been going on about. He took a sip of water, blinked a couple of times and cleared his throat, mechanisms he'd developed to stall for time while his brain tried to turn over, like an old engine on a cold morning. There ought to be a Diehard for the human brain, he had thought many times. Something to spark it when things get hazy.

He looked around him. He was in some small space, a room in a little apartment or a trailer, maybe. A woman looked at him expectantly, small and frail and familiar. He had seen pictures of her, maybe, or met her once a long time ago. He hadn't expected to see a woman here, though he wasn't entirely sure why not. He stood and went to a window, looked out at a strip of cement and brown, barren hills beyond. He realized then that he'd been expecting to see green hedgerows under a gray sky, and it came back to him, and he picked up the sentence where he'd left off, returning to his place on the sofa.

"—July seventh, it was, a foggy, rainy day—we were taking heavy fire. The Nazis set their 88s on us and the shelling was terrible. I remember I was running with five guys, keeping our heads down, looking for cover, and we ran in between some of the buildings in town. But then we heard a shell whistling in and we all hit the dirt, and it landed close by. When I opened my eyes again my ears were ringing so loud I could barely hear, and there was all this smoke in the air, and I couldn't see any of my buddies. I found out later that I'd been blown about twenty feet by the blast and they thought I was dead. There were more coming all the time, so they couldn't stop to pick me up. They'd have come back for me, though. That was how we did it there.

"So now I'm all alone, half-deaf and I might as well be blind from the smoke. And still the shells are coming in, so I figure that there must be some of my guys in the town, only I can't find them."

Harold realized his breathing had quickened and a film of sweat covered his forehead. He picked up the glass of ice water, took a sip, and held it against his brow. The memory was vivid, more so than his memory of the Grape Nuts he'd had for breakfast this morning. Confusion and panic had warred in him, and to this day he wasn't sure which had won out or if they'd in fact just been opposite sides of the same coin.

"I guess I kind of stumbled farther into town," he went on. "I still had my rifle in my hands and my helmet on my head, but I was worried, I don't mind telling you, because I couldn't find the guys and I didn't know where the Germans were or if the next shell was going to be the one that would finish me off.

"A couple of minutes later I found myself in the town square. It was completely deserted. The church was on one side, with its tower facing the square, and the town hall on another, and a couple of other buildings. In the center the square was cobblestoned. It must have been hundreds of years old, I remember thinking that. The streets and houses must have been in the same position they'd been in since before Europeans settled North America. But the Nazis didn't care about that, and I guess at that moment we didn't either. The two sides in a war are never as far apart as they think they are, I guess. Their goals are different but not how they go about them.

"Anyway, I was there in the town square and I could hear artillery pounding in the distance: our guys, hammering the German positions. But then I heard another 88 shell, the whistle like one of those fireworks that make so much noise, only louder, and I dove for the ground again, but there was no place to go except onto the hard cobblestones. I flattened there, and the whistle kept coming, and then I did something I never should have done.

"I looked up.

"I crooked my neck and looked up and I actually saw the thing coming, the shell spinning as it flew into the square like something in slow motion. I guess it was, or I never would have been able to make out any detail. I turned back and looked at where it was headed, and I knew it was going to hit the church.

"Which is just what it did. It hit the church and exploded, and the air right over my head was filled with what must have been tons of stone and glass and flaming wood. You know those pictures on the TV of the World Trade Center?"

"Yes," Virginia said. "How could I not?"

"It wasn't the same as that, not by a long shot. But it was similar. Not tens of thousands of people on the ground, but just me, and just one building coming down on my head, but it was the biggest building in town and any one of those chunks of stone that hit me, that would've been the end right there."

Virginia squeezed his leg. "I'm glad they didn't."

"Oh, they did," Harold said. "See, that's why I'm telling you all this. Because that morning when I woke up, July seventh, 1944, there was a funny taste in my mouth.

All my food—and it wasn't much, some hardtack and a cup of coffee and we'd managed to get some bread from a bakery—all my food tasted bad that morning."

"Like today?" Virginia pointed at his water glass, barely touched.

"Yes. Like yesterday, and today. I've since come to think of those days, when the taste gets really strong in my mouth like it has today, as magic days."

"Magic?"

"Let me finish," Harold said. "I'm down there on the ground, kind of twisted around though because I'm watching everything that's going on above me, and the church is blown to smithereens and I'm looking up at all the debris that's going to crush me, and there was nothing I could do about it. Just nothing. I was going to die there in St. Fromond-Eglise.

"And then the magic happened. That's the only way I can think about it, the only way I've ever been able to explain it. Instead of a few tons of stone and glass and wood falling on me, in mid-air, right over my head, all of it turned into some kind of glittery powder or dust, like that fairy dust in Peter Pan or something. Like that shiny confetti they throw at parades. Suddenly it's all that, and it's practically weightless, washing over me like a gentle snowfall. I stood up and put my arms out, put my hands in the air to catch it, and it was still falling, still falling. Just as soft and gentle as could be. And then it started to rain, a heavy, pounding shower.

"When the dust hit the ground it just vanished, as if it was washed away by the sudden downpour. Just gone, like it was never there at all. I couldn't even save any of it, it vanished from my hands, my shoulders, wherever it landed. An entire church tower turned into this snowfall of glittering dust, and then it was gone."

Harold chuckled. "Now you see why I never told anyone," he said. "They'd have called me crazy. They'd have sent me back home and put me in the loony bin, I can guarantee you. Because how could I explain that? How could I explain that it was a magic day—my first magic day, for that matter? Even I didn't really understand it, not then. I was grateful as hell, but I couldn't understand what had saved me."

He stopped then, picturing himself as a young man, facing the sky, arms spread wide. In his mind's eye he was among the flakes of glitter, drifting down toward himself. He saw his own huge smile, watched himself laugh out loud as he realized that whatever this stuff was, it wasn't going to hurt him. A man didn't get many moments like that in life, moments where happiness was pure and undiluted by stress or fear or anxiety, and that moment was one of Harold's. It still made him grin to think of it.

Virginia put an arm across his chest, and pressed her face against his. "I can't explain it either," she said. "Except I guess God wanted you here with me."

"I never presumed that He paid attention to me," Harold said. "But if that's what you want to think, I guess it's as good an explanation as any."

"And that's why you're telling me today?" she asked him. "Because the magic's back?"

"The magic's back," he confirmed. "Stronger than ever. I don't know what's going to happen, Gin. I never do. But something is. And I have a feeling it's going to be something big."

Virginia stood at the pump basin, washing off the dishes in the water-efficient way that had become second nature to her over their years on the Slab, thinking about her husband. She was delighted that his memory was so good today—it was rare that he could remember that much detail about anything, and if the "magic" explanation seemed a bit bizarre, she was willing to accept that he believed in it, at least. She hadn't known him until after the war, when he'd come to New Mexico to work on the interstate highway that spread across the American West in the postwar years. They'd met in a luncheonette where she, fresh out of high school, was applying for a job, and he had come in while working with his road gang. After chatting for a few minutes, he'd asked her out to dinner that night, and they had never looked back.

That had been fifty years ago this past June.

She hadn't regretted a day of it, anyway. But Harold had. He had never been satisfied with his lot—his jobs never led to the promotions he wanted. He looked for a big score, a main chance, that never came. And when it didn't, he thought he'd failed at life. She tried to tell him that wasn't true, that he had her and the love and respect of their friends, and why couldn't he be content if she was? He wouldn't buy that argument, though, and sometimes she found his recalcitrance infuriating.

As she dried the saucers, she thought about the way he looked in his Army pictures, not so terribly different than when she'd first met him except that he'd been in uniform and his brown hair had been a bit shorter. He still had a good bit of that hair, white now, as hers was, but enough for him to palm some Vitalis into every morning and comb back off his forehead. She imagined him in his Army days, laden with full pack and a rifle in his arms, as the church tower exploded and rained rubble down on him.

But in her version, the tons of broken stone and sharp glass didn't turn into some kind of mystical pixie dust. Instead, as Harold squirmed on the ground, his face contorted with terror, the rocks slammed into him, breaking bone, tearing flesh, smashing him into the cobblestones. The horrific downpour continued, even as the rocks ripped his body into pieces, an arm coming off and flopping onto the stones here, a section of skull bouncing under the steady assault there. Blood mixed with rain and ran between the cobblestones like grout between bathroom tiles. When at last the storm abated and the village square was quiet, the man with whom Virginia Shipp had shared a bed and a life for the last fifty years was torn into pieces no bigger than scattered coins, in her mind's eye, and the only sound she could hear was the faint trickle of his blood as it flowed toward the lowest ground.

She put the dishes back into the cabinet and looked in on Harold, who had drifted off to sleep on the couch, head back, mouth open. For a moment she was surprised; the vision had been almost more real than this, her real life, living in a trailer in the middle of nowhere with a man who had somehow become old. Life had always been full of promise, getting out of bed in the morning had always held an expectation that something wonderful might happen that day. But now Virginia looked at Harold, a man near the end of his life, and realized that she was only twelve years younger than his eighty-one years. If his life was virtually over, what did that say about hers?

She sat down in a chair across from him, where she could see him but not touch him, and watched him as he slept, her daydream all but forgotten now except for the faint, warm tingle she'd felt as it happened.

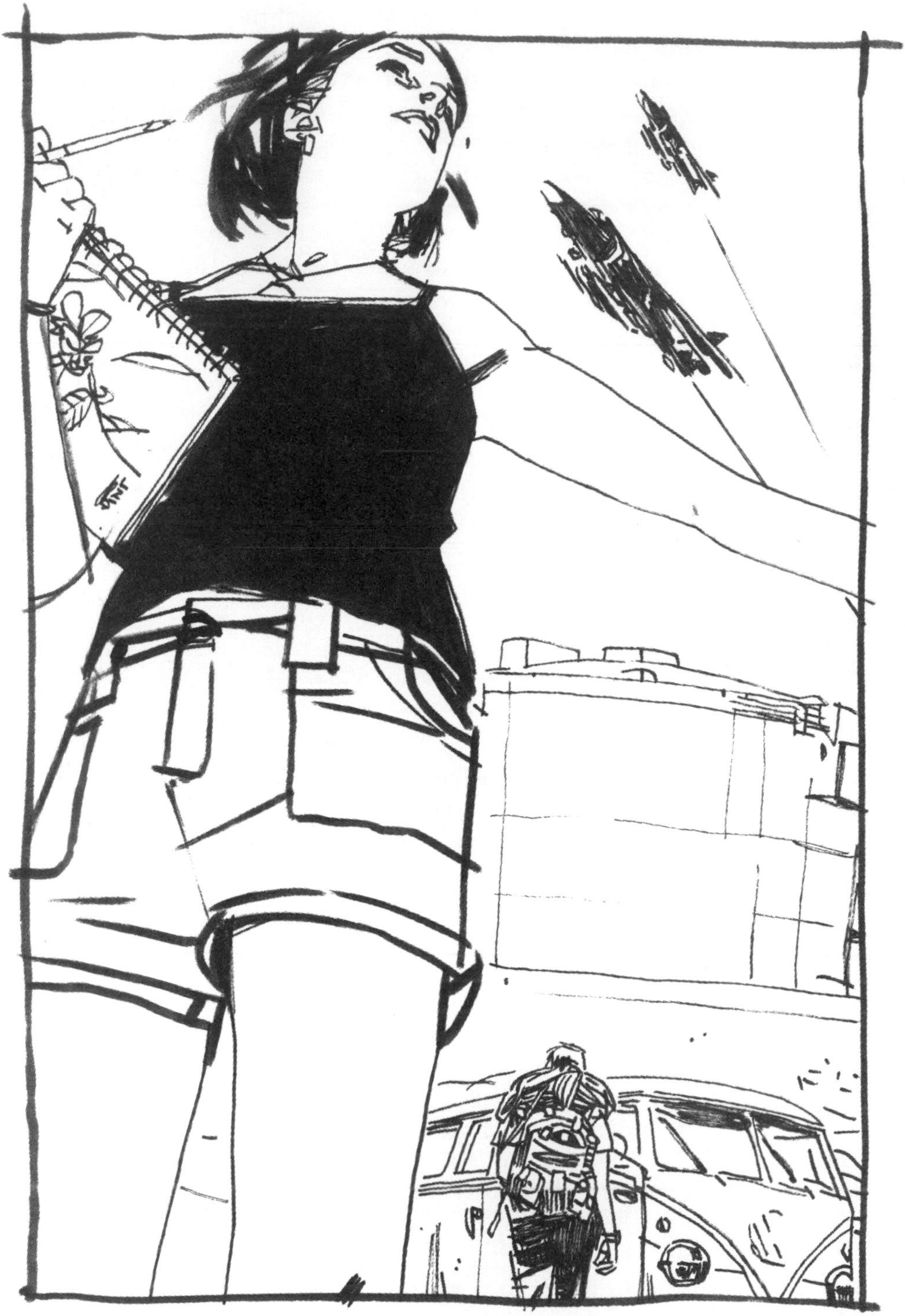

Mick had packed his gear and started down the trail, back toward where he'd parked the van—after two more hugs—when the first Harrier flew overhead. Penny froze in mid-squat, a sketchpad across her knees and a pencil between her fingers. She had left camp when Mick did, to catalogue and sketch some of the abundant plant life in the area. She was no artist but she could do fairly accurate representational work if she had a subject in front of her.

The warplane passed over quickly, and she turned to watch it as it circled and came back for another pass. It didn't drop any bombs or fire any weapons—she highly doubted that there would be any live fire practice with a real war in the offing—so she guessed that its purpose was to take a second look at the messages her group had written on the ground, in letters big enough to be seen from a thousand feet up.

After the Harrier's second pass Penny closed her sketchpad and hurried back to camp. She hoped that Mick had sense enough to find cover, or at least drop and freeze, when he heard the planes, but honestly she doubted that he would. He seemed to go through life with a big red flag that he waved at every metaphorical bull he encountered, she thought. Instead of hiding from the planes, he'd be more likely to fire flares in their direction just to make sure they got his message. His heart was definitely in the right place, but his brain often seemed MIA.

She stayed in the shade of her camo net, making some notes and reading a book, for the next forty minutes, putting it down only when she heard the unmistakable sound of Mick Beachum returning to camp. The plane had been gone and the air silent since the second pass.

She met him at the edge of camp, coming out from under the net. "I thought you'd be at the van by now," she said, shaking her head in dismay.

"I got worried when that jet came back for a second time," he said. "I thought that meant they'd seen the message."

"They're supposed to see it," she reminded him. "That's kind of the point, right?"

"Well, of course. But…I don't know, Pen. I just didn't want them to find you."

Penny shook her head. "That's why we took such pains to wipe away our tracks," she told him. "That's why we hiked for an hour before we wrote it. It's a big desert out here—even if they put troops on the ground it'll take them a while to find us. By then we'll have moved on. Only it was supposed to be just me, because one person is harder to find than two. Remember the plan?"

"I remember," Mick snapped. He grabbed Penny's shoulders and shook her, suddenly enraged. "Remember flexibility? I was worried about you, for fuck's sake."

She shrugged out of his grip, her voice like ice. "Take your hands off me, and don't ever touch me again."

Mick's face fell. He looked stricken. "Oh, Jesus Christ, Penny, I am so sorry. I don't know what...really, I'm sorry."

"That's fine, Mick. You're sorry. Just don't do it again. I mean it. No hugs for luck, no squeezing my ass like a football player or copping a cheap feel disguised as adjusting my backpack's straps or anything like that. If I ever feel your hand on me again I'll break your arm."

"Jesus, Penny, do you think maybe you're overreacting a little?"

She ignored the question, working on keeping her voice level. If she relaxed it would quaver with emotion and she didn't want that. "Don't think I can't do it."

He stood before her for a moment, blinking under the fury of her onslaught but not making any reply. Softening her voice a bit, she continued. "Do you know how to win a war, Mick?" she asked him. "You outlast the other side. That's why we lost in Vietnam—we found out that no matter what we threw at them, they could outlast us. That's why in the Gulf and then in Kosovo we pounded them so hard while keeping our own people out of their reach. If we'd been taking heavy casualties, public opinion might have gone against us and we wouldn't have outlasted them. I don't know if our war, right here in these mountains, is one we can win—I doubt it, though. So all I want to do is last as long as I can before I let them win. That means staying on this range, undiscovered. And I can do that better by myself than with you here. I've been trained." She laughed once, harshly. "Those guys trained me! The United States military. I know what they know. All you're going to do is get in the way, slow me down, make me a target. Do you understand that? If you want this action to work at all, I have to stay in here, to keep writing new messages, to keep obstructing their ability to drop bombs because they don't know where I am or how many I am or what I'm up to."

"I get that, Penny," Mick said. "I know the plan."

"You're not acting like you do."

"So what you're saying is that I should turn around and go back to the van, go back and get a motel room."

"Yes," she agreed flatly. "That's what I'm saying."

"Okay, then." Mick started to move as if to hug Penny, then caught himself and backed away, running a hand through his dreadlocks. "I, uhh...I guess I'll see you, then."

"I guess so."

But Mick had only taken a few steps from camp when Penny heard the distant stutter of helicopters, coming from the east, over the hills. "Shit," she breathed. She ran after Mick, caught his arm.

"Get under the net!" she said. "Now!"

Mick turned, surprisingly light on his feet when he wasn't being contrary. They both ran back to the tarp spread under the camo netting. He tossed his gear down and they sat, legs crossed, watching the sky.

The helicopters came closer. Two of them, Penny thought. "Hueys."

"That's not the one that keeps crashing, is it?" Mick asked.

"No, that's the Osprey. It's a Marine bird, too, though."

The pitch of one of them changed, deepening.

"One's landing," she said. "The other's not."

"You can tell that from here?" Mick asked.

"I told you, I know these people."

"What are they doing, then?"

"The one that's landing will be dropping off a ground force. They'll undo our message, and look for our tracks so they can find out who wrote it. We were careful enough that they won't find any tracks, at least not right away. The second bird will fly low, in an organized search pattern, looking for us."

"How many men do they carry?"

"Probably ten, fully loaded. If they're traveling light they could squeeze another couple on board, but they probably don't need to."

"Will they find us?"

"They have satellites that can take pictures clear enough to read the logo on your backpack, Mick. If they want to find us bad enough, they will. The 'copter probably won't. The ground troops will, eventually, but it'll take them a while. In the meantime, we'll be ready to move whenever they get too close."

"I guess you're stuck with me for a while."

"I guess I am," Penny agreed. "Do what I tell you, though, or I'll feed you to them."

"You're the boss."

"Don't forget that."

Terrance Berkley hated the silence.

When he was at home, he always had the radio playing or a CD going or the TV on. He didn't much care what he was listening to as long as it wasn't that rap shit. Classic rock, Top 40, shit-kickin' country, even Rush Limbaugh was better than silence. A lot better. Fact was, the man just made sense and there was no getting around that.

But today, he had nothing to listen to except the breeze that blew up occasionally and scratched the leaves of low-growing plants against sand, the random caws of a raven, the faster flutter of a starling's wings. He didn't like Kerry's order to stay at the cabin, alone and silent, but he understood it. And if the girl did what Kerry suspected she might and doubled back, trying to steal the SUV, then Terrance would be damn glad it was him.

Whoever brought in the Dove got first crack at her. Terrance had never had first crack, not in nine years of Dove Hunts. Maybe this one was as smart as Kerry thought she was. A guy could always hope, anyway.

Terrance had taken up a position in the bare rocks overlooking the cabin and the SUV. If she came back to either one, he'd spot her. But he'd been sitting here for more than an hour, in the hot sun. Big guys had a tendency to sweat, and Terrance was a big guy. He'd already finished off the two quarts of water he carried. Good thing I'm not on the trail, he thought. Walking would only make it worse.

There was no sign of the girl anywhere, so he figured it couldn't hurt to head back down to the cabin and refill his canteen. Anyway, Kerry had told him to walk the perimeter from time to time, not just watch the house. Which he hadn't done. So he'd get some water, take a leak in the outhouse, and then make a circuit of the area. If she was hiding out there, he'd find her. He hoisted his bulk off the ground, his wooden-stocked Steyr Forester rifle—if he ever did shoot a real dove there wouldn't be enough left of it to roast over a fire, but it'd stop a person, which was the important thing—in his hands, and hiked back down off the rocks.

The cabin was quiet and empty. He went to the kitchen and refilled his canteen from the five-gallon jugs they'd hauled in, and left it on the counter while he went outside to offload some. The outhouse was empty, too.

He leaned the Steyr against the wall while he urinated. The stench was almost unbearable in here. Most outhouses were emptied once in a while, he knew. Serviced. But there could be no public acknowledgement of this one. It had been stolen from a construction site outside Redlands and brought here in the back of Rock's pick-up truck. Once a year, they brought a bag of lime and dumped it down the hole, but all that really accomplished was changing the quality of the stink. If a terrorist really wanted to cause havoc, Terrance thought, all he'd need to do would be to steal the contents of this Port-a Potty and dump it over an inhabited area.

Finished, Terrance zipped up, then peered through the ventilation slits before stepping outside again. Still no sign of their Dove.

Back in the kitchen, he found his canteen where he'd left it. He was tempted by the coolers of beer and soft drinks, and by the relative comfort of the living room's chairs. But if the guys came back and found him inside…best not to even think about what their reaction would be. He didn't hang around, but stepped back into the punishing heat for his reconnaissance mission.

The cabin was in a narrow, boulder-strewn valley a few miles from the Eastern Mojave National Monument. This land was government-owned as well, managed by the BLM, but no one could think of anything to do with it so it was left alone. Anything worth mining had been taken long ago, there was no timber to harvest unless a sudden market for Joshua trees opened up, and there were no particularly stunning natural features to draw hikers or tourists. The nearest town was twenty miles away, most of that grueling, washboard dirt road. It was almost ten miles to a paved highway.

Terrance had spent most of the morning on the north side of the cabin, where the rocks combined with the natural rise of the valley to make the elevated bluff from which he'd stood guard. But to the southeast the ground fell away rapidly, a rocky slope that bottomed out in a tangle of thick brush, edging a wash where water ran during the rare winter rains.

This was where they dug the graves.

Terrance went that way, because it wouldn't be impossible for someone to hide down there in the brush until the cabin was empty, and if she had gone that route, he wouldn't have been able to see her from his earlier perch. He used the barrel of the rifle to push aside thorny branches as he plucked his way down the slope. At the very bottom the growth was thickest, almost as if the branches had been woven together by hand, but when he was all the way through the worst of it, he stepped out into the wide, sandy wash.

The sand was a bitch to dig in, he remembered. You'd dig and you'd dig but the sides would continually cave in on you. Fortunately they didn't have to dig too far down—just enough to make sure animals didn't get at the bodies. And the graves almost filled themselves in, once the bodies were down here. A few shovels of sand, then they all stomped around on top to flatten it out. By the next year, it was impossible to know for sure where a body had gone. Once, in fact, they had accidentally dug up a Dove from a couple of years before when trying to bury a new one, so they'd just shoved the new corpse in with the desiccated old one.

But it only took a moment for Terrance to know that something was very wrong. The floor of the wash was disturbed, with a big pile of sand next to a depression. He hurried over to it and could see in an instant that someone had been digging there. And he was sure that whoever it was had been digging over one of the graves—he remembered the position of the paloverde tree just beyond it, one of the immovable landmarks of the wash. None of the guys had been down here during this trip, Terrance knew.

Which had to mean that someone else had been in the wash, snooping around. Someone who knew where to dig. It couldn't have been too long ago, or the winds and occasional flash flood would have leveled the ground again. No rain had fallen out here for months, but wind was a constant factor.

Terrance had no shovel with him, just a hunting rifle. He knelt in the sand and scooped up double handfuls of earth, throwing it to the side. Whoever had dug this hole hadn't worried about refilling it at all—in just a few minutes, he had found the skeletal remains of one of their Doves, from five or six years ago if he remembered right. She'd been buried nude, as they all were, so there were no clothes in the pit, just bones.

There was also no skull.

Breathing faster, feeling the onset of panic, he dug around some more, in case the skull had somehow become separated from the rest of the skeleton. Sand and dirt sprayed from the hole like splashes of water; Terrance got grit in his eyes and mouth, and ignored it.

No skull at all.

This isn't good, he thought. Kerry needs to know about this. Everybody needs to know.

He scrambled back up the hill, shoving through the brush, mindless now of the thorns that tore his clothes and skin. By the time he reached the cabin he knew his skin was flushed, his heart slamming. All's I need's a fucking heart attack now, he thought. That would put a capper on a fine day. He stumbled into the cabin. He had a cell phone in his bag, but it wouldn't work here, there was never any signal here, so even if Kerry's was receiving, which was unlikely, he still couldn't get through.

He dug it out anyway, just in case. No signal. He shoved it into the pocket of his pants and stalked from room to room as if an answer would present itself in their gear, in the D-rings set into the floor to hold down the Dove, in the coolers of drinks and meat.

Hidden on the back of one of the kitchen's drawers, though, they always kept a key to whichever vehicle they'd come out in, just in case there was some sort of emergency. It wouldn't do for the only key to be in the pocket of one of the guys if that guy happened to be at the bottom of a cliff with two broken legs. Terrance tugged the drawer out and snagged the key. The path the girl had taken had—at least initially—followed the track of an old mining road. Terrance could make up some ground by taking the SUV, if they'd stuck close to the road. And if they hadn't, he'd see what the thing's real off-road capability was. He ran outside, threw the rifle into the passenger seat footwell, and cranked the engine.

Diego had the wheel, his father cramped between them on the bench seat, legs straddling the gearshift, and Jorge against the other window, trying to keep the three rifles between his legs from rattling too much.

The law had done nothing, which wasn't surprising but was upsetting anyway. Henry Rios had forgotten what it meant to be a Mexican in this world—it was like when he put a uniform on, his skin turned white. So they were out again, in Diego's truck, looking for any sign of their sister. No one would help them; they had to help themselves. The way it was, the way it had always been.

They'd all skipped work that day. If they got fired, they'd just find other work. Lucy was more important than any construction job. But they'd been out for hours— and they'd cruised for hours the day before, too, as long as it stayed light out—and so far, nothing.

They worked their way north now, having gone south before. They covered the roads away from Mecca, up through Thermal and Indio, then into the strip of wealth that became Palm Desert and Palm Springs. The guys had driven a luxury SUV, according to the witness, so it made sense that they might be up this way. But mostly they'd seen pick-ups, Explorers, Jeep Cherokees, a couple of old Toyota Land Cruisers. Except for the islands of excess in Palm Springs, where Mercedes and Lexus became the standard, they saw nothing fancy and dark, like they were looking for. None of the expensive ones in the rich neighborhoods carried the right assortment of passengers, and they didn't really think that kidnappers would hang out in one of the more heavily populated areas of the county.

"They're in a garage by now," Jorge said. "There's no way they'd leave it sitting around in the open, not after someone saw them."

"They don't know anybody saw them," Raul argued. "They think they're clear."

"Even if they garaged it, they might go out for something," Diego insisted. "We stay out long enough, we'll find them."

"There!" Raul shouted suddenly, grabbing Diego's right arm as he did. Diego fought to maintain control of the truck. "Don't do that," he said. "What?"

Raul was pointing forward, and then Diego saw it too, a quarter-mile or so ahead. A big, black luxury SUV pulling out of a dirt drive onto the paved road, turning to travel the same direction they were. "What is that?" Diego asked.

"I don't know, Expedition, Lincoln, Lexus, something like that," Jorge said. "I can't tell from here. But it's one of those expensive ones. Look at the way it shines."

The windows were darkened, too, which fit what the witness had told Sheriff Rios. Diego mashed the accelerator to the floor.

"Those guns are loaded, right?"

"You shot anything today?" Jorge came back. "I haven't."

"Just checking." Diego leaned forward as if doing so could squeeze every ounce of speed from the old GMC. It wasn't much of a truck but it had been built to last and it had served the family well for many years. He was pretty sure that Lucy had lost her virginity in its bed—he knew he had—but he'd never been able to find out to whom, so he hadn't been able to beat the guy up.

Ahead of them, the SUV picked up speed, as if suddenly aware that it was being chased. Its burst of speed was tentative, though, while Diego's was sustained. He had already made up most of the ground between the two vehicles. The SUV's tail was right ahead of him now. Diego flashed his headlights and honked, but the driver refused to pull over, and instead leaned on the gas more. The other vehicle started to pull away.

"Come on!" Jorge pleaded. "Catch it!"

"I'm trying," Diego said.

The SUV leaned into a blind curve, and its brake lights flashed. The driver didn't want to lose control of the big car. Diego had no such compunctions. He pulled out into the oncoming lane to go around the thing, block it off.

Only there was a farm truck, loaded with sugar beets, barreling at them in that lane. Raul let out a scream and grabbed Diego's arm again. Shaking him off, Diego heard his father muttering prayers in rapid Spanish.

Diego pushed farther to his left, going around the truck on its right shoulder. The truck's horn blared in his ears, and his pick-up's tires slipped when they hit the dirt on the shoulder, kicking up a blinding plume of dust. But within seconds he was back on the highway, farm truck past him, rocketing toward the SUV. The driver of that vehicle had either thought he was dead, or had been watching the near-miss instead of the road, because Diego had hardly lost any ground at all. A minute later Diego had pulled ahead of it, and he stomped on the brake, fishtailing to a stop across two lanes. Smoke coming from tires and brakes, the SUV screeched to a halt just behind it.

Diego, Raul, and Jorge threw open their doors and jumped to the ground, rifles raised and pointed at the SUV.

Inside, a young couple sat, hands over their heads. The guy looked like an accountant or a computer programmer, right down to the pens in the pocket of his blue Oxford shirt. The woman seemed a little hardier, dressed in a denim jumper over a white cotton blouse. Both had tears streaming down their cheeks.

"It's not them," Diego said. He spat onto the hot pavement. "Shit, it's not even them."

Jorge gave the couple a friendly wave. "Sorry," he said. "Drive safely."

As the couple sped away, Diego jabbed with the toe of his snakeskin boot at a strange-looking mushroom growing in the shade of a scraggly tree. He bent over it and examined it more closely, then picked it up for a closer look. "Check this out," he said. The mushroom was that shade of sickly pale white reserved for things that never see the sun, but its surface was dotted with red spots, like it had measles or maybe like someone had dripped blood on it, Diego thought. Connecting the spots was a network of fine red lines that could have been capillaries.

"It's a fucking mushroom, that's all," Jorge said. "Let's go."

Diego crushed the thing in his hands and tossed it to the side of the road, then got back in behind the wheel.

"Well?" Colonel Wardlaw asked. He looked out his office window at the base's dusty parade ground. Everything in Yuma is dusty, dry and hot, he thought. Some soldiers get Europe, some get Hawaii for Christ's sake. Even Pendleton would be better than this. He was from Michigan originally, where nature was green unless it was covered with snow, and he couldn't get used to how different the landscape was here.

Behind him, he knew, Captain Yato stood at attention. "Sir, we landed at each of the three target locations. The messages our aircraft had observed were written with rocks, so we erased them by moving the rocks."

Wardlaw turned around to face the young officer. It was a different Corps when a Japanese-American could be a Captain. Wardlaw wasn't entirely sure how he felt about that. "Did you find whoever wrote the messages?"

"No, sir. Not yet, sir."

"At ease, Captain." Yato spread his legs a little, but otherwise his posture remained rigid.

"Thank you, sir."

"I want them, Captain," Wardlaw said. He had seen photos of the messages. WAR NO MORE my ass, he thought. The Pentagon would almost certainly see photos within a matter of days. Probably only the fact that the brass back in Arlington was occupied with more important things had kept them from seeing satellite pictures already. He had to keep a lid on this, and the only way to do that was to get the perpetrators in custody before they could repeat themselves. Yuma was a shithole, but it was his shithole and he didn't want to lose it. "There are traitors in my gunnery area. I want them in my brig instead, and I want them today."

"We're continuing to search for any parties who might have been involved, sir."

"Will, I know we're short-handed. There's a Goddamn war effort going on out there, so we can't be expected to commit a lot of man-hours into finding what could charitably be described as a few vandals, right?"

"Basically, sir."

"Except for one thing."

"What's that, sir?"

"I want them!" Wardlaw roared. "Anyone writing messages like those in a time of war is guilty of treason, and I won't have it on my land!"

"Yes, sir."

"Get back out there, William. And don't come back until you can bring me some traitors."

Ken finished his lunch and threw the wrappers in the metal wastebasket that stood at the end of his desk. He needed to get back up to the Slab, though so far no one he'd spoken to had known anything at all about the mystery skull. He didn't have anything to go on in the way of forensic evidence, though, so he had to go with what he had, which was the hope that someone might have seen someone else put it in the fire pit.

Risa at the Coroner's Office in El Centro had called with some more details on the skull during the morning. The victim was Mexican, from the interior, maybe Oaxaca, judging from the dental work. She was having a facial reconstruction done so they'd be able to get a reasonable likeness, though that kind of thing was always largely guess-work and didn't take into account scars, piercings, tattoos, or any number of other ways people could alter their appearance without disfiguring their skulls. She believed the victim was fairly young—late teens, early twenties. She'd call again when she had more.

Ken was on his feet and halfway to the door when he saw his Bronco pull up outside. He went back to lean against his desk and wait for the deputy to enter.

Billy's face was flushed and tense when he came in. "What's up, boss?"

"Bad day?" Ken asked him.

"Now I know why Osama bin Laden's so damn hard to find," Billy said. "I can't find one stinking Navigator in a county I know like my own back yard."

"It's a challenge," Ken agreed.

"But I was thinking," Billy went on. "With all that shit back East. Do you think we ought to come up with some kind of terrorist safety plan? Preparedness, and all that?"

Ken made an effort not to laugh. "Billy, on the list of targets terrorists might have in mind, I think the Imperial Valley would come near the bottom."

Billy mulled on that. "I guess so. But there is lots of agriculture here, you know? Someone could fly over with a crop duster full of anthrax gas or whatever and really cause some problems."

Ken drummed his fingers on the edge of his desk. "Anthrax is a biological agent, not a gas, to begin with. Maybe it could be spread with a crop duster, I don't know."

"Maybe I should check it out," Billy suggested. "Go look at all the crop dusters in the area, make sure there's no ragheads flyin' 'em."

Ken came up off his desk and stood close to Billy, his expression no longer one of bemusement. "You check it out," he said. "Then you report to me, and don't approach anyone or take any action on your own. And don't use terms like that—it's disrespectful and it reflects badly on me and the entire Imperial County Sheriff's Office. One more racial slur and you're looking for a new job, do you understand me?"

"Yes, sir," Billy said. "Sorry, Ken."

"I don't think we have but a dozen or so Islamic families in the whole county, that I know about," Ken said. "But those that are here are American citizens, and don't forget that."

"In World War Two we put Japanese-Americans in camps," Billy reminded him.

A historical fact coming from Billy Cobb, Ken thought. That was kind of like watching a pig do math. It didn't so much matter whether or not his answer was right, just watching him hold the pencil was impressive. "That's right," he said. "And it was a mistake. But we've learned better since then. Anyway, that was a different kind of war. I don't think we'll see an effort like that put in here."

"You don't think we're really going to war?" Billy asked. He sounded surprised.

"We declared war on crime, on racism, on poverty and on drugs," Ken said. "We haven't won any of those yet."

"But this is different," Billy said. He took off his hat and scratched his sweaty scalp. "They attacked us."

"Yes, they did," Ken agreed. "And killed six thousand of us or so, and they need to be brought to justice for that. But remember, firearms kill thirty thousand Americans every year. Alcohol kills four hundred thousand. Is it really about how many people were killed?"

"Then what is it about?"

"I don't know for sure," Ken said. He went back to his desk, scooted out the chair and sat down. Trying to educate Billy might be a long process. "It's partly that, and partly the fact that we believe we should be safe within our own borders. But as far as it being a real war—well, I don't claim to be an expert, but as far as I'm concerned, there are three things any military action needs to be successful."

"What are those?" Billy asked. He leaned forward, hands resting on the back of Ken's guest chair.

Ken counted off on his fingers. "You need to know who the enemy is, that's number one."

"Bin Laden."

"He's one of many. Thousands, probably. He's a target, but he's not the only terrorist or even the king of all terrorists by any means. It's a much bigger fight than that. And if you stretch it to cover everyone who's ever provided his network aid and support, then do you launch strikes at Ronald Reagan and President Bush's dad? William Casey's already dead, but those three armed and trained bin Laden's troops if anyone did."

"No way," Billy said.

"Way. Do a little outside reading. You might just learn something. But okay, second, you need to know to know where you're going to fight this war. Again, Afghanistan is just the beginning. What about Libya, Somalia, Syria? What about the IRA—are they terrorists? Do we attack Ireland? What about some of our own activities in Latin America? A lot of people consider us terrorists."

"What's the third thing?" Billy asked.

"You need to be able to define success or failure. This is the trickiest one. How do you know if you've beaten terrorism? When they stop attacking us?"

"I guess you got a point there, Ken."

"Damn right I have a point. You launch a military operation without answering those three questions, all you're really doing is swinging your dick. Now, we may be good at swinging our dick, but this time people are going to die with every swing. We need to be a little careful."

"Which comes back around to me checking out the crop dusters," Billy observed. Proving once again that he's smarter than I usually gave him credit for, Ken thought. "That's right. You go out and have a look. It's not a bad idea. But don't go arresting or accusing anybody before you check with me."

"Got it, Ken."

"Okay, Billy. I'm going back up to the Slab, see what more I can come up with on our dead lady. I'll see you later on."

Billy replaced his hat, touched the brim in salute, and walked out.

Lucy knew that a twenty-minute head start was virtually meaningless when comparing the speed she could travel through the desert on platform-soled sandals with that of men in real hiking boots, carrying water. So she did the best she could to increase her lead. Initially, she took her sandals off, knowing that she would be able to move faster barefoot, and also knowing that her feet would cut and bleed fairly quickly. Convinced that she was leaving obvious footprints, she tore some strips from her shirt and bound the wounds on her feet, then backtracked down the path she had taken and chose a different route. Her hope was that they'd follow the bloody prints down a canyon she had no intention of taking, and when the footprints stopped they'd continue on that path.

That bit of misinformation planted, she put the sandals back on and scrambled over a series of sandstone boulders. She had no idea where she was, except that the desert was Mojave, not the Sonoran to which she was accustomed. The same creosote bushes were omnipresent, but there were Joshua trees, which didn't grow at home, and other yuccas with which she wasn't familiar. Which put her north of home, probably by a couple of hours, given the length of the car ride. Spying a range of low mountains to the south, she headed for those. She'd be thirsty soon enough, and if there was water to be found anywhere, it'd be among the hills.

Lucy worked as a file clerk in an insurance office up in Coachella, where she had to know the alphabet but not necessarily the ins and outs of risk versus benefit calculations. But she heard those terms bandied about, and understood the basic concepts. She knew enough to know that, while just being out in the desert by herself was dangerous, the risk of letting those guys catch her was pretty much identical to the risk of doing it without water. Both would be equally fatal.

Coming down from the rocks, she found a narrow canyon heading in the right direction, so she allowed herself the luxury of moving along its relatively smooth, soft floor for a while. She left footprints in the sand, but she made good time and counted on having thrown off her pursuers for long enough.

As the sun rose higher and began to beat down between the canyon walls, she started to wonder if this had been a good idea. The walls rose higher and higher, effectively trapping her there, and the air inside the canyon seemed superheated, bouncing off the sandy floor and the slick walls like microwaves in an oven. She had to slow to a walk or risk heatstroke. But she was committed now, so she continued, the canyon's smooth walls coming closer and closer together until it was a slot canyon. Extending her arms, Lucy's fingertips could touch both sides at once. The advantage was that as the canyon narrowed to the extreme, the upper lip overhung the floor and blocked some of the sun. Now it was like a furnace, but not a furnace with a huge ball of flaming gas attached.

Finally, the two walls met, creating a barrier about waist-high. Lucy didn't hesitate, but pressed her palms against the edge and hoisted herself up and into the next, slightly more elevated branch of the slot canyon. She repeated the process twice more; it was like a boat working through a canal by shunting from lock to lock.

With each rise, the canyon got narrower—but, as she was counting on, the top edge of the wall grew closer as well. At the point where she needed to turn sideways and edge through the canyon, the lip of the wall was less than ten feet above her. Time to go up. Her back against one wall and feet on the opposite, she pushed herself up to the top of the wall. Breaking out into the sun again, she learned that she had made real progress toward the hills, and that the other side of the canyon was a gentle slope that ended at a broad Joshua tree forest. She left the canyon behind and struck out across the plain, its floor shimmering in the day's heat and casting mirage greenery several feet above the actual brush. The hills were close enough now to make out details.

Forty minutes or so later, Lucy guessed, she reached the hills. Every step now was agony. The skin on her arms and face was burned. She knew she needed water soon—she was dehydrated, and heatstroke would follow soon if she couldn't get water and some shade.

But from halfway across the plain she'd seen a dark streak on a cliff wall, and now, closer, she could see a leafy green plant at the base of the cliff, and she knew what that meant. She pointed herself at that spot, and a few minutes later she was there, in front of a tall sandstone face with a narrow black mark running down it from a point midway up. A spring. She couldn't even see the water, just where it had discolored the stone over the years. But it was there, nonetheless. She pressed her mouth to the stone and held it there, letting the moisture seep into her. Not nearly as satisfying as a mouthful of water, or the long drink she craved, but it would be enough to save her life, she knew.

If she could continue to evade the men who chased her.

And that didn't look good, because when she pulled her mouth away from the wall—holding her hand there to catch what water she could—and looked back over the plain she had just crossed, she saw several figures, following her path. She had bought herself some time but she hadn't lost them. Which just meant things would be harder from here out—she was weak, tired, hungry, burned, and used up. They were maybe not much fresher, but they had the right clothes and gear.

And guns.

Lucy turned and pressed her face to the cliff again. She'd need to find a better source of water than this soon, but at least it was something. She stayed as long as she dared and then left the cliff wall, following it around until it opened into a wide, rocky canyon.

She scouted the canyon for a few minutes, always aware that the hunters were less than a half hour behind her. Running away was looking less and less like a possibility, which left her only two options. Giving up seemed like a bad choice.

So, to be honest, did making a stand.

But if she was going to die, then she'd by God do everything she could to take some of those men with her.

Exploring the canyon, though, gave her a glimmer of hope.

A side canyon branched off this main one, its entrance blending so well with the main canyon's wall as to be virtually invisible unless one were walking the canyon's edge as Lucy had done, looking for precisely this kind of thing. The narrow side canyon led uphill, and its walls were a dozen feet or so tall, and climbable, with plenty of hand and footholds. Lucy scaled one to see what was on the other side and spotted an inset in the canyon wall—an indentation big enough for a person, if she was small enough and maybe a little flexible.

She poked her head inside, looking for snakes or scorpions, but it was clear. And shaded by the overhang. She climbed inside, fitting herself into the indentation's natural curve. Pluses and minuses, she knew. If they climbed the canyon wall in the same place she did, they'd spot her, and she'd have nowhere to hide or run. Her back was, quite literally, to the wall.

But if they didn't climb the wall, they'd never see her. They'd go up the main canyon, or maybe even up the side canyon, but the only place from which they could see into this indentation was from up on the opposite wall of the side canyon itself, and what were the chances they'd be up there when the canyon floor was easier walking?

With a few minutes to spare, Lucy climbed back down and went out into the canyon to make a few more adjustments. Stepping as firmly as she could bear to, she made a trail of deep footprints leading up the main canyon a ways, ending at a rocky patch where sandaled feet wouldn't leave marks anyway. Then she backtracked, walking backward, stepping in her own footprints. Finally, she cut over to the side canyon, using a fallen branch of greasewood to brush away the footprints she made. Her hope was that they'd believe the obvious footprints and go straight up the main canyon, leading them far away from her. In the meantime, she'd be inside her hidey-hole, in the shade, waiting for them to clear out so she could get back to the important business of finding water and food.

She worked her way back up-canyon and was starting to climb when she heard them behind her, entering the main canyon. If her camouflage didn't work, they'd spot the side canyon within minutes, and see her before she got back to the indentation. Climbing all the way to that would leave her visible for too long, so instead she picked a flat shelf of rock, lower than she was comfortable with but well above the head of any of the men, and flattened herself against it, waiting to see which way they'd go.

Carter Haynes had to shove a pile of newspapers—the most recent seemed to be from late 1998—over to one side of the chair he was offered in the semi-random collection of debris that was Gray Boonton's little piece of the Slab. Where most of the locals at least had something resembling a mobile home, Gray had connected sheets of cast-off corrugated sheet metal, possibly with chewing gum and kite string, and added cardboard, plywood, and other artifacts (the hood of a Ford Fairlane, for instance, had become a front door). There were mushrooms, for God's sake, growing up through a scrap of cheap remnant carpeting that covered the broken cement slab and served as a floor; broad-headed, red-spotted things with a fine red tracery connecting the spots. Sandra, Carter's wife, would probably have his clothes sterilized if she saw this place. She was a clean freak, which didn't bother Carter as long as she dealt with her neuroses while he was away from the condo. And there was something to be said for coming back to a neat home every night.

Despite the crushing heat inside the place, Boonton wore a moth-eaten cardigan sweater the color of his name over a one-piece orange polyester jumpsuit, open to the navel. Sweat gleamed across his chest and the exposed swell of his belly. Giving Boonton two grand for this mess was absurd—it would probably cost nearly that to haul it all to a dump, and if he'd spent a penny on it Carter would be surprised. But a deal was a deal, and if Boonton would sign the contract, he'd get the dough, same as anybody else on the Slab. It was worth it to Carter to avoid the bad publicity that might come from forcible evictions. Not to mention the possibility that any of these people could come back with a can of gasoline and a match if they weren't treated with what passed for respect.

He was perilously close to losing his cool with Boonton, though.

The old man turned the contract this way and that, upside down and over, as if he not only couldn't read but didn't actually understand that the side with the words on it was the side that mattered. "All I got to do is sign this paper and you give me the money?" he asked, for what must have been the thirtieth time.

"That's right. You sign that and then you move off the Slab."

"Why do I got to move?"

Carter bit his lip. Behind him, he could tell Nick Postak was working hard to keep from cracking up—he could hear his bodyguard's breathing catch and hold as he made a supreme effort.

Gray Boonton was a hundred and fifty if he was a day, Carter thought, and resembled nothing so much as an older version of Professor Irwin Corey. The man still had a wild shock of long hair, lots of it for someone who should have been dead decades past. His chin and cheeks were grizzled and white, and his teeth sat abandoned in an empty glass on top of an upside down tortoise shell that rested on a broken-slatted fruit crate turned on end to function as—well, apparently as a base for the turtle shell, Carter decided. Unless the shell and crate were both meant to be part of a pedestal for the teeth. Hard to tell, really.

"Because that's the whole point," Carter reminded him. "We're building houses here."

"Well, as soon as you start to build on this spot, why then I'll move," Boonton said. He sounded totally convinced of his own reasonableness.

"No, you need to move right away. Everybody else is."

"They are?" Boonton asked. "Why?"

"Because that's the deal. They agree to move, they get the money. Then they can use the money to pay for the move."

"Two thousand dollars?" The man had a lock on that particular figure, if nothing else.

"That's right."

"Can I buy one of these new houses for that?"

"No," Carter replied. "I'm afraid not. Not even close."

"Well, then what good does it do me? I ain't got any other money."

"I don't care where you move to," Carter said. "As long as it's ten miles or more from the Slab."

"You going to give me a ruler?"

"With two grand you can buy a whole yardstick."

Boonton sprang to his feet from the old truck bench he'd been using as a chair and began rummaging around on a card table. One leg was broken off and that corner wedged between the slats of a kitchen chair, keeping it somewhere in the general vicinity of level. Watching him dig through the detritus of his life, Carter had the sense that Boonton was an impersonation of a man, maybe a bunch of squirrels in a human suit trying to pass.

"So…" Boonton muttered, seemingly to himself, "…so, two thousand dollars for me. But that won't buy me one of your fine houses. But if you have money for me in that case, maybe you have money for everybody else, hey? Hey?"

The last word came out louder, almost shouted. With it, Boonton drew a long, wicked-looking knife from underneath the piles of crap on his slanted card table. It looked like a fish-scaling knife with a rusted, serrated blade. He pointed it at Carter.

"Just hand that suitcase over here, you," he said. "Let me see all that pretty money inside."

Nick Postak was already in motion. Having decided the old man wasn't a significant enough threat to use the gun on, Carter guessed, he planted himself between Boonton and Carter and grabbed the wrist of Boonton's knife hand. His bulk blocked the next move, but Carter heard the crack of bone and Boonton's scream. Nick's left arm shot out in a jab, and Boonton flew backward, crashing into his barely-balanced card table and upending the whole thing. Boonton flipped over the table as it fell, paper and animal bones and aluminum cans and bottles and broken appliances flew through the room as if catapulted. Carter ducked as a green beer bottle jetted past his head, slipping somehow through the barricade that Nick's body provided.

He looked up again to see Gray Boonton, still in motion, seeming to cartwheel over the card table into the rear wall of his dwelling. Into, and through—as Boonton slammed into the rickety structure, the wall gave way behind him. The old man, arms and legs flailing, burst through into the bright sunshine on the other side. As the corrugated tin wall hit the cement of the Slab, the rest of the makeshift cabin shuddered as if an earthquake were striking it. Carter Haynes bolted from his seat for the Fairlane hood door, shoving it aside and running away from Boonton's collapsing home. Nick Postak followed, his gun clenched in his meaty fist now.

As he and Carter stood there, catching their breaths, the little shack fell in on itself with a rumble and a cloud of dust.

On the other side, Gray Boonton knelt on the Slab, shaking a fist at them. "You broke my God-damned house, you bastards! You owe me a lot more than two thousand dollars now, by God!"

Nick looked at Carter. "I could just shoot him."

"Don't tempt me," Carter said. He looked past Gray, where a familiar figure came toward them at a trot. "But I'd advise against it. That's the local law."

Ken Butler came up behind Boonton, still screaming bloody murder over the collapse of his house of cards. Half a dozen mangy-looking mongrels converged from different points of the Slab, barking and sniffing at the wreckage. "You gentlemen having a disagreement of some kind?" Butler asked.

"They knocked down my house," Boonton insisted. "And that big fucker hit me!"

"This is Nick Postak, my bodyguard," Carter explained quickly. "He did strike Mr. Boonton, after Boonton pulled a knife on me and tried to steal my briefcase."

"I see," Butler said. "And you have a concealed carry permit for that weapon, Mr. Postak?"

"I sure do, Lieutenant," Nick said. "I can show it to you."

"Not just yet, please. That true, Gray? You tried to get the man's briefcase?"

"He's trying to give me two thousand bucks," Boonton said. "But he's got a lot more than that in the case. Figure I need it more than he does if I got to find a new place to live."

Butler did a chuckle that reminded Carter once again of Andy Griffith. "Looks like you need one anyway," he said. "I'm going to make a suggestion, gentlemen. I'm going to suggest that no one presses charges for any of the variety of criminal acts that may have occurred here, because I just don't think a judge or jury will be able to keep a straight face long enough to hear the facts. Mr. Haynes, I recommend you wrap it up for today and continue again tomorrow. Further, Gray, I'm going to suggest that you sign Mr. Haynes's contract, and take the two thousand dollars, and move off the Slab right away."

Boonton rose unsteadily to his feet, with Butler helping him. A trickle of blood ran from the corner of his mouth. Considering Nick's size, the old coot's lucky his jaw wasn't broken, Carter thought. The bodyguard had probably pulled his punch so as not to kill the old fool.

"I reckon that's the best thing," Boonton said. He looked at the pile of wreckage that had once been his shelter and kicked at a stray bottle that had rolled out of it. "Shoot, I gotta find my teeth."

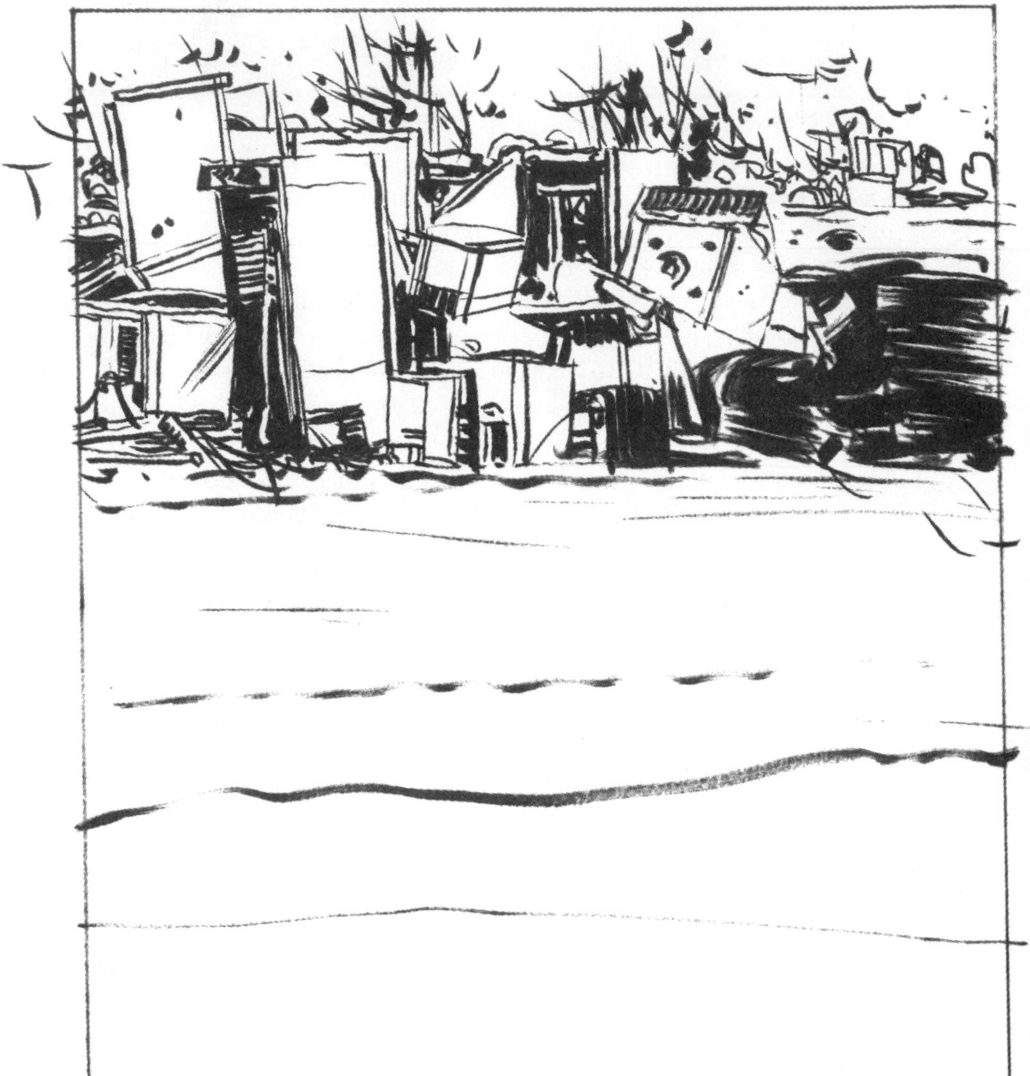

chapter 12

Cam had a bad feeling about this whole deal, and his bad feeling got worse and worse as the day wore on. The Dove had managed to elude them for far longer than they usually did—usually, within an hour or so, they could be found sitting and crying against a rock somewhere. This one had stones, though. Without food or water or even decent shoes, she did an Energizer bunny routine that was wearing Cam out. His shoulders ached from the backpack, his arms were tired from carrying the gun, his feet felt like he'd tromped barefoot on hot glass. This girl was going to pay for running them ragged…if they had the energy to extract the price.

"We're not far behind her," Kerry insisted. That had been his usual refrain, today. But every time he was convinced they were right on top of her, she was nowhere to be found.

"You keep saying that, Kerry," Rock said.

Kerry shot him a death look. "And I mean it. These tracks are fresh."

"It's the desert, Kerry," Vic pointed out. "It's a pretty still day. Hard to tell if a track was made an hour ago or a day ago."

Vic was right, Cam knew. There were still marks from wagon wheels in parts of the desert, not that far away, on land that he owned, made during the westward migration that followed the gold rush of 1849. The desert healed slowly and showed its scars for a long time.

He wasn't used to this kind of physical exertion—he was getting up there, anyway, the double-nickel had come and gone since the last time he'd done this, and he paid people—maybe this Dove's family, for that matter—to do the manual labor on his property. For Cam, farming was about sitting in front of a computer, meeting with accountants and lawyers, being driven in a pick-up truck or flown overhead in a helicopter occasionally. Not as hands-on as some, but at least he was actually farming his land. Other landowners in the Valley were absentees, big corporate interests that owned tens of thousands of acres each, farming little, mostly holding onto the property so that at some point they could sell water, not produce, to the increasingly thirsty megalopolises of coastal California. Cam had little patience for those outsiders. Cam double-planted when he could, bringing in his lettuce, for instance, and then planting Sudan grass on the same acreage. Used more water, but he was thinking about installing a drip irrigation system which would be much more efficient than the old-fashioned flood irrigation most of the Valley's farms had. If you were going to go up against the big agribusinesses, he thought, you had to be leaner and smarter.

Thinking about irrigation made him realize how thirsty he was. He stopped in the shade from the canyon wall's overhang to catch his breath and take a swig from his canteen. Standing there, feeling the warm water splash down his dry throat, he noticed that the wall actually led off the main canyon, up a smaller side canyon.

"Guys!" he called. "Got a branch canyon over here."

Kerry stopped in his tracks, looking back at Cam. "The footprints are here," he said. "So it's unlikely the Dove even saw that branch. But check it out for a few minutes, Cam, see if she's trying to pull a fast one. If you don't see her in ten minutes, come back down and join us in this one."

Cam resisted the urge to salute. "Ten minutes," he repeated. He capped his canteen and started up the side canyon. The floor was rockier and more uneven than the main canyon's, so he immediately regretted having even said anything when he'd found it. The last thing he needed, though, was for her to be sitting up some side canyon while they continued to cover ground in the wrong direction. Already, he was starting to wonder if they'd make it back to the cabin before dark. He just hoped the Dove would be able to walk when they found her, and not make them carry her. Seemed unlikely any of them would be up to that, especially if she struggled like he had every expectation she would. He supposed they could just knock her out and drag her, though.

As he made his way up the canyon, he wondered if maybe he ought to think about dropping out after this year. Kerry had presented it as a foolproof plan, and so far he'd been right. But every year presented new possibilities for mistakes. Cam had a wife and two kids in college and a successful, respected business. If word ever got out about how he spent his annual vacation, all that would be ruined. He would deserve whatever happened, he knew. But he knew that in life you don't always get what you deserve, and he was hoping this was one of those occasions.

Christ, it was hot. He knew he'd just hit the canteen a few minutes ago, but he needed another drink. His canteen hung on a strap across his chest, so he stopped, set his gun down, and pulled the canteen off. Then he picked the gun up again and continued up the uneven canyon floor, tilting his head back for a drink. Another couple of minutes here and he'd turn around to rejoin the others.

She wasn't up here. He screwed the cap back onto the canteen, ready to give up. He barely saw the flash of light off metal, the motion of an arm arcing toward him, before the pain swallowed him alive.

The pain drove him to his knees, pain that was unimaginable, indescribable. He clapped both hands to his left eye. His glasses were already gone, the lens shattered, the frames knocked off his head by the blow. He held his hands there, over his eye, but it was like throwing up a makeshift dam before a rushing river. When he moved them away for a moment—anything to quash the pain, and maybe God maybe air would do it since cupping his hands didn't—the river, released, splashed wetly down his shirt. Blood, and he was afraid to think what else.

There was screaming, and Cam knew it was him screaming but he couldn't bring himself to stop it. Where the hell were the other guys, that's what he wanted to know.

He couldn't see, couldn't hear anything over his own wordless wail. She could be anywhere, even now, sneaking up to finish him off.

He forced himself to his feet and ran, down-canyon, keeping his right hand outstretched to feel the rough canyon wall as he went. The left hand stayed over his eye. After four steps he fell, then dragged himself to his feet, three more steps, fell again. The skin on his knees was shredding, knees and palms bleeding now, he was sure, but that awareness was secondary, somewhere deep in his brain, and he paid it no mind. His attention was focused on the pain and the girl who was surely out there somewhere, stalking him.

As he hauled himself once again to his feet, finally hearing the shouts of his friends as they came from the main canyon toward this side one, he realized what she must have used, with what weapon the bitch had attacked him.

The fork. Kerry had let her keep her fucking fork, from breakfast.

And that fork had gone into his eye.

Penny went up the hill to get away from Mick.

Officially, the reason was to gather some reconnaissance. From the hilltop she thought she could see where the troops were, and if they were making any progress finding the tracks that she believed she and Mick had done a good job of covering up. Lying on her stomach she could look back across their path, and if the marines were following the tracks, she'd know and have enough warning to move out.

But as important as that was, it was just as vital that she get away from Mick before she completely lost her patience with him. He meant well, she kept telling herself. His heart was in the right place. But he was just freaking annoying. She had a high tolerance—a girl didn't have two younger brothers without developing tolerance for the annoying. Or committing fratricide, which she had considered but never resorted to.

It was harder for her, probably, because she agreed with most of what he said. The nation was drifting to war—no, strapping on rocket engines and rocketing toward it, more likely. She believed that with absolute certainty, and that's what Mick thought, too, only he couldn't stop talking about it. He was right—the thought depressed her, almost brought tears to her eyes as she bellied into the sand and watched the hillsides through binoculars—but there was only so much listening to it one person could stand. She was here to work for peace, she believed that peace was, in almost all circumstances, better than war, and she believed that a peaceful approach in this particular case—or at least, a law enforcement approach, taking the case to a world court and convicting bin Laden there, if he was indeed responsible, was the best way to make sure that more attacks didn't shake America's foundations. But if she had to listen to one more of Mick's lectures about it she thought she'd rip his tongue out and force it down his throat.

She figured the entire nation had been depressed since September eleventh. It needed a good long session on the couch of some omnipotent psychiatrist—not a Freudian, who'd get all hung up on the imagery of the airplanes penetrating the two buildings, like the upraised legs of some Whore of Commerce. Someone who could make sense of things, who could ask questions other than "How do you feel about six thousand deaths?" Questions that would lead to dialogue, to healing, or at least to some kind of coming to terms with the horror.

Hell, she realized, she'd been depressed since the previous December, when it had become plain that while a minority of voters had felt that Dubya was presidential material, it was a large enough minority to put him within Supreme Court distance of the White House. She hadn't been terribly excited about Gore, and considered Nader little more than a glory-seeking opportunist, despite the fact that most of her friends were voting for him. But both seemed like better choices than Bush, who had never accomplished anything positive in his life that she could see.

Something had torn for her the day the Supreme Court's decision came down, though. A lifetime's faith in the political process she loved had been shattered. The terror attacks were just one more sign that the world had changed, that the things she had taken for granted—every vote counts, the branches of government are distinct and separate, Americans are safe in their own country—were not the sure things she had believed.

Maybe she was really depressed, she thought. Clinically depressed. That could explain the lack of patience with Mick, who had been a friend and who wanted to be more. She had spent extended periods of time with him before, traveling around the country to meetings or actions, and never felt this urge to physical assault, though she'd always made clear that his advances were unwanted. She had left him with specific instructions to remain under the netting, knowing that her nerves were frayed enough that if he followed her up the hill she'd tear into him.

And they might be out here together for days. It seemed to be what Mick wanted; she hoped he survived the experience.

Virginia's thoughts blared in Hal Shipp's mind like one of those cars that pulls up next to you at a light, stereo screaming so loud your ears start to bleed in spite of rolled-up windows. This was new; not something he'd ever experienced on any other magic day, but at the same time not entirely surprising. This day had seemed different from earlier ones, and since he had touched Lieutenant Butler it had taken on new undertones and overtones, a familiar song with a different arrangement.

The Virginia thing had started while he napped. It had infected his dreams, turned them dark and savage and bloody, and finally he'd awakened, still sitting on the sofa. He'd tried to shake off the sense of dread he felt, but then he caught a glimpse of Virginia and it was rolling off her in waves, almost tangible. He didn't think she really meant it—it was very unlike her to wish anyone ill, especially him—but who ever knew what was in another person's heart?

Nevertheless, he couldn't remain in their mobile home—it felt like trying to stay inside a bath that had begun to boil because it had felt so nice before the heat was turned up. He stood, suddenly. Virginia saw him.

"Oh, you're up."

"Yes," he said. "I'm going to take a walk."

"Just a minute," she said, drying a plate with an old white towel. "I'll come with you."

"No, that's okay," Hal said. "I'd like to go alone."

Virginia frowned. "I'd rather you didn't."

"I'm fine, Virginia," he said. "Really. I feel better than I have in years; my memory is perfect. If anything changes I'll come right back."

"But, Harold—"

"Gin, I really need to do this alone," he said, his tone more insistent. He didn't know what he'd do if she couldn't be persuaded. Point out what she'd been thinking about, he supposed. Describe the way she'd envisioned wrapping one edge of a shard of glass with heavy duct tape and driving the other, the pointed side, into his throat. That would at least get her off his back for a few minutes, he figured.

But she didn't protest, and he left the trailer, stepping out onto the hot slab.

As he walked around its perimeter, he realized that it wasn't limited to Virginia. He could "hear" the people in just about every home, and the thoughts were remarkably similar—violent and twisted and full of inappropriate rage. Heather Justice plotted to smother her husband Royal with a pillow—not long enough to kill him, but long enough to cause him to lose consciousness so she could shave his back for once. After twenty-eight years of making love to him, feeling the thick tufts under her hands, she just couldn't take it any more. Royal, for his part, was giving serious thought to taking the two grand that Carter Haynes offered and leaving Heather behind, to drive up to Reno and look for a cocktail waitress he'd had a brief flirtation with while on vacation six years before. Heather had fended for herself before they were married—Royal had always suspected that she'd had a sugar daddy of some kind, before her looks had faded—and could do so again.

Dickie Rawlingson had something more concrete in mind for his sister Bettina, with whom he'd lived since childhood. Devout Catholics, neither had ever married, and though they'd held minimum wage jobs from time to time, most of their income had gone to the Church. Now they lived on the Slab and Bettina worked part-time cleaning houses in Indio and Palm Desert. Dickie hadn't had a job since he'd been injured in a car accident. Now he walked with a cane and a pronounced limp, and his left arm hung uselessly at his side. Despite his handicap, however, he thought he'd come up with a way to tie Bettina into her bed, following which he'd empty a five gallon can of gasoline onto and around her, and set a fuse that would give him just time enough to get into the old LeSabre she drove to her jobs and race away. Bettina wasn't home, presently, but her comment from earlier in the day, when she'd accused Dickie of being a leech who had killed their mother with his neediness, hung on the air like a mildew stain on wallpaper.

Hal felt like he was eavesdropping on all these people, but he was powerless to do anything about it. The voices of his friends and neighbors screamed at him, shouts of murder and torment and the willful infliction of pain without mercy. He shuddered, but plugging his ears did no good; the voices were inside his head, not outside. Underneath it all he thought he heard another voice, low and compelling, urging them all on, inciting their base impulses. He wasn't sure about that one, though. He could have been imagining it, because he could only "hear" it when the others were quiet, and the din of all the voices on the Slab threatened to overwhelm him.

Finally he decided the only answer was to strike away from the Slab and off into the desert, where things might be quieter.

chapter 13

He had told Cam to take ten minutes, then to rejoin them. When he heard the screams, Kerry glanced at his Tag Heuer. Eight minutes, and the farmer had already run into trouble.

"Let's go," he told the others. "Double time."

They all turned, without questioning the order or his right to give it, and started down the canyon at a trot. Cam's cries continued.

"Fuck, man," Rock said. "He sounds bad."

He'd better be, Kerry thought, but he didn't say it. Cam was turning into a liability on these hunts—getting too soft, too rich, too successful. Cam knew it, too. Kerry thought this would be Cam's last year with them. If the panic in his screams was warranted, it was entirely possible that this would be his last day with them.

"Bitch pulled something," he said. "Cam's not the kind of man to cry like a baby."

"But he might be the kind of man who'd let a chick get the drop on him," Ray observed. "Maybe he was wiping his glasses or something—goddamn guy's always cleaning his glasses. I hate that. Breathes on them and wipes them on his shirt tails."

"Let up on him," Vic said, panting with the effort. "He's in trouble, you can hear that."

When they made it back to the entrance to the side canyon, Kerry glanced at his chronograph again. Another four minutes had elapsed—the difference between the slight slope down, versus up, and moving at a jog instead of walking, trying to follow tracks that had been distinct but then just came to a dead stop at a patch of bare rock. He took the lead up the side canyon, his M-4 at the ready.

Two minutes up the canyon, they found Cam stumbling toward them. His pants were in tatters, his gun and glasses missing, his shirt drenched with blood. He moved like a blind man, with his left hand covering his left eye and his right thrown out for balance. He looked like he'd rolled down the canyon instead of walking—gashes on his head and arms bled along with those on his legs.

But the worst was the river that flowed from underneath his hand.

"Cam!" Kerry shouted when he saw the man. Cam didn't respond, just kept up his insistent whimpering and continued pitching blindly toward them. "Cam!" Kerry called again, more forcefully.

This time, Cam stopped short.

"K-Kerry? I'm...I'm hurt. She..."

"Where is she?" Kerry swept the area behind Cam with the M-4's muzzle but saw no sign of her.

"I don't…I don't…she hurt me."

Kerry caught up to Cam, put his hands on the man's arms and stopped him in his tracks. "Let me see," he said. "Move your hand, Cam."

Cam didn't reply, just whined like a whipped puppy.

"Move your hand or I'll break your arm."

Cam trembled under Kerry's touch. The other men crowded around, now, but they didn't bother Kerry and Cam likely didn't even know they were there. The eye Kerry could see was wide open but the panic was in it, and panic drove out sight, drove out senses. Panic killed. Kerry had seen it plenty of times. In Nicaragua an American nun who should have known better had panicked when Kerry had been forced to kill some villagers—their heads needed to go up on stakes, as a warning to some who were feeding information to the Sandinistas. She'd panicked and run from Kerry right out into a field she knew perfectly well had been seeded with antipersonnel mines. That nun had vaporized herself, and then Kerry had been forced to deal with two of her Sisters who'd seen the whole thing. Panic killed, and there was no getting around that, and its targets weren't all that picky and there was no getting around that either.

Cam, shaking like an aspen in fall, moved his hand away from his face. Where his eyeball should have been there was only a wet, red mess.

"Oh, Christ," Kerry heard Vic say, behind him. Then he heard retching. He stayed focused on Cam, though.

"It was the fork, Kerry. You let her keep the fork and it was the fork, she put the fork in my eye and it hurts, oh God it really hurts, Kerry. It really hurts. The fork, you see what I'm saying, she used the fucking fork—"

"Okay, Cam," Kerry interrupted. "You're hurt but you'll be okay. We're going to get you out of here, get you to a doctor, all right? Keep your hand over your eye, like you had it, okay? That's a good idea. That's what we'll do." He ripped a strip of fabric from his own shirt and folded it into a square, then placed the square under Cam's hand to help staunch the flow. Cam allowed Kerry to move his hand about, offering no resistance at all. He was in shock, Kerry was sure. He stepped around to Cam's side, so he could put an arm over the man's shoulders and guide him the rest of the way out of the canyon. Now he could see Vic, doubled over at the base of the canyon's wall, wiping his mouth on his arm

"Vic, pull yourself together," he said. "We have to move fast. You and Rock come with me."

"What about me?" Ray asked. "What do you want me to—"

"Find the bitch," Kerry said. "Find her and kill her. She's in this canyon somewhere."

"I can do that," Ray said. "No problem. I can do that easy."

"I know you can," Kerry replied. "That's why I picked you." He'd rather have done it himself, but he couldn't. When a decision had to be made about what to do with Cam, it was going to have to be the right decision and it would have to be made and executed with quick efficiency. Kerry trusted only himself with that responsibility.

"When you're finished come back to the cabin, Ray, and we'll meet up there."

"Don't worry about me, Kerry," he said. "I'll enjoy doing this bitch, after what she done to Cam."

"Just remember," Kerry said. "She has Cam's gun now. And she's already demonstrated that she's dangerous."

"Don't worry about me," Ray repeated.

But Kerry couldn't help worrying. If he could be in two places at once, he'd feel a lot better about this whole fucking mess.

Well, okay, Lucy thought. Water and a gun. Two unexpected bonuses, just like buying Ginsu knives from a TV commercial and getting the vegetable peeler for nothing.

When she'd realized that only one guy was coming up the canyon she had taken—and that she couldn't make it back to her hidey-hole in time—she had remembered the fork that had been riding against her ass all day long. She had lain flat against a rock shelf until the guy had come along—she could just see the top of his head, bobbing along as he walked, and she heard him because not only was he not taking pains to be quiet, but he stopped for a water break just before coming into range, so she heard the sounds of the canteen being opened, the glug-glug of him downing the stuff, and then the sounds of the cap going back on. It was bald guy, guayabera shirt guy, not the curly-haired leader she'd been hoping for.

But one was better than none.

From her prone position on her stomach, she had started the arc of attack at her hip, and just drove the fork forward with all her might. He hadn't seen it coming, she was sure—there was no gasp of surprise, no intake of breath, as she'd been expecting. There was only the desert silence, the faint rustle of her jeans against the rock as she struck, and then the shattering of glass and the delicious wet splurting sound as the fork broke through the glasses and sank into his eye. She couldn't quite see his eye from her vantage point, but that was the target she'd been hoping for. Either an eye itself, or a head wound that would blind him with his own blood.

In his shock and pain, he'd dropped his rifle and the canteen he'd been guzzling from. As soon as he went scrambling down the canyon, she had silently come to the floor and scooped up those treasures, then taken to the wall again. Now she was ensconced in her hidey-hole, waiting. She drank deep from the canteen and she made sure the safety was off on the gun. If she saw someone's face, she would shoot. No question about that—the fork in the eye thing had convinced her of her own seriousness, her own resolve, as surely it had convinced her enemies. Though she had always been a determined sort she was not, by nature, a violent woman. But circumstances brought out new sides of people, she was learning. It certainly had for her.

From her hiding place, Lucy could hear the voices of the men conversing, their tones too low for her to make out the words. At least the guy she'd stabbed had stopped his godawful screaming. The way that had echoed up and down the canyon made her wish she'd managed to kill him with the first blow, or had finished him off with the gun once she had it.

But that would be suicide, she knew. Leaving him alive was a much better way to go. Leaving him alive but injured meant, she hoped, that they'd split up. At least some of them would take their friend to try to get him medical attention. Maybe others would stay and look for her. But if she'd killed the guy outright, then they'd all stay and look for her, and they wouldn't rest until they'd killed her.

She hadn't thought this through at first—she had struck out of rage and opportunity, and what happened happened. But in retrospect, she thought it had worked out the best way it could. Guayabera guy might still die—she hoped he did. She just wanted him to live long enough to divide the enemy for a while. Divide and conquer, that's what she'd always heard. She'd just find out if it really worked that way.

"Isn't this Ken's Bronco?"

"You worried he'll smell your perfume?"

"I saw him today. He bought lunch."

"You see him just about every day, don't you? Man has a major league crush on you."

Mindy Sesno sighed. "If he does, he sure hasn't done anything about it."

Billy had picked her up a block from the Shop-R Mart, as he usually did. When she'd seen the Bronco rounding the corner instead of the usual Crown Vic, she'd tried to melt into the wall. But then she realized it was Billy behind the wheel and broke into a relieved grin.

"You're better off," Billy said. "What could that old man do for you that I can't?"

"I hear older men are better lovers," Mindy replied.

He put a hand on her thigh, squeezing hard enough to leave finger marks in the tender flesh there. "You got any complaints about me?"

Her laugh was low and throaty when she was aroused, he knew. That's how it sounded now. "No. No complaints."

"So don't worry about a guy that's too shy to make a move," Billy said. "Just be glad you got back-up."

Ten minutes later they were at her place. Billy parked the Bronco around back, so it wouldn't be noticed by anyone passing by, and stepped out. Walking around to her side, his boot slipped in something. "Goddamnit," he said. "You don't have a dog, do you?"

"Of course not," Mindy laughed. "Why?"

But when he looked, he saw that it hadn't been dogshit he'd stepped in, but a wide mushroom, as big around as a saucer. What was left of its head was pale, with red spots, and where he'd torn it open it seemed to seep a thick reddish liquid, like half-coagulated blood.

"Nothing," he said. "Ugly fucking mushroom. I stepped right in it."

He picked bits of it off his boot and tossed them back onto the gravel yard as she unlocked the kitchen door of her little cottage. "That's funny," she said. "It wasn't there this morning when I left. I didn't see it, anyway." She shook her head and opened the door.

"How long's it been?" Billy asked, following her inside. "A month? I've been so horny for you."

Truth was, he'd been half out of his mind with lust since his trip to El Centro and the supposedly free bj down there that had turned out not to be free at all.

"More like three days," Mindy said. She unbuttoned the top three buttons of her pink blouse and slipped it off her shoulder, revealing the mark that Billy had left on her collarbone last time. "Your hickey's still fresh," she said. "I can't even wear a tank top."

"Not like you ever do," he said. He reached around from behind her, cupped her small breasts in his hands, and ground his crotch against her rear. He felt her nipples harden beneath his palms. "Sun might get on your precious skin then."

"I thought you liked me pale," she said with a laugh. Her breath was coming harder now, blowing out through her mouth and inhaling deeply. "Rather have skin cancer all over me?"

"I like you just fine," Billy said. He continued rubbing her breasts, slipping his hands underneath her blouse now and shoving her bra out of the way. "Right now I'd rather like you naked than with all these clothes on."

"That could maybe be arranged," she said. "But don't you think we ought to get into the bedroom?"

He pushed her up against the tile-topped kitchen cabinet. "This'll do just fine," he said. "I can't wait that long."

Ray was glad Kerry had picked him to stay behind. It was pathetic that five grown men couldn't catch one lone, unarmed woman in platform sandals. But his theory was that it was because they had five men that they were having such a hard time. This Dove was smarter, trickier, and more ruthless than past ones, she had proven that. She was no doubt paying attention. Five men walking raise dust, make noise. One man could move more silently, more discreetly. One man could get the drop on her, where five couldn't. Ray was convinced of that.

Ray had never served in the military, though he'd often dreamed of it. But he was small, and he had a heart murmur, and that had kept him from being allowed to serve his country. Anyway, he'd been born just a little too late for Vietnam and a little too early for the Gulf War, so even if he'd been allowed to enlist chances were he wouldn't have seen action.

He'd give his left nut to be on the ground in Afghanistan right now, though. Hiking through a canyon just like this, but wearing a uniform with an American flag on his shoulder. Serving with the Rangers, or Delta Force, maybe even the SEALs, though he didn't think there was much water in Afghanistan so they might be out of their element. He was sure Special Forces were already over there, tracking down Osama, identifying targets for the bombers that were surely on the way, working to win the hearts and minds of the Afghani populace even while plotting to destroy their leaders.

And if that didn't work, to level the whole damn country. It wasn't like it was good for anything. And somebody had to pay for September eleventh. They couldn't just take aim at the U.S. and expect to survive unscathed. If they weren't punished, what would stop the next nut with a grievance, and the one after that? These people were just plain evil, and evil had to be dealt with.

Just like someone had to punish the Dove for what she'd done to Cam. Kerry wanted her dead. Ray thought that was for the best. But he thought about the big hunting knife in its sheath on his belt, with its serrated top edge and razor-like blade, and he thought that before he actually killed her he just might want to have a little fun. No one would ever find her body out here—he'd leave it for the carrion eaters. Some hiker found her bones ten years from now, they'd never be able to tell if her flesh was a little cut up before she died.

Like wearing a uniform, carving up a human was something Ray had never done, but had dreamed about since childhood. Maybe he'd never get a chance to defend America, but he could at least do something about that other dream.

He started back up the canyon, rifle at the ready, walking silently. Each step had to be thought through, figured out before his foot touched the ground, so as not to kick up any pebbles or make crunching noises on sticks or sand. It made movement slow, but still, he thought, faster than five guys arguing over which way to go, or how old this or that footprint was. He'd speed up later—his guess was that as soon as she'd forked Cam she'd taken off running, and he'd be able to tell that when he got to the scene of the attack. Until then, though, he would assume that she was still waiting in ambush—only with Cam's gun this time.

Ray worked processing sugar, and if that wasn't boring then boring had never been invented. Once a year, he came out with Kerry and the guys and cut loose—really letting themselves be men for a change, taking what they wanted instead of begging for it like most men did their whole lives. It had taken amazing courage to do this, and the experience had bonded them, made them closer than brothers. No Dove had ever run them such a wild chase, that much was for sure.

Ray was glad that this one had. Made the whole thing that much more special. And he'd enjoy killing her, once he finally caught her. He had no doubt about that, none at all.

Yes indeed, he was glad that Kerry had picked him.

Ken sat in his office in the dark, eyes shut, face buried in his hands, trying to see.

He'd been interviewing people up on the Slab, to no apparent effect, when he realized that he was having trouble concentrating on their faces because other images kept trying to force themselves to the forefront of his mind. He couldn't quite bring those pictures into focus, though—trying to was like watching a TV screen hopelessly clogged with snow, or looking through a sandblasted camera lens.

Finally he gave up on his interrogations, which weren't going anywhere to begin with, and drove back to his office, hoping that solitude and silence would allow him to clarify the half-formed images in his head. To a degree, it seemed to be working. The distortion cleared, and for a moment the picture swam into view, floating up from the soup of his own mind. Ken didn't question the origins of these visions—it was a magic day and touching Hal Shipp's hand had somehow kicked the magic up into a higher gear than before, so he just accepted that it all stemmed from that.

The first fractured image had involved hands on a shovel's handle and a booted foot pushing its head deep into packed earth. Everything was dark, lit occasionally by a flickering circle of light. The hands were vague, almost formless and colorless, just hand-shaped blobs of light. Ken could tell they were hands only because of their position on the handle. He could almost feel the effort of digging, the cold metal of the shovel handle against his palms, the hard rim of the shovel's head pressing against the sole of his foot. As he watched the shovel churn up dirt and toss it to the side and return for more, he could tell that this was hard work for someone unaccustomed to physically demanding manual labor, but that the person he couldn't quite make out— a woman, he was pretty sure, it felt like she was a woman, though he couldn't see her—was spurred on by anger. Anger, and fear. And not for herself, but for someone else.

Ken shook his head and slammed his palm on his desktop. Why can't I see more? he asked himself. Or feel more? Not being able to tell who he was looking at was more frustrating than being up on the Slab, asking questions to which no one knew the answers. This time, the answers were there, in his head, and he couldn't get at them. He knew the problem was that he was seeing these things through her eyes, so he couldn't get a look at her face. She was focused on the effort of moving dirt, so that's what he saw—not who held the flashlight that wobbled off to one side, casting an uneven beam over the dig, not even, yet, what she was digging for.

Though he had a pretty good idea what that would be anyway. This had all started with a skull in a fire pit, and what better place to find a skull than by digging it up?

Maybe he just needed to give it more time. Some things couldn't be rushed, he guessed, and whoever the skull had originally belonged to was certainly in no hurry to get it back. Ken stood and went to the coffee maker to brew a fresh cup, hoping that to focus on mundane tasks might free his mind to make some progress on its own.

Lucy Alvarez had grown up around guns.

Her big brothers both owned guns, as did her father and grandfather. She'd never been a particular fan of them, but neither was she afraid of them. She had fired them, had gone out into the desert with her brothers plinking, shooting at cans and bottles and on one memorable occasion, a wide-screen TV they'd found abandoned in an alleyway. The TV had made wonderful popping sounds and small explosions when they'd hit it.

Even her husband had owned a couple of guns, though they, in fact, had been a factor in ending the marriage. It still made her heart catch a little to picture Dag. He'd been twenty-seven when they'd met, and she only eighteen, still easily impressed by a deep chest and broad shoulders and bulging arms. Besides a powerful build, Dagoberto Morales had been blessed with an angel's face. His features were movie-star perfect, right down to the dimples that carved his cheeks when he smiled, revealing even, white teeth. His eyes were dark and soulful and seemed, to Lucy, like the ones that had been under discussion when the phrase "window to the soul" had been coined. They clouded over like a stormy day when he was troubled, shone like the summer sun when he was happy, wept like the winter rain when he felt sorrow. He'd been funny and charming and seemed to have plenty of money to shower on a young lady, and it was no wonder she'd fallen in love with him. The only wonder would have been if she hadn't.

But after they'd married, Dag had changed. He lost his job, for one thing, when the Palm Desert restaurant he'd been managing had closed its doors. Lucy was working retail in a poster gallery at the mall there, so they weren't broke, but they were suddenly much less flush than they had been. As the money crunch continued, Dag's temper started to flare, revealing a side of him that she hadn't encountered before. His drinking, once seemingly part of his social life but lately more and more common at any time or opportunity, exacerbated the problem. The first time he'd struck her she had tried to excuse it, blaming stress, blaming herself. The second time she blamed the booze. The third time, he had reminded her of his guns, and she'd moved out.

She was born and raised a good Catholic and good Catholics didn't divorce, but Lucy decided that her safety and sanity were more important than decisions made long ago by men who would never understand what it was to be female and vulnerable, and she'd divorced him anyway. He had pleaded and wept and promised to change, scolded and threatened, called her every name in the book, but eventually he had agreed to the divorce and had signed the papers that freed her.

Lucy hadn't spoken with him since that day, though it took some doing. At night she went out with high school friends, or sometimes a couple of people from the insurance agency she worked at. Drinking, shooting pool, partying by the Salton on hot weekend days. She'd grown up in the tiny community of Mecca, and so far seemed to be stuck there, though she couldn't imagine that she would stay forever. But being in such a small town made it hard to avoid places where she might run into Dag again.

She made the effort, though. She didn't want to risk falling in love with the physical perfection of him all over again; couldn't risk being blinded to his dark side. Avoidance was her best bet.

Guns? No friends of hers, but no strangers either.

She heard the man coming when he was still halfway down the canyon. He moved slowly, and he thought that translated as quietly, but he was wrong. The desert was truly quiet, with only the occasional breeze and the distant cries of a raven disrupting the silence. From where the man was, down-canyon, every sound was captured by the stone walls and funneled up-canyon to where Lucy waited, safe within her indentation atop the canyon's wall. His breathing, slow and steady. The scrape of his foot on sand, of equipment, maybe his backpack, against the canyon walls. The occasional clink of his gun or creak of its strap. The shuffling when he rearranged his grip on it. He broadcast his location every step of the way.

Waiting was hard, especially when he moved so slowly, but she forced herself. She kept telling herself that he'd pick up speed, move past her. She needed to pee but she tried to force that out of her mind, promising herself that when he was dead she'd drop her pants and have the most satisfying pee of her life.

Finally, she could tell, he reached the spot where she had stabbed his friend. She remembered the spurt of blood when she'd driven the fork into his face—there was still a brown streak of it on her hand and up her arm—and knew that it must have splashed the canyon walls as well. And there would be remains of his glasses—she was pretty sure he'd lost the whole deal, frame and all, so that would be on the ground. The location would be easy to determine and even the method would be clear. He'd be able to look up and see the shelf upon which she'd waited. If he ventured up there, it wouldn't take much more climbing to bring him to a point where he could look down into the indentation she hid in now. She held the stolen rifle pointed in that direction, though, and if he showed himself, she would fire.

But she didn't hear him climb. She heard him pause and move around the site, his clothes rustling as he did. He even kicked at the glasses, it sounded like, sending them scuffing over the ground. But then he kept on, heading up the canyon at a slightly faster clip, as if he'd already decided that's where she had gone.

Lucy's heart started to pound. She'd almost hoped that he would climb, because that would force the issue. Now, though, she had to make the decision, and fast, before he was out of sight around a bend. She would have to choose to kill him—no longer in legitimate self-defense, but out of a longing for justice. (Or revenge.)

She realized she'd already made the decision, long ago. He was a rapist and a killer and there was nothing she could do to him that was worse than what he intended for her. She rolled out of her indentation in the stone and flattened herself against the upper rim of the canyon. Now she could see him. They'd sent the black man, the short, muscular one after her, the one who looked like a soldier in his buzz cut and rigid bearing. He carried a mean-looking weapon, a semiautomatic or automatic rifle. A military weapon, she thought.

Lucy sighted down the barrel of the rifle. She aimed at the mass of his back. A shot there would probably prove fatal, if not immediately, and the target was bigger than his head. All she really had to do was drop him, and she'd be able to finish him off, as long as he was wounded badly enough that he couldn't turn his gun on her. High in the upper back, that's where she needed to take him. If she missed a little she might get the neck or head or the small of his back or the ribs, and any of those would do. He wore a small day pack, slung low on his back, and it could be a problem, she thought, if she hit that, but there really was nothing to do but try to miss it.

He was no beer can or soda bottle, no household appliance, but a flesh and blood man. And he wasn't sitting still on a rock or a fence, but moving away from her, fairly quickly now. He wouldn't remain a target for long. She sighted the way she had been taught to do, getting a bead on him, and she blew out her breath and she squeezed the trigger.

In the canyon, the shot echoed like thunder.

She missed.

She saw the man throw himself to the ground, flattening himself, but the bullet had torn out a chunk of wall six feet from him. Lucy threw herself back into her hidey-hole before her target was able to look up and behind him—at least, she thought so, unless he'd caught a glimpse of her as he fell. She didn't think that was very likely, but it was possible, and since he would be hunting her now, she had to accept that if it was even remotely possible then it was probable.

Her heart had been pounding before but now it jackhammered inside her, making it hard to even catch her breath. She tried to still herself so she could hear him, but now he really was silent.

She could only assume the minutes were ticking by. Time seemed to both stop and stretch—she felt like it had already been an hour since the echo of her shot had died off, but she still hadn't heard the slightest sound from the man she'd fired at. She wore no watch, and the upper edge of the indentation blocked the sun from her view. She could judge time only by the shadows she could see, and they were long, making it late in the afternoon, but she didn't know how much they had changed since she had come out of hiding to shoot a man.

More time passed, and still, not the faintest sound. She began to wonder if in fact she had killed him after all—if maybe the bullet had passed through him and then hit the wall, or if he'd been killed by a ricochet. She could well be stuck in here, still needing to pee, forever if she waited for a dead man to make noise.

She waited what seemed like another long stretch and then decided she had to find out. There was every likelihood that he was simply waiting her out, watching for her to show herself so he could unload that wicked-looking automatic rifle at her. But she'd die anyway if she never came out of hiding.

It was her turn to move silently. She scooted from the impression in the rock, weapon in her hands held just inches above the stone so it wouldn't scrape. Keeping her head low, she inched out onto the rim—not as far as she'd gone before, just enough to raise her head to the level from which she'd be able to spot him if he was still flat on the canyon floor where she'd last seen him.

He wasn't there.

She raised a little more, just in case she'd misjudged where he'd fallen. Still no sign of him.

Which could only mean that he was out there somewhere, on the move, no doubt closing in on her.

She was lowering her head again when a brown-skinned hand came over the rim, quietly flattening itself on the rock, four feet from her face. A gun barrel, black and ominous, followed, sticking up into the air. She watched the barrel rise like a shark in the sea, knowing that there would be another hand coming along behind, finger on the trigger guard, ready to slip inside and fire. The barrel shifted, lowering, pointing almost straight at her, and she stifled a gasp of surprise. But it was just a natural shift as the man continued to hoist himself up. She saw the hand, knuckles paling with exertion against the rock as it bore most of its weight. Then the top of his head, the short, razor-cut dark hair, the skin of his forehead. Then his eyes, brown as those glass bottles she and her brother had shot so long ago. As the eyes cleared the rim of stone, they saw her and widened in surprise.

She pulled her trigger.

The gun boomed and the face exploded, a red haze filling the air where his head had been a moment before. A fine spray of blood spattered against the rock rim, and then a louder sound, his body thudding to the canyon floor below. As before, the gunshot's echo bounced among the canyon walls for a while before it finally faded away.

She waited on top of the canyon wall for several minutes, letting herself settle again, before she tried to climb down. Reaching the ground, she hiked around a bend, not wanting him to see her even in death, and took down her pants for her long-delayed pee. She'd probably get a urinary tract infection because of this bastard, she knew, but compared to what he'd had in mind for her, that was something she could live with.

When she was finished, she fastened her jeans again and went to investigate the body. He had landed on his back, facing the sky. Just below the spot where his nose met his brow, and a little to the left, was a neat round hole, red with black edges. Blood had pooled under his head, and she imagined that there was an exit wound back there considerably larger than the entry wound.

The rifle's strap had been wrapped around his wrist so the gun remained with him when he fell. He also had a hunting knife in a sheath on his belt. She almost couldn't bring herself to do it, but she knew she had to so she forced herself to dig through the pockets of his camouflage fatigue pants.

Inside his right rear pocket, she found a wallet. Ray Dixon, his name was. And he lived in Brawley.

Now she had a starting point.

chapter 15

In the desert, a distant rainfall can set off a flash flood miles away. Rain hits hard-packed earth that is unused to absorbing water and runs along the surface, seeking a low point, rather than soaking in. As it goes, it's joined by more rain. Finally, in a stream channel or road bed or wash, it turns into a raging flood until it finally finds ground willing to allow it to penetrate.

Hal Shipp felt like he was faced with a flash flood of memories, as if all the ones he hadn't been able to grasp for the last couple of years, since his Alzheimer's had really set in, were rushing through his brain at once. At the Slab, he'd been unable to unleash the flood—the noise from everyone's disturbed and violent daydreams had blocked it—but now that he'd wandered off into open desert, far from the world, the dam was breached.

Not surprisingly, given his vivid recall earlier of the events at St. Fromond-Eglise, the times that limned themselves most clearly in his mind were the magic days. He had lived a long time since 1944, and there had been plenty of those days. Few had seemed as significant, in the living of them, as that day in France, but taken as a whole, he knew, they had shaped his life, pointed him in a certain direction and kept him on track. Does anyone ever know which days are really the telling ones? he wondered. You figured your wedding day, the day you landed the job you kept for most of your adult life, maybe the day you retired from it, the days your kids were born. But maybe the wedding day was a foregone conclusion, part of the arc of a relationship but not the key to it. Maybe the really significant day was the day you found out she was cheating on you and went ballistic, or the day you realized you didn't care if she did, because either of those days could set the course for the rest of your time together. When you landed that job, you couldn't have known it would last longer than all the rest— couldn't the significant day be the one on which it suddenly occurred to you that you hadn't been looking for a new career and weren't going to bother?

Probably you never knew, even on the day you died, which days really counted and which were just marking time. But at least Hal could point to certain days, magic days, and know that they had made a definite impact on his life.

The first postwar magic day had been the day he'd met Virginia. That strange electric taste had been in his mouth that morning, and while it tasted familiar he didn't, at first, connect it to the day in France. He wondered, instead, if he was getting a cold or something—the sensation was not unlike having a mouth full of metal or blood, and he thought it signified something wrong with him. It was a Saturday, he knew, a day off for him, and he was scheduled to drive into the hills outside Albuquerque for a picnic with a young lady named JoAnn Perski. They had dated several times, and seemed already to be falling into a kind of semi-domestic arrangement, as if both were ready to be married and were willing to accept the other as spouse material.

But looking out the window of his boarding house room that morning, Hal, tasting the familiar yet strange flavor in his mouth, had noticed that the sky had clouded over dramatically during the night. As he watched, the heavens opened up and an Olympian rainfall drenched the city. By the time Hal got downstairs, people were already talking about building arks.

The rain continued through the morning. Picnic cancelled, Hal was still in the boarding house when a call came in for him. A half-mile of recently-completed highway had collapsed, and the whole road gang was needed to get out and help contain the damage. Hal met his crew at the site, took a look around, and retreated to a nearby diner to get out of the rain and plan a strategy.

Inside the diner, he met Virginia Winfield. An apple-cheeked young blonde, applying for a post-high school job, she had looked at the dripping wet road crew foreman and burst into peals of infectious laughter. Hal found himself drawn to her on the spot and fished a wet quarter out of a pocket to buy her a cup of coffee.

After they had talked for a while and made a dinner date for later, Hal had his conference, then went back outside to find that the rain had stopped as quickly as it had appeared, and the damage wasn't as bad as it had first seemed. He had never dated JoAnn Perski again, and never looked back.

Definitely a magic day, Hal thought. And one of the best ones.

Another one he remembered fondly was the day that Tim was born. Timothy Braddock Shipp, named for Hal and Virginia's fathers, respectively, had come into the world on a brilliant June day in 1953. June fourteenth, that had been. Hal, by now out of the road-building field and instead selling business machines across the Southwest, had needed to make an unexpected trip to Austin. Knowing that his wife was due any time with their first child, he hadn't wanted to go, but the client considered their situation an emergency, and if he wanted to support his wife and new baby in decent style, he couldn't afford to write off a customer who added several hundred thousand dollars a year to the company's bottom line. He and Virginia had settled just outside Albuquerque, so he made the trip by car, dealt with the situation, and then set off for home all on the same very long day.

He hadn't been able to get very far from Austin that night, but he'd stopped in a small motel by the highway to catch a few hours of sleep. When he woke up, just after four in the morning, the now-familiar metallic taste was in his mouth and the motel room was bathed in an odd, golden light. He didn't know what it meant, but he knew what was on his mind so he went to a pay phone outside the lobby and called home. No one answered.

Leaving the motel key and twenty dollars in the room, he got back into his Buick and stepped on the gas. He was still hundreds of miles from home, and the only reason he could imagine that Virginia wouldn't answer the phone was that she'd gone to the hospital to have the baby.

As he drove, he gradually realized something—his Buick's speedometer needle remained poised at the sixty-five mark, but he was passing every car on the road. Not just passing, but flying past, like an Indy 500 driver tearing past a bunch of grandmothers out for a Sunday drive in the country.

He must have been doing a hundred miles an hour. More. Maybe close to one-twenty, he thought, watching the other cars blur as he tore past them. If it was even possible for the old Buick to travel so quickly, it should have been shaking apart, as it tried to do when he pushed it up to seventy on a normal day. But it gave no sign of any strain. As far as the car was concerned, he might have been cruising at fifty. Not only did it not seem to feel the speed, but it didn't handle like a car going double the speed limit. He never even came close to losing control or running into anything. And no one seemed to take note of him, not even the Highway Patrol cars he rocketed past. It was as if he were invisible, hidden inside a pocket of motion.

Hal kept thinking he'd have to stop for gas, but the fuel indicator dropped only the tiniest bit during his journey, so he just pressed on. He reached the hospital in downtown Albuquerque an hour before his son did.

On the seventeenth of December, 1973, he had once again felt the presence of the magic. It was as strong in him as it had ever been, tingling in his mouth, making the fine hairs on the back of his neck stand on end as if he moved in a field of static electricity. All that day he'd waited—recognizing the symptoms by now, as easily as one might the onset of a cold or flu—for the magic to happen, for the next twist in a life that sometimes seemed directed by the whims of a force he could neither understand nor control.

But it didn't. He went to work, he had lunch with a colleague, he came home, dined with Virginia, listening to her talk about her own day. After dinner they had done the dishes together, as was their habit, and then watched TV for a while. *The Flip Wilson Show* had been on, Hal remembered, and Virginia, who couldn't stand Flip, had read a magazine while Hal laughed himself silly. Afterward, they'd watched *Ironside* together, switching to *The Streets of San Francisco* before finally turning in for the night. By morning, the magic had faded.

It wasn't until more than a week had passed before he finally figured out what had happened.

In a camp somewhere in the Vietnamese jungle, Tim had been in a hut with a few of his friends. Someone was drunk, or high on drugs the Army had never really specified—and fooled around with a live hand grenade. Which probably would have been okay, except that just then a Viet Cong mortar round had landed nearby, causing the drunk or stoned soldier to drop the grenade on the floor of the hut.

And then the magic kicked in. The other guys dove for the door. So did Tim, but, according to one of the G.I.s who was there and who later wrote to Hal and Virginia about it, he seemed to be moving in slow motion, as if he was underwater and couldn't get any momentum going. He'd moved just inches when the grenade went off, killing him instantly. That had happened at what would have been 8:30 p.m. on December the seventeenth.

Until that day, Hal had always believed the magic was somehow a blessing, a favorable if inexplicable curiosity. He couldn't quite bring himself to think that God was personally watching over him, but one of his angels? Maybe.

That day, though—the day he found out what had really taken place on his magic day—all that had changed. Hal came to believe that the magic was malicious, or if not that then at least capricious, with no concern for how Hal might be affected by its interference. He had thought once that he had been spared, back at St. Fromond-Eglise, for some specific reason. That he had something to contribute, something worthwhile.

Had he been spared so that he could later take part in the rape and murder of thirteen women? Where was the blessing in that? Looking back at it now, though, at the pattern of his life, at the turns that had sent him here, to the Slab, that conclusion seemed almost inescapable.

His last magic day had been seventeen years before. Tim's death, and Hal's subsequent loss of faith in the beneficial nature of the magic, had changed his life in significant ways, and not for the better. He had started drinking, heavily. His marriage had suffered, though Virginia, showing more patience than he would have if circumstances had been reversed, had worked hard to hold things together in spite of his bad behavior. He'd lost one job, then another, until he was, he thought, virtually unemployable—too old to be hired anywhere even if he had a clean record and hadn't burned bridge after bridge. Virginia's temporary job as an administrative assistant at a real estate office had turned into a permanent job and she paid what bills she could, and rent on a series of ever-cheaper apartments.

Finally, he had told Virginia he was going on an out of town job hunt and had taken the last fifty dollars out of his savings account and drove their old Ford Fairlane—praying all the way that it wouldn't die until he got there—to Las Vegas.

Where the magic came back, strong, almost the minute he crossed into the city. The car, on its last legs, made it to a used car lot where he sold it for three hundred dollars to a mustached man named Slim.

For a second, he felt unbridled optimism. He was in Vegas with a few hundred bucks in his pocket, and the magic flowed within him.

But then he remembered Tim, remembered that the magic wasn't always a good thing. When he got inside a casino, he was nervous. He bought a roll of quarters and hit a quarter slot machine. Lost it. Bought another, lost that too. A roll of nickels. Lost it.

As the money, the last of the money he and Virginia had to live on, to make rent, to buy groceries, trickled through his fingers, he began to have doubts. Bringing the money to Las Vegas without even telling Virginia had been patently stupid, but he hadn't thought it through, had only believed that he'd be able to go back to her with pockets full and then explain where it had come from.

Only now, it was looking like he'd go back to her more broke than before, and have to explain where it had gone.

He backed off the slots for a while and wandered the casino floor. The din was awful, the sounds of slots and voices and cards slapping felt and tumbling dice, all of it somehow magnified by the surroundings as if to keep people unsettled, off their guard. He hadn't spent much time in casinos, and now he understood why he'd never bothered.

He watched roulette, craps, blackjack. Looked over the rail at poker games. None of it appealed; all of it scared him. Finally, he changed another ten and sat down at a video poker machine, which he'd never seen before. He put four quarters in and pressed the DEAL button.

And came up with a royal flush, winning four thousand dollars.

Finally, he thought, the magic is back.

His next few hands were losers, but then he hit a straight flush. Another royal flush. Four kings.

Twenty minutes after he'd first sat down, he had won nineteen thousand dollars. And the magic was still powerful within him; he could taste it, feel it in his veins.

But video poker was too slow.

He wanted to make some real money, and he wanted it fast. He took his winnings and bought into a roulette game. Put five thousand dollars on nine, because it seemed like a good number.

The croupier spun the wheel. Eleven. Five grand gone. He chased it with another five, then one at a time. Every time the croupier spun the wheel he could feel the energy build up in him, knowing that the ball would stop on the number he had chosen. And every time, it skipped past his number and landed somewhere nearby.

When he finally stopped, after going to five dollar bets for a while, he had just under three hundred dollars left. He had no idea what time it was but his eyes burned and stubble had sprouted on his cheeks and he felt a gnawing hunger that had been growing throughout the night and now, as he walked away from the table, threatened to double him over. He stumbled from the casino and walked to a coffee shop he'd seen on the way in, wondering how he could face Virginia again. At least he had a little something to show—enough for a bus ticket to get back to Albuquerque.

It was still dark out, with the morning's last stars fading before the dawn, and the desert air was cold. He pulled his jacket tight around him and made for the glow of the coffee shop's windows.

Inside he saw the sign that said PLEASE BE SEATED, and he selected a booth. The restaurant was nearly empty. After a few minutes a waitress named Ella gave him coffee and took his order. She came back fifteen minutes after that with a plate of scrambled eggs and sourdough toast and bacon, and put it down in front of him. Then she put the check down and looked at him with a barely restrained, almost frantic grin. "I'll take that when you're ready," she said. "And you might want to pay it right now."

"Can it wait until after I eat?" he asked, the hunger pains even worse now.

"It could, I guess," Ella answered. "But...just pay it. I'll take it up for you." Ella was blonde and heavy and her eyes twinkled like starlight, and something about the way she wiggled in her white polyester uniform, almost as if she had to pee and had been holding it in for hours, or days, made him want to please her. So he fished out his billfold and removed a twenty and put it on top of the check without even turning the piece of paper over. Ella let out a squeal of delight, scraped them both from the table, and ran them to the register. "He's the one!" she said, and the rest of the coffee shop's staff joined her at the counter while she rang up his order and made change. When she returned to the table a procession followed her, including a man who was presumably the manager, in a short-sleeved blue shirt and a cheap patterned tie. He held a manila envelope in his hand and the smile plastered on his face was just as broad as Ella's. Harold began to wonder if he'd accidentally stumbled into some kind of mental asylum.

The manager pushed past Ella and stuck his hand out. Reflexively, Hal shook it.

"Sir, congratulations," he said.

"What'd I do?" Hal asked him.

"You're our one hundred thousandth customer since the new owners took over," the manager said. He handed Hal the envelope. "So you win the big prize!"

Hal felt the envelope the man had given him, turning it between his fingers, not really believing the whole situation. People didn't do this kind of thing in real life, did they?

But then again, it was a magic day—real life rules didn't apply.

The something hard contained within the envelope turned out to be the keys to a brand new RV, and inside the RV's kitchen cabinet was five thousand dollars in cash and a pink slip for the vehicle. The restaurant's entire staff, including fry cooks in stained whites with baseball caps and greasy shoes, as well as the handful of customers, trailed Hal out to the parking lot in back of the restaurant where the 1983 Winnebago Minnie Winnie sat bathed by floodlights, a spectacle in earth tones and fiberglass.

Finally convinced that it was really his—the RV and the cash—Hal Shipp went home. Back in Albuquerque, he and Virginia spent only two weeks selling off a few remaining possessions and settling accounts, before they loaded up the Winnebago and hit the road, ultimately landing on the Slab.

Magic days.

"It's a world war in the making," Mick insisted. He sat cross-legged on a blanket, hugging his own arms, head bowed, looking at her with his eyes rolled up in his head. If he'd had a guitar or a joint he'd have looked like guys at a hundred college parties she'd seen, serious and self-absorbed and utterly convinced of their own wisdom. On the other side of the netting the shadows grew long. Helicopters had been buzzing the range for hours, preventing Penny from doing any of the field research she'd wanted to work on.

"Here's how it goes," he continued. "We pound Afghanistan into rubble. But then, under some pretext, we go after Iraq as well. Bush's dad got no end of shit for not finishing off Saddam Hussein, and since his presidency is all about restoring his dad's reputation after getting his ass kicked by Clinton, Bush Junior is going to want to finish that battle too. Maybe bin Laden will escape and get into Iraq, or there'll be another terrorist attack of some kind traceable to Iraq, whatever. Something. And we'll attack there too.

"Which is the final straw, as far as the Islamic world is concerned, because they understand by now that what the war is really about is oil."

"Oil?" Penny echoed, enthralled in spite of herself. She'd had the same thought, but wanted to see where Mick would go with it.

"Of course," Mick said. "Bush is an oil guy, so was his dad, so is Cheney. Oil contributed millions to his campaign. Oil and defense industries, those are the places to buy stock during a Bush administration, I'm telling you. You can get rich enough to become a Republican."

"Get back to the oil," Penny prompted.

"Okay, yeah. It's about the oil. Central Asia is full of it, but there hasn't been a good way to get it out without taking it through Afghanistan, which hasn't exactly been friendly, or dealing with the Russians. So our plan is to go in and kick ass all over the region so we can put the pipelines wherever the hell we want. You watch, at the same time, the oil interests are going to go back to demanding we drill in ANWR and Yellowstone and wherever else they want to rape the Earth. How many planes have flown since September eleventh? How many people are canceling trips, staying home? Oil consumption's already dropping, but they'll claim we need it anyway. Just like they said before this all happened that we needed it because there was an energy crisis, that California was going to be blackout central all summer. Didn't happen, because Californians conserved. And everyone knew that Arctic oil wouldn't be on the market for six to ten years, and even then would only be a drop in the bucket. Because they lie, Penny. They just lie."

He was speaking faster now, bobbing his head as he went as if in time with some internal metronome. The more agitated he made himself the faster he bobbed and the faster he talked. Sometimes winding him up and turning him loose was fascinating to watch.

"So instead of turning to conservation, Bush and Cheney and those guys are going to try to ram through drilling in national parks and monuments and refuges, dressing it all in the flag and patriotism and the war effort. And at the same time they'll be killing Muslims for their oil, and in fact the result will be that we will increase, not decrease, our dependence on oil because they refuse to consider any kind of reduction in demand."

"Sounds about right," Penny agreed.

"But at some point the Muslim world isn't going to take it any more. Pakistan and India start throwing nukes at each other, the Israelis and the Palestinians start killing each other faster and faster, and every Islamic nation from Indonesia to Saudi Arabia declares war on us and whatever allies we're left with. World war. All to line the pockets of Cheney's pals at Halliburton. With a few bucks going to Enron and Lockheed and the Carlyle Group, for good measure."

He shook his head, blowing out a breath. "I can see it all lined up like dominoes, but there's not a fucking thing I can do to stop it, Penny. Do you know how frustrating that is?"

Yeah, she thought. I know.

The sensation of powerlessness she'd been feeling all year came rushing back to her. She had hoped to defeat it by joining this project, taking on this mission. But now she realized just how ridiculous the whole thing was. Even if they managed to shut down this bombing range for a month, what good would that do? It was just one range. One of how many? She didn't even know.

And of course, when they'd planned this, there had been no terrorist attacks, no "war on terrorism," to contend with. The statement they'd wanted to make might have fallen on ears that were ready to hear it. But that was two weeks ago. Today, no one wanted to hear talk of peace, of nonviolence. No one cared how the Earth could heal them. They wanted to see blood flow.

She started to lean forward to put a hand on Mick's knee. A calming hand, she hoped, not a leading one. "I know, Mick. I do." Before it even got there, she drew the hand back, as if from a hot oven, knowing that Mick would take it the way he wanted it instead of the way it was really meant. He was already reaching for it as she snatched it back.

Kerry Williams was tired and pissed off and his legs hurt and his back and neck and shoulders ached and he thought if he had to listen to Cam Hensley fucking complain one more time about "my eye oh for God's sake my eye!" he was going to fucking lose it and unload on the man. Rock had it the worst, he had an arm wrapped around Cam's ribs, Cam's arm over his shoulders and was bearing most of the wounded man's weight, which also meant that Cam's incessant whining was right in his ear.

Kerry had been on a sortie in Nicaragua when a soldier had taken a Sandinista bullet in the shoulder, twenty klicks from civilization. Every step had hurt, of course, and the guy had started whimpering about halfway back. His companions let it continue for fifteen minutes before warning him, and after that, the third time he'd forgotten and let another whine escape his lips, someone had stuck the barrel of an M-16 against the base of his skull and pulled the trigger.

The lesson? Nobody likes losing a friend, but everybody hates a whiner. Kerry never forgot it.

Of course, that stay down south had cemented a few other things in Kerry, like a taste for black-haired, brown-eyed women on their knees, willing to take everything a group of strange men could think of to give them and then beg for more, knowing that the alternative was a short burst and a shallow grave. That was a taste a man had to indulge in from time to time, which was why Kerry had started up the Dove Hunts years before with some acquaintances from the area. These men weren't his best friends—some things a man didn't share with those closest to him, after all, not if he wanted to keep them close. But they were men he felt would be amenable to his idea of a good time, and able to keep their mouths shut about it once they'd experienced the joy to be had. And so far, he'd been right about every single one of them.

But then, knowing how to pick men was crucial to building a team, and Kerry had always excelled at that. Whether the goal of the team was to go out and kill commies, as in Nicaragua, or to get laid, the theory was the same. Put together the men who can do the job without thinking about it too much. It was when you got all intellectual that things turned messy.

These men all looked up to Kerry, and came to him for his opinion about any number of topics. He was definitely the expert when it came to military matters, of course. A few days ago, on the first day of the Hunt, he had been in a men's room behind a tavern in Indio, he and Ray Dixon, unloading some excess beer. Ray had glanced up from the urinal, and said, "You know what, Kerry?"

"What?"

"I don't do drugs harder than beer, but I'll be damned if I'll take self-improvement tips from something that spends all day getting pissed on."

Kerry looked down at the rubber splash guard inside the urinal he used, which had DON'T DO DRUGS imprinted on it alongside the manufacturer's logo. He laughed, and Ray joined him, and they were still laughing as they washed their hands and dried them on rough paper towels. When they had parked themselves at their table again, Ray had put his Coors to his lips and taken a long tug and then looked seriously at Kerry.

"Hey, Kerry, you think we're gonna really go to war over there?" he asked.

"What, Afghanistan?" Kerry asked. "We have to, Ray. What, seven thousand dead? We can't just turn our backs on that."

"Can we win?"

Kerry turned his bottle around in his hands, listening to the sound it made rolling against the wet wood of the tabletop. "There is no finer military force—has been no finer military force in the history of the world—than the U.S. armed forces. We can win any conflict we put our hearts and minds to. Whether we have the balls—as a nation, I'm talking—to stick it out for long enough to win, I can't say. But if we do, then we can. That make sense?"

"That seems to go for a lotta stuff," Ray said. "If you got the balls and the desire, you can do it."

Kerry put his bottle down on the ring of condensation and rubbed a hand across his scalp, pulling his hair back from his forehead. "That's the only way to live, Ray. The only way life is worth living."

Ray's phrase had been Kerry's motto for years, though he'd never encapsulated it into words like that. The same attitude was what he looked for in men to join him on the Dove Hunt. He had found an inordinate number of them on or near the Slab, as it turned out. He had a theory about that, and it was this: men who lived on the Slab were men who cared less about material belongings than about freedom, that precious concept that no government could really give to anyone, but which every free man had to carve out for himself. Kerry was all for laws and regulations—they helped provide structure for those people who were willing to allow themselves to be so constrained. But for him, and those like him, they were ultimately meaningless, as much vapor as the latest pop song or TV sitcom that dulled the drones into submission.

He had every faith that Ray Dixon would take care of the bitch who had done this to Cam. The men wouldn't get their fun—she had seen to that, ruining the first Dove Hunt in fourteen years that hadn't been one hundred percent successful. But neither would she get away without paying for it. Already, he'd heard an exchange of fire. The girl was resourceful and tough, but Ray was smarter and tougher and knew what he was doing when it came to firearms. Kerry half-expected him to catch up before they even made it back to the cabin and the car. When they'd heard the faraway thunder, Vic had wanted to turn around and go back, but Kerry ordered him to stay with the rest of them. They needed to get Cam back to civilization or they'd have a dead man on their hands, and if it came to it they'd have to carry him.

They had covered about five miles, he guessed, when they found Terrance.

The sun was dipping toward the hills, and when it finally went behind them the nearly unbearable heat of the day would break. Cam had stopped his moaning, or at least lowered the volume. Vic and Rock were both supporting him now, and he shuffled along, barely moving his legs. He looked dead already, his skin pasty, his lips dried and cracked, his eye torn and seeping.

They came around a rocky bend and Terrance was there, sitting next to the trail, his back bent so his face, which was buried in both hands, rested on his enormous gut. At the sound of the walking men, he looked up. Dirt on his face was caked but streaked by sweat at his forehead and what looked like tears on his cheeks. His eyes were puffy, his nose red.

"Have you been crying?" Kerry asked him. "Are you fucking crying?"

Terrance wiped at his nose with one hand and looked away, as if embarrassed. Which he should be, Kerry thought. Fucking pussy. "What are you doing here?" he asked. "I thought you were supposed to stay at the cabin."

"I—I was," Terrance said, sniffling like a first grader. "I...Kerry, man, someone dug up one of the girls!"

At first Kerry didn't understand what he was saying. The girls? But then it sank in. "What do you mean? How do you know?"

Terrance spoke frantically, like if he didn't get it all out in one breath he never would. "I was...I was walking around, keeping an eye out for the girl, you know. Like you told me to. And I went down into the wash where we buried them, and one of the graves was all dug up. Most of her was still in there but her head, her skull or whatever, was missing."

"So you decided to walk all the way out here and tell us?" Kerry demanded. "What part of that involved sitting on a rock crying like a teenager whose boyfriend just dumped her?"

Terrance looked at the other guys for the first time, and when his gaze fell on Cam his mouth dropped open. "The fuck happened to him?"

"Never mind him," Kerry said. "I'm talking to you."

"I...I brought the Navigator," Terrance said. He swallowed, looked at the ground, at the sky—everywhere but at Kerry. "But...but I think I fucked it up."

Kerry felt rage boiling up inside him, nearly uncontrollable now. He took a step closer to Terrance. The fat man was taller than him, and outweighed him by almost a hundred pounds, but right now Kerry was ready to pick him up and smash him against the rocks.

"Fucked it up how?" he asked slowly, teeth clenched.

"I high-centered it on some rocks and when I came off, one of the wheels ran into the ground at a weird angle," Terrance explained, almost sobbing now. "I...I should have backed off it, I guess, but I didn't want to...to get hung up again, and now the wheel is all bent weird. It's...it's a mile or so back there. I just started walking then, until I couldn't walk any more."

"Ah, shit," Rock said. He spat into the dirt. "Now what do we do with him?" He still had Cam's weight pressing down on him. "We got to walk him the rest of the way to civilization?"

Kerry rubbed his hands together in frustration. He wanted to hit somebody but he didn't know for sure who, or what good it would do him. Terrance had screwed the pooch, as they said, screwed it good. That dog wouldn't be able to walk right for weeks, now that good old Terrance was done with her.

Vic sat down on a ledge of rock, shaking his head slowly. "God damn it, Terrance," he said. "God damn it to hell."

"Hey, I didn't fucking do it on purpose, you know!" Terrance shouted.

"Accidents happen, right?" Kerry asked. "Things go bad. Nothing you can do about it, right? Just bad luck, right?" Terrance didn't rise to the bait, just stood there, shoulders slumped, gut hanging out. The sight of him made Kerry sick.

And so did the situation they faced. They'd already been on their feet most of the day. To get to pavement, they'd have to hike another ten miles—on dirt roads, not cross-country, so it wouldn't be as bad as the rest of the day had been, but it was still a long haul, especially with an injured man. Even in good shape, they'd have to rest for a while once they made it back to the cabin, and then move out through the dark to get to anyplace where they could reasonably expect to catch a ride.

They had always come out in just one car, in order to reduce the chance of being noticed by anyone and to keep the number of tire tracks headed to the cabin to a minimum. But they'd always used a vehicle in good condition, well-maintained, with four-wheel drive. So far, none of them had been stupid enough to wreck it.

Of course, it had to happen now. In concert with Cam's eye being jabbed and someone—and what was up with that, Kerry wondered—digging up the skull of one of the earlier Doves. When the sun had come up this morning it had looked like any other sun, the sky was blue, the Earth turning in its usual direction. So how had everything—*everything*—turned to shit?

As Kerry examined the situation, turning it over in his mind like a jeweler holding a diamond under his lens, he thought he saw an angle that might salvage something out of this colossal clusterfuck. He caught Rock's eye and crooked his finger. "Rock, come here."

"But...Cam..." Rock said.

"He'll be okay for a minute. Won't you, Cam?"

Cam opened his mouth to answer, but only a single, incomprehensible croak came out. That was good enough for Rock, though. He disentangled himself from Cam, who swayed unsteadily, and he came to Kerry's side. "Yeah?" he asked.

Kerry just looked away from him and drew his .50-caliber Desert Eagle from its holster. The thing was a cannon; the first time he'd held it, he thought he was holding Death himself, encased in steel.

"What the fuck?" Rock asked.

"Just stand aside," Kerry said.

He heard Vic's sharp intake of breath, and a gasp from Terrance. Cam probably couldn't even see the thing, Kerry figured, he was so far gone.

"K-kerry, man," Terrance protested, still blubbering. "You…you can't…"

"I'm not going to shoot anyone," Kerry said, trying hard to sound reassuring. Then he spun the .50 around in his hand, and held it out to Terrance, who took it reflexively. When Terrance's hand was on the grip, Kerry let go. "You are."

"What?" Terrance asked, eyes widening in horror. "No way."

"Yes," Kerry told him flatly. "You've got to do it, Terrance. You've got to put Cam out of his misery. One shot, right in the eye." He walked over to Cam, touched him on the cheek, right below the mass of jelly that had been his eye. "Right here. That's all it takes."

"But, Kerry…"

"But nothing, Terrance. There's no choice. He'll never make it to a doctor, not now that you've fucked up and ruined the car. Cam's car, I should point out. Thing set him back, what, thirty-five grand? More? How happy do you think he'd be if he was capable of understanding what's going on? Look at him, Terrance, he's already dead. Death on toast, that's Cam. You're doing him a favor. Since you fucked up, this is the only way." He lowered his voice for this last part, talking to Terrance as if he were trying to seduce him. "And, by the way, if you don't do it, then we'll just have to shoot you. And then Cam. Your call, really."

Terrance was shaking like a leaf in a windstorm. "But I…I…"

"Do it, Terrance."

"Just fucking pull the trigger," Rock chimed in.

Kerry knew this was the only way things could go, now. No way would Cam make it to civilization, or survive long enough for help to get back if they had to hike out. This way, Terrance would be the one with powder burns on his skin from the gun that had killed Cam. If there was an investigation, that would come in handy, since Terrance would have to take the rap as punishment for abandoning his post and breaking the car. And even if there was no formal investigation, by doing it at Kerry's urging, Terrance would deliver his own life into Kerry's hands even more surely than killing the Doves did, because Cam was one of their own, not a lesser human. Kerry would own Terrance. He didn't know what he'd do with such a fat pathetic loser, but life had a way of presenting opportunities, if you were strong enough to take them.

He kept his gaze steady on Terrance, willing the big man to show some spine for once and do what had to be done. Tears ran down Terrance's already-streaked face, rolling off his round cheeks and thwipping into the dirt. He kept quiet for a change, his open-mouthed breathing catching, but his sobs soundless. Some small relief, Kerry thought. Hands quivering, eyes flooding, Terrance raised the gun.

Cam seemed to snap into consciousness and realize what was going on, because his mouth started to work again, and he said "No, no, no, no" in a weak voice that sounded as dry as the desert that surrounded them. But Terrance was in motion. His mouth closed as if drawn shut by a string, his eyes narrowed. He had made his decision, Kerry thought, and that decision called for him to shut down some part of himself, some aspect of his humanity. Even his eyes dried up as he aimed the weapon, his hands steady now, at Cam's head.

Cam tried to raise his hands to ward off the shot but the movement knocked him off balance and he swayed at the same moment that Terrance fired. The shot didn't hit him in the eye—Kerry was impressed that Terrance's aim had been so true, after all—but in the forehead, above the left eye, skating under the skin just below that bizarre tuft of misplaced black hair, and penetrating the skull and then blasting out the top of Cam's head even as the man continued his fall, spraying the rocks behind him with a sheen of red like an airbrush had passed over them.

Whatever, Kerry thought. Done's done.

They were all silent, and all looking at him. He straightened his spine, met their gazes, one by one. "The way it had to be," he said. "Now let's get the fuck out of here."

"Why do you lead him on?" Billy Cobb asked. He used Mindy's belly as a pillow, and his right hand traced random patterns on her thigh. They had moved, at some point, to the living room of her little cottage, and she sat with her head against the foot of the couch, partially upright, her ass on a throw rug she'd bought at the Big K in El Centro.

"Who?" she asked.

"Ken. Who else? You got some other guys I don't know about?"

"I don't lead Ken on."

"What do you call it, then? Why do we have to hide from him, if you're not trying to keep him on a string? You know he likes you, right? Think he buys his lunch from you three or four times a week cause you got good food? That's his way of asking you to marry him!"

Mindy slapped his naked stomach. "I'm sure he doesn't want that!" she said, laughing.

"How do you know?" Billy asked. "You asked him?"

"He hasn't asked me."

"It's a modern world. Women can ask too, you know."

She shifted a little, putting a hand on his chest to hold him in place as she did. The rug was beginning to tickle her butt, but she liked his weight on her and didn't want him to get up, because if he got up he'd leave, and she'd be left alone in her tiny house with her TV and her cassettes and probably a frozen dinner from the Shop-R Mart.

Billy wasn't the kind of man she'd ever want to settle down with, but that didn't keep him from being the kind she wouldn't mind making breakfast for from time to time, and God knew there weren't a lot of adequate choices in the Valley. Not that there was anything wrong with Ken. He was almost old enough to be her father, if he'd procreated young, she guessed. Handsome enough, in that kind of rugged, manly way, and hell, there was nothing wrong with that.

But if he was interested in her—and he was interested in her, a woman could almost always tell these things and she was certain of it—he had never taken even the first step of asking her to a movie, or lunch, or even coffee. Yes, this was the modern world but that didn't mean that some things shouldn't remain the same, and this was one of them. The man, Mindy thought, should be the one to make the first move. A person had to have some rules for life, and that was one of hers.

Outside, the sky grew darker. Billy hadn't gone anywhere, but he hadn't fallen asleep on her either. His hand continued to draw designs on her legs, and she thought maybe she saw signs of life returning to his penis. Maybe she could keep him here for a while longer, after all. Talking about Ken seemed to get a rise out of him, so she'd continue in that vein, see how far she could push it. She leaned forward, let her breast press against his cheek, and teased the hair around his navel. Yes, definitely some movement down there.

chapter 17

Jorge, Raul, and Diego stopped off in a bar before heading home. The sun was slipping behind the western hills. It would be dark soon, and they'd been crammed into Diego's truck all day long and nothing had come of it. Diego pulled the truck into the parking lot of The Rig ("OUR WELL NEVER RUNS DRY") and stopped it between a cream colored Toyota Tercel hatchback and a Datsun B-210 that had once been dark blue but now was kind of a glazed-white from sun and oxidation. A field worker in a mud-caked T-shirt and a baseball cap too big for his skinny head leaned against a low half-wall edging the parking lot, smoking a cigarette and bopping to a tune only he could hear.

The bar was dark inside, and cooler than out, with ceiling fans that turned lazily overhead, fluttering the red white and blue bunting that had been strewn almost haphazardly around the room's interior. Besides the bartender, a stocky Hispanic in a white wife-beater T that showed off the multiple tattoos on his arms and shoulders, the joint was nearly empty, with one barstool occupied by a sad-looking Anglo drunk bent over a glass of tequila, and a blonde woman sitting alone at a table, spinning her empty bottle between her palms. She looked up expectantly when the men entered, as if hoping to see whoever would be buying her next drink come in. She tossed them a toothy smile, which Jorge returned. Diego just scowled at her and beelined for the bar. His mood had turned increasingly foul during the afternoon and the last thing he wanted was some barroom skank gluing herself to them.

"Cerveza," he ordered.

The bartender met his eyes briefly and then turned away, setting down the glass he'd been toweling off and reaching for a clean beer mug. At the same time, the man at the bar clicked his tequila glass on the counter, hard. "Hit me again, Pablo," he said.

The bartender glanced at Diego again and showed some gold teeth in what was probably, Diego figured, supposed to be a friendly grin. "My name ain't even Pablo," he said. "S'Isidro."

"I give a fuck?" Diego said. "Get me a beer." He flicked his thumbs toward Raul and Jorge. "Three beers."

The drunk at the end of the bar slammed his glass down, louder than before. "I said hit me," he said.

"I'll hit you, *madrone*," Diego offered.

The drunk spun slowly on his stool and eyed Diego, letting his rheumy gaze slide briefly over Jorge and Raul as well. He looked like he'd been sitting there long enough to have become part of the barstool itself. But except for his typical barroom pallor, he seemed healthy enough, with muscles that rippled beneath his tight T-shirt and strong, bandy legs straining the pants of his jeans. Steel-toed work boots were hooked over the rail of the stool's footrest.

"You say something to me?" he asked. "Pablo, I'm a regular customer and I asked for another drink. You're not going to serve these wetbacks before you serve me, are you? They still smell like the Rio Grande. Or is that the Mexicali sewer system?"

"Look, man," Jorge said, beginning to push forward. "We didn't come in here to—"

Diego cut him off, putting a hand out in front of his brother's chest. "We didn't come in to start nothing but that don't mean we got to take this kind of shit," he said. He locked eyes with the drunk for a long moment, sizing him up. The three of them, he decided, could take the guy, easy. Strong or not, he was hardly able to stand up straight. But a better idea occurred to Diego. Without another word, he turned and pushed between his brother and father, heading for the blue leatherette strips that shielded the doorway.

Jorge and Raul were out the door by the time he reached the truck. "What are you doing?" Raul demanded.

"Finishing what that *puta* started," Diego said simply. He unlocked the truck and wrapped his fist around the barrel of his Winchester Model 94 Trails End rifle. Raul was on him as he turned around, pulling it from the truck's footwell.

"I asked you a question," he said.

"Get out of the way, Papa," Diego said. "I didn't start this, but I'll end it."

"You can't just shoot the dude!" Jorge put in.

"Watch me."

Raul had impressed upon the whole family that if they were going to live in America they had to speak English, and they'd all worked hard at doing so between themselves. But when he was really emotional, it became harder. Diego started to think in Spanish, and then the languages got mixed up in his head and he started to think in pictures because it was easier than words, and that was happening now, but the pictures were all of that Anglo fuck at the bar choking on his own blood with a hole in his lungs. Raul and Jorge both had their hands on him now, but he knocked them away, swinging the Winchester's butt to keep his path clear. He couldn't even see his brother or father now, his vision was a red blur, a tunnel leading back through the barroom door and ending with the drunken fool dead on its floor. He knew they were speaking to him, in Spanish now as well as English, but he couldn't hear their words, any more than if he'd been underwater and being called to from dry land. The roaring in his ears drowned out everything else.

The drunk looked up in surprise when he came back in, and fear when he realized Diego held a gun. Diego's mind was hazy but alert enough to know he hadn't fired the gun today, which meant it still held eleven rounds. The bartender and the drunk both screamed, their mouths turning into ovals, and the screams joined the general cymbal crash that was his only experience of sound at that moment, a crash punctuated with the boom of the rifle as he pulled the trigger and pumped the lever and pulled and pumped and pulled again. The drunk flew backwards off his stool then, as if he'd been yanked back by a wire, and roses of blood bloomed on his T-shirt, and fountains of it sprayed out behind him, then into the air as he fell from the stool and spun and dropped toward the floor.

Diego's senses began to return to him once the drunk was down. He could hear screaming now, and he thought he heard another sharp report, and another, and he looked and saw the bartender stagger back against his back shelf, breaking glasses and bottles as he went, and then slide down behind the bar. But he hadn't shot the bartender, he was sure. Then still another gun boomed and he turned again and the woman at the table, hiding under it now as if its one skinny center pole provided any cover at all, was jerking like she was having some kind of a spasm, and blood gushed from her, pooling on the ground. She slipped in her own blood and fell still. Diego took all this in before he bothered to look back to see Jorge and Raul standing behind him, each with his own rifle in his hands. Raul looked grim but there was a smile on Jorge's face.

"Couldn't let there be any witnesses, you did what we thought you were going to do," he said.

"Get out of here," Raul urged. "*Vamonos.*"

Diego clapped his brother on the shoulder and led the way back into the dusk. The migrant picker they'd seen in the parking lot on their way in was on the move now, starting to run from the lot but looking back over his shoulder with a fearful expression.

Witnesses, Diego thought. He raised the Winchester, sighted carefully, and squeezed the trigger once. He was much more calm, taking this shot, than he had been previously. The red haze had lifted and he knew exactly what he was doing. The slug hit the worker between the shoulder blades and propelled him forward, carried along by his own momentum, and he must have covered ten feet before he hit the ground, skidding along the pavement when he did.

Jorge high-fived him and they climbed back into the truck. There would be beer someplace else, he knew.

He felt better than he had all day.

The trilling phone roused Ken out of the half-doze he'd slipped into. He had kept his gaze focused on a bare patch of wall and worked on clearing his mind. He no longer focused so intently on trying to figure out where the mystery skull had come from, until his vision blurred and he drifted away. But he grabbed for the phone now, instantly alert. "Sheriff's Office."

There was a pause during which all he could hear was cell phone static, and then a small voice spoke. "Lieutenant Butler," the voice said. It sounded female and familiar, but he couldn't place it right off. "This is Virginia Shipp." She didn't sound well.

"Hello, Virginia," he said. "What is it?"

"Harold, Lieutenant Butler. He's wandered off somewhere. He was doing so well today, since we saw you, and he wanted to take a walk by himself and I thought it was all right to let him. But now it's been hours and I can't find him anywhere."

Great, Ken thought. An old, forgetful man out in the desert, with dark coming on. "I'll come up and have a look around, Virginia. Don't worry about him. There's not too much trouble he can get into out there, and with sunset coming up, well, he might get a little chilly but it's better than if he was out at midday."

"I suppose that's true," she admitted, not sounding completely convinced.

"Sure it is," Ken said. "I'll be up there in just a few minutes, okay?"

He hung up the phone and glanced out the window. Where the hell was Billy, anyway? That kid had taken to disappearing lately. He tried to raise the Deputy by radio and by pager, but neither one got a response. Which meant he'd have to take Billy's Crown Vic up to the Slab, when, if old Hal Shipp really had wandered into the desert, the Bronco would do him a lot more good.

And if he couldn't get a line on Hal pretty quick, then he'd have to call in help, raise some volunteers to go hunting for him. Being lost in the desert at night wasn't really that much better than on a hot summer day. Temperatures would drop fast, and Hal would still have a hard time finding water, which he most likely hadn't thought to carry with him.

Any way he looked at it, he didn't like it. And he didn't like that Billy Cobb was missing, either.

He was heading for the door when the phone rang again. He debated whether to answer it or let it shunt automatically to El Centro, but decided it might be Virginia Shipp calling to tell him that Hal had shown up, so he grabbed it.

"Sheriff's office."

"Hi, Ken." This voice, he knew instantly. Clara Bishop was a dispatcher in the El Centro office.

"What's up, Clara? I'm just on my way out the door. Got an old man, an Alzheimer's case, wandered off the Slab."

"I won't keep you then," she said. "Just wanted to let you know there's been a shooting incident, just outside Coachella. Four dead in and around a bar just off the one-eleven, called The Rig."

"I know the place," Ken said. "Real dive. Any suspects?"

"No suspects, no witnesses."

"Those Riverside boys are having a bad week, aren't they?" Ken said, thinking of the abduction in Mecca.

"Sounds like ours isn't much better," Clara reminded him. "You want any help with your stray? Need me to round up a Search and Rescue team?"

"I'll take a look around first and let you know," Ken said. He wanted to find Hal Shipp himself, if there was a way to do that. And he had a feeling there was. "I think I know where he'd go, though, so I'll let you know."

"Okay, Ken. That'll work. In the meantime, keep an eye out for anyone who looks like he just killed four people up road from you."

"Got it, Clara. Thanks." He hung up the phone and went out to the Crown Vic, wondering just what steaming pile of trouble he'd run into next.

"No, not tomorrow," Carter said into his cell phone. "Maybe in a couple more days. There's still a long way to go out here, babe. I know. I know. Listen, I can barely hear you in here. I'll talk to you soon, okay? Bye, honey."

He ended the call, folded the phone and slipped it back into his pocket. He and Nick Postak were in a nice steak house in Palm Springs, with heavy leather-backed chairs and substantial carving knives and white linen tablecloths. Candles glowed on the tabletops. Sinatra played in the background.

He glanced at Nick, who was slicing into his prime rib. "She doesn't understand business," Carter said. "My wife. She thinks I should just be able to wave my magic wand and make everything okay, so I can come home and make babies. Well, I'll tell you something. It isn't that simple, and I'm not ready for babies. Not that there's anything wrong with practicing."

"I hear you," Nick said, stuffing a big chunk of beef into his mouth.

"I guess it's a guy thing," Carter continued. "Although, come to think of it, my dad was just as bad as my mom when it came to business."

John Haynes, Carter's father, had led his small family from one western boomtown to another in search of the elusive goal of financial self-sufficiency. He had mined for uranium, coal, methane, copper—whatever was in demand at the moment. John Haynes kept his ears to the wind, and when he heard a whisper of a strike, even if the last one wasn't played out, he packed the car and hit the road, chasing the dream to the next place, and the next, and the one after that. His wife, Helen, tagged along without complaint, even though the thankless job of turning one shoddy trailer or shabby apartment into a home was left entirely to her. For Carter, who moved from school to school almost as soon as he's made a single friend in any one, the constant uprooting was hard to take. But his voice carried no weight in family discussions, which were called only so John Haynes could announce to his dependents which small mountain town they'd be moving to next. These pronouncements were usually accompanied by exaggerated accounts of the wonders these towns had to offer: friendly people, free public swimming pools, great schools, ski runs, movie palaces. What the boomtowns usually contained, though, was somewhat less grand than advertised. There were always a few bars and usually a church, a company-owned store, sometimes a bowling alley, a school, and row after row of hastily-erected housing for the families of those who would extract some mineral from the earth until it had no more to give. One town they lived in had five thousand residents at its peak and forty-seven two years later. But by then, of course, John was already on to the next big strike.

What struck Carter Haynes early, though his father never seemed to catch on, was that only the owners got rich off these operations. The people who worked the mineral claims in exchange for a salary never got ahead; they spent their lives scraping and struggling, while the people who owned the companies—usually living in far-off big cities, Carter noted—raked in the dough. Determined not to make his father's mistake, as soon as he was old enough to leave home he went to Los Angeles and then to San Diego, still a bit of a boom town then but not an extractive town. San Diego was a place where growth could still happen and fortunes could be made. Carter put himself through school, emerging with an MBA, and took a well-paying job with a brokerage firm. But instead of depending on the salary he made, he put all his money into buying a piece of property, a lovely but worn-down old Victorian house a few miles from downtown. Into this house, Carter put his own efforts, the sweat of his brow and the blood from his veins, and within a year had restored it to its original glory. He sold it for more than three times what he'd paid just a year before, quit his job at the brokerage, bought two houses and hired a crew.

You only get rich by owning things, he had decided. Not by working for the guy who owns things. That had been his way of doing business ever since, and it had worked for him.

He speared a piece of a rare, bloody porterhouse with his heavy silver fork. Postak had been talking, and he'd been ignoring the guy.

"I understand why you're trying to get those losers off the Slab," he was saying. "But how are you gonna get rich people to buy houses there?"

Carter savored the taste of the steak for a moment, swallowed, and chased it with a splash of red wine. "They'll buy," he said. "Because even though the houses will be expensive, they'll be the nicest, least expensive homes in America's newest luxury enclave. Salton Estates will be transformed, and the homes up on the Slab will have the primo views, looking out over the tops of the lakefront homes, over the lake and the hills on the other side, and back onto the Chocolate Mountains behind them."

"You're going to put houses on the lake too?" Nick asked. "But the lake stinks. It's nasty."

"It is now," Carter said. "But it won't always be."

"What's going to happen to it?"

Carter cut another piece of steak, enjoying the easy way it parted before the sharp blade. "The Salton Sea has a few problems, but they all stem from one main one," he said. "Water flows in but it doesn't flow out. The only way the water gets out is by evaporation. And the water that's flowing in is salty, it picks up chemicals from fertilizers used in the valley around it, and it has an abundance of life forms, most of which die in it, so it's overly abundant with nutrients. And it's full of shit because of the inflow from the New River, which brings untreated water in from Mexico and is the filthiest, most polluted water in the country. What we're going to do is build some evaporation flats and, in a couple of spots, spray water out of the sea onto them. This'll evaporate the water faster and allow us to trap the salts. We're going to take steps to counteract the nutrients, including removing the dead fish that pile up and contribute to the problem. We can use some of the water to feed lawns, golf courses, fountains, and pools. We treat the water from the New and Alamo Rivers before it reaches the Sea—I can get the government to do that for me. Eventually, I hope to pump water out of the Salton and back down to the Gulf of Mexico, where it'll be someone else's problem. Once that's underway, then the water will clean up nicely. The Salton will be America's newest aquatic playground, with boating, fishing, skiing, swimming. Imagine if Palm Springs had a huge, natural body of water."

"That'd be pretty cool," Nick agreed.

"It'd be a gold mine," Carter said.

"But it sounds pretty expensive."

"Oh, it is," Carter admitted. "And a substantial part of the expense will be mine. Well, mine and my partners'. But there's an administration in Washington, finally, that understands who its friends are. And I've made a healthy number of campaign contributions into certain coffers. The Interior Department, I have every reason to believe, will look kindly on my attempts to single-handedly reinvigorate an unhealthy ecosystem. It's even possible that environmental groups will kick in to help the process. A partnership between private enterprise, environmental activists, and federal government. Everybody wins."

"Especially you."

"Of course." Carter laughed. "Of course me."

"So what's on for tomorrow?" Nick asked. "More visits to the Slab residents?"

"Tomorrow," Carter replied, "I have something a little different in mind. We're going to need to round up some men. Good men, who we can count on, and who aren't afraid to get their hands dirty. Do you think you can do that?"

"Sure," Nick said. "I can do that."

chapter 18

"Captain Yato wants to see you, sir." Marcus Jenkins, Wardlaw's aide-de-camp, was as Marine as they came. Ramrod straight, hair clipped to the shortest nubs, tall and strong and true. Wardlaw liked having him sitting in the outer office, just because he was such a good example of an American fighting man. And being African-American, he created the appearance of diversity, as well. Wardlaw had a real secretary, but he liked to dismiss her early and let Jenkins sit in her chair now and again, just to remind him who was in charge. "As soon as possible, he said. He said he had someone he wanted you to meet."

Wardlaw had told Yato not to come back until he had prisoners. He dearly hoped that Yato hadn't taken that as some kind of rhetorical request rather than an outright command. He must have some kind of results to report, Wardlaw thought, if he had left a message that he wanted to see me right away. If he had failed, he'd be hiding out.

"Call him. Get him in here. I'll be in my office," Wardlaw said. He went inside and closed the door. He was sitting behind his desk, staring out the window at his base, a shining beacon against the night sky, a few minutes later when his phone buzzed. "Yeah," he said.

"Captain Yato to see you," Marcus's voice said.

"Send him in."

The office door opened and Yato walked in. Behind him, flanked by two Marine guards, was a scrawny hippie type with dirty hair and a ragged beard, wearing a Green Party T-shirt and camo fatigue pants. He had wire-rimmed glasses and he looked scared to death.

"Sir," Yato said. "I thought you might want to see our prisoner."

Wardlaw was actually impressed. Yato had come through after all. "This is the guy who's been vandalizing my gunnery area?" Wardlaw asked.

"We believe it is, sir. We picked him up in the central section of the range, in a bivouac he'd put up. Tracked him there from one of the sites, the one that said 'Wage Peace.'"

"He offer any resistance?"

"No, sir."

"Very well," Wardlaw said. "Leave him here with me. I'd like to have a conversation with this boy."

"Sir?" Yato began.

"You have a problem with that, William? I'm not afraid to be left alone in a room with a pencilnecked geek like him."

"Yes sir." Yato and the Marine guards left and Wardlaw walked slowly around the prisoner, examining him. Looked like the Sierra Club type, all right. Fancy hiking boots. Nice tan on his arms and neck and face, where you could see his face under all the hair and beard. Looked like the tan ended under the shirtsleeves, though. Soft looking hands.

"What's your name, son?" he asked.

"Dieter," the young man replied. "Dieter Holtz."

Kid had a foreign accent.

Wardlaw hated foreign accents.

"You're not even an American."

"No. I am from Germany."

"You have a visa?"

"Yes. I am here on a student visa."

"Some of those terrorists were in the country on student visas," Wardlaw said. He leaned back against his desk, crossed his arms. "Did you know that?"

"I have heard that."

"Is that how it works? You come here on a student visa so you can get into our country, and then you attack it from the inside?"

"I have attacked nothing," Dieter said.

"You're not a terrorist?"

"No. I am not a terrorist."

"Then what are you doing trespassing on a United States Marine Corps facility?"

"I believe in peace, environmental protection, and social justice," Dieter said. "I was merely making a statement about my beliefs."

"By breaking the law."

"Yes. Which I believe is a noble tradition in the United States, yes? The Boston Tea Party? Martin Luther King? Freedom Riders?"

"You don't have to give me a history lesson about my own country, son," Wardlaw said. "I could give you some history of your own. World War One, we kicked your asses. World War Two, we kicked them again. Remember?"

"Yes. I am not here as a citizen of Germany. I am here as a citizen of the world, concerned about things that affect the entire world."

"Let me get this straight," Wardlaw said. He moved around to the front of his desk and sat down in his chair. "What we do on my bombing range affects the whole world?"

"Yes. The destruction of natural habitat affects the world. War in Central Asia affects the world. Geopolitical borders are imaginary lines on a map, not real things."

"So by writing silly messages with rocks, you're putting an end to war and environmental destruction? I'm having a hard time wrapping my head around this idea, boy."

Dieter remained still, in the center of the room. His evident fear had gone and he seemed composed, even calm. This just pissed Wardlaw off all the more. "My hope was to stimulate dialogue," Dieter replied. "To encourage people to seek to understand the link between military aggression and the natural world."

Wardlaw picked up a pencil from his desktop pencil cup and tapped it on the desk, eraser-side down. Kind of bouncing it on the rubber end. Johnny Carson had done that, and Wardlaw had always liked it when Johnny did it. Sometimes he tried it to soothe his nerves, but it never seemed to work. "Do you think you're better than I am, son?"

"Excuse me?"

"Better. Superior to. In any way smarter, more informed, more ethical. A superior human being."

This was the first question the kid didn't have a ready answer to. He blinked several times as if that would help him arrive at one. "Not better. Possibly more informed, in some areas, as I'm sure you are more informed than I in others."

Wardlaw caught the pencil in both hands and snapped it with a sharp, loud crack. "More informed than me?" he echoed. "Boy, I am probably double your age. I have lived a long time and seen a lot of things. I've fought in wars, have you done that? I've killed men, have you? I've raised children and held my wife's hand as she died. Have you done those things?"

"I have not," Dieter replied. The more Wardlaw raged the calmer the kid seemed. "But I have summitted eleven fourteen-thousand-foot peaks. I have held the hand of my partner as he died of AIDS-related pneumonia. I have chained myself to friends and colleagues and lain across a roadway to block the transport of nuclear waste. Have you done those things?"

So the kid was not only a Kraut but he was a queer Kraut to boot. Wardlaw felt his blood pressure rising, like steam in a pot. "Were you alone out there in my bombing range, or are there others?"

The kid looked straight ahead but didn't answer. Wardlaw stood, coming around the desk fast and stopping right in front of him, his face inches from the German's. "Were you alone?"

No answer.

"Are there others? Are there still people on my range?"

No answer.

"Do you have any idea what kind of trouble you're in, boy?"

"I believe so."

"Are there others?"

No answer.

Wardlaw lost it then. He drew back his fist and drove it into the kid's gut as hard as he could. Dieter doubled over, blowing out his breath and grunting, and Wardlaw wrapped an arm around his neck and twisted. Dieter tried to kick, his hands flailed around ineffectually. Wardlaw kept twisting until he heard a satisfying snap and felt the kid go still.

Now he just had to deal with the problem of the kid's body. A sudden inspiration struck him and he lifted the dead weight, hoisting it over his head, and hurled it through the glass of his window. There was a huge crash, and the body thumped onto the parade ground below, accompanied by the tinkling of a thousand shards of glass, like so many tiny bells.

Marcus Jenkins rushed into the room. "Sir?"

Wardlaw pointed at the window. "Little shit tried to escape by going through my window," he said. He looked down as Marcus joined him by the broken glass. "Doesn't look like he landed well. Better get him cleaned up."

"I'll take care of it," Marcus said. He hurried from the office.

Wardlaw hadn't killed a man since the Gulf War. Until just this minute, he hadn't realized how much he missed it. He felt suddenly very relaxed. This is the best moment of my day, he thought. The very best. He brushed some glass out of his chair and sat back down, folding his hands behind his head and leaning back. If only every day could end on a high note.

Ken had stayed and talked to Virginia for a while, knowing that each minute he spent with her was another minute that something could be happening to her husband. She seemed to need it, though—sitting alone in their RV, she clung to Ken's arm as if it were a lifeline, and she'd drown if she let go.

Finally, though, he persuaded her that he needed to be on his way, that if he were going to find Hal he should be out looking, not sitting in here. She understood and released him, and he walked across the Slab in the quickly gathering dark. He'd brought a flashlight and a day pack with some food and water and blankets in it. Virginia said Hal was just wearing a light blue short-sleeved shirt and some old Sansabelt slacks and his loafers—not desert survival gear by any stretch.

He was taking a risk and he knew it. Maybe he should have called out a volunteer Search and Rescue team, a bunch of off-road enthusiasts and would-be cops who'd beat the bushes looking for the old man. But he was playing a hunch here—maybe a little more than a hunch, but a hell of a lot less than a sure thing—and his hunch was that, since he and Hal Shipp had felt some kind of bizarre connection earlier in the day, some kind of bond, he'd be able to find the man on his own.

Just like those "pictures" he'd seen of somebody digging, he figured. If he concentrated hard enough on Hal, he'd be able to see where the man was. And a bunch of other yahoos racing around on ATVs and calling pseudo police code into walkie-talkies would only interfere with that process. He zipped up his jacket and tugged his Smokey hat down on his head against the night's coming chill and went to work.

Standing in the center of the Slab, he closed his eyes and tried to summon up Hal Shipp's face. Remembering the details of someone's appearance, Ken knew, as opposed to the general overview, or what you tended to think of when you thought about a certain individual, was a pretty tricky job. Within a month of his own wife's death, he had realized he could no longer even conjure a complete image of her face. He could get the details: the tiny mole near her ear, the curve of her nose, the slight tilt of her eyes that gave her an exotic air, the fullness of her lips. But he couldn't put them together in a whole that approximated the real person, and he had taken to spending hours looking at photos as if they'd keep her appearance more clear in his mind and heart.

His method was to start at the top and work down. Hal's hair was white and wispy, thinning as a man's of that age will do, but he still had plenty. It was an inch or so long, and he combed it back off his forehead but it never stayed there. The old man usually had a lock of it hanging down over his forehead, almost boyishly.

The skin of that forehead was pale pink, almost porcelain-looking, like the surface of a cameo, with fine lines running parallel to one another above his eyes. The skin was smooth there, and looked soft as a baby's.

Set into that skin, behind fleshy folds that had always reminded Ken of Robert Mitchum's eyes, Hal had two sparkling chips of sky blue surrounded by whites clear enough, even at his age, to model for Visine commercials. In spite of what sounded to Ken like a rough life, Hal had loved to laugh, and years of that had etched dozens of fine creases at the corners of his eyes.

His cheeks were round and plump, also sunburn pink, Santa Claus cheeks, almost. They pressed against his eyes from below, as if forehead and cheeks conspired to blind the man, but the piercing blue always managed to show through anyway.

Hal's nose was generous, pocked with large pores and mottled with broken capillaries, making it red enough to stand out even against the pink skin of the rest of his face. A testament, Ken figured, to the man's hard-drinking days. A man couldn't have a nose like that and not be reminded by every mirror of his mistakes.

But Hal had overcome his mistakes, and when Ken tried to envision his mouth he could only see it slightly open and curved in a wide smile. His teeth were white and all his own, he claimed. His lips were thin but sharply-drawn, handsome and masculine. The corners of his mouth dimpled when he grinned, creating a mischievous, almost elfin effect in one so aged.

Finally, Hal's chin—a strong jaw, giving way in age to the folds of flesh that hung there, but still the lines of his original jaw were evident as they swept down to a serious chin, a chin of substance and character, Ken thought, with a small cleft right in its center.

Having picked out the individual pieces, Ken assembled them and came up with what he thought was a reasonably good picture of the man's face. He put that on top of a basic representation of Hal's body—a heavy-set guy, collapsing in on himself as people did when they reached his age. He still filled out a shirt but probably weighed less than he had at any time since reaching his full growth. Ken had noticed before that old people seemed to hollow out, as if their bones became empty tubes and their skin kept an approximation of its former shape but without the mass behind it.

With this image in his mind's eye and his real eyes shut, Ken focused on Hal. Suddenly a flash of light blinded him, like a strobe going off, and then he saw a section of the Slab, the eastern edge of it, facing the Chocolate Mountains. That spot was just a little ways from where he stood, so he hurried there. Two minutes later, he stood on the same spot, and it looked just like it had in his vision, right down to the plastic grocery bag snared on a jumping cholla and fluttering in a night breeze. Ken flicked on his flashlight and looked for footprints.

There were dozens here, of course. There was a path leading off the Slab, and he didn't know where it led but of course people walked on it occasionally. Even the most steadfast Slab dweller didn't spend all his time on those strips of cement. He followed the path a little ways, and the footprints tapered off, and eventually he found a set that he believed were Hal's. Keeping the light swaying from side to side across the path, he followed them off into the dark.

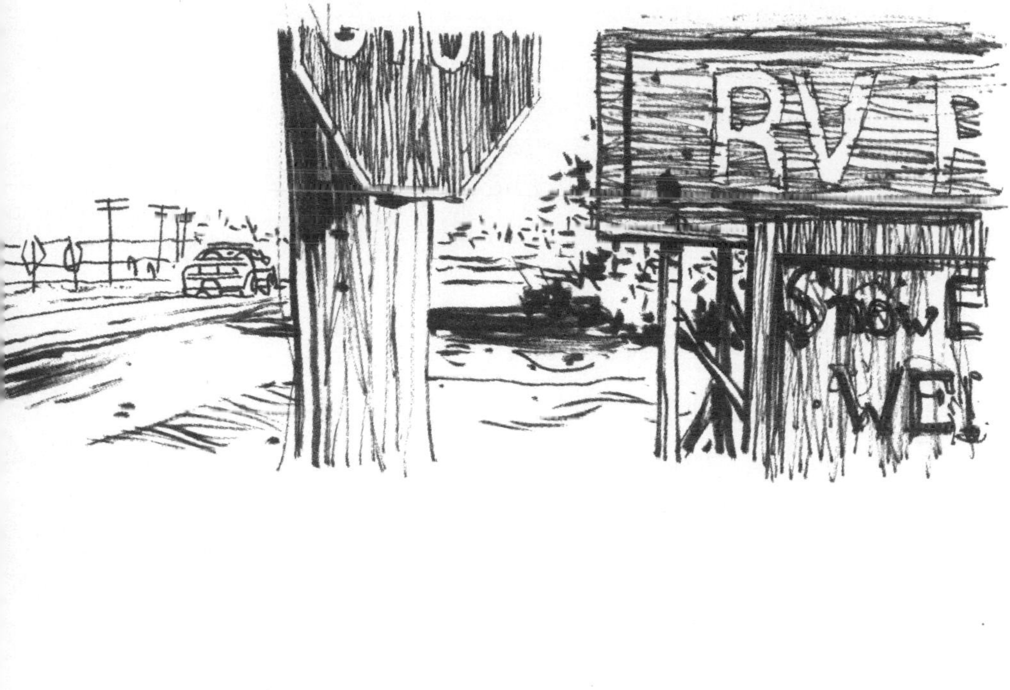
RV
SHOW
WE

part 3

penny rice

Penny clapped a hand across Mick's mouth, interrupting a diatribe about the environmental costs of globalization. His eyes widened and he looked at her as if she'd lost her mind.

"Shhh," she cautioned. "Listen."

She pulled her hand away and raised a finger to her lips, in case he needed reminding. But he kept his mouth shut, and after a moment he nodded. The evening air definitely carried voices, the tramping of feet, the creak and jangle of equipment.

"They're coming," Penny whispered. "They're not far. We need to get out of here."

"And go where?" Mick asked, fear making his voice rise.

"Keep quiet!" she instructed. "Listen, I saw a cave when I was exploring before. We'll go there. They won't find us inside it in the dark."

This was not exactly true. She had seen a cave, but not in the actual physical sense of the word. It was more the vague, undefined knowledge of a cave. She knew where it was—was, in fact, willing to bet her life that it was where she somehow knew it would be. But she didn't know precisely how she knew that, and had not, in fact, ever been to it. The cave's mouth was in a valley she hadn't even bothered to explore yet.

No time like the present, she thought. From the noises she heard, it sounded like the soldiers were about to top the rise that would lead them into this valley. The camp she had set up was most of the way up the far hill, so that she'd be able to slip up and over the hill if necessary. It looked like that necessity had arrived.

"We have to go," she insisted. Mick was still sitting, even though she was up and stuffing things into her backpack—water, notebooks, personal items. She had kept most of her stuff in the pack anyway, ready to move out on short notice. "Mick, I'm not kidding, let's go."

It was hard to see him—the night was virtually moonless and they were under the camo netting, but she thought he blinked a few times. "Okay," he finally said, and slowly got to his feet. She couldn't tell if he didn't believe the danger that they were in was real, or thought they wouldn't be spotted, or if he was stoned or something, but she determined to just move out when she was ready and let him worry about himself. Even if they caught him, he didn't know where the cave was so he couldn't give her up. For a moment a thought flitted across her mind—why be so worried about getting caught, she wondered, when you knew all along you probably would be? She didn't have an answer for that one; it just seemed urgent, all of a sudden, that she not be removed from this bombing range yet.

The sounds of the approaching soldiers grew louder. She slung her backpack over her shoulders and, with a final word to Mick, left the camp. He scrambled behind her, still holding his own pack by its straps and struggling to zip it shut as he walked. The night sky cast very little light, but she had already walked this path several times, in practice, and was able to pick her way up the hill, around the rocks and brush that studded the slope. In just a few minutes, she reached the top of the hill. She waited there for Mick, scanning the opposite hilltop, across the valley. The soldiers would have metal surfaces with matte finishes to avoid any telltale glints from the faint starlight, their faces would be painted, and they'd have night vision goggles, but she was sure she could see forms moving there, blobs of deeper black against the sky, blotting out the stars on the horizon. It could have been her imagination, but she didn't think so.

When Mick reached her she turned without a word or a look back and led the way down the hill on the opposite side. They made their way in silence, down to the bottom of this slope where a sandy wash cut north-south, and went to the right, heading north along the valley floor. At the end of this valley there was a low rise and then another, deeper valley on the other side, she knew. It was in that valley, on the west-facing slope, that the cave's mouth was.

If her mind—which, she reminded herself, had never seen this so-called cave—was to be believed.

She didn't think it was a good idea to start second-guessing herself now, though. She had come this far, convinced of the cave's reality. No harm in remaining convinced. At worst, they were putting more space between them and the soldiers, covering ground on which it would be hard for the soldiers to follow their tracks in the dark, for the most part. The wash was the exception; their footprints here in the soft sand were deep and readily apparent. But it was still the fastest way to move, and the soldiers would have to get to the wash before they could find prints there.

With his long-legged gait, Mick caught up to her easily here.

"You do know where you're going, right?" he asked. "Because it'd really suck if we went to all this trouble and just walked right into another troop or whatever."

"I know where I'm going," she assured him. "Just trust me. And I don't think there are any soldiers in that direction—they came just the way I thought they would. Basically, they made circles around the rock message we left, until they eventually cut across our trail. Did you notice they were coming right along the same path we took when we came back from there?"

"No, because I couldn't really see a damn thing. But I'll take your word for it, I guess."

"That's good enough."

"It's a good thing I have you out here," he said. "I don't think I'd know what to do on my own in a situation like this. With the Marines or whatever."

She had to fight back a wry laugh. "You weren't supposed to be out here in the first place, remember? You're supposed to be sitting in some nice safe motel room coordinating things."

"I know, I know. We've been over all that."

"Right." She was willing to let it go at that.

"I wonder what Larry and Dieter are up to," he said. "Haven't heard from them at all." They'd agreed to only use cell phones in the case of extreme emergency, since they didn't want to risk giving the authorities any signals to hone in on. "You think this counts as an emergency?"

"I wouldn't bother them yet," Penny said. "Surely they've heard the helicopters. If it looks like we're going to get caught, then you can call and give them the word to get out."

"Yeah, that's probably best," Mick agreed. "That's what I'll do."

"That's good," Penny said. She walked fast, almost at a jog, as long as they were in the wash and obstacles were few. At one point, they surprised a coyote out for its evening hunt and the beast loped away into the brush, casting occasional glances back over its shoulder to be sure they weren't following. But otherwise, the nighttime desert was as empty as it was dark, which Penny thought was strange. There should be bats, she thought, and kangaroo rats, ground squirrels. Something. For as pristine as the bombing range was, and as many birds and lizards and snakes as she'd seen during the day, there wasn't really as much fauna as she'd expected, and very little sign of the large animals, like mule deer and bighorn sheep, that she knew inhabited the area. And tonight was the quietest she'd seen it yet, with none of the nocturnal critters who should have been out and about. She thought it might have had something to do with the presence of all the people on the ground, far more than was usual.

And she thought it might have something to do with the electric taste in her mouth, the taste that seemed to grow ever more intense as they neared the cave.

The stars were cold pinpricks against the night sky, and the thin sliver of moon provided precious little light, so Lucy heard the road before she could see it and saw it only when she was practically on top of it.

From a mile away, or maybe a little more, she had heard the unmistakable rumble of a big rig rolling along. The noise had spurred her to new efforts. She had been going since afternoon, when she had taken the knife and canteen from her second victim of the day and struck out across the hills, heading south, getting her bearings from the sun and sticking to as straight a course as the landscape would allow. Since the sun had gone down, though, and the sky darkened, progress had been more difficult and she had been on the verge of giving up for the night when she heard the truck. Renewed, she pressed on through the dark desert, trying her best to dodge the cholla and ocotillo and broad, sharp-tipped yucca leaves that lurked around her.

Finally, she staggered out onto the surface of the roadway itself, its black asphalt shedding the heat it had stored from the day, and fell down to her knees, placing her palms on the road as if to reassure herself of its solidity. The road meant civilization. Safety. She felt herself beginning to weep, and sniffed it back.

It was just a road, she knew. She had no idea where it was, or where it led, or how well trafficked it was. For all she knew, the truck that had passed was the only vehicle that would come along all night. The next one might contain her kidnappers. It wouldn't do to ascribe too much power to a simple strip of tar.

Lucy needed some rest. As much as she'd have loved to just start walking along the road, she could just as easily walk ten miles in the wrong direction, straight toward those who were certainly still pursuing her, and kill herself from exhaustion in the process. So instead of walking, she found a spot in the desert, a dozen feet from the road, sheltered from it by darkness and the mass of a spreading creosote bush, and lay down.

The passing of a car woke her. She scrambled to her knees just in time to see its taillights disappearing in the distance. Damn it! she thought. She cursed herself for not having woken up on its approach. It was a passenger car, by the looks of the lights, low to the ground. Not the SUV she'd been snatched in. She needed the sleep, but if a ride could be had, that would be good too. She moved closer to the road, and sat instead of laying down. After a few minutes she rested her head on her knees and dozed again.

When she snapped to alertness again, it was because she heard the drone of a vehicle in the distance, growing nearer. She hurried to the roadside and put the rifle down in the dirt, just off the edge of the road. The stolen knife was tucked through her belt, its handle hidden by her shirt, so she didn't bother trying to disguise it any further. Then she checked herself, as carefully as she could. She knew she was a mess, her hair a tangle rivaling that of Brer Rabbit's briar patch, her skin filthy and torn, her clothes ragged. But the ragged clothes, at least, could work for her, if the vehicle's driver was a heterosexual male. She grabbed the ripped neckline of her tight top and tore it farther, exposing an expanse of breast. If she'd had time, she would have taken her pants off altogether, but the car's headlights were already splitting the darkness and heading toward her. She stepped onto the edge of the road and began waving her hands frantically.

The headlights swooshed across her and passed on. But as soon as it was past her, its brake lights flashed and then glowed as it shifted into reverse and backed toward her. The car, a small Japanese model she couldn't even identify in the dark, came to a stop right next to her. In the dark, she saw the driver lean over and pop open his passenger door.

"Sorry I passed you," he said. "When I saw you there, I thought I'd fallen asleep and was dreaming or something."

He was a white guy in a business shirt and khakis, with dark hair and a neatly trimmed beard. His eyes looked puffy, as if he had in fact been sleeping, but he had a smile on his face as he looked at Lucy. "That's okay," she said. "You stopped, anyway. Can I get a ride? I've had kind of a rough day."

"Sure, sure, no problem," he said. "Get in."

She turned away and stooped down, grabbing the rifle off the ground. Keeping her body between him and the gun to block his view of it, she backed into the car. She gave her ass an extra wiggle as she did, figuring he'd be checking that out anyway. At the last moment, before she was fully in the car but while she could still maneuver, she turned and pointed the weapon at his head.

"I hate to do this," she said. "You seem like a nice guy and all, and you did stop for me. But someone will stop for you, and you'll be fine, and you'll have a great story to tell your kids. So you need to get out of the car now."

"Wh—are you kidding me? You have got to be fucking joking," he said. His voice was quaking, though, and she saw his knuckles whiten against the wheel.

"I'm not joking," she said. "I told you I've had a bad day, so don't push it. Get out, and leave the keys where they are." She nudged his temple with the rifle's barrel. "Go."

He moved his left hand robotically from the wheel to the door handle and opened his door. "That's good," Lucy said. "Keep going."

The guy slid from the driver's seat and stood up in the middle of the road, next to the car. He looked half-amused, as if she were going to start laughing any moment and invite him back into his own car. But that wasn't happening. "Close the door," she instructed. He did.

Keeping the gun pointed at him as well as she could, she shifted into the driver's seat, reaching over and closing the passenger door as she did so. She slammed down the door lock button, and at the same time he began pounding on the roof and window. "You can't do this!" he shouted. "You can't just leave me out here!"

She didn't bother to answer, just dropped the rifle across her lap and the passenger seat and stepped on the gas. In just a few seconds she couldn't even see him in the rear-view mirror any more. She felt bad about stealing his car—she'd told the truth about that. But, frankly, she thought, I need it more than you do right now.

She wondered how he would adjust the story when he told it. Would she be sexier? More cruel? Completely nude? Maybe she'd be turned into a vicious gang of female thugs.

At any rate, she had a car. She still didn't know where she was, but that could be fixed, if she could only stay awake. She stayed on the road, going in the same direction the guy had been traveling. After about twenty minutes, this road intersected a wider road, so she turned right onto that road and drove for a while longer. Finally, up ahead she saw the glow of an all-night gas station and mini-mart, sitting by the side of what looked like a major freeway. The gas tank was three quarters full, and she didn't have any money anyway, so she pulled up to the side of the building and let herself into the washroom. There was no mirror and only the cold water worked. She let it run and washed herself up as best she could, using a rough paper towel to dab at her various wounds. When she was somewhat awake and dried off, she went back outside and looked at the map posted in the mini-mart's window. Someone had conveniently written YOU ARE HERE and drawn an arrow with a blue ball-point pen on the map, so she learned that she was ten miles from the Mojave desert town of Blythe, and that the freeway she could hear was the I-10.

The guy working behind the counter inside the mini-mart had noticed her and blatantly stared at her as she studied the map, but she wanted to avoid talking to him because she knew that police would come around asking questions at some point, and she didn't want him to be able to tell what direction she was going, or what her destination was. But the more she glanced inside, the more she realized just how hungry she was. And the shop was full of food. Making up her mind, she went inside and strode confidently to the counter, feeling his gaze measuring her as she did.

"Hi," she said. "I don't have any money, so we can do this a couple of ways. You can take pity on me because I've been kidnapped and had to escape, and I'm really hungry, and give me some food. Or I can go back out to my car and get my gun and shoot you. Your choice."

The guy—a kid, really, younger than her, with an acne-pocked face and spiky hair, a Metallica T-shirt underneath his polyester red, white and blue uniform shirt—didn't take his eyes of her. His lips curled into a smile. "Show me your boobs," he said, nerves cracking his voice.

"What?"

"You got some big boobs. Show me them and you can take whatever you want to eat."

Lucy shrugged and rolled up what was left of her tank top, then popped her breasts free of her bra. She didn't really mind people looking—there had been times when she'd have flashed this guy for the fun of it, just to see the look on his face. And, by comparison to what she had just escaped, this barely registered on the scale of degradation. This was nothing but commerce, goods for services. She let him have an eyeful and then put them away.

"Niiiice," he said. She ignored him and went to the heating trays where she grabbed two burritos and a foil-wrapped burger. From a cooler she snagged a few plastic bottles of water. A box of Cheez-its, a few napkins and a tray of mini-donuts completed the menu. She waved her handful of food at the guy and walked out. Getting into her stolen car, which she had discovered was a dark green Nissan Altima, she had another thought. She put her loot on the passenger seat and went back inside.

"I need to make a phone call," she said. "I need some change."

The guy punched open his register drawer and scooped out some quarters, which he handed her, the smile still on his face and his gaze still on her chest. She closed her fist over the coins. "See you in your wet dreams," she said, and went back outside, to the phone booth at a corner of the lot. Chunking a few quarters into the slot, she dialed home. After several rings, her mother answered.

"Mama, it's me, Lucia," she said. "I'm okay, I'm fine."

"Oh my God, Lucia, where are you? Are you all right?" The poor woman sounded frantic. Lucy could already hear her voice wavering, and figured tears would be running down her cheeks within seconds.

"I'm fine, mama. I'm coming home."

"Oh, good. When? Do you need anything? Your brothers, they—"

"I'll be home sometime tomorrow," Lucy told her. "I don't know when. I have some things to take care of first. Tell my brothers not to worry about me. I'm fine, I just need to do some things before I can come home."

She hung up then, cutting off her mother's urgent pleadings. It wouldn't do to talk for long—she might be talked out of doing what she knew she had to. So she left the phone and returned to the Altima and started the engine, then unwrapped the first burrito and began eating that with one hand as she steered out of the gas station and up the freeway onramp with the other.

She hit the 10, merging with the few other cars that were on the road at this time of night. Moving back toward civilization felt strange, as if she'd spent months in a foreign country and had just been deposited back home. The familiar—taillights ahead of her, lane markings on the road, green signs with white lettering—were new and wonderful. She felt like a child who's discovered a lost barrel of favorite toys in the back of a closet.

But after a few miles, the novelty wore off as a new wave of exhaustion hit her. She rolled down her window, letting a blast of cold air wash over her face. Even with that, she could barely keep her eyes open, and she knew she had to sleep. She pulled off the freeway at the first exit and took a narrow two-lane road into the desert until she found an empty stretch of wilderness. Here she crawled along until a rutted dirt road presented itself. She took this path until she was out of sight from the paved road and shut off the engine and crawled into the back seat, hugging the rifle to her like a stuffed animal as she went to sleep.

The desert at night, out where no city lights cast an umbrella glow over the sky and blocked the stars and moon's reflected luminescence, reminded Ken of Illinois nights of his youth. At night it was easier to feel a part of nature. The works of man were harder to see, and they felt less important, insignificant really in the face of all those stars and planets, all the boundless space around, all the rocks and hills and plants and creatures nature provided. Man, if he tried hard enough, could cause a species to become extinct. But he'd never learned how to create a new one.

Continued flashes of insight throughout the night had kept Ken on what he believed was the right course. Any time he lost the tracks or was confused by another set of footprints, he could summon an image of the trail from Hal's point of view, and from those, determine which path Hal had chosen.

Hal's course seemed random at first, as he meandered around the landscape. But eventually it became clear that he was always moving, however indirectly, toward the east, toward the Chocolates. This suspicion was confirmed when Ken saw a vision of the USMC's DANGER signs at the line that separated their bombing range from the canal and ultimately the Slab. Ken hesitated a moment—he should have called the Marines at this point. They'd want their own people on it, though, he reasoned. Which would mean flying in from Yuma and wasting precious time during which Hal could be freezing, or dying of exposure, or stepping on unexploded ordnance. No, there was no time for that. He ignored the imaginary line and continued his pursuit.

Once the signs were behind him and out of sight, he had the epiphany about how much this was like those long-ago days, running outside at night, through fields of corn or long grass, playing baseball on a summer night, catching fireflies or crickets in jars, laying back on a blanket and counting the endless stars in the sky.

Now, though, he walked through a different world. He'd been in the military, though that was decades past. He could barely imagine what kind of technology flew above this bombing range every day. Stuff that would have seemed absurd in the science fiction stories he read as a young man. Tom Swift's Triphibian Atomicar would have paled in comparison to a modern fighter jet, he knew.

It wasn't, he thought, that he didn't like change, so much as that he despised the increasing rate of change. Once, things had made sense to him. When he'd been a boy in the middle of the last century, he'd understood life. In so many ways, the nation seemed to grow up with him, gradually and at a steady pace a person could keep up with. It wasn't like the sixties had just suddenly hit. They came on slowly, with television and Hugh Hefner and Madison Avenue leading the way, breaking down little by little the standards and mores of the Eisenhower years; and Elvis and the Beatles and the Rolling Stones kicked the changes in the pants, made them come a little faster, those and the assassination of JFK; but still you could keep up with things, you could anticipate the era of the hippies, the Summer of Love, that had came from someplace and you could trace the connecting lines, Ken thought, and Civil Rights and Vietnam hung over that whole era as constants, bloody and divisive but always there like a security blanket and they led into Nixon and Watergate and the scandals, and that seemed to Ken to be when things started to speed up a little; he turned around and Gerald Ford was President and then he turned around and it was Carter and there were American hostages overseas and a general malaise which was undeniable but which Americans didn't want broadcast; he turned around and it was Reagan and arms for hostages, Iran-Contra, a booming stock market and greed ruled and it was all about Me; he turned around and Reagan was gone but Bush was still there, Bush who had called Reagan's economic vision voodoo economics and now it looked like he was right because Reagan had spent until there was nothing left to spend and then some and the economy collapsed and idealism was out of fashion; he turned around and Bush got Noriega and pushed Saddam back; he turned around and Bush was gone and there was Clinton; he turned around and rap was called hip hop and people wore their hats backwards; he turned around and everything was digital, personal computers and the online world fueling another boom, and once he had been in a men's room while a broker sold stocks on a cell phone standing at a urinal taking a loud piss; he turned around and Gingrich had led a revolution; he turned around and you needed to press a button to unlock your car and you couldn't get a person on the phone without listening to a menu, which had once been something you looked at by choice; he turned around and people were screaming about oral sex, calling for blood, and civility was out the window, seemingly forever; he turned around and there was an impeachment hearing; he turned around and a flawed election failed the nation; and he turned around and no one cared about what had happened because they cared about movie grosses and someone named Chandra Levy; and then he turned around and it was September eleventh and terrorists attacked American shores, and he turned around, and he turned around, and he turned around.

He had turned his back and America had slipped away, everyone he'd known gone, leaving behind only strangers in American skins. And nothing would ever be the same as it had been, and if these changes were for the better he couldn't see it. People hated, people distrusted, people accused. Good people died and evil ones prospered. Foolish to long for the days you could leave your doors unlocked, foolish to remember when people could leave their keys in the car, when people could let their kids walk to school, when people knew who lived next door. He was a foolish old man now, not as old as Hal but closing in, and anyway Hal wouldn't have to live to see the next turns, which was just as well, Ken thought, because he had stopped believing things would turn for the better. You couldn't affect things on any significant level, he believed, because only a few people could do that, and they did so in service of only one thing, only money. Not even money, he realized, just bits of information that stood for money. Flashes of data streaming along wires controlled everything, from the colors of cars you could buy to the shoes on your feet to the quality of the air and water.

All a man could do was to get up in the morning and go about his day, do the best job he could, try not to hurt anybody, maybe help someone if he could, and go back to bed. The rest of it was in someone else's hands.

Ken hiked through the dark, because that was what it took to do the job.

They slept for a few hours, Kerry and Rock and Terrance and Vic, slept because they had to, because after a day on the move and all the things they'd gone through, Cam's death and the apparent escape of their Dove, they'd been too exhausted to continue. Ray hadn't made it back to the cabin, and the later it got the less likely it seemed that he would. They'd been less than an hour away from him when they'd heard the gunfire. If he'd hit her, he could have caught up before they made it back, since they were hauling Cam much of the way and he was on his own. If not, he should still have reached the cabin by now.

Kerry was awake first. He had a gift, a totally reliable internal clock, and could wake himself at any hour he chose. Vic started when he felt Kerry's toe nudge his ribs. He rolled over and looked up at Kerry, already dressed and moving on to wake Rock. A lantern glowed on the counter that separated the kitchen area from the rest of the room, throwing Kerry's shadow across the walls as he stepped among the sleeping men like a fairy tale ogre's. Vic glanced at his watch. A little past four. It had been well past dark by the time they'd stumbled in, dropping onto unrolled sleeping bags in the main room. They'd had less than five hours of sleep.

"Up and at 'em, ladies," Kerry said. His ultimate insult, Vic thought, realizing for the first time the extent to which Kerry truly disliked women. He'd never married and rarely seemed to date. He was definitely heterosexual, but when he talked of women he'd been with, they were usually whores or tramps or sluts. Hispanic, usually. Vic understood suddenly, laying there on a sleeping bag in a room with three men he'd once considered friends, that they were all just here to enable Kerry's addiction. He got off on mistreating and abusing brown-skinned, black-haired women. Somehow he'd convinced the rest of them that there was not only nothing wrong with that, but that it was an experience to be shared. Cherished.

He felt ashamed that he'd never reached this conclusion before. It had been years. Years. He'd been coming on these Dove Hunts almost as long as he'd been married. With the horrible clarity of four a.m. he understood that he'd never met a woman as sexy as Cathy, his own wife. Even more than a little overweight, with hair the color of dirty straw and an unpretty face that nevertheless beamed like spring sunshine when she looked at him, none of the Doves over the years could do for him what Cathy did. Girls who took whatever they could hand out and begged for more, girls who accepted their treatment with blank expressions and slack bodies, girls who fought and bit and kicked, giving all the men bruises they'd have to hide from wives and loved ones—none even compared to the way Vic felt when Cathy happily, greedily took him in her mouth or stroked him hard and then guided him into her waiting heat.

He pushed back the flap of the sleeping bag he'd slept in that night. This was it, then, he decided. No more Dove Hunts for him. He'd see this one through until they all got home—with all that had happened, there was no getting around that, now—but then he was done. Without another glance at the others, he went outside to piss.

When he returned, Kerry shot a narrow-eyed, angry glance at him and pointedly looked at his watch. "Two minutes gone, Vic," he said. "You've got eight minutes to pack whatever you can carry on a double-time hike.

Kerry's backpack, stuffed to the brim, already leaned against the kitchen counter. Rock and Terrance were busily cramming personal belongings and food items from the coolers into theirs. Vic didn't reply, just found his own backpack and began to fill it.

When the eight minutes had passed—it felt like less—Kerry whistled as if he were hailing a Manhattan taxi. "Time's up, gentlemen," he said. "Let's move out."

Terrance and Rock were pretty much packed up by that point, and both men rose and shouldered their packs. But Vic wasn't quite finished—he was trying to pack his things in some kind of reasonable fashion so he could carry the thing on Kerry's forced march. Kerry was apparently serious about his deadline, though. He squirted fuel from a can of charcoal lighter fluid, which Terrance had brought along with a portable Weber grill, toward Vic, a finger of it sketching up the side of his backpack. "Move it out, Bradford," Kerry commanded.

Vic hoisted his pack off the floor. "Okay, geez," he said. Kerry looked away from him and continued squirting the fluid around the room's outside walls, then played it over a pile he'd made of propane cans for the stove and lanterns. "Having a cookout, Kerry?" Vic asked.

"We're not coming back here." Kerry said. He went around the corner, squirting into the other room, and called back after him. "You want to leave a bunch of fingerprints and DNA evidence around, by my guest. But I plan to make it as hard as I can for anyone to know who's been here."

Vic looked at Terrance, who shrugged, and Rock, whose sleepy face was as impassive as if he hadn't heard at all. "Makes sense," Terrance said.

Vic didn't answer. It made sense. It made as much sense as any of it. Kerry wasn't turned on by fucking these Hispanic girls, he was turned on by the knowledge that he was going to kill them. That had been his whole motivation from the start. He'd wanted to share it because that's what he was used to, sex and death in the company of men. Now the premeditated way he went about his clean-up process proved that he'd had an escape plan from the beginning, too. He had known from the beginning that there would be a last time, at least for this killing ground, and he'd made sure there would be a way to erase the clues.

Back in the main room, Kerry set the now-empty lighter fluid can down on the pile of propane tanks and pulled a box of matches from his pocket. He picked up his backpack, slipping his shoulders through the straps, and looked at the other guys.

"Better get going," he said. "I don't know how long it's going to take to get to the propane, but when it does it's going to blow." He was, Vic noted, smiling as he said it.

Vic followed the other two outside. It was still full dark, stars glittering in the cold reaches of space. "Where to?" Terrance asked.

Rock simply pointed down the dirt track they had driven in on. "Home," he said.

"It's the fastest way to civilization," Vic said. "And the easiest to hike."

"What about Kerry?"

"He'll catch up, Terrance," Vic said. "Let's go."

Penny and Mick spent the first part of the night sitting with their backs against the dry, cool cave wall. She dozed a few times, falling into a sleep deep enough to dream once, but her dreams made no sense: full of crazy images of half-naked people carrying torches, their faces wracked with fear, speaking a language she couldn't even begin to comprehend.

They had found the cave just where she had thought it would be, and flicked on flashlights only long enough to ascertain that it wasn't home to bobcats or any other predator big enough to cause them harm. The mouth was only about three feet across, but they could see that it widened rapidly inside. With a fallen ocotillo wand they whisked away the spider webs and they made their way around the first bend, so that no cursory glance by soldiers would reveal their presence. That was as far as they wanted to explore in the dead of night, so they had taken their positions, scooping out reasonably comfortable seats from the sand but remaining semi-upright instead of stretching out in case a quick escape farther into the cave became necessary.

In the twilight space between waking and sleeping, Penny saw, or thought she saw, something glowing deeper inside the cave. She was on her feet before she really came to full consciousness. By then, she decided, she was already committed so she felt for her flashlight—she'd left it on top of her backpack next to where she'd sat—and, finding it, started down the cave, her empty left hand waving about before her to keep spider webs or stray bats out of her way.

The roof of the cave was higher than she could reach now, and without turning on her light, which she didn't want to do, she couldn't see it. The walls were far enough apart that she couldn't touch both at once. The cave took another bend, to the left this time, and she followed it. So far there had been no side-tunnels, so even though she had left Mick snoring away where they'd both slept, she knew she couldn't lose him. Anyway, she thought, it's surprising this thing is so deep—almost more like a mineshaft than a simple cave. But there was nothing man-made about it, as far as she could see.

Of course, the farther into it she went, the less she could see. She considered switching on her flashlight but didn't, for no reason that she could articulate. By scraping her fingertips along the walls, she followed the cave's path as it led her away from Mick and toward—well, she didn't know what. Not-Mick. Something that glowed.

Rounding yet another curve, she finally found them. Mushrooms, glowing with their own internal phosphorescence like little gaslights. Not tiny, though—the heads of some of them were plate-sized or bigger. Their stems and heads were mostly white, which was what glowed, dotted with darker spots. She was no botanist but she thought that mushrooms were out of place in the desert to begin with—didn't they like moist climates?

But then she remembered something she'd read about while researching dry-climate flora, as part of her preparation for this trip. She hadn't paid much attention because it was about a place in Oregon—eastern Oregon, on the dry side of that state, where the Cascades held off the coast's traditionally high rainfall. A mushroom had been found there that had been determined to be the largest single living organism in the world. She couldn't remember the exact dimensions now—something like the size of sixteen hundred football fields, three and a half miles long, three feet thick, living mostly underground except where it sprouted up mushrooms above the surface. DNA testing had shown that all these mushrooms were part of the same massive fungus. It killed trees as it grew underground, poisoning their roots and cutting them off from needed nutrients in the soil.

The previous record-holder for biggest single organism had also been a mushroom—in Washington, she thought. But this Oregon one dwarfed even that. It turned out that dry climates were useful for this kind of growth, because the aridity prevented a lot of competition.

So maybe a mushroom in a dry California desert wasn't so unusual, after all. The fact that these glowed like deep-sea fish was strange, though, no getting around that.

She bent closer to look at them, but Penny had never been a fan of mushrooms under any circumstances, and this freakish variety wasn't about to change that. She had seen what she'd come down here for. It was time she headed back. If Mick woke up and she was gone, the poor baby would freak.

But before she turned around, she decided to click on her light for a moment, just to see what else was here.

In the circle of light she cast on the wall, she saw writing. Years' worth—centuries, even. Some of the languages were immediately apparent—English, German, French, Russian maybe. Others were not. Some, she wasn't sure were even human languages. She saw seemingly random jumbles of marks that had presumably meant something to someone, once, but probably couldn't be translated now without a new Rosetta Stone.

The expected markings were there, and mostly on the top layers, evidence of relatively recent visitations: EMMETT LOVES JUNITA, RHM + RMD 4-EVER, I LUV RANDY, JACK WAS HERE 11/17/86. On what seemed to be the next level down she began to see earlier dates, a 1901 and an 1892 among them. Disturbingly, threaded through all this, in such a way that she couldn't quite make out the chronology of the graffiti, was a more sinister series of quotes. KILL EDDY was one, and SLIC HER OPEN AND WATCH HER BLEED and ALL MEXES MUST DIE and more, words it sickened her to read. And under and over and between all the rest of it someone had written what appeared to be a treatise, in small, cramped handwriting that went on for what would have been the equivalent of pages and pages. Penny sat on the cave's sandy floor and played the light over the wall, trying to make it out.

"The Evil that results is shurely the work of Man and Devil but not God because God is the Creator who made the Heavens Above and the evil is of the Hell Below, tempting, taunting, leading Mankind to shure and definate Ruine. Whores and temtresses and dark women are inside the Evil and from the Evil. Men who worship not at the Lord's feet and fear not the Lord's wrathe are from the Evil and of the Evil. The only way out for these Lost Souls from the Evil is Deathe only in Deathe will they be guided toward the Light and the true path and the true way that God intended for them. Deathe is not an Ending but a passage through to a better life in servitude of the Lord's Will. Deathe is a gift bestowed upon the Evil, a reflexion of the Lord's Mercy Deathe blood flows on the sands and streetes and skin is cut open parted heads removed entrails spilt wicked Flesh seared with righteous fire bubbles the smell the stenk of Deathe is strong—"

"What are you doing?"

Penny jumped and dropped the flashlight, startled out of her near-stupor by the sound of Mick's voice behind her. She hadn't heard him approach, so enthralled was she by the horrific text she pieced together through all the other markings on the cave wall. She snatched the flashlight, still beaming, from the floor and aimed it behind her. Mick leaned against the opposite wall, holding one of the big mushrooms in his hands and picking it apart bit by bit, like a kid playing "loves me, loves me not" with a daisy, dropping the shreds on the cave floor.

"Jesus, you nearly gave me a heart attack," Penny said. Hyperbole, sure, but her heart was indeed pounding in her chest and she couldn't quite catch her breath. "Why did you sneak up on me like that?"

"I didn't," Mick replied. "I just walked down here, making as much noise as I ever make, I guess. You were just so engrossed in whatever you were doing there, I guess you didn't hear me."

"I was reading," she tried to explain. "All this freaky graffiti on the wall."

"Reading?" Mick echoed. "What graffiti?"

Penny turned the flashlight's beam away from him and toward the wall she'd been examining before.

It was blank, solid rock—a few scrapes and chinks from the occasional explorer's passing the only sign that humans had ever been here.

The busy chitter of small birds woke Lucy up in the morning. Sunlight angled in through the car's windshield but hadn't reached her yet, curled up as she was in the back seat. She felt behind her head for the door handle and opened it, then fell out into the still-cool morning air. Every muscle in her body seemed to have its own individual ache or pain; she felt like she'd been dragged behind the Altima last night, instead of driving it.

She hadn't wanted to sleep this late, but figured maybe it was better than fighting exhaustion all day. She had a lot to take care of before she could sleep again. Opening the front passenger door, she found a couple of mini-donuts, some napkins, and a bottle of the water that she'd taken the night before. She ate the donuts walking, stretching her thigh and calf muscles. Then she found a dense bush and squatted behind it to pee, wiping herself with one of the napkins. After fastening her jeans again, she broke the seal on the water bottle and guzzled it. When it was nearly gone she fingerbrushed her teeth and used the last little bit of water to rinse and spit.

Her morning ablutions done, she climbed back behind the wheel and keyed the stolen car to life. She made her way back to the freeway, a little busier at this time of the day than it had been the night before, and drove it for about twenty minutes, until she found the exit for the 111. There she headed south, through the wealthy communities of Palm Springs and Palm Desert, and farther down, through Indio. At Mecca, worried that she might be recognized, she tried to keep her face down as much as possible, looking at the road through the tops of her eyes. Still she stayed on the road, leaving Riverside County and entering Imperial. She knew nobody down here, so she relaxed a little.

Finally she left the Salton Sea behind her and drove into Brawley, the sugar plant rising up on her left, the town spreading ahead of her. She fished Ray Dixon's driver's license out of her jeans pocket and looked at the address on it. She had to drive around for a little while before she could find his apartment on Gilmour Street, but finally she did and she pulled the car to a stop in front of it and sat looking at it. The building was nothing special, a two-story stucco construction that faced onto a parking area and an empty cement pool. It looked like maybe it had been a motel once, though why on Earth anyone would stay here at the edge of Brawley if they didn't have to was beyond her. Probably why it was a motel no longer, she guessed.

From what she could tell sitting here in the car, the building was deserted this time of day. It was after ten now, later than she had hoped to arrive, but that sleeping-in thing had thrown off her whole schedule. It didn't really matter, she supposed. She didn't know much about Ray Dixon, but he had worn a wedding ring and in his wallet there had been a photo of him with a skinny brown-haired woman at least four inches taller than him, so Lucy assumed that he'd been married at one time, and maybe still was.

She spotted the apartment door with the number 8 on it, upstairs, second door from the stairway. Not ideal, but she'd make do. She pulled the rifle from the car and carried it close to her side, hand down casually, keeping her body between the apartment building and the gun. At the stairs, she climbed quickly, and then hid the gun with herself again as she covered the walkway to apartment 8. There was a doorbell button in the center of the door, with a peephole above it. She pushed the button and didn't hear anything so she rapped on the flimsy door, loud, with her knuckles. She waited. Nothing. She knocked again, and this time she heard a rustling from inside.

A moment later the door pulled open to the maximum width that the inside chain lock would allow, and a woman—the one from the photo, just as scrawny and tall as she'd looked—peered out at her through sleepy eyes, her brown hair in matted clumps. "Yeah?" she asked. "I'm sleepin', what do you want?"

"I need to talk to you," Lucy said calmly. "Let me in."

"About what? I don't even know you," Ray Dixon's wife said. She hadn't noticed the rifle yet. Shaking her head, she began to close the door.

Lucy raised the gun and drove its stock against the chain, slamming it into the door and pushing as hard as she could. The chain snapped out of the jamb and the door flew open. Dixon's wife turned and stared at her, eyes wide, and started to say something, but only "What—" came out before she saw the gun and her jaw shut with an audible thump. Lucy spun the weapon around so that the muzzle was pointed at Dixon's wife, and stepped inside, backing the other woman up with the gun. Once inside the apartment she closed the door firmly with her foot.

"Wh-what d-do you want?" Dixon's wife asked, her eyes filling with tears. "I don't have any m-money."

"I'm not after money," Lucy said.

"Then what? Why are you here? I don't have anything for you."

"Maybe you do. Is Ray Dixon your husband?"

The woman sniffed and held a knuckle under her nose. She paused before answering, as if trying to decide what would be the best way to reply. Impatient, Lucy retrieved the driver's license from her pocket and flung it at the woman. It hit her in the chest and she snagged it with both hands. She wore a tattered bathrobe over an oversized tee. "Is that your husband?" Lucy asked again.

The thin woman fumbled with the license, but got it turned over and looked at it. She nodded and the tears started to really flow now, streaming down her cheeks and rolling off to fall onto the plain gray carpet. "What, are you sleeping with him or something?" she asked.

"Where is he now?" Lucy demanded.

"He's…he's hunting."

"Dove hunting."

"That's right."

"I need to know who's with him. I need names, addresses, everything. You got that?"

"Why?" Dixon's wife sniffled again. "What's this all about?"

Lucy wagged the gun at her. "Lady, you're not in a position to ask a lot of questions. Do you have that information or don't you?"

The woman dragged her hands through her stiff hair and looked at Lucy as if measuring how far she'd go. He decision apparently made, she heaved a big sigh. "Ray is good about being organized," she said. "A place for everything, everything in its place, you know?"

"I don't care about his personal habits," Lucy prompted. "Just get me the details. Five guys."

Dixon's wife nodded. "Okay." She sniffled again and wiped her nose on the back of her ratty pink bathrobe sleeve. "It'll take me a minute."

"Faster is better," Lucy pointed out.

"Yeah, okay," the woman said, sounding resigned. She went to a little table underneath a wall-mounted telephone and opened the single drawer, taking out a red address book. She laid that on a kitchen counter and tore a piece of paper from a pad kept on top of the table, took a pen from beside the pad, and flipped through the address book.

Lucy looked at the apartment as Dixon's wife wrote. It was nothing special, she decided. The focal points of the living room were a widescreen color TV and a gun rack with a couple of empty spaces. The furniture was serviceable, but nothing more. A couple of framed prints that had probably come from a poster store, with no particular significance other than that the colors blended with the gray of the carpet and the tans and light blues of the couch, decorated the walls. Everything was neat and clean. The place felt like a model apartment, not like somebody's home. Lucy figured that Dixon's wife probably worked a night shift, and maybe Dixon worked days and they only saw each other in passing. The apartment reflected that kind of marriage, she thought, one in which the parties were husband and wife in name but not in much more than that. Their emotional lives were probably as barren as the walls.

A minute or two later the wife held out a piece of paper with shaking hands. Keeping the index finger of her right hand near the trigger, Lucy let go with her left and took the paper, scanning it quickly before stuffing it into a jeans pocket. "If this isn't right I'll be back for your skinny white ass," she warned.

"Those are the addresses in his book," Dixon's wife swore. "He writes in pencil so when he has to change them he can just erase the old ones. He's very meticulous."

Lucy started to back toward the door, but Dixon's wife kept talking, almost as if she didn't want to be left alone. "He's really done it this time, hasn't he?" she asked. "Screwed something up big time."

"You could say that," Lucy said. Then the door was at her back so she pulled it open and slipped through, lowering the rifle back to her side as she did. She hurried to the Altima, got in, and sped off. Four blocks away she stopped and, with hands shaking even more than Dixon's wife's had been, she unfolded the piece of paper and read what the woman had put down there.

The names of her attackers.

Kerry Williams.

R. J. Rocknowski.

Vic Bradford.

Terrance Berkley.

Cam Hensley.

She had some visits to make.

Kerry tossed a match at a tendril of lighter fluid and watched the flames leap up. It wouldn't be long before the ancient, bone-dry wood caught, and the propane cans—if they didn't blow so forcefully that they knocked the cabin apart before it burned fully—should only help speed things along. He'd saved some fluid for the outhouse, too. Investigators would be able to, he was certain, find bits of DNA evidence around the place if they looked hard enough. He was hoping they wouldn't bother to. He for damn sure didn't have time to stick around here and sterilize. The Dove had been gone for hours and could be leading a posse back here even now. He shouldn't have let the guys sleep as long as they did. But they needed it, he supposed, after the day they'd had. He certainly felt restored.

He'd caught up to them after they'd been gone about fifteen minutes, right before the propane cans went off, one after another like a stuttering bass drum. For the rest of the morning, he set the pace, cajoling and browbeating the others into keeping up with him. Eventually the sun glimmered on the Eastern horizon and then broke over the distant hilltops and the day began to warm, and with that Kerry's mood improved as well. He was where he liked to be: one step ahead of trouble.

He couldn't say as much for the moods of his fellow travelers. Terrance was virtually silent, almost completely shut down. He plodded along, his enormous bulk making him the slowest of them all. When Kerry poked or prodded he didn't react at all, not a smile or a grimace or a growl. He just walked faster for a little while, and then slowed again.

All in all, that was pretty much exactly what Kerry wanted from the fat man. He had broken Terrance Berkley, now he could remake him in whatever mold he saw fit. He'd lost Cam Hensley, who had money, and Ray Dixon, who had some skills. Terrance at least had a steady job and some brains, but he was physically useless and had never shown as much zeal as he should have. Kerry anticipated fixing those problems, shaming him into losing weight and working out, and transforming him into a kind of sidekick who'd do Kerry's bidding without question or complaint.

And it was all, Kerry thought, because of gender inequality. Together these men had killed thirteen women, and Terrance hadn't suffered, so far as Kerry knew, a single sleepless night over it. But kill one man—one friend—and guilt destroyed him.

That left Rock and Vic Bradford. Rock was his name—hard, solid, dependable, and with only a single other characteristic that mattered. He was a horndog of the highest order, which was how Kerry controlled him. Once triggered, he would soldier on until

Kerry released him. Vic, though…Vic was another matter. Kerry thought he'd been seeing signs of defiance in Vic. Rebellion brewing, maybe. Vic would most likely have refused to kill Cam, even if he'd been ordered to. That was a problem.

Kerry thought that perhaps Vic would not survive this particular Dove Hunt either. He'd just have to see.

They found the house around six-thirty in the morning. It was a small, wood-frame job with a little dry yard surrounded by a wrought-iron fence, painted white. A red GMC pick-up idled in the drive, the driver's door open. Kerry motioned the other guys to get down as he approached the house alone, staying low and keeping the fence between himself and the building's windows. As he squatted in wait, a man came out of the house in a faded brown tee and jeans, carrying a metal lunchbox in his hand. Kerry gave him time to almost reach the car, then shouldered his M-4 and squeezed out one round. The crack was deafening in the quiet morning air, with only the rumble of the truck's engine to compete with it, and seemed to echo for minutes. But it dropped the guy, his lunchbox breaking open and spilling into the dirt drive. Kerry gestured for the other guys to join him, and as they were running he scanned the house.

What he was afraid of. A woman stared out the window at him, fear twisting her face and making her into an ugly crone. He raised his weapon again and fired a short burst in her direction. The window and her head exploded at the same time.

"Jesus, Kerry!" Vic complained. "What are you doing?"

Kerry pointed the barrel of his gun at the truck. "Hitching a ride," he said. "What's it look like?"

He could have found Hal Shipp a whole lot easier, Ken figured, if the guy had stuck to preexisting paths or gotten himself lost in daylight, or both. As it was—even using the trick he'd so recently learned of closing his eyes and concentrating and looking at the landscape through Hal's eyes—the sun had been up for hours before he finally tracked the old man down. During the night, looking through Hal's eyes hadn't done much good—starry skies and moonlit desert shrubs looked basically the same all over. Come daylight, he'd been able to recognize landmarks again—though not many, since Hal had crossed over onto the bombing range the day before and Ken had never spent time over there. But he got an angle of one of the more notable hills, a tall one with a sharp peak offset to the left and a sudden drop-off beside it, so he headed to where the view ought to be the same and eventually found Hal sound asleep in the shade of a smoke tree in the middle of a wash.

At first he thought the man was dead. He spotted Hal from a hundred feet away or so, his blue shirt plainly visible against the brown earth. But he was under a tree, not moving, and he'd just spent the last afternoon and night exposed to the often-cruel elements. The deserts of the Southwest killed hundreds of people every year, most of them Mexicans crossing over in search of jobs and opportunity, using the empty spaces to dodge *la Migra*. But there was also the occasional Anglo hiker, too, lost in the wilderness without enough water, or too little cover for the cold nights. Anything could have happened to Hal out here. Ken started to run.

By the time he reached Hal, though, the old man had awakened and started to shift his body. Ken called to him, and Hal turned over and opened his eyes, surprised to see Ken bearing down on him. His expression was at first closed off, defensive, but then he opened up.

"Hal, are you okay?" Ken asked him. "You shouldn't wander around by yourself, you know that. You've been out here all night?"

"Think I don't know that, young fella?" Hal replied. "I may be old but I'm no idiot. When the sun goes down and the moon comes up, that's nighttime."

"Are you cold?" Ken asked. "Hungry?" He slipped a canteen off his shoulder and handed it to Hal, who had moved to a sitting position. Hal unscrewed the lid and tipped his head back, drinking deep. After a few moments he pulled the canteen away and wiped his mouth with the back of his hand. "Ahh, that's good," he said, and then he launched into a coughing fit so severe that Ken was afraid he was going to vomit.

"Easy," he said. "Take it slow. You probably haven't had any water all night, have you?"

Hal brought his coughing under control, though when he looked up at Ken his blue eyes were teary. "No, I don't...I don't think so," he said. "I guess not, anyhow."

"Come on, Hal," Ken said. "Let's get you back home. Virginia's worried half to death about you."

"Virginia?" Hal asked. "Is that my sister?"

And Ken knew that the Alzheimer's had come back, with a vengeance—probably why Hal had roamed off in the first place, he thought. Poor guy probably couldn't remember how to get home even if he'd wanted to.

But he thought there was something he could do about that.

He extended a hand to Hal. "Let me help you up there, partner," he said. Hal reached out and clasped Ken's hand with his own, and sure enough, it happened again, the magic coursing through both of them like a transfusion of energy and strength and wisdom, like all of his blood had been driven from his body and replaced with trumpet music.

Hal felt it too. Ken could tell by the sudden focus and intensity in the older man's eyes, the increased strength of his grip, the way he practically lunged to his feet in spite of a night lost in the wilderness.

"What the hell are we doing here, Ken?" Hal asked, speaking with more vigor than he had exhibited just moments ago. "Where are we?"

Ken chuckled. "That's two questions, Hal. Number one, what we're doing here is you took a little walk last night and got yourself lost. Number two is, we're somewhere in the Chocolate Mountains bombing range."

Hal took a quick look around, as if to orient himself. "Guess I'm lucky I didn't step on some unexploded ordnance, huh? Or make myself a target."

"Lucky, right," Ken agreed. "Just the same, I think it'd be an excellent idea if we got out of here now."

"I'm with you there," Hal said. "Lead the way."

As they walked, Hal told Ken what he remembered about his adventure of the night before, wandering away from the Slab, lost in thought and paying no attention to his course or his destination. When they reached the hole in the fence, the sun now high in the sky and the morning heating up fast, Hal suddenly grabbed Ken's arm and faced him with a worried expression.

"Where are we going?" he asked.

Ken thought for a moment that Hal's memory had slipped again. But his eyes were still sharp and his grip strong. "Back home. Virginia's scared to death about you."

"No," Hal said adamantly. "I don't want to go back to the Slab."

"But your wife's there, Hal," Ken said. "Anyway, my car's parked there, I have to go back."

"There's something bad there, Ken," Hal said. "Something, I don't know, wrong about that place."

Ken held the fence back for Hal to pass through. "What kind of wrong? You've lived up there for years."

"I know it, Ken. But...I don't know. I guess I hadn't touched you and had that...well, you know, that kind of electrical charge go through me before. It's like it opened these shutters in my mind or something. I can hear lots of things—not really hear, but you know..."

"I think I do," Ken admitted, remembering the strange images he'd been able to call up since he and Hal had connected yesterday.

"I call 'em magic days," Hal said. "When I think about 'em at all. And these last few days, they've been magic days, for sure. But since you and I touched over there, on the Slab, the magic's been even stronger than before. If I'm not careful I can hear all the things my neighbors are thinking about, and what they're thinking, well, I don't want any part of it. It's foul, Ken, it's evil. They're thinking about killing each other, hurting each other, they're full of anger and fear and misery."

"Seems like that's true of most people," Ken suggested.

"No, more than that, though. Way more. Like wading through some kind of cesspool, barefoot and with open cuts on my feet. I can't go back there."

Ken thought for a moment as they walked. The hike back hadn't felt strenuous at all—he actually felt refreshed, as if he'd had a good night's sleep and a shower. "Okay," he said finally. "I left the car near Virginia's place—your place. I'll pick it up and I'll stop in to tell her that I've got you but I'm going to take you to a doctor just to be checked out—that you're fine but as a precaution I want someone to take a look at you. That way she won't worry about you so much, and I'll be able to come and pick you up in the car."

"If she wants to come with you, Ken," Hal said, his tone somber, "don't let her. I don't want to see her right now either."

Ken was surprised by this news—Virginia Shipp was one of the sweetest women he'd ever known, the kind every kid wishes his grandmother could be, or believes she is. "Are you sure?"

"Absolutely sure," Hal replied. "I can't trust her. I know it's not her—it's that place.It's the Slab. But she's, she's under its influence, I guess. That's the only way I can put it. That place has an evil influence, and she's fallen under it."

"What about taking her away from it?"

"I don't know for sure," Hal said. "But I don't think that'll help. I think once it's in someone, it's in there."

"Okay, Hal," Ken said. "I believe what you're telling me."

"Are you sure? Because if I didn't know myself I'd think I was completely insane."

"I'm sure, Hal. Because I have them too. The magic days. Like you. And like you, since we touched yesterday it's all been different. I don't hear things, but I can see— strange things. Like I'm looking through someone else's eyes. That's how I found you, out there. Seeing through your eyes."

"Figured you just followed my footprints," Hal said. "I wasn't exactly hiding 'em."

"I did some of that too," Ken confessed. "But it was a little tough in the dark."

They had approached the Slab now, it was just on the other side of a battered dirt path and the next little rise, and Hal stopped, planting his feet in the sand. "No farther," he said. "This is an old Jeep road you can take from the edge of the Slab, you know the one?"

"I know it," Ken said.

"It's pretty passable, even with a passenger car. Pick me up here. I'm not taking another step closer to that place."

"All right, Hal," Ken said. "It'll be a little while. Twenty minutes, half hour maybe. You'll be okay?"

"I'll be fine," Hal said.

"And Hal? How'd you know I was driving a passenger car and not the Bronco?"

Hal Shipp smiled. "Like I said, I can hear things."

Ken laughed and turned away from the old man, heading toward the Slab—a place he had always thought of as off-beat, a little strange, but never particularly evil. He trusted Hal's judgement, though, especially now, in the wake of the magic that had enveloped them both. That, he accepted without hesitation, since he'd felt it himself. As he walked, peeling off his jacket as the day warmed, he still had a spring in his step that was unexpected considering how long he'd been on his feet. He didn't necessarily feel younger, but he felt stronger, more composed, more optimistic somehow.

And immediately, Mindy Sesno flitted into his mind. She would go out with me, he thought. He couldn't actually figure out why he had believed that she wouldn't, or that there would be any harm done in asking her. So he decided that he would, as soon as he finished dealing with Hal Shipp.

Today, though. For sure. Before it was too late and she hooked up with some other guy.

But then, as he stepped up onto the first of the many cement slabs that made up the community called the Slab, he put her out of his mind. If there was any basis to what Hal had said, he'd have to keep a close watch while he was here.

"Do you trust me?"

Colonel Franklin Wardlaw looked at William Yato and Marcus Jenkins as if he could see all the way through their uniforms, through their bags of flesh, through their interwoven masses of muscles, through the skeletal structure that gave them shape, to the faint blue outline that he believed was the embodiment of the human soul. They were strapped into their seats in the otherwise-empty belly of a Bell UH-1 Iroquois, a Marine Corps utility helicopter that could transport twelve, currently buzzing across the range at a speed of around one hundred knots. The chatter of the rotor and the buzz of the interior made conversation hard, but not impossible, if you shouted. Wardlaw was used to shouting. You didn't make Colonel in the USMC with a soft voice, he thought. A man needed to make himself heard.

Neither of them answered, so he asked the question again. "Do you trust me?"

Marcus smiled. "Yes, sir," he replied eagerly. He was young, and not particularly bright, but he was eager and that was something.

Yato only watched, but didn't answer. He'd take some observation, Captain Yato would, Wardlaw thought. Some testing. If a man needed to make himself heard, which he did, a man also needed to know where he stood.

"We'll know, soon enough," Wardlaw shouted, settling back into his seat. The chopper roared to the west, away from the rising sun. Ten minutes later, it had deposited its passengers, picked up nine new ones, and headed back to Yuma.

And on the ground, Franklin Wardlaw and his entourage had taken over custody of the prisoner. Larry Melton had been located during the night, near the southern end of the Impact Area, not far from the border with the gold mining operation that capped the bottom of the mountain range.

Melton himself was not much to see. He sat on a rock, hands cuffed behind his back. He was a furry thing, with long wavy hair that billowed out from his head, a thick beard, and a hairy neck, back, and shoulders, all growing together so thickly that one couldn't really tell where the hair from one left off and became something else. He wore a plain red tank top, as if to expose more of his fur to the morning air, with faded blue jeans and hiking boots. His eyes were small, pig-like, Wardlaw thought, as if the man were only part human and still trying to overcome some animal past. A fugitive from Morcau's island, maybe, with all that fur and those small bloodshot eyes.

"So your name is Larry Melton," Wardlaw said to him. He paced in front of the prisoner, back and forth, back and forth, as they talked. Marcus and Yato stood off to one side, at ease but alert. Weird red and white mushrooms poked out of the ground near their feet. "What else can you tell us about you, Mr. Melton? Your driver's license says you're from Indiana. Is that a fact?"

"Yes."

"A Hoosier. And what would a Hoosier be doing out here in the extreme desert Southwest, I wonder?"

Melton didn't answer, so Wardlaw tried a more direct question. "What are you doing on my gunnery range?"

"Working for peace," Melton said simply.

"'Working for peace.' That's precious, really it is. And to you, arranging rocks into clever little messages like 'War No More,' that's a form of working for peace?"

"Yes."

"In what way?" Wardlaw demanded.

"It works to raise public consciousness."

"What about flying airplanes into skyscrapers? Did that raise public consciousness too?"

"I guess, in a way."

"You guess. Don't you think that raised the public's consciousness to the idea that not all war is bad, that sometimes it's a necessary response to global conditions? You do know that the American public stands firmly behind the idea of a war against terrorism, don't you?"

"I don't find it surprising, given what happened. But I don't think the public really knows what it's asking for."

"Maybe not. Maybe not." Wardlaw stopped pacing and faced the young man directly. "If the public ever really knew what war was like, maybe they wouldn't support one under any circumstances. Do you think that's true?"

"It probably is," Melton agreed.

"Which is why the public has to be left in the dark about some things. Because some wars are just, some wars are necessary, and some wars have to be fought and won. We're a nation forged in war, built by war, protected by war and enriched by war, Mr. Melton. But you come into my Impact Area, in the midst of one of the greatest national crises our country has ever faced, and you try to disrupt our mobilization efforts, try to turn public opinion against us. Do you think you speak for the people, Mr. Melton?"

"I think so, yes."

"When I look at you, do you know what I see? A spoiled, middle class white kid. Your friend Dieter—ex-friend, I should say, may he rest in piece—" He watched Melton's face as he dropped this news tidbit; to his credit, the young half-man barely flinched. "—he wasn't even an American, he was a German. Middle class white kid, just the same. Your rich and your poor, they don't have time for such nonsense. The poor are too busy trying to scrape out a living, and the rich are too busy building a great nation. It's the middle class, with too much time on their hands and not enough to do but watch TV, that are always out causing trouble. Look at us!" He thumped his own chest. "A white man." He gestured at Yato and Jenkins. "An Asian man and a black man. The few, the proud, the multicultural. We're America, boy. We represent America, not you!"

"I notice which one's in charge," Melton said.

"Nobody asked you for your opinion, son. You vandalize United States property. You evade our troops, forcing us to spend thousands of dollars and dozens, maybe hundreds, of man-hours, to find you. That money and those man-hours would be better spent keeping America safe from terrorism, but here we are, throwing them away—" He made a sweeping motion with his arms and raised his voice, so that it boomed up the scrub-strewn slope and echoed back to him. "Throwing them away! On you!"

He stepped closer to the prisoner and lowered his voice again. "And do you know what that makes you, Mr. Melton? Do you?"

"A patriot?" Melton asked smugly. Wardlaw wanted to bash his face in with the nearest heavy rock, or maybe with his fists. But he didn't, because he still had something to find out.

"A traitor," he explained. "You are guilty of treason, Mr. Melton. That's a crime punishable by death."

"Isn't that up to a jury to decide?"

"We're at war, Mr. Melton. Rules change. You're on my turf, you come under my law."

Melton's eyes ticked over to where Marcus Jenkins and William Yato were standing, listening impassively. He looked nervous.

"Don't look at them for help, Mr. Melton," Wardlaw said. "They're with me." He turned to face the other two Marines. "Right, men? You're with me."

"Yes, sir," they both said.

"Do you trust me?"

"Yes, sir," Jenkins said again. Yato nodded.

"Then kill him."

"Excuse me?" Yato asked.

"If you trust me, then kill this traitor. Both of you, firing at once. Like a firing squad. Then we're all in this together."

Neither man moved.

"Do you trust me?" Wardlaw asked again.

Still calm, unreadable, Yato drew his sidearm. Marcus Jenkins did the same. Wardlaw stepped aside, trying to keep his smile restrained, as they took aim and squeezed their triggers.

Melton's body twitched twice in quick succession as the slugs hit it, then collapsed in a furry, treacherous heap on the dirt. Yato barked out a short laugh, an unfamiliar sound to Wardlaw, who couldn't remember ever having heard the Captain laugh out loud, and stood over the body, pointing his weapon at the head. He fired again and again, emptying his clip. Melton's head, pulverized by the onslaught, leaked red and gray all over the dun colored sand. Jenkins joined in then, using a series of carefully-placed shots to cut a strip down the middle of Melton's chest.

When both guns were empty and the echoes had faded, the desert seemed more quiet than usual. "What should we do with him, sir?" Jenkins asked, in a tone one might use in church.

Wardlaw pointed to the area where they'd been standing. "Just drag him over there," he said. "Leave him for the mushrooms." Yato looked questioningly at him, and he didn't even know for sure what it meant himself.

But it didn't matter. It would work. That's all that counted.

It would work.

Penny put her fingertips to the wall, as if she'd be able to feel the writing she could no longer see. I know what I was reading, she thought. It was as clear as anything. Where could it have gone?

She wasn't willing to believe that it had been a hallucination. Her mind couldn't make up something as twisted as what she'd seen—she wasn't imaginative enough for that. Penny had always been the realist, pragmatic Penny, unwilling or unable to wander off the paths that had been established for her life.

Still on her knees before the cave wall, she turned and shined the light on Mick again. He still had the remnants of the freaky glowing mushroom in his hands, and had brought a tiny portion up to his lips to taste. She'd hurl if she did something like that, she knew, taking a taste of what could very well be a poisonous mushroom. Who knew what kind of thing would grow in a cave like this? But Mick knew the natural world a lot better than she did, she realized. She was still a relative novice compared to him. For all she knew, he'd encountered these mushrooms a dozen times before and considered them a delicacy.

But she didn't like it, and she didn't like the way he flicked his tongue across the mushroom's stem and stared at her over the top of it, like some second-rate Don Juan from a low budget romance. She didn't know what he could see in the dark, since she held the only visible flashlight, but she didn't care for the way his eyes narrowed as he examined her.

"What?" she finally asked.

"Just watching you," he said. His voice sounded different—less whiny, more self-assured, than usual. "It looks like you have a little problem."

"What is it?" Penny demanded. "What's my problem, Mick? I'm sure you've catalogued all of them."

"Well, since you ask," Mick replied. "Your immediate problem is that you're seeing things on the wall that clearly aren't there. That's just a little scary, don't you think?"

"Sure, a little, but—"

"But your bigger problem—the mother of all your problems, I believe, is that you're just too uptight. You need to get laid once in a while."

She clicked the flashlight off, but found that there was still enough light—from the mushrooms? she couldn't tell—for her to see Mick clearly. His expression hadn't changed, though he'd taken the mushroom away from his lips. "Don't start, Mick, for God's sake not now."

"Yes, that's definitely it, Penny," he said, continuing as if he couldn't even hear her. "A little nookie, a little horizontal bop, bit of the old in and out. Straighten you right out. Right out."

Penny had been annoyed but now she started to feel genuine fear. This wasn't Mick—wasn't talking like Mick, didn't look like Mick. The body was still Mick's but he was holding himself differently, somehow more composed, less gangly and awkward, than she was accustomed to.

"So whaddya say?" he went on. "Give a little up to old Mick, why don't you?" Saying this, he dropped the mushroom fragments and lunged at her. She tried to back away but the wall was right behind her and she was still down on her knees, so all she succeeded in doing was slamming her own head into the hard rock. Bright flashes of light blinded her momentarily—long enough for Mick to grope, seemingly everywhere, hands pawing at her breasts, her cheeks, her crotch. He clamped his lips over hers and she breathed in mushroom-fouled breath.

Trying to get her footing, she writhed, twisting her head away from his, and hit him on the back with both hands. She couldn't get any leverage, any momentum for her punches, and he kept up his assault. His hand rubbed her groin through her jeans, rough and fast, in time with his own rapid breathing.

But Penny had survived basic training and hand-to-hand combat training and a fucking war, for Christ's sake, and she wasn't going to let some 'shroom-addled adolescent asswipe have his way with her in his idea of a tunnel of love. She gained her balance, brought her arms together inside his grasp, and threw then up and out, breaking his grip. Then she shot to her feet and aimed a snap-kick at his groin, connecting with a satisfying impact. The breath blew out of him. He doubled over in pain. She pressed the advantage, locking her fists together and swinging, baseball-style, as his head drooped toward her. Her balled fists rammed into his nose, with more force than she had expected, and his head snapped backward.

When he bounced off the other wall, it was much harder than she had hit. Blood and spit flew from his suddenly slack mouth and he dropped to the cave floor.

Oh God, Penny thought, scrambling for the flashlight she'd dropped when Mick had first attacked her. Oh God, oh God. She found the light and clicked it on. A dark pool was already spreading from beneath Mick's head. "Mick?" she asked hesitantly. But he was still and he wasn't breathing and when she pressed her hands against his neck and his wrist and his chest, she could find no heartbeat. She felt his head and the tip of her finger slipped into a deep indentation, which gave beneath the pressure like an overripe cantaloupe. Her hands came away sticky with his blood.

She fought back panic. He'd been attacking her, ready to rape her. But she hadn't meant to kill him. That was not part of her plan at all. She just wanted him off her, away from her. Not dead.

She even asked herself if she was lying, if she had been trying to kill him. The answer remained no. He was dead, but it was an accident, not a purposeful act.

He was dead, though. No changing that.

She had to get out of there.

Before she went—and if she'd ever had to do anything more difficult in her life she couldn't remember it—she patted down his pants pockets and found his keys. She'd need the van.

Penny took a last look at Mick—just in case, she thought, though if he got up now she'd be even more terrified than she was already—and turned to go, the powerful flashlight's beam sweeping across the far wall as she did.

And illuminated there, as clearly as it had been earlier, was the graffiti of those who had been here before. She took a moment to scan the wall as it led farther and farther back into the cave, and she saw that the writing extended as far as the light's beam could shine.

She couldn't take the time to study it now, though. With any luck at all, she would never come back here and never look at it again. She hurried back through the cave toward the entrance. When she got to the place she and Mick had spent the night, she snatched up her own backpack. As she picked it up, she remembered the cell phone inside, the way to contact Dieter and Larry, and they had to be told what had happened, they needed to be warned to get off the bombing range and to some safe ground where she could find them. She was frantic now, hands shaking as she dug through her pack. Finally she found the phone, in an inside pocket. It slipped through her fingers twice as she tried to extract it, but then she finally had it. She shouldered the backpack as she rounded the corner, heading for the light. As the cave's ceiling lowered she dropped to her hands and knees, crawling through the mouth and into the blistering heat of the day.

A quick glance around assured her that the soldiers had not found this place yet, though certainly they would have found the campsite last night. They couldn't be too far from here—in the dark and their haste, she and Mick hadn't done a very good job of concealing their tracks. It didn't matter now—if she could just stay ahead of them long enough to get out, she'd be okay. All she wanted was out.

As she hiked, she scrolled through the speed dial menu and punched the button for Dieter. His phone rang twice, and then a male voice answered it.

"Hello?"

But the voice wasn't Dieter's, didn't bear the slightest resemblance to his rather high-pitched German accent. She hit the END button immediately and scrolled again. This time, she saw Mick's number, and a flash of guilt struck her. She bit it back and scrolled down to where Larry's name was and pushed the CALL button again. And again, two rings, followed by the same male voice. "Who is this?"

She hung up and reached around to stuff the phone back into her backpack.

She had thought she was in trouble before, but now she knew that her worst fears were true, and then some.

Lucy sat in the stolen car looking at the house where Kerry Williams lived, according to the address list Ray Dixon's wife had given her. It was on Lotus Lane, in what passed for the wealthier neighborhood of El Centro, a street of big stucco houses with red tile roofs and fenced back yards. Through many of the fences she'd glimpsed pools.

She was pretty sure that Kerry Williams was the guy with the curly silver hair, the one who had seemed like the leader of the group that had kidnapped her. She was also sure there was no one at home. She'd been sitting here for twenty minutes and there hadn't been so much as a flicker of movement in any of the windows. At one point she had walked up to the door and peered in through the full-length window beside it, and inside there was a wrought-iron table with a metal surface piled high with several days' worth of newspapers, as if someone brought the paper in for him each day. Today's paper still sat in the yard where it had landed when the paper carrier tossed it. She remembered no wedding band on his finger, or pale line on his darkly tanned skin, so she didn't think he was married. She didn't know what a single man would need with a house this size, though. She guessed he just had the money to spend, so why not?

Lucy suspected that she was extremely conspicuous, sitting in a stolen Altima outside an empty house on a relatively quiet street. The occasional vehicle passed her—a gardener's pick-up truck, laden with workers and equipment, long-handled rakes turning idly in tubes as it rumbled past; a brown UPS truck, its doors open, driver clad in brown shorts and a short-sleeved shirt and visibly sweating anyway; a Hispanic woman, a maid, Lucy guessed, driving a Mercedes with two blond preschoolers in their safety seats in back. Sooner or later, if she stayed here, she was going to see a police car show up behind her. And she didn't want that to happen until after she'd done what she needed to do.

She ate a few of her precious Cheez-its and chased them with some water. Her supplies were getting low, and at some point she'd have to replenish. She had no cash, though; her purse with her wallet and ATM card and checkbook had been left back at the cabin. So she'd have to steal again, or she'd have to go home. Going home would almost certainly entail turning herself in.

There would come a time for that, she knew. There would be an aftermath to all this, some kind of fallout. She didn't want to think that far in advance. She didn't want to think beyond the moment when she found the men who had taken her. She was already pressing her luck, sitting here outside Kerry Williams's place, and it was obvious that he wasn't home yet. She cranked the engine and drove away, headed for the next place on her list.

Hal Shipp was uncomfortable this close to the Slab. Once, he thought he heard the voices again, whispering their evil thoughts, but it turned out to be simply the susurrus of the wind whistling through creosote. Another time, what he believed was a litany of horrors turned out to be the skritch skritch of a yucca leaf, the point of which inscribed a semi-circle in the sand as the breeze blew it and then ceased, blew and ceased.

He missed Virginia, he really did. They'd probably been apart fewer than a dozen nights since they'd married, and not being with her was the hardest part of his self-imposed exile from the Slab. Last night, of course, he hadn't even remembered her, and he thought that the loss of memory was probably a blessing if he had to spend more time away from her. He was just so accustomed to her being there—especially in these last years, since he'd retired, knowing that he could always, with just a few steps, feel the softness of her skin or smell her hair or taste her lips.

Now, though, she'd been taken over by something, some force outside of herself. That was what Hal believed, anyway, that some malevolent presence had taken over everyone on the Slab, except himself. And he'd been spared only because he had been gifted with the magic, he figured. Somehow Sheriff Butler brought the magic to the surface again, which was both a blessing and a curse.

Blessing because it gave him strength, and Hal, who had once been strong, was strong no more. He was frail and weak and he knew it, and that was part of what scared him. He relied on Virginia, but if she was no longer in control of her own actions she could turn on him. She could easily knock him down, strangle him, stab him, and there would be nothing he could do to prevent it. Curse, because, if he couldn't be with her he didn't want to remember when he had been. He had always known they both would die some day; he wanted to go first, because he knew that she could get along without him better than he without her.

Memory could be brutal, a dagger to the heart. He remembered the way Timmy's hand had felt in his on the first day of school, when they had walked into his new classroom and the boy's trepidation had mingled with excitement, causing his hand to flutter like a small bird's wings. But Tim was gone now. He remembered the boys he'd gone to college with, and the men he'd served with overseas. They were dead or otherwise absent from his life. He remembered the friends he and Virginia had made in Albuquerque, and then on the Slab. Gone now, gone from his life. As long as whatever it was had control of the people on the Slab, he would not be setting foot there again, would not be seeing those people. Each one of them, each face, each voice, each individual style of laughter, left a hole in him as though a piece had been carved out with a kitchen knife.

He didn't realize that he'd started to cry, arms wrapped around himself like a lost little boy, until the sound of Ken Butler's car interrupted the flow of his thoughts.

Once they were headed west on the 10, Kerry fished a cell phone out of one of his pockets and dialed without telling the others who he was calling, or why. Vic thought that Kerry seemed to be retreating into himself, keeping his own counsel. Almost as if he didn't trust the others.

That's good, Kerry, Vic thought. Don't trust me. I'll turn on you in a second.

Every mile they covered was a mile closer to home, a mile closer to the time he'd say goodbye forever to Kerry and the other guys. It was a mile closer to Cathy, and the new, normal life Vic craved. It meant going back to work, ten at night to six the next morning pushing brooms and waxing floors for a janitorial service, when there was work at all, for just enough money to scrape by rent-free on the Slab.

Still, he'd take it. It was hard and it was wearying, but it was a life. Kerry Williams only offered death. No bargain there.

"Hi, Margie?" he heard Kerry say. That was a surprise—Margie was Cam Hensley's wife. Widow, now, he supposed. "Is Cam there?"

Kerry was quiet a moment, listening. He turned his head slowly so his passengers could see the wide smile on his face, the smile that contradicted the sincere tone with which he spoke. "You're kidding! No!" He paused a moment, shaking his head and screwing his face into an exaggerated frown. "No, we had a big fight, the very first night out. Cam got mad and said he was going home. He took his car and left us stranded out there. We haven't seen him since. You haven't heard from him at all?"

Vic had to appreciate Kerry's cruel brilliance. Cam and his car were both missing in the desert. By tying them together—and distancing Cam from the rest of them—Kerry would deflect suspicion. Sure, their fingerprints would be found in the Navigator, but they'd driven out to their hunting area in it—an area that they'd already picked out, years ago, in case they were ever asked, and which was nowhere near the cabin they'd burned or the bodies they'd buried. The bullet in Cam's brain had come from Kerry's precious Desert Eagle, so he'd have to ditch the gun somewhere, but he could do that and get another one down the line.

"No, I really—I don't know what to say, Margie. We've—well, you know, we've been out in the boonies, not in cell phone range or anything. When he never showed up again, we...we just...you know, assumed. That he was home. Yeah."

Vic could hear Margie' voice now, growing louder on the other end of the connection. She was probably crying, probably beginning to panic, now. And still, Kerry kept his cool. Vic was impressed in spite of himself.

"No, no, totally. I understand. Listen, Marg. We'll look for him, okay. I mean, we won't even come home. We'll just start looking for him, anyplace we can think of. In the meantime, I hate to say it, but maybe you should call the police, okay? Okay? Yeah. What?"

He was quiet again, listening to another extended monologue. This time, his expression of concern seemed real.

"I don't know, Margie. I don't know what he's gotten mixed up in. Maybe it's nothing. I know how it sounds, but who knows? You just keep yourself safe. And thanks for the heads up. As soon as I know anything at all, I'll let you know, okay? Okay. Bye, Margie."

He closed the phone, and after a second's pause, he said, "Well, shit."

"What is it, Kerry?" Terrance asked. Terrance was in the front passenger seat, while Rock and Vic were squeezed into the extended cab's cramped rear seat.

"The bitch showed up at Ray's house," Kerry replied.

"Who? Margie?"

"No, dumbfuck," Kerry said. "The Dove. The Mexican girl. Dixon's wife said she smashed her way in, waving a gun around. Made her write out a list of all our addresses."

"Which of course Ray would have," Rock put in. "Fucker's so anal about everything."

"Past tense," Kerry said. "If she's still alive—and ahead of us, even—then Ray's dead."

"Shit," Vic said. This trip had turned into the biggest pile of dogshit he could imagine, and apparently it was still getting worse.

"So what's that mean?" Terrance asked. "What do we do? We can't go look for Cam, we know what happened to him."

"Yeah, and now there's someone to blame it on," Kerry said. "An angle we can use. Maybe Cam was having an affair with this chick, using our Dove Hunt to hide it from his wife. That's why he faked getting pissed off at us and left—so he could go meet up with her. Except she turned out to be loony tunes. She offed him, then decided to go after the rest of us."

"Hey, I like that," Rock said. "That's good."

"You think she's really coming after us all?" Vic asked.

"I don't see why she'd want the list if she wasn't."

"But Vic and I, we don't even have addresses," Rock said. "No street numbers on the Slab."

"That's right," Kerry agreed. "That's why we'll make our stand at your place. She's got to come searching for us. We sit tight and wait for her. Then we kill her, in self-defense, and we put the Cam story together for the cops."

"Not at my place," Vic protested. "We're not endangering Cathy that way."

"Rock's place is better anyway," Kerry said. "It's far enough away from the neighbors to limit any collateral damage. Your place, Vic, anyone shot the bitch from there the bullet'd probably kill two or three other people in the bargain."

Kerry was right, Vic knew. Rock lived alone, and his trailer was both more isolated and more defensible. And he had to hand it to the bastard—he seemed to have a knack for turning shit into gold. If they could really kill the Dove, after all this, they might have a good chance of being able to pin Cam's murder on her. Two birds, and all that.

There was a kind of genius to it, he thought. Sick, but genius just the same.

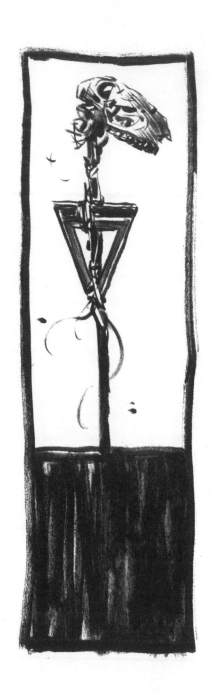

chapter 23

The ride out was much smoother than the one in had been. Mick wasn't used to driving on dirt roads and jeep tracks, and the novice's instinct was to slow down on washboard roads, which only served to maximize the jolt of every little bump. But Penny had driven huge trucks through Kuwaiti deserts, and knew that the way to get over the washboard with a minimum of aggravation was to speed up to the fastest safe speed, which served to even out the road.

Comfort wasn't her priority anyway. She was pushing it as fast as she dared, given the regularity with which the old jeep track dropped away in the middle, or rose up, or had big rocks laying across the path, or broke into a sandy wash that made the wheels slip and shimmy. Too fast could be dangerous, but too slow was, well, too slow. She had killed somebody, and that was something you didn't mess around with.

She had a hard time even imagining how it had come to that. Certainly when she had felt the oddly familiar, tingling taste in her mouth the other day, she had not anticipated that it would somehow lead to her committing manslaughter, even in self-defense. She remembered the date she'd first experienced it, of course. March fourteenth, in the year of the Gulf War 1991. The ground war that would last for a hundred days had just begun. Penny, assigned as a truck driver to the King Khalid Military City in Saudi Arabia, which everyone just called KKMC, was behind the wheel of a five-ton truck heading for Iraqi territory via the Euphrates River. "Convoy" was just a glorified word for the procession: there were three trucks on the road, two five tonners and a refrigerated truck. The refrigerator was to bring back American bodies. The group was assigned to bury Iraqi corpses, but in case anything had been captured that needed to be seen back in Saudi, or any POWs needed to be brought back, the cargo capacity of the big trucks would come into play.

Sand and dust got everywhere, in her teeth and hair, eyes and underpants—a problem throughout her Gulf War experience but even more so when they were driving long distance. Condoms were used less for birth control or disease prevention than for stretching over the muzzle of your M-16 to keep the grit out. Penny's company on this drive was Sergeant Aaron Tippetts of Athens, Georgia. He outranked her, he'd been in the Army longer than she had, and he hated the very idea of women in the military, much less anywhere near the front lines. So the trip wasn't her favorite duty.

When she first started to feel the odd metallic taste on her tongue, she thought maybe it was just that she'd opened her mouth to breathe and got dust on it. Then it occurred to her that maybe it was one of the chemical agents the Iraqis were expected to use against the Coalition forces. They'd already been given Cipro and pyridiostigmine bromide pills and some sort of vaccine they were warned not to talk about with anybody—none of which did much to put a person's mind to rest, she thought. But she mentioned it to Tippetts, who shrugged it off; he hadn't felt or tasted anything, he said. Her MOPP suit remained tucked away for later use, if necessary.

As they rolled through Kuwait toward Iraq, Tippetts, sitting in the passenger seat and "navigating," spotted what he was sure was a shorter route than the one they'd been told to take. Penny was wary of shortcuts, but Tippetts had insisted that it would save them a day of driving time. Four hours later, they reached the reason it wasn't the officially prescribed route—retreating Iraqi soldiers had left behind a gift in the form of a vast field of land mines. The field had been marked by Allied forces, but with the rush of the ground war on, it hadn't been cleared. The road was the road, though—to go around the minefield and cross-country could result in the heavy trucks getting caught in the sand, and backtracking to the suggested route would cost most of another day. Penny deferred to Tippetts, who gave the order to drive through.

That was when it clicked in. She felt a rushing of her blood, as if her veins were suddenly full to overloading, and a sharpening of her senses. It seemed that she could see every grain of sand, every inch of ground, in intricate detail. Somehow it all felt natural to her, not like something she should be concerned about, or even wonder about. Imagination had never been her strong point—even as a child, while Penny had been fine with board games or structured play, she'd never really enjoyed games of pure pretend, house or astronauts or princesses and dragons, because she couldn't set aside what she knew of the real world and immerse herself in the fantasy. Her pragmatic streak was a mile wide. So when things changed for her—when the magic happened—part of the magic, she decided, was that it was able to convince her without argument or second-guessing that it was genuine and not something to be afraid of, not a manifestation of mental illness or a drug-induced hallucination.

To top it all off, she could "see," in her mind's eye, glowing red spots on the ground ahead of her. Each of those spots, she believed, was a buried mine. She put the big truck into its lowest gear and crawled across the desert floor. There was enough room to negotiate between the mines if she was cautious and precise. Her hands gripped the wheel hard and turned it without letting go, hand over hand as she inched to the right to avoid one of the red spots and then corrected back to the left immediately. The other two trucks followed in her tracks, and Tippetts stared at her in amazement as she picked out her course.

"What the hell are you doing?" he demanded after about fifteen minutes of torturous progress.

"Avoiding the mines," Penny answered matter-of-factly, as if anyone should be able to see the luminous markers that she did. Sweat poured off her body, soaking the truck's bench seat.

"I can tell," Tippetts said. "What I want to know is how."

"Hard to explain," Penny said. "But I kind of have to concentrate, you know? So if you'd just let me—"

"I'll take over now, soldier."

"What?"

"I said, I'll take over." She hazarded a glance at him, and he wasn't kidding. The set of his jaw and the glare in his eyes told her that. She'd offended his male ego or military tradition or something, and he wasn't going to let her drive them all the way across this minefield.

Penny argued, but it did no good. Tippetts outranked her and he had given an order. Rather than risk being brought up on charges, Penny surrendered the wheel. Tippets climbed out of his seat and walked around, while she slid over to the passenger side. He hauled himself up behind the wheel, released the brake, and started forward.

"On the left," Penny warned. "Avoid the left."

"I've got it under control," he growled at her.

Fine, she thought. He had it under control. Maybe he really did—maybe they both shared the same gift, and he really could see the mines under the buff-colored earth. After all, if she could, what was to keep the same thing from happening to him? She had never felt the kind of power running through her body that she did today. What if it was the place, imbuing her with its magic? Then Tippetts would be just as likely to feel it as she did. She sat back in the seat and wiped her dripping head on a bandanna.

It was then, when she closed her eyes and put the cloth over them, that he hit the mine.

Her first indication that something had happened was a soft *whump* sound, as if a big hammer had struck thick sand. Then a bright flash, like the sun itself exploding in her eyes, and she felt herself flying into the air. She was blinded by this point, but she felt the air rushing all around her body, felt the heat of the blast wash over her like an ocean's wave.

She didn't feel the impact. She hit the ground a hundred feet from the truck—or the flaming, twisted wreckage that had once been the truck. She must have hit hard, and she should have been hurt—broken ribs, fractured skull, concussion. By all rights, the explosion should at least have left her bleeding from the eyes and ears. But no. She had a gash in her upper chest, which she later figured must have been from windshield glass cutting her as she flew away from the truck. She was sore, and bruised in several places, but otherwise uninjured. The cut left a scar that she kept to this day.

Sergeant Tippetts was blown into such small pieces there was hardly enough to scrape up and put in the reefer truck. Their first bit of human cargo.

That truck and the other five-ton turned around and returned to the route that had been mapped out for them, arriving at the front a full day behind schedule. The metallic taste in Penny's mouth and the strange sensation of power went away. She had almost forgotten about it, until the day it came back. The day that she sat down at a table in a coffee shop, which she'd entered hoping to wash away the odd, but somehow familiar taste. Someone had left a newspaper at the table, open to the classifieds, and an ad for office help at the Wilderness Peace Initiative had caught her eye. She had been thinking a lot about the connection between environmental degradation and war, and this ad seemed to hit home. She applied that day. By the end of the week she had an offer. And the magic went away again.

Only twice, she thought. Not so often that it couldn't be coincidence. But both times she'd felt this way, major events happened that had shaped her life. Saved her life.

Until today, when she had taken a life. That is not how it's supposed to work, she thought. Who do I complain to?

Ken knew he should be exhausted, but somehow the magic still thrummed inside him, keeping him fresh and alert. He sat behind his desk, filling out some of the paperwork that El Centro would need about his overnight missing persons hunt. Hal had taken a visitor's chair by the window and entertained himself flipping through a news magazine—if cover-to-cover information about the thousands lost in the World Trade Center attacks could pass for entertainment.

Ken recognized the sound of the Bronco's engine from blocks away, even before he could see his beloved vehicle. Leaving the paperwork behind for the moment, he went to the door and watched Billy Cobb drive up to one of the slanted parking spaces in front of the storefront office. Billy shot him a wide, innocent grin as he stepped down from the Bronco. Ken held the door open for him, and Billy walked inside, with a glance at Hal.

"Hey, Mr. Shipp," he said. "What's up, Boss?"

"Hello, Billy," Hal replied.

Ken didn't bother with the pleasantries. "Where the hell have you been, Billy? I haven't heard from you in eighteen hours, probably."

Billy's face registered surprise. "Doing my job, Lieutenant Butler. Looking for that missing girl—except last night, we got a notice that she had contacted her family and she's fine. Last night I caught Jake Bell driving drunk, took him home and gave him a warning. A couple of kids from over in Holtville were parking over on the abandoned streets, trying to find enough privacy to do the deed, but I put the fear of God in 'em. Stuff like that, you know?"

"Out of radio contact?"

"I've been in radio contact with El Centro. Haven't heard anything from you, though. Maybe your radio's busted."

Kid had a point there. The only times he'd talked to El Centro in the past day or so had been from the office and in the Crown Vic. His portable Motorola had been silent the whole night, and he'd been so involved in trying to mentally track Hal that he hadn't really thought about it. Since finding Hal, his mind had been racing and he hadn't given any thought or effort to trying to locate Billy.

"Yeah, maybe it is," he admitted.

"I'm just glad to see you're okay, Lieutenant," Billy said. "I kind of had a busy night, taking care of everything by myself."

"I'm fine."

"It okay if I go home and get some sleep, then?"

"Couple hours," Ken told him. "Then I want you out at the Slab. There's something going on up there, I think. And Carter Haynes is going to be back up there today, with his bodyguard. It's all too touchy to not have one of us around most of the time." Plus he was worried about what Hal had said—he had every reason to believe that when the old man said he could hear trouble brewing on the Slab, he was correct.

"What about you?"

"I'll be there later on, too," Ken said. "I've got some other stuff to take care of first, but I'll be up by this afternoon."

"Okay, then," Billy said. "I'll get two hours of shut-eye and then get over there."

"And take the Crown Vic," Ken instructed. "Leave my Bronco here."

Billy nodded and touched the brim of his Smokey hat. "Good to see you, Mr. Shipp."

"You too, son," Hal said. Billy left, pulling the door closed behind him with a bang. Ken shook his head in bemusement. He guessed Billy would never change. His idea of working all night had probably meant that he hadn't bothered to punch out before going off duty at six, because Ken hadn't been here to make him.

"There's something not right about that boy," Hal announced.

"You aren't kidding about that," Ken agreed.

He hadn't even made it back to his desk when he heard the sound of another vehicle approaching. He glanced out the window and saw a van that looked somehow familiar, a mud-red Dodge Ram 250, pulling into the space next to the Bronco, from which Billy had just taken the Crown Vic. Ken tried to remember vehicles—not too many strange ones really passed through here, at least compared to what a city cop would face, and he knew he'd seen this one before.

A tall brunette, maybe pretty but you couldn't tell, her face all twisted by emotion, climbed down from behind the wheel. She'd been crying, and while she'd brought her tears under control, her face still carried a frantic aspect. This isn't going to be good, he thought. Not good at all. Once again, he held the door open, and she brushed past him as if looking for whoever was in charge. Inside, she stopped in the middle of the room, swiveling to look at Hal and back at Ken.

"Something I can do for you, ma'am?"

She blinked a couple of times and stared at him with eyes that looked like they'd seen more than they wanted to. He'd seen eyes like that before, haunted by unexpected horrors. If that was indeed the case, no amount of blinking would clear them.

"Yes. Yes, I…" She stopped as if the right words just wouldn't come to her. "Yes," she said again. "I…I've killed someone."

Yeah, that would do it, he thought. "Why don't you come over here, ma'am, and have a seat." He touched the bare skin on her forearm, to direct her to the guest chair nearest his desk, and he felt the charge again, just like when he touched Hal. He almost yanked his hand away in surprise.

In the same instant, the expression on the woman's face changed from shock and remorse to one of almost pure bliss. "Oh," she said. "Oh, wow." She reached out to him, linked her fingers with his. Ken allowed it to happen, as hungry for the rush as she seemed to be. "Oh, man," she said. "We have got to have sex sometime."

Ken let go again and felt his face going crimson. "Now, ma'am, you could be in a bit of a situation here, and talk like that isn't going to help anything."

"I know, but…just imagine what it would be like."

"You could have a point," Ken said. "But let's take care of this first, why don't we?" He noticed Hal observing them with some interest.

"She's one of us too, isn't she?" Hal asked.

Ken nodded. "Yep," he said. "Ma'am, that's Hal Shipp. I'm Ken Butler. We're thinking that the three of us have something in common—something most folks don't share, or even know about."

The woman took the seat Ken had indicated, in front of his desk. He sat down in his regular chair and watched her. She looked at Hal, then back at Ken, understanding seeming to be reflected in her eyes. "Yes," she said. "Magic days, right?"

"That's right, that's what I call them. Hal too, I guess. Now, why don't you tell me what happened."

Lupe Alvarez hung up the phone quietly, as if to make any excessive noise with the receiver would somehow magnify the bad news. Raul watched her from his chair across the room, gazing out over the tops of his glasses. He could tell by her posture, slightly hunched and withdrawn, that the phone call hadn't been a good one.

"Lucia?" he asked.

She shook her head. "Henry Rios."

"You told him to stop looking for her, right? That she called last night and she's fine?"

"I told him. But he says he needs to talk to her anyway, and the sooner the better. He wanted to know if she has been home, or if I know where she is."

"What did you tell him?" Raul asked.

"You were sitting right there, weren't you? I said she hasn't called since last night, and we haven't seen her. But he's coming over anyway."

"But she's not here. What good will that do?"

"Not to talk to her, not right now. He wants to talk to the boys."

Raul felt his stomach churn. "About what?" He tried to keep his voice firm, his lip from quaking.

"He wouldn't say."

"Did you tell him they were here?"

"He said he—"

"Did you tell him they were here!" He came out of his chair at her. She shrank away from him, and he backed off, suddenly ashamed of himself. For that, for scaring Lupe, and for so much more.

"Hey, hey," Lupe's father said from his chair. He waved an old, liver-spotted hand at them "Not so much noise, eh?"

"Yes," Lupe admitted, looking at the floor.

"They won't be," he said "Not by the time he gets here. They'll be out of the county."

"But Raul—"

"We don't know where they are. Do you understand?"

A single tear traced her cheek, and she nodded, lips clamped together tight as if to prevent a single word from escaping. Raul felt terrible. But it had to be done. The boys needed to get out of the county fast, someplace they couldn't be found for a while. Two weeks ago, he'd have sent them to Mexico, but not now, not since September eleventh. The borders were being watched closely now. No, they'd have to go someplace local, but out of Henry Rios's territory. Someplace they could hide out.

He would take his own chances.

The first woman Kerry Williams had killed had almost turned him off to the joy of it altogether.

She barely qualified as a woman. She was seventeen, he recalled, and he was eighteen. She was a blonde of Norwegian descent. It was a Michigan springtime, the frozen ground had thawed and new green leaves were beginning to sprout on tree branches, and they'd walked home from school together, flirting, stopping in a culvert beneath the roadway for a spirited make-out session. She'd let him slip a hand up under her sweater, outside her bra, and his other hand had, almost by its own accord, gone to her neck, caressing the tender flesh there. When he put a little pressure on her throat, closing his hand on her, she moaned with pleasure and pressed her breast against his other hand. He squeezed it, then took that hand away from her breast and added it to the one at her throat.

Her eyes had opened wide, then, and the pleasure noises stopped, and she started to say something but by that time he was really putting on the pressure, and all she could make were inarticulate choking sounds. She kicked and hit and bucked against him but couldn't break his grip, strengthened as it was by weight training and school athletics. Almost sooner than he expected, she was still, and she stank, and his heart was pounding as he realized what he'd done. What if people had seen them leaving school together? What if they found his fingerprints on her body? The act of murder had been an interesting sensation, almost fun—borderline erotic, in fact, but not worth spending the rest of his life in jail for.

Trying hard to keep his cool, he'd gone home for a shovel. Fifty yards from the culvert was the tree line of the local woods. He found a spot where he was screened by trees from the road and dug a shallow grave in the hard earth. During a long break in the sparse traffic, he hauled her body out of the culvert and carried her to the grave. He tossed dirt over her and left her there. Because their friendship was well known, he was later questioned by the cops, but he denied having seen her after school that day, and the questions eventually stopped. By spring, when her body was finally found, there wasn't enough left of it to give the cops any incriminating evidence at all.

It wasn't until El Salvador, seven years later, that Kerry realized what had been lacking. Blondes had never held much attraction for him. But when he saw a raven-haired beauty on her knees, begging for her life, her dark eyes imploring him not to pull the trigger of the pistol he had jammed against her temple, full lips pleading in Spanish…that was heaven. That was when he really knew what it was all about—life, death, the whole enchilada, as it were. It was about power: getting it, keeping it, using it. Love, sex, wealth, the rest of the things for which the unenlightened strove, were only outward indicators of the real goal. Only power, applied in the right way, with the proper erotic/fetishistic attributes, was ultimately fulfilling.

Kerry remembered every woman he'd ever killed, though the number was at thirty-one now. They were each, in their own way, special to him, even sacred. The ones who had died from bullets, from strangulation, from knives, from being beaten to death, from asphyxiation…there were almost as many ways to die as there were people to kill, and each woman's face stayed locked in his memory with her means of death, kept there like precious mementos.

He realized he'd driven the last stretch of road to the Slab almost on autopilot, his attention focused on the women he'd known. The other guys were quiet, as they often were at this stage of a Dove Hunt. But this one, he knew, was different. They'd never come home unsuccessful before. Not only had they failed miserably, but some of their friends were dead and the bitch was out there somewhere, hunting them. He almost laughed at the injustice of it. Hunting them!

Not far from Rocknowski's trailer, which perched on the West-facing edge of the Slab like a vulture on a cliff, there was a deep gully not quite big enough, Kerry supposed, to be called a canyon. The dirt tracks that spiderwebbed around the Slab led into it. At Rock's suggestion, he stopped the stolen truck there and nestled it up against one of the gully's walls. Since they'd gone out in Cam's Navigator, they had left their own vehicles at his farm, and since they were supposed to be out looking for him no one wanted to face Cam's wife yet. They all piled out, weapons and packs in their hands, glad to have some space to move around again. From here, it was just a short scramble up the dirt face to Rock's place. Kerry shouldered his M-4. The Desert Eagle had gone into the Salton Sea, up near Bombay Beach. Damn, he'd miss that gun. They'd stopped at a gun store in Palm Desert on the way down, since Kerry was convinced that they'd need more ammo, before this was all over and done with, than they had carried with them, and he'd considered buying a new handgun. But he thought it might be wiser not to have one on him for a while.

Just in case they had to answer any awkward questions.

And speaking of law enforcement, as they dragged their weary asses up the last rise to the Slab, Kerry saw Deputy Cobb watching them with interest. He couldn't lower the M-4 into firing position without drawing attention, but he figured out how he'd make his move if it came to it—tossing the backpack he carried in his left hand toward the deputy to distract him, then continuing the motion, bringing his left up to grip the underside of the M-4, drawing it down and into position as he squeezed the trigger with his right. Cobb would have to be fast to stop him—faster than he believed the young Deputy was.

"Hey, guys," Cobb said. He didn't act like he was here to arrest them, or had any suspicions whatsoever. "Back from the big hunt?"

Everyone pretty much knew about their annual hunts—though no one except those who took part knew their real nature—and it didn't seem to bother most people that they took place a week or two out of dove season, since they never really came home with much in the way of dead birds. Rock stepped up onto the concrete slab. "Yeah," he said. "We're just stoppin' off at my place for a couple of final beers to commemorate."

"Get any?" Cobb asked.

Rock shrugged. "Just couldn't seem to find 'em this year," he said. "What about you, what are you doin' up here?"

Cobb's turn to shrug. "That crazy old Carrie Provost found a skull in the fire pit. Turns out it's human and killed with a bullet, so Ken Butler's been on a tear ever since, trying to find out whose it was and how it came to be up here. He's off with Hal Shipp now, doing God knows what, so I'm supposed to be here. In case a clue comes around and bites me on the ass, I guess."

"Human skull, huh?" Kerry repeated. "Guess that is kind of a mystery."

"Yeah. You see Sherlock Holmes, you send him my way, okay?"

"You got it, Billy," Rock said.

Cobb wandered off then, stepping on his own shadow, foreshortened by the overhead sun, maybe in search of that wayward clue. In the distance, the Slab's concrete wavered from heat distortion. Kerry turned away from the hapless Deputy and led the way toward Rock's trailer, accompanied by the other three, one of whom most likely carried the gun that had killed the person whose skull had been found. And Kerry had an idea who had planted the skull in the fire pit.

Rock's trailer was fifteen years old, powered by solar panels on its roof, and with a kind of patio built from found two-by-fours and sheets of plywood in front of it. He'd done a half assed job of painting an American flag on it in the days immediately after September eleventh. The number of stripes was right, Kerry noticed, but the fifty stars had turned into twenty-some blobs.

Inside—this was Rock's place, after all—the walls and cabinets were covered with cheesecake photos, nudie mag centerfolds, and pages ripped from hardcore porn magazines. At least they were carefully applied. Rock was surprisingly tidy for a bachelor and pervert, Kerry thought. The floors were picked up, the surfaces of the galley and the little washbasin were clean, as was his chemical toilet. Rock was a scrapper—when the military did bombing practice in the mountains, Rock jumped on his ATV and raced out into the range, looking for scrap metal—bomb parts, or the remnants of whatever had been targeted—and hauled it down to a junk dealer in Calipatria to sell. Some days he could make as much as six hundred bucks, but others— most days, in fact, he made nothing.

As soon as they were inside, Rock switched on a battery-operated radio, which somehow, even here in the middle of nowhere, pulled in a heavy metal station from Los Angeles. As soon as he had it on, Kerry went behind him and turned it down. Rock shot him a glare but didn't protest.

"Fucking hot in here," Terrance complained.

"Yeah, well, I forgot to pay the air conditioning bill," Rock replied. "Live with it."

"You all heard what Deputy Dawg said out there, right?" Kerry asked.

"About the skull, you mean?" Terrance said.

"Yes, about the skull." He figured Terrance would get it, since Terrance was the one who found the open grave missing a skull, outside the cabin. Vic and Rock, he wasn't so sure of.

"You think it's one of ours?" Rock asked.

"Do I think it's one of ours?" Kerry echoed, sarcasm dripping in his tone. "Of course it is. And I know how it got here. So would you, if you thought about it for ten seconds."

Again, Terrance came through. "Hal Shipp?"

"Got to be," Kerry said. "We know a grave was dug up and a skull taken. We know a skull turned up here while we were all out on the Hunt. Who else could have planted it?"

"Jeez," Vic said. Kerry didn't think he'd heard Vic's voice in hours. "Old Hal finally grew him some."

Kerry spun on him. "Grew some? That's what you think it is? Turned traitor on his friends, and you think it means he's got balls?"

Vic just shrugged, which infuriated Kerry all the more. "Sometimes I wonder about you, Bradford," he said. "I hope you're not thinking about growing some. Wouldn't really fit you."

"What are we gonna do about Hal?" Rock asked. He opened an icebox powered by his solar panels and took out some cans of Bud.

"We'll wait until it's dark," Kerry said. "Then we'll kill the fucker."

Sitting in the shade of a creosote bush up on the hill overlooking the Slab, Lucy lined up the sights of her stolen gun on the four men. She wasn't good enough to hit them from here, she knew. And anyway, they were talking to a cop. As soon as the cop left they headed inside a trailer, and a corner of another trailer blocked her view of that trailer's door from here.

What she needed was to get closer. The trailer they'd disappeared into was at the far edge of the Slab from her, the side facing the Salton Sea, and she was on the inland side, on the highest hill around in hopes of spotting them when they showed up. That part, at least, had worked. Now she just had the hard part ahead—killing four men, all of whom were probably better with guns than she was.

She had checked all the addresses on her list—Cam Hensley, who she didn't see here and hoped had died from her attack with the fork, Terrance Berkley, Kerry Williams. All empty. But two names remained, Vic Bradford and R. J. Rocknowski. No street addresses were listed for them, just "the Slab." Lucy knew what that meant, of course, anyone who lived near the shores of the Salton did. And her brothers had a friend, Eddie Trujillo, who lived on the Slab—they'd taken her down to his place a couple of times, a crappy mobile home with no roof, only sheets of corrugated metal lashed on top to keep the very occasional rain out. So she knew her way there. But she didn't know how to find her prey, short of asking people, and she figured that if she did that, they'd hear about it. She tried this approach instead, claiming the high ground, waiting and watching. Staying awake had been a challenge, and it was hotter than hell, but the creosote offered some shade and also provided cover in case anyone looked up this way. And it had worked.

As reluctant as she was to give up what shade the creosote offered, she needed to start working her way around the Slab—crossing it was out of the question. When it was dark, maybe they could be lured out of the trailer. It could catch on fire or something, she supposed. That might work…

Lieutenant Butler seemed reluctant at first to accompany Penny back to the Aerial Gunnery Range. But the connection they'd made when they touched—she was still tingling from it, in a kind of pseudo-orgasmic afterglow—had somehow convinced him to trust her. She wasn't even sure why she felt so adamantly about not involving the Marines. Sure, she'd been hiding from them for a couple of days, but that all changed the minute she killed Mick. Suddenly, the political action receded in importance. Recovering Mick's body, without the military catching them, did seem vital, though. She also wanted to find out what had happened to Dieter and Larry, but she believed they'd be showing up on the evening news, soon enough. Most likely in shackles.

So Butler and the older man, Hal Shipp, accompanied her back to the break in the fence, and then the three of them trespassed together. Hal, it turned out, had spent the previous night on the range himself, though he wasn't quite sure why or how he had ended up there. And Ken had spent the night looking for him. Neither man looked the worse for the experience, a fact that she attributed to the beneficial effects of the magic. They told her they'd felt the same thing, upon touching, that she felt when she touched Ken—that sense of power, like a battery getting an instant recharge, and a nearly exultant sense of well-being.

They spent a little time getting acquainted on the trip in—both men were, like her, combat veterans, both had moved here to the Imperial Valley from points east—but mostly, they passed the time in a comfortable silence, as if they were old friends who were rarely apart. The only moment of conflict occurred when she tried to explain what she and Mick and the others had been doing inside the bombing range in the first place.

Hal had taken offense. "So you don't support going to war against people who killed six thousand of your own countrymen?" he challenged.

"I don't support going to war, no," she said.

"We should just leave them alone? A rap on the knuckles?"

"I don't think they should just get away with it, but there must be some other way to punish them, don't you think? Y'know, if it is bin Laden, and we find him and kill him, how do we know that won't just make him a martyr and breed ten thousand new terrorists?"

"Maybe we have to hit them with enough firepower to make anyone who might want to become a terrorist change his mind," Hal offered. "We can't just sit back and do nothing, though. And this isn't something the FBI can fix. We need to use military force, and we need to do it soon while our resolve holds."

"Do you really think it'll do any good?" she asked him.

"I think sometimes there comes a time in world events when military force is the answer. I think that's why nations have armies. Even good nations. To stand up for those who are at risk. Unless we do something, and right away, every American is at risk from these people."

"I see your point, I guess," Penny relented. "But I don't agree. From what I've seen, war is never the best answer. It's often the easiest answer, but it's not the best."

"You believe what you want," Hal said. "You're wrong. But you just go ahead and believe it." He chuckled, and that was the end of the conversation. No raised voices, no frayed tempers, no insistence upon changing the other person's point of view. Had Mick been here he'd be red-faced and screaming by now, hoping to persuade Hal by sheer volume if nothing else. Hal's face, shaded from the cruel sun by the brim of a baseball cap left behind in Ken's office by some long-forgotten miscreant, was red, but just from the heat and exertion.

Somehow, through all this, Penny had managed to keep her own soft, wide-brimmed hat, and Ken had his Smokey hat and, thankfully, several canteens full of water. The shared magic strengthened them all, but didn't make them entirely immune to the effects of heat and sun and thirst.

At the top of the rise that led down to the cave, Ken insisted they stop while he scoured the landscape with binoculars. Penny thought she'd die in those few minutes—knowing precious shade lay below, and yet standing here in the punishing sun as he carefully combed every inch of the desert. When he was finished, he capped the lenses. "Nothing," he said. "Anybody's watching the cave, they're doing it from a satellite or a damn good hiding place."

"Let's go, then," Penny said.

"Slow, though," Ken warned. "When we get closer I want to stop again, see if there's any footprints around the outside besides yours and the boy's."

"His name's Mick, and he's no boy."

"Mick, then. Whatever. I just don't want to be surprised if they found the cave and are waiting inside." He started down the hill, and Penny, thankful to be almost to the shade, went right behind him. Hal followed her, beaming as if this were some great adventure.

True to his word, Ken slowed again when they were able to make out the disturbed dirt at the cave's mouth. Her footprints going away were clearly evident, and there were scuffled marks that could have been the two of them going in the first time. Just the night before, she realized. Eighteen hours or so, maybe. Lifetimes.

"Looks okay," Ken announced. "I got to tell you though, I don't much care for tunnels and caves and such."

"Think how I feel about it," Penny said. "At least you haven't killed anybody in there."

"No, that's true. But when you've been in law enforcement for long enough, you look at every situation as a possible ambush. Once we go inside that cave there's no back door that we know of, no escape route. Anything's laying for us in there, we'll be walking right into it."

She had the sense that there was something he was leaving unsaid. But then he pulled a mini-Mag flashlight from a pouch on his leather belt, switched it on, ducked his head and went into the cave opening. Penny clicked on her own flashlight and followed. She had told Ken and Hal about the mushrooms, the writing on the walls, the whole story. It sounded unbelievable coming out of her mouth, but she knew that when three people had shared an experience that most other people on Earth would find just as outlandish, their tendency to trust one another's perceptions was raised quite a bit. Having experienced the magic for themselves, each was more open than the average person to new experiences and the not-quite-explicable. Hell, she thought, Martians could land now and we'd just take it in stride.

Inside, the air was considerably cooler than out in the merciless desert sun. But the goosebumps that rose on Penny's flesh as they made their way through, away and down from the opening on a course that seemed as if it might lead ultimately to the Slab or the Salton, weren't just attributable to the drop in temperature. She was nervous about what they would find. Ken's ambush theory hadn't helped.

Worse, she couldn't "see" anything—not even the mushrooms she had keyed into before. The cave looked vaguely familiar, but she didn't know for sure what was around the next corner.

Or the one after that.

"We ought to be getting close," she said after a while. They had passed the spot where Mick's backpack was abandoned on the ground, and the cave walls continued to narrow, closing in like some kind of trap. Lieutenant Butler had to walk with his head bowed to keep from scraping it on the ceiling. His hat was held in his left hand, his flashlight in his right.

"I was thinking that too," the Lieutenant said. "Then I thought I must be wrong, because I haven't been here before."

"It's the connection between us," Hal observed. "Haven't you noticed that we don't even need to be touching any more? Just proximity is good enough to link us up."

Penny thought the old man was right. It wasn't like mind-reading—or what she thought mind-reading must be like. More like sharing, she believed, shared perceptions—again, like three people might experience if they had been together for a long time, and constantly, so that they looked at the world from very similar viewpoints.

This was a day for new experiences, she guessed.

Notwithstanding that, she wasn't prepared for what she saw when they finally rounded the bend and came into the stretch where she'd left Mick's body.

It wasn't there.

"He's gone," she said, surprised and not a little scared. She pointed at the base of the wall, amidst the glowing mushrooms. "He was there."

"What do you mean, gone? You think he wasn't really dead?"

"He was dead. When I checked him my finger slipped inside his skull. I think I felt brain. He was definitely dead, trust me."

"Then where is he?" Ken toed through the mushrooms and shining his flashlight's beam down. "I don't even see any blood here."

"I don't know," Penny replied. The same sense of panic that had attacked her when she first realized Mick had died threatened to return. "He was there, that's all I know."

Then she looked again at Ken's boot pushing the mushrooms around, and a ghastly realization came to her. She tried to blink it away but it wouldn't let go.

"But…but there are more mushrooms now," she said. "A lot more."

"More mushrooms?" Hal echoed.

"Yeah, like four or five times more." They had been confined to the wall before, she remembered. Now they had spread to the cave's floor, and grew thicker, closer together. In fact, their pattern of growth seemed to follow the same basic line as Mick's body, filling in the space where she'd left him. The obvious thought came to her. "They were just up on the wall before, not down here, where his body was. Not on the floor. It's almost like they've replaced him."

"Or like they've been fed."

Ken made a face at that idea. "Well, he's not here now," Ken said. "So what do we do? Keep looking? Give up?"

"Ken, I killed somebody."

"So you tell me, Penny. I don't have a body, I don't have anybody claiming that someone's missing. There's some blood on your clothes, but that's the only evidence I see. Not a drop of it in this cave."

She shrugged. She had played her light across the opposite wall and saw the writing again, and remembered the argument with Mick that had preceded his attack. "Do you see that?" she asked. "The writing there?"

"Sure," Hal said. "Plain as the nose on your face."

"He couldn't see it. Mick."

"It's there," Ken put in.

"Yeah," Penny said. She began to read it again, as if compelled by some force she couldn't resist. Her world narrowed to the width of her flashlight's beam. She started right where she had left off, and the words flowed effortlessly, seemingly moving from the wall to her brain without having to even pass through her eyes. She had earlier nearly exhausted the writing she could see from this spot, so she moved around a bend in the cave wall and continued reading.

As she moved farther back in the cave, the writing was older and older. What she was seeing was no longer in English, but that didn't slow her down for a second. She saw it and understood it, and then the words—drawings, really, scratched on the stone with primitive edged tools, marked with sharp-edged rocks—that formed the bottom layer, over which all the rest was written, swam into focus. Circles and squiggles and lines no human had seen for centuries, and she understood all those as well.

"Penny? Penny…"

Voices from far away called her name but she didn't respond. She couldn't respond. She was no longer in the cave, but had been sucked into the world of the people who had first marked on these walls. Another time, long, long ago. She knew it was all

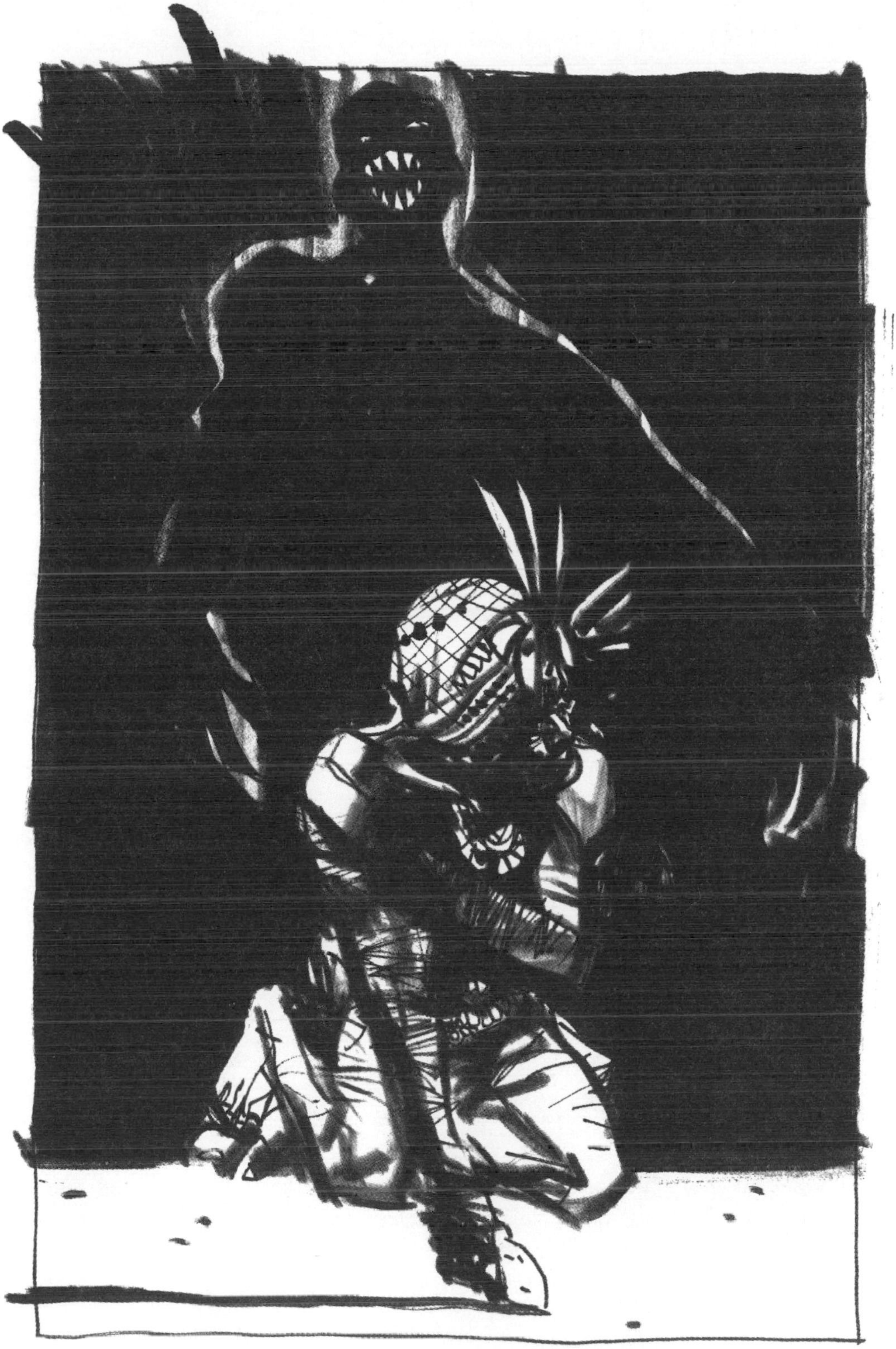

in her head, that she was stooped over in the dank cave looking at indecipherable markings, but the markings played a scene in her mind like a silent movie on a screen, and she was helpless to do anything but watch.

Tall, bronze-skinned people, naked but painted and tattooed—here a man's leg was all black with a row of red dots up the back, here a woman's face and left breast were aqua, there red and yellow stripes encircled a man's barrel-shaped torso—moved before her on a desert hillside. The sky overhead was dark and tormented, with angry clouds piled one on top of another like stones marking a trail. Powerful winds swept up the slope of desert, raising whitecaps on a flat body of water that lapped just below their position on the hill.

At the center of the painted people was a strange looking man, taller than the rest by half, which would have made him almost nine feet tall, she thought. His muscular arms and legs were scarred, and his skin, though it didn't seem to be painted, was as gray as the ash of a day-old fire. He turned, slowly, trying to keep all the others in sight, even though they surrounded him like hunters around prey. This impression was furthered by the weapons in their hands—crude axes, knives, spears with stone points. The man in the center was unarmed, except for the nails of his hands, long and claw-like, and the clubs of his fists, and the gnashing teeth he bared at them, spittle flying in the stiff wind.

One man made his move, lunging with a spear. The gray man sidestepped and caught the weapon, using it to tug the other off-balance. The attacker fell to one knee and the gray man swiped a hand at him, as casually as a grizzly might, and sharp claws ripped through the man's flesh, trailing blood. The man collapsed, bleeding out onto the packed earth, as his comrades watched. Penny had the impression that this stalemate had gone on for some time.

Then her field of vision changed, and she saw the same scene but from a different angle. Now she could see more people, women and children as well as the men. And more—what at first glance she took to be some kind of forest, she realized, was dozens of the bronze men raised off the earth, skewered on poles that ran red from their grisly decorations. Women and a few men sat beneath these poles, weeping and wailing, though Penny could only see their faces and not hear their cries. But watching, she understood that, while the gray man was ultimately responsible for this scene, he was not the one who had impaled these people and raised them for all to see. The painted people had done this to their own kind. Persuaded or compelled by the gray man, to be sure, but his hands were not soiled by these crimes—the only blood under his horned nails was that spilled in self-defense against the angry mob surrounding him.

The angle changed again, each change a vertiginous swirl that made her stomach lurch, and she saw yet another painted man, older than most of the others, squatting close to the ground. Tattoos covered almost every inch of his nude body, and jewelry encircled his neck, wrists, and ankles. He held a sharp, hard rock, and made markings with it on a flat shard of stone that must have measured eight feet long and four across. Observing him, she realized that he was a shaman or medicine man of some kind, and that the marks he made functioned as the casting of some kind of spell. And he was very nearly finished; his marks, each made with the sure swiftness of a well-practiced hand, closed on the bottom of the slab of rock.

Beyond him—and he kept an eye on this scene, as well, as if he knew what was at stake—the warriors continued to try to bring down the gray man. But more of them had fallen; their bodies littered the ground around him now, and the sand was red and wet. Finally, as Penny watched him, the shaman finished his spell, and the gray man suddenly stopped, his arms dropping to his sides, head lowering to his chest, as if he'd been a puppet and his strings had been cut. She could see his eyes, red and glaring with defiance, but his muscles were no longer under his control. Now the men were able to reach him and they did so, cutting and scoring his flesh—which, she noticed, did not bleed—then throwing aside their weapons and closing their hands around him, picking him up and bringing him to the shaman's side.

For the first time, Penny noticed the pit next to where he worked. It almost matched the dimensions of the stone on which he marked, and was rimmed with low stone walls, like a well. The warriors threw the gray man into the pit, then spat at his still form, pissed on him, kicked rocks and dirt down onto him. The shaman watched this for a while and then spoke up, and the warriors came to him, helped him lift the heavy slab of stone and place it on top of the rock walls. The gray man was sealed inside.

And the water, until now just a lake in the distance, spilled onto the shelf of land on which they stood, and kept rising, covering the people's feet, their ankles. They shouted and laughed and moved up the side of the hill, seeking higher ground, even as the water covered the inscribed slab of rock and the poles bearing their impaled brothers.

And the water kept rising and rising, drowning the world.

Ken and Hal looked at each other. Penny had left the building, Ken thought. Her eyes were open, the flashlight in her hand still shone on the cave walls, and her feet moved her along as if she were really reading the hieroglyphics there. But he had waved a hand right in front of her eyes, snapped his fingers next to her ears, called her name, and she had not responded.

"Can't just leave her here," Hal pointed out.

"Whatever she's doing, it must be important," Ken suggested. He knew how absurd that sounded—she might as well have slipped into a coma, how could that be important? But he knew it was true. Any man whose had accepted magic into his life had to be willing to let intuition triumph over reason from time to time. "We can wait a few minutes." Not that he wanted to spend any more time than necessary here—he'd had enough of tunnels and caves to last a lifetime.

Sure enough, after a couple of minutes, she returned from wherever she'd been. She blinked and blew out a ragged breath, and her rigid body relaxed. Ken moved to catch her in case she fell, but she put a hand out and steadied herself against the wall. "Wow," she said. "What was that?" Her tone was strange, as if she were in a cathedral, filled with awe at the glory of God.

"I don't know," Ken said. "But we should probably get—damn."

His radio crackled—not broken after all, unless it had fixed itself. "Ken?" He recognized Clara Bishop's voice, from down in El Centro.

"Yeah, Clara. What is it?"

"I've had a call from Lamont Hardy at the Shop-R Mart up there," Clara said. "He says Mindy Sesno hasn't shown up for work. He went by her place, and her car's there but the doors are locked. He's worried about her. He asked for you, said he thought you were friends with her."

Before Ken could even answer, the radio crackled again as Billy Cobb broke in. "I don't know where you are, Ken, but I could go down and have a look, you want me to."

"No, Billy. You stay where you are. I'm on my way." He turned to the others. "I have to go. Now. You two can stay here if you want or come with, but I'm going to be moving fast. You come, you have to keep up."

"No trouble," Hal said. "I feel, quite literally, stronger than I have in years. Maybe decades. You can't outrun me."

"You're not leaving me here," Penny said. "This place creeps me out."

"You were kind of creeping us out," Ken pointed out, already making his way back toward the cave's entrance. "What was going on with you back there?"

"I'll tell you on the way," she said. "Let's go."

Penny explained what she'd seen in the cave as the Bronco bounced toward Salton Estates. Ken acted like he barely heard her. Whoever this Mindy Sesno was, she must have been important to him. But he nodded and grunted in the right places, and when she was done, he was silent for a moment, mulling it all over.

"I can't claim to know what you saw," he said after a time. "But it sounds right, somehow."

"What do you mean?" Hal asked him. Hal had the shotgun seat while Penny rode in the back, leaning forward, her arms over the seats between the two men.

"The Cahuilla Indians used to live in the Salton Sink, back in the old days. When white settlers first came through here, but even before that, for who knows how long? Thousands of years, maybe. They were a pretty basic, primitive people. But we know they painted and tattooed themselves, like you described, Penny. We know they went mostly naked. And we know something else." The Salton Sea filled the middle distance, out the windshield, and he pointed toward it. "The Salton is basically an accidental sea, an error in judgment made back in 1905 when the Colorado River was allowed to run free for two years and filled this vast, low space. But it's not the first time there's been water here. See that line on the hills?"

He pointed now at a distinct line, a little more than halfway up the hills on both sides of the Sea. The rock was noticeably darker below the line, lighter above it. "This land was all underwater once, part of the Gulf of California. As the Colorado River wore through the Earth, carving out the Grand Canyon and the like, it carried its silt down here and made the Delta that's out there now, effectively damming it up. But even so, some years there was a lake here, Lake Cahuilla, it's called now, even before the Salton Sea. It was bigger and deeper, and it came and went with very little notice. When the Colorado and Gila Rivers overflowed their banks powerfully enough, the lake came back, and it happened with what the Cahuilla Indians must have considered depressing regularity. Their oral tradition, at least, is full of it. They liked it when there was a little water around. They could farm, grow some crops, have plenty to drink. When there was a lot of water, though, they had to move to higher ground, sometimes in a hurry."

Now the dirt road met the pavement of Highway 111, and Ken squealed out onto the roadway. A couple of cars and a big rig were in the lane ahead of him, but he hit lights and siren and bore down on them. "So the part you describe, Penny, about the water coming in and forcing them off their land, is accurate. This 'gray man,' I've never heard stories about him. The Cahuilla weren't especially warlike, that I remember hearing about, so that whole thing with the stakes is a little strange."

Penny shut her eyes, trying to remember not what she saw but what she felt about what she saw. "I had the impression that he was one of them, but not," she said. "Not their God, but sort of—the way we tend to think of God as a guy, you know, a man who sits on a chair, that you could talk to if only you were in Heaven. It was like the gray guy was some kind supernatural entity, but not one who was strange or unknown to them. More like he was around a lot, and he was a nuisance. Not a nuisance, that's understating it."

She decided to tell them what she had really felt, watching him. Even though it scared her to think about. "It was like he was evil. Or maybe Evil, with a capital 'E.' The personification of it. Like they held him responsible for the bad things they'd done to each other, and wanted to punish him for that."

"And they punished him by putting him in a hole in the ground?" Hal asked.

"Right. Not just under the ground, though. Under this magical slab, in a place where they knew the water would cover him. He was supposed to be kept under the sea. I don't think these people would have had a safer place they could have put him. He'd have been at the bottom of the ocean, as far as they were concerned, for what? A generation? More?"

"I don't know precisely how long the deluge lasted when it came," Ken said. "Long enough to make it into their stories. And not the happy ones. If they managed to capture Evil and put it under the sea, that'd probably help explain why they weren't happy ones."

The town of Salton Estates rushed past the Bronco's windows. Between the buildings, Penny caught glimpses of the Salton Sea, strobing in the last light of the sinking sun. Ken drove like a maniac, whipping into the oncoming traffic lane of the two-lane highway when someone wouldn't get out of his way fast enough. Capture Evil? Penny thought. Somehow, evil had gotten out. She doubted whether there had ever been a time, in the history of mankind, when evil had been entirely encapsulated in a single individual, even such a big, freaky looking one as the gray man. Maybe before people had come along to spoil things there had been no evil, but there certainly was now. If the Cahuilla had managed to seal away evil beneath their stone slab and their rising sea, then more power to them. But they hadn't locked it away completely or forever.

A minute later, Ken brought the Bronco to a shuddering halt in front of a small house. The stucco had been pink once but was faded and cracked. Colorful curtains covered the windows and the little patch of gravel in front, where a couple of golden barrel cacti and an ocotillo grew, was well manicured. A window air conditioner dripped onto the gravel near the house, and a couple of dandelions grew up where the water fell. Not far away, a couple of mushrooms had sprouted, white with red, like the ones they'd seen in the cave. Ken jumped from his seat as soon as the engine died and ran to the door. He pounded on it, calling Mindy's name. When no one answered, he reared back and kicked the door, next to the knob. Wood splintered and the door gave way, and Ken disappeared inside.

Hal turned in his seat and looked at Penny. She had changed in the few short hours he'd known her, he realized. When she had first walked into the Sheriff's office she'd been distraught, an emotional train wreck. Surely she'd been through a lot since then—discovering that others shared the same kind of magic that had touched her life; finding that the body of her friend was gone, maybe eaten by impossibly fast-growing mushrooms; somehow seeing or being transported through the mists of history to the distant past. And yet, she looked better than ever—clear-eyed, alert, almost happy. She was a pretty young woman, even reminded him a little of Virginia when they'd first met. It was the intelligence about her eyes, he thought, and the way she held her mouth when she was about to say something and then decided against it. So many people, they never decided against it. Just said whatever flitted into their minds.

She ticked her eyes toward the little house. "He going to be okay?" she asked.

"He's plenty worried about that young lady," Hal answered. "I think she means a lot to him."

"Because he didn't talk about her all the way down here."

"I've never heard him talk about her," Hal said. "That's how I know how much he thinks of her."

"Have you known him long?"

"Ken? As long as I've lived on the Slab, I guess. But really known him, just the last day or so. Since the…"

"Since the magic kicked in," she finished.

"Right. Since then."

"It's funny, isn't it? Feeling like you've known someone your whole life when you barely know their name."

"Funny?" he repeated. "I guess. But nice, too. We could all use more people to be close to, right? I mean, really close."

"Yeah, you're right," she said. "I suppose we could."

Hal looked back toward the house, its door gaping open on a dark interior. "And Kenneth, I think he had his heart set on a closeness he may never get now."

He knew she was dead as soon as he got inside the front door. The a/c was blasting and had been for some time, cooling the house far below the temperature at which he knew Mindy, a lifelong desert dweller, was comfortable. The air conditioner had helped to dilute the smell of her, but it still hung in the air.

He found her in her bedroom, nude, laying on her back on top of sheets which she had soiled in death. A ligature around her throat—the sash of a pink silk robe he saw wadded in a corner—and hemorrhaging there instantly revealed how she had died. He fought back tears at the sight of her body, so vulnerable in its nakedness, so slight. Trying to maintain an air of professionalism, he looked at the condition of her body—*the* body, he corrected himself, keep it straightforward, it's a crime scene investigation now.

Cyanosis had blued her lips and the tips of her fingers. Her eyes were open, covered with a filmy glaze. The body had paled as blood settled to her back, lividity showing when he raised one shoulder and looked at the blotchy redness on her back. The corpse was cold and the muscles were stiff, so rigor mortis had set in.

Touching Mindy, though, he couldn't hold back his personal feelings for her any longer. He sank to his knees beside the bed and awkwardly cradled the rigid form in his arms, getting just a whiff of her perfume from her hair, the scent that had always appealed so to him when he leaned close to her in the store or spoke to her on the street.

As he held her and breathed her in, a dozen images of Mindy flooded his brain, but then they fell away and he was here, in this room, but frantic, anger and fear and pain fighting for primacy in him and he knew he was looking out through Mindy's eyes. "If you want the old man so much why don't you just go to him?" a voice raged at her, and then a hand slapped her, backhanded her, and she took a deep gasping breath until the hand resumed tugging on the silken sash, cutting into her throat and then she couldn't breathe, and "You'd be perfect together, you're both used up old ladies!" and then tighter, he pulled the silk still tighter, and she tried to twist, to writhe out of his grasp but her strength was already going, arms and legs and hips not responding to the desperate commands her mind sent, black dots filling her vision, swarming before her, blocking everything.

Blocking his face.

Billy Cobb.

Ken put Mindy Sesno back down on her bed, gently, as if she could tell. He reached for his radio, but then stopped himself. The coroner would need to examine the scene at some point, but Ken didn't need a complete crime scene investigation. It didn't matter what traces there were of DNA evidence, hairs or saliva or semen or bits of fuzz from the carpeting in his car—which, he realized, would be from the Bronco anyway since Billy had been driving that—because Billy Cobb would never stand trial for this crime.

He wouldn't live that long.

Kerry moved from window to window like a gangster in a bad hostage movie, a second-rate Bogey checking for John Law to come sneaking up on him. Rock's windows were covered with curtains made from torn strips of fabric: old sheets, a Gold Medal flour bag that must have been older than he was, a flattened cardboard box he'd simply taped over the window with masking tape. But in the movie the gangster would have worn a gray suit and hat, not stained and torn desert camo trousers with a sweat-rimmed olive drab tee, and he'd have carried a snub-nosed .38 instead of the utilitarian killing machine that was Kerry's M-4.

"She's out there," Kerry said. "I know she is."

"How do you know she hasn't just called the cops?" Terrance asked him. Vic thought it was wishful thinking on Terrance's part—with everything their Dove had put them through, it might have been easier to just deal with the criminal justice system.

"She wouldn't have barged in on Ray's wife if she were going to do that," Kerry replied. "No, she's gone vigilante on us."

"So you guys are just gonna camp out in my place until she comes after us?" Rock asked.

"We're staying put until full dark," Kerry said. "At which point I'm going to go out and kill Hal Shipp, that traitorous bastard. After that we'll figure out what to do about the bitch."

Vic didn't like that idea. He'd always been friendly with Hal, even though the man was so much older than him. But he couldn't see any flaw in Kerry's reasoning—it pretty much had to be Hal who had planted the skull. Hal's mind was going, this last year or two, and he supposed Hal hadn't even remembered that he was supposed to keep the Dove Hunts a secret. Although, in that case, why wouldn't he have just gone to the law or started talking about it to his friends and neighbors? Sticking the skull in a fire pit sounded like someone trying to tip people off while still keeping his own identity secret, and that didn't point to a person who couldn't think clearly. Downright clever was what it was.

But he was already losing his patience with Kerry, and didn't want to open up another can of worms with the man. They were both on edge—all of them were, and they were all armed, and it wouldn't take much, he thought, penned up in this tiny trailer, to start a firefight.

That was the last thing any of them needed.

Carter Haynes stared in the rear-view mirror of his Town Car, his attention suddenly caught by motion in the far distance. Behind him, lost in darkness now, was the Salton Sea. But what had struck him was an enormous flock of birds—egrets, maybe, what looked like thousands of them—taking wing from its surface and flying up to where the sun's last rays, angling in over the hills of the Anza-Borrego Desert State Park, on the Sea's west side, caught their white feathers, an explosion of light on an otherwise dark backdrop.

It had taken him and Nick Postak all day to pull together the men and machines they needed. Now they all rolled in a convoy, up the low grade toward the Slab, the huge tires of flatbed trucks chewing up the dirt road, two rented vans full of men leading the way and Carter's Town Car bringing up the rear. Bright headlights illuminated the desert scrub, brutalized and dirt-caked by the amount of vehicle traffic this stretch of road carried. As the pink of the western sky purpled toward indigo, they arrived at their destination.

Many of the Slab-dwellers had heard the trucks approaching, and some, seeing what was coming, may have figured out its goal. Carter didn't care. That's what the men in the first van were for. The men in the second van would drive the big machines—two massive 939C Hystat track loaders, with cabs, and two smaller but more maneuverable 277 Multi Terrain loaders outfitted with industrial grapple buckets, all rented from Williams Caterpillar in El Centro. In the harsh glare of headlights, Carter could see people lined up at the edge of the Slab, as if to step off the concrete was the same as walking off the edge of the world. So far, there was nothing more threatening in their hands than beer bottles and maybe the occasional flame-cooked hot dog.

The men in the first van, armed with .44 caliber Magnums and Remington shotguns, would keep it that way.

Diego Alvarez cocked his head toward the north wall of Eddie Trujillo's shitheap of a mobile home. "Mobile," in this case, Diego thought, meant that a good stiff wind could move the whole thing a mile away. A tornado wouldn't even give this place the time of day.

"What's that noise?" he asked.

"Sounds like trucks or something," Eddie said.

"That common, around here?" Jorge asked him. Diego and Jorge were both anxious about Henry Rios's threatened visit, anticipating police choppers and SWAT teams to show up looking for them at any moment. Their guns—including Raul's, which he'd decided he wanted out of the house when Rios came over—were leaned up against a table Eddie had made by laying half a door across the top of an old wooden crate.

Eddie shook his head and fished another cold one out of the ice-filled cooler of beer the Alvarez brothers had bought him, as thanks for letting them hide out with him for a while. "No, it's usually pretty quiet."

Eddie was plenty strong and healthy, a handsome guy in his mid-thirties with long straight hair and only a hint of a bulge at his gut, but he hated to work. Every now and then he disappeared for a while, and he told them he was off doing just enough seasonal labor to keep himself in beer and food for the rest of the year. Diego had never seen him working, though, and had never known anyone else so utterly lacking in ambition. He couldn't even figure out what Eddie did around here all the time—his place had no electricity, there never seemed to be books or magazines around, he had no hobbies that they knew of. When he'd asked, Eddie usually said he played cards with "the guys," meaning the old retirees who populated the Slab.

"You think we should see what's up?" Diego asked. The noise grew louder, and Diego began to recognize it as trucks. Maybe a bunch of them. Big ones.

"If you want to," Eddie offered. "Up to you." He sounded as if he'd be just as happy staying put. He tilted his head back and poured beer down his throat, and Diego thought maybe he'd just do the same. If the noise was anything important, they'd know soon enough.

Lucy had used the afternoon's last light to make her way far from the Slab, then down, cross-country, past it. Cross-country wasn't difficult in this region—the yuccas and cacti, greasewood and mesquite didn't grow so thick that one couldn't negotiate a path around them, and it was only unexpected ravines now and again that slowed her down. When she felt like she'd gone far enough to be well beyond the downhill, western side of the Slab, she turned and doubled back. As she had hoped, she was now coming up from downslope of it, on the side nearest the trailer into which the men she was hunting had gone. Of course, they could have left in the interim, but it really looked like they were there to stay for a while. Anyway, she had passed a truck parked in a nearby gully, which she suspected was the vehicle that had brought them here.

The new difficulty was that she had to get much closer to the Slab than she had been, and from this side she didn't even have the advantage of altitude. She had to stay low, running at a crouch from the scant shelter of one bush to the next. Getting in close was good—she was no marksman and her ammo was probably very limited. At close range, though, she might at least have a hope of killing some of them before they got her.

Lucy had given up thinking that she'd have to face legal charges when this was done. What she was determined to do now went well beyond self-defense. She was out for vengeance, no use kidding herself about that, and this vengeance would cost dearly. The chance that she'd be alive when this was finished was minuscule, barely worth considering. She had come to accept that this was her final day on Earth, and that her final act would be trying to take out as many of those men as she could. Her revenge would have the additional benefit of ensuring that those men couldn't do to any other women what they had tried to do to her, and part of her was comforted by the knowledge that she was paying them back for thirteen previous victims as well.

When she was close enough to see light through the windows of the trailer they had gone into, she settled down, once again finding a little cover behind a dense creosote bush. Sooner or later they'd show themselves. When they did...well, judgment day was here.

Hearing the sounds of the trucks, Billy Cobb started walking across the Slab to the far north side, where the road up from Salton Estates narrowed and turned into a vague set of ruts that threaded between the individual concrete slabs that comprised this desert community. When he got closer and glimpsed men on trucks pulling out stops and preparing to guide bulldozers off their beds, he walked faster. When he saw men emerging from a van with shotguns in their fists, he started to run.

As he approached them, the men closed ranks in front of Carter Haynes. But Carter seemed to recognize him. "Let him through," he told them, and they parted. Billy stopped in front of Carter, working to catch his breath. Before he spoke he brought himself up to his full height and rested his right hand on the grip of his gun.

"Mr. Haynes, what—"

"This is all legal, Deputy."

"—the fuck is—legal?"

"That's right."

"Those guys have shotguns!"

"That's right, and they're permitted. They're a security team."

"And those bulldozers?"

"They call them loaders, it turns out. I made the same mistake, at first. Those big ones are track loaders. Because of having tracks, I'd guess, instead of wheels."

Billy began to sense that he wasn't going to get anywhere with Carter Haynes. Rich bastard was used to getting his way, no matter what. The bitch of it was people like him usually did.

"What do you think you're—"

"I'm sure you'll agree that this is my land, Deputy Cobb. I hold title to it, legally and fairly, transferred to me by the government of the United States of America. And these people are trespassing. I've tried to work it out with them, but they are belligerent and recalcitrant and they won't leave. Tonight, they'll leave."

"You're—" Billy looked back at the Slab, at the people standing and watching him argue with Haynes. He waved a hand at them. "You're just going to demolish their homes?"

"That's a pretty generous term for what these are, but yes. That's the general idea."

"And you think they're just going to stand back and let you?"

Haynes gestured toward the men with the guns. His "security team." They were uniformly big men, wearing flak vests and combat trousers. They looked tough, like they knew how to handle the shotguns but didn't necessarily need them to raise hell. Billy began to feel glad that Haynes was doing this legally. If, in fact, he was. That wasn't his call to make, though.

"Looks like you've got your bases covered, Mr. Haynes," he said.

"I certainly do."

"Mind if I try to get these people to back off, maybe pack up what they can?"

"If they hurry," Haynes said. "We're just about ready to roll here."

"Okay," Billy said. "Give me five minutes, okay? Five minutes."

Haynes glanced at the progress the men were making getting the loaders down off the truck. "You probably have that," he said. "But not much more."

Lettie Bosworth was in the trailer's cramped galley trying to put together a dinner that her husband Will would both eat and not notice the rat poison in. She'd put tiny doses into his food for a couple of days, but so far, except for him maybe being a little less obnoxious than usual, she hadn't noticed any change in his health or overall demeanor. She didn't know if the rat poison accounted for the improvement, but if it did that was just one more reason why using a bigger dose this time was a good idea.

A radio was playing big band music from down in El Centro, and she swayed gently to the beat as she—wearing rubber kitchen gloves—worked the poison into Will's seasoned chicken breast. Because of the music she didn't really notice the truck noises at first. But when Will's voice started calling to her, its familiar timbre caught her attention and she turned down the volume on the portable boombox.

"Lettie!" he was hollering. "Get my gun! I need my gun!"

Without hesitation, she went to the shelf over the settee where he kept his hunting rifle and reached for it. He was still screaming, and now she heard other voices raised in alarm, and the trucks idling and some other kind of heavy machinery moving toward the Slab, and she levered a cartridge into the breech. When he appeared in the doorway, yanking open the spring-closing screen and bursting inside, he was red-faced, winded from the run.

"They're trying to mow us down!" he shouted.

Lettie stared at him, feeling nothing. His face changed as he looked at her, rifle in her hands, pointed at him. His eyes went wide, and white splotches appeared on his red cheeks. His mouth worked for a moment, with only a small, strangled sound coming out. Then she pulled the trigger and he flew backward, through the screen door, tearing it from its hinges as he went, and landed on the concrete outside. The interior of the trailer seemed to ring with the noise, and a cloud of acrid smoke burned Lettie's nostrils.

The first shot had been fired.

part 4
triad

By the time Ken's Bronco rolled up to the Slab, the four big Cats were making their way across the cement. Their head- and roof-lights illuminated the dwellings, picking out run-down trailers and jerrybuilt additions against the dark sky. Between the machines, the armed men walked, shotguns held at the ready.

Ken stopped the SUV and jumped out, running up to Carter Haynes, who leaned on his Town Car, speaking almost casually into a cell phone. His hired muscle—Postak was his name, Ken remembered—stood next to him, at attention, a SIG Sauer P226 looking miniature in his beefy hand. "What in the hell is going on here!" Ken demanded. Somehow those Caterpillars might as well have had HAYNES plastered across them.

Carter closed his phone slowly and turned to face him. "I've already explained to your deputy, Lieutenant, that I'm simply exercising my right as the landowner to evict those who are illegally encamped on my land."

"Billy's here?" Ken's eagerness to find Billy Cobb had been only briefly sidelined by the sight of bulldozers closing in on Slab trailers. "Where?"

"He was around a few minutes ago," Carter explained. "He said he was going to try to get people to pack their things and move out while they still could."

"So those 'dozers are yours?"

"That's right."

"Men with the guns too?"

"Yes," Carter affirmed.

"They shoot anybody yet?"

Carter shook his head. "I've heard one shot fired," he said. "Not by my guys, and apparently not at them, either. I haven't heard anything about who was shooting at whom. But as you can see, my men aren't the only ones with guns."

Ken looked across the Slab. The developer was right; silhouetted through clouds of dust kicked up by the big machines were men and women Ken recognized as Slab residents, their own guns in their hands, facing down the heavy equipment as it rolled toward their homes. He thought he could make out the enormous bulk of Jim Trainor, the lanky form of Darren Cook, maybe Dickie Rawlingson and some others.

"You've got to call off your guys," Ken said. "Or there's gonna be a bloodbath."

"If that's what it takes, so be it," Carter replied. "They could always just choose to get off my land. If they don't, they're trespassers, and here illegally, and if they attack my people we have every right to defend ourselves and our property."

He said it with such finality that Ken was sure he meant it—and just as sure that the man had completely lost his mind.

"What's going on?" Hal asked from behind him. Ken had been so involved in thinking about Mindy and Billy—so mentally wrapped up in his revenge scenario— that he'd practically forgotten he still had Hal and Penny with him. They must have followed him over from the Bronco, because both were here now.

"Trouble," Ken said simply. Before he had a chance to elaborate, one of the big track loaders plowed into a trailer that an old couple named Vassallo had lived in for years. Metal screamed as the loader pushed through aluminum walls and steel infrastructure. Beneath the unstoppable blade of the earth-moving machine, the trailer collapsed, folding in on itself as it if had fallen into a trash compactor. Sparks flew, but the huge machine just kept advancing.

"Big trouble," Ken said.

Darren Cook had been itching to kill someone for days. He'd never done it, but that didn't mean anything. He'd never been to New York City, either, but people did it every day. Didn't mean he never would, just that he hadn't accomplished that goal yet.

When he'd thought about it over the last few days, it had always been Maryjane he had in mind. But not now. Now he was sighting down the length of his rifle at the driver of a bulldozer. His Jamboree was next in line after Merry and Lou's place, and not only was Maryjane inside it but so were his collections of hockey cards and beer bottles—those he'd emptied himself and those he'd found in the desert and stacked up on the windowsills to catch the light when it streamed through. So he aimed and he squeezed the trigger and he felt the rifle kick against his shoulder.

He couldn't see where the bullet went, but he thought it spanged off the big blade of the machine. He levered another round in to fire again.

"Taking fire," Mike Zanatapolous said into a wireless microphone clipped to his collar. The other guys on the detail all wore them too, and earphones, so they could stay in touch with each other and command during this operation, even with the racket of the 'dozers next to them. Mike Zanatopolous, more commonly known simply as Mikey Zee, headed up this crew, providing personal defense, security, and bodyguard services throughout the Palm Springs area. He'd known Nick Postak for years, and when Nick had warned him that this assignment carried certain dangers, Mikey Zee had just smiled. "If it didn't, you wouldn't be talking to me," he said. "And I wouldn't be talking to you."

"I've got him," Neil Woodward's voice replied. Woody was on the other side of the Cat 277 from him. Mikey glanced past the machine and saw Woody raising his shotgun. He wouldn't miss. Another bullet thudded harmlessly into the dirt ahead of them— guy was too scared to shoot straight, Mikey figured, and with good reason. Woody fired once, a bright muzzle burst and a loud crack, and the gunman was blown clean off his feet.

"Subject's down," Woody said.

He didn't have to point out that there were still a dozen or so that they could see, and who knew how many more hiding inside their homes, any of whom could be pointing weapons at them right now.

Vic thought Kerry would jump out of his skin when he heard the shooting start. "What's that?" he asked, as if any of them had been outside Rock's trailer since late afternoon. "What's going on?" He returned to the windows he'd abandoned only minutes before, peering into the dark outside as if it would tell him something. "You hear that?"

"I hear guns, man," Rock said. "And something else, like tanks or something."

The military? Vic thought. No way could that girl have sicced the Marines on them. "That doesn't make any sense," he said.

"Well, it's something big," Rock insisted. "Hear it?"

Vic strained to listen. Rock was right. It was coming from the far end of the Slab—the end closest to the road—but it definitely sounded like big vehicles of some kind. And the gunfire continued, scattered bursts of it.

He made up his mind suddenly. "I'm going to Cathy," he announced, grabbing Cam's Ithaca pump-action 12 gauge. "Got to make sure she's okay."

"Nobody breaks ranks," Kerry said, his voice sharp. "Especially now." His command voice, Vic knew. Fuck that.

"Fuck you," he said. "My wife is out there and people are shooting off guns. I'm gonna make sure she's okay."

"You go out that door, you don't come back," Kerry said. "We don't protect you any more. You're on your own."

"And that's different from ten seconds ago how?" Arguing with Kerry would be pointless. He shoved open the door and ran out into the night.

All the noise had worried Lucy. When she'd heard the vehicles coming up the grade, her first thought had been that the hunters she was hunting had called in reinforcements of some kind. But that was unlikely, she realized. They couldn't call the police, not without explaining their own crimes. She stayed put, moving about from time to time to keep her limbs from falling asleep, but keeping within the cover offered by the creosote bushes and now the darkness.

Once the shooting started, she hoped that the fireworks would draw out her quarry. Anticipating a shot, she flattened herself on her stomach and propped the barrel of the gun up on a flat slab of rock, helping to angle it up the hill. Sure enough, after just a couple of minutes, the trailer door banged open and someone dashed out. She led him for a moment and pulled the trigger, and the man went down with a shout, his gun skittering off across the concrete. She swiveled the gun back toward the trailer's door, in case someone else followed. But the trailer remained quiet.

Earlier, she thought she'd glimpsed someone looking out through the one small window that faced off in her direction—a vague shape against the curtain. Now that the sun was down and the trailer lit from within, that shape, if that's what it had been, would be more distinct. She'd watch the window now, too, and if no one came out the door to check on the one she'd hit, maybe she'd put a slug through the glass.

One by one or all at once. She didn't care how she took them down.

Only that they fell.

When the firing began, Billy Cobb made a quick exit from the Carnahans' trailer. They hadn't been in there anyway—he thought he'd seen Alex running toward the commotion with some kind of handgun, and Stephanie had been staying with her sister in Calexico since September eleventh. He'd gone in to warn them, as he was warning everyone, that bulldozers were coming to knock down their homes, but since the place was empty he took a few minutes to see if they had anything that looked valuable. Desert rats for years, the Carnahans had amassed an amazing collection of junk— antique glass, old horseshoes and bullet molds and badges, rusted food tins, animal skulls and horns, and the like—and Billy had always half-suspected they had some good stuff among the trash.

He wasn't finding it now, though, and since there were guns going off he decided that it was probably best not to be inside someone else's trailer. He thought the wisest course of action was to take cover somewhere, maybe get off the Slab altogether, until whatever was going on had played itself out.

Leaving their trailer empty-handed, he plotted out the safest way off the Slab— past the Bryants' and Barry Lichter's, then around Eddie Trujillo's place and he was home free. Sparing only a glance toward where all the gunfire was coming from, he started to run.

Jorge and Diego had gone to separate windows when the shooting started, their own rifles in their fists. Eddie stayed put on his couch, munching from a bag of tortilla chips. "Can you see what's going on?" Jorge asked frantically. "Turn out that fucking light, I can't see shit!"

Almost reluctantly, it seemed, Eddie switched off the lamp next to his couch. Nearly everything in the place was next to the couch, Diego realized—if Eddie leaned far enough over the back of it he could get to the refrigerator and pantry, and the remote lived on the couch arm, pointed at a TV that was just beyond the reach of his toes if he stretched them out. If he didn't need a toilet once in a while, he'd never have to move.

When the trailer went dark it was easier to see outside, but what he could see in the distance looked like a nightmare—lights from some kind of big machines moving inexorably forward, men walking between them with guns raised, other men scattering to take up positions behind rocks or outdoor furniture or trailers, and taking shots toward the machines and the armed force that seemed intent on occupying the Slab. There was a hole where at least one trailer had stood, but most of it was flattened now, and bits of it still stuck out from the blade of the big bulldozer. Smoke hung on the air, giving everything a surrealistic, filtered look, like something out of a movie.

"I can't tell exactly," he reported. "I don't think it's the cops, but I can't really see too well."

"I can't see from here either," Jorge said from his own vantage point. "But it looks like those things are flattening the houses."

A flurry of sudden motion caught Diego's eye: a man in a Sheriff's uniform, a pistol in his hand, breaking from the cover of another trailer and running straight toward this one.

"Cops!" Diego shouted, near panic. Without pausing to think it over, he jammed the barrel of his gun through Eddie's window and fired. Outside, the lawman hit the ground with a skid, fired a shot that went high, sailing over the roof of Eddie's trailer, and rolled into the darkness beneath the next mobile home over from them. Diego lost him in the dark.

"Damn," he said. His brother and Eddie were staring at him. Which, he thought, was exactly the wrong thing to do. The threat lay outside, not within. "I couldn't tell if I hit him or not. Can't see him, now. Keep your eyes open, Jorge, in case there's more."

Carter's eyes were open but he wasn't seeing the scene of Armageddon that unfolded in front of him, the bodies falling, the homes burning as primitive electrical systems were forcibly torn apart, the men he employed staying behind the cover of giant steel machines and firing round after round from powerful guns. He was already thinking ahead, to what would happen after the loaders had moved all the pitiful dwellings off the Slab. To the time that they would start tearing apart the multiple concrete slabs themselves. He'd have to bring in jackhammers to break up the concrete where it had survived the years intact. But it would only be a day's work, maybe two, with enough equipment and money thrown at the job. Then the big machines could begin the task of moving the earth itself.

Because, he understood now, the real prize wasn't in building houses on this forsaken hillside.

It lay beneath the earth, no longer slumbering but awake. Wanting to get out.

And it had chosen Carter Haynes to make that happen.

Carter had no intention of disappointing it...

"I have to get to Virginia," Hal said. "She's probably terrified."

Ken thought about it for only a moment. He wanted to find Billy. What he really needed to do was to put a lid on this whole mess before more people got hurt, but he wasn't sure precisely how to do that. Even with a bullhorn, he doubted he could be heard over the heavy equipment, the crash of trailers being crushed under steel blades, and the gunfire and shouting coming from all over the Slab. With a few well-aimed shots, he could maybe take down the equipment operators from behind, where their shovels and big chunks of mobile home didn't shield them. But Carter Haynes's crew would turn on him and blow him away before he'd fired more than a shot or two, so unless he could persuade Carter to call them off, that wouldn't really help the situation any. And, while Carter's body stood right next to his Town Car just like it had been, Carter's mind didn't seem to be there with it. Ken had tried to engage the developer in conversation a couple of times, but Carter just stared right through him, a malicious half-smile on his face and a thin line of spittle trickling from the corner of his mouth. His cell phone lay abandoned in the dirt by his feet, resting next to a couple of mushrooms.

So going with Hal to find Virginia seemed like maybe it wasn't such a bad idea. Maybe the only way to deal with the insanity of this night was one person at a time. He touched Penny's hand, feeling the now-familiar surge of power. "Come on," he said. "Let's go with him."

She nodded, and he could see the fear glowing in her big moist eyes. "Okay," she agreed, though it was clear that going up onto the Slab was the last thing she wanted to do. Well, he could relate to that feeling. But getting back in the Bronco and driving away—while probably the wisest course of action—also seemed like a gross dereliction of his duty.

Besides, Billy was still here somewhere.

"He's hit," Rock said. He'd dashed to the window to watch Vic when the man left his trailer to find his wife, and saw Vic go down, blood gouting from his side as he did.

"Screw him," Kerry replied. "He's a traitor. Is he dead?"

"I don't think so," Rock said. "Not yet."

"I ought to go finish him myself."

"You do, and whoever shot him will probably just shoot you too," Terrance pointed out.

"What do you mean, whoever shot him? The bitch did it. Who else?"

But by now, gunfire sounded from every part of the Slab. Even Kerry, who had sat down heavily on a rickety metal-legged dining chair when Vic left, looked a little worried, Rock thought. "She's not firing all those guns, Kerry," he said. "Something's going on out there."

"Then we're safest in here."

Rock didn't like the sound of that. For one thing, he wasn't sure they were, in fact, safe in here. For another, this was his trailer, his home, and if they were going to become targets while they were in here, that meant his home was on the firing line as well.

"It sounds like the whole Slab is under attack," he observed. "I'm not sure we wouldn't be better off out in the brush somewhere."

"You think that way, feel free to go outside," Kerry said. "Not me. I'm staying right here."

Rock swallowed hard. "Kerry, this is my home, you know? If I say you guys have to go then you guys have to go."

Kerry came off the chair like a young fighter off his stool at the bell and put himself right in Rock's face. "Are you telling us we have to go?" he demanded. Rock knew Kerry could take him in a fight. Rock was bigger, and plenty strong, but he didn't have Kerry's years of special ops experience or whatever it was—Kerry refused to talk much about his past, but he alluded to it often enough to keep everybody wondering. And his talk was convincing enough to make Rock worried about the prospect of going against him.

He put up both hands, palm out, as a kind of warding-off gesture but also defensively, just in case. "No, I'm not saying that, man," he insisted. "Just, if I did, you know? I have a right to protect my place."

"And we have a right to protect our asses," Kerry countered. "You want us all to end up like Vic out there, bleeding out onto the concrete? Knowing that anyone who came to help him would get shot too?"

"Guess you weren't a Ranger," Terrance said.

"The fuck you mean by that?"

"Isn't it the Rangers who won't leave one of their own behind, alive or dead? A Ranger would risk it to go help Vic."

"Vic stopped being one of our own when he went out that door," Kerry said. "You two, you can make the same choice. We can stick together or you can turn traitor. But I warn you—anybody turns traitor, I'll kill them myself before they can take two steps." His voice was cold and as calm as if he were ordering lunch in a nice restaurant. "I promise you that."

Billy dove to the hard ground when he heard the glass break nearby, and the bullet whistled over his head. In the commotion he couldn't hear where it landed. He rolled over, pausing only momentarily to fire a round in the general direction of the muzzle burst he'd seen, then he rolled again. The nearest home was a double-wide trailer mounted on blocks, and he shoved himself underneath it, pushing his way through spider webs and trash and who knew what else had grown or been blown under here by the desert winds. But at least he was in shadow here, and presumably couldn't be seen by whoever had shot at him.

Scrambling to get underneath, he accidentally kicked the underside of the double-wide, and the impact was almost immediately followed by a loud "What the hell was that?" Billy froze. Maybe the liberal bleeding hearts were right, there were way too many people around here with guns, and it didn't take much to imagine one being aimed through the floor of the double-wide at him right now. The mobile home creaked and shifted as someone walked across the floor. Billy decided he needed to be away from it before somebody came out and trapped him under here—the last thing he wanted was to be caught in a crossfire with no room to maneuver. He pushed himself forward with his hands and feet, belly scraping the Slab, crushing mushrooms between himself and the cement, until he was at the front of the double-wide. Going this way would put him back out onto the Slab, not into the desert like he'd wanted, but as unpleasant as the prospect was it was better than backing out blindly. When he'd gone under he hadn't had time to strategize. Now he'd just have to make do.

At the other end of the stretch of desert that formed the eastern section of Imperial County, over the Arizona line in Yuma, past the confluence of rivers that had formed the Salton Sea, Colonel Franklin Wardlaw could barely refrain from rubbing his hands together in glee. It was too much of a cliché, he thought, so he bit back the urge. But he still experienced the glee, because Captain William Yato and Marcus Jenkins were taxiing an F/A-18 Hornet to an imminent take-off. The aircraft was armed—in addition its usual assortment of Sidewinders, Sparrows, and M61 Vulcan rotary cannon—with a centerline Guided Bomb Unit-12. The GBU carried a five-hundred-pound warhead that would plow through the concrete of the Slab like a hot knife through butter.

Wardlaw knew that Jenkins and Yato were on his side in this. The Slab needed to be gone. What waited beneath it needed to be free. Nothing else mattered. Back in some cobwebbed corner of his military mind, Wardlaw knew that he could face serious charges for authorizing this mission. But would anyone bring those charges? What would the face of the Earth resemble when Wardlaw's task was complete? Who would be in charge? He didn't know the answers to those questions…he only knew that everything would be different, and he, who had obliterated the Slab, would be held in much favor.

He paced in his office now, watching the aircraft take off in the dark. A corpse lay on his carpet, two bullet holes in its head. A Captain who had come in to protest the unscheduled mission, claiming that neither Yato nor Jenkins were flight certified, that there was no paperwork—paperwork! In a time of crisis this guy had been worried about marks on paper. Wardlaw had taken care of him, and no one else seemed to be complaining.

Soon…soon enough, listening to the complaints of whiners would be a thing of the past for Franklin Wardlaw. He reveled in the roar of the jet as it banked toward the west.

Toward the Slab.

"Keep your head down!" Ken shouted. Hal did as he was told, though it seemed like somewhat vague and unhelpful advice when he'd just seen one man torn almost in half at the waist by a shotgun blast, the homes of friends and neighbors flattened like used cardboard boxes after a move, and bullets flying every which way from every corner of the community he'd called home for so long. As he ran—head down—he could barely believe that this was all really happening. But the hammering in his chest was real. So was the ringing in his ears, and the furious, inescapable noise—guns, bulldozers, the screaming and wailing of people he knew, the faint, faraway-seeming patter of his own feet on the cement, running at a speed he hadn't been able to attain in years, if not decades. All those things were undeniable.

He and Virginia lived on the third of the various Slabs. Ken knew the way, and as fast as Hal was, Ken was faster. So Ken led the way and Hal followed. He stayed on the dirt path, at least at first, Hal guessed because the big machines were sticking to the concrete and most of the gunplay seemed centered around those.

Most, but not all.

After a couple of minutes, their familiar Minnie Winnie loomed ahead, a dark island in a sea of concrete dotted with mushrooms, like whitecaps on the ocean of night. No lights burned inside, and in the dim, crazy illumination of flames and reflected headlights and what moonlight could penetrate the haze of smoke and dust overhanging the Slab, he thought he could make out a bullet hole in the Winnie's outer skin.

When he saw that he pushed harder, passing Ken and barely slowing in time to keep from slamming into the RV's door. The screen door confounded him for a moment, as he tried to open it and succeeded only in bouncing it off his own leg and face, but then he got it wide, and he shoved through the inside door, trying to look everywhere at once in the dark interior. "Virginia!" he called. "Gin!"

The world seemed to go silent for a moment, and his heart rose to his throat, but then he heard a rustling sound and Virginia's voice, speaking through a quiet sob, said, "I'm in here."

The voice came from the head, the only space inside with no window exposure to the mad world beyond. Hal crossed to it and gently tapped on the door. "It's okay, Virginia," he said. "You can come out."

"Are you sure?" she asked him, her voice plaintive. "I don't..."

"Come on out, Gin," he said. "Please. I just want to see you."

He heard the door latch work, and then it opened and she rushed out and into his arms. He wrapped his arms around her. Her back hitched as she sobbed, great, sorrowful noises that shook her and made him feel regret that he had ever left her side. He moved his hands in a slow, circular pattern that he hoped was comforting. It'll be okay now, Virginia," he said. "Now we're together."

"But—" she began, and her voice caught, and she had to start again after two more racking sobs. "But I was so scared. And I didn't know where you were. And I thought the most horrible things…"

"I know," Hal said soothingly.

"No, I mean, before, the things I was thinking about…"

"I know," he said again. "I really do know."

"Everything?"

"Everything. Don't worry. It's not your fault."

Outside, the racket continued. It had never stopped, but he felt that it had, that the whole world had dropped away when he'd come inside and couldn't find Virginia, when he had feared that she was already gone. The magic that had happened to him hadn't changed anything; he still wanted to go first, didn't want to live on an Earth that didn't have Virginia Winfield Shipp on it, and when he heard her voice it was like a wish granted, a miracle.

The screen door opened and he started, but it was just Ken and Penny coming in. The RV dipped a little as they stepped up into it. "Everything okay?" Ken asked.

"Fine," Hal said. "Just fine."

"I'll see that you two are safe in here," Ken said.

"Don't you worry about us," Hal argued. "We'll be fine. We've got the magic on our side, remember?"

Ken took a step closer, and Hal felt Virginia shift in his arms, backing her face away from his chest to look at the lawman. "Harold's right," she said. You don't need to worry about us. I'm sure you have much more important things to take care of."

"There isn't anything more important," Ken said. He reached out and stroked the exposed skin of Virginia's arm, as if to reassure her, but when he touched her, Hal thought his face clouded over for a moment. Lowering his hand, Ken looked straight into Hal's eyes.

"Okay," he said. "I'll leave you here for now, while I try to go stop whatever it is that's going on here tonight. But when this is all over, Hal, you and me, we need to have a talk about some things. A serious talk."

Hal knew what he meant. He knew about the bodies, somehow. The dead women. His horrific legacy. "You're right, Ken. We do."

"Stay with them, Penny," Ken said on his way out the door. "I'll be back soon's I can."

"You can't do everything by yourself, Ken," she argued. But he just pressed his pistol into her hands.

"You know how to use that," he said. "If you need to, don't hesitate." Armed now with only his service shotgun, he tromped down the steps and banged the door shut.

Penny shrugged and went to the window to look outside. "How do we even know who the good guys are?" she asked.

Hal gave a deep-throated chuckle. "Good guys?" he echoed. "There aren't any good guys. You saw it yourself."

"What do you mean?" she wondered, turning away from the window to regard him. "You mean that vision or whatever? The Indians?"

"I wouldn't call it a vision," he said. He and Virginia sat down side by side on the living area's sofa, holding hands. "You were reading the pictographs on the walls, and you saw the story in your head, that's all. And what you saw may be what was written there but it was filtered through your own brain, your own perceptions. You saw a guy who was, you said, maybe the personification of evil. But he was gray, right?"

"Yes…" she said hesitantly.

"Because it's not a black and white world. Evil isn't absolute and it lives in all of us. So does good. Those bastards who flew airplanes into the World Trade Center had some good in them somewhere, and the cops who gave their lives to save others, they were heroes but they were human beings, they had some evil too. You said yourself that some of the victims you saw in that Indian camp had been killed by one another, not by the gray guy, right?"

"Well, yeah…I think they were under his influence, but…okay, I see your point."

"It's simplistic as all heck, but it's always been true, and I expect it always will be."

Virginia squeezed Hal's hand with her own. "Whatever are you two talking about?" she asked. She always had possessed a streak of curiosity as wide as the Mississippi, he thought.

"I guess there's a lot to tell you," he said. He leaned over and kissed the soft skin of his wife's cheek. "Now may not be the best time, but soon, okay?"

"Real soon," she said with a laugh. "Or I'm going to start thinking you two are keeping secrets from me."

"Never," Hal promised. "Never again."

Virginia Shipp tried to join in the conversation, tried to get Hal to share some of what he'd obviously been through with this young lady and Kenneth Butler. But she could only force herself to be mildly interested. She was relieved that he'd come back, relieved and happy. But those emotions warred inside her with another one, an urge so strong that she could barely suppress it.

She wanted to get her hands on the gun that Penny held. Ken's gun. That was her overwhelming priority at this moment. She could almost feel its cool steel skin, the way it would buck in her hands as she discharged it, the jets of flame that would erupt from its barrel, the matching jets of blood that would erupt from those she pointed it at.

Including Harold. Oh, God, especially Harold…

Vic writhed on the cement slab, trying to drag himself away from Rock's trailer to someplace he might reasonably expect to get some help. Better yet, to someone who could find Cathy for him.

The bullet had smashed his left hip and he couldn't even raise himself up onto hands and knees, could only tug himself by pressing his hands against the flat concrete and pushing as much as he could stand with his right leg. The more he moved, the more it hurt, but he had to move, couldn't just stay where he'd fallen so whoever had shot him could finish him off at will.

When he'd heard the firefight start up in earnest, he was heartened, thinking that maybe it wasn't the Dove, maybe it was Muslim terrorists or something. But he gave up on that notion in a hurry, since there was nothing on the Slab to attract the attention or interest of terrorists of any stripe. No, it was the Dove, he was sure. She was out there, down in the brush, most likely, where she couldn't see him as long as he was flat and she didn't change her position. Not that she'd need to, she seemed to have a pretty good angle on the trailer's door.

Fucking Kerry, he thought, fucking Kerry had talked him into all this. If he could only walk he'd go back in there and kill the bastard himself.

But even as he thought it, he knew it wasn't true. Yes, Kerry had brought him in, had persuaded him to join in the fun. But there was something inside himself that had responded to the offer, that had made him think that rape and murder sounded like a good time. Killing Kerry wouldn't kill that. Vic thought it was already dead, thought that it had died in the moment at the cabin when he'd first realized that it lived. But he couldn't be sure. Even now, crawling like a slug because he couldn't stand up, as helpless as a newborn, he couldn't deny that it would feel good, someplace deep inside that he didn't want to examine too closely, to hold a gun to someone's head and pull the trigger and breathe in the rank odors of blood and brain and smoke and lead and death.

Biting his lower lip until it bled, trying to stifle the pain, Vic dragged himself forward another foot.

Mikey Zee and his men had no casualties other than one man with a cheek scraped by shrapnel, metal chips that had flown when someone's bullet had struck the Multi Terrain loader near his face. The men moved with the loaders, always staying behind the cover of the heavy metal equipment, and used their shotguns sparingly to guarantee the safety of the vehicle operators. So far more than a dozen of the ramshackle residences had fallen before their onslaught, and Mikey estimated that they'd only had to shoot six of the locals.

Nick had anticipated armed resistance, but not on this level. From listening to Nick's comments in his ear, he had the sense that his friend would rather be out here with them, where things were happening, than back at the car with the principal. But Haynes was his job and he had to stay with the man no matter what.

Mikey Zee himself had yet to shoot anyone. He carried his favorite big gun, a gas-operated, semi-auto Benelli Super 90 M3 12 gauge with the shoulder stock/pistol grip combination, and the more he was out here, breathing in the sharp-edged smoke and listening to the lead fly past him like so many mosquitoes, the more he longed to unload it on somebody.

He poked his head above the edge of the big track loader and saw someone running across in front of them, pistol in his hand, firing one shot after another toward them. Good enough, he thought, raising the Benelli to his shoulder. He led the runner and fired. The runner stopped as if he'd encountered a brick wall, jerked to his right, and the middle part of him disintegrated in a fine mist, black in the smoky light. Mikey liked the shotgun's kick against him, like a punch to the shoulder, and liked the way it had done its job. Nick hadn't promised this would be as fun as it was turning out.

"Another one down," he said.

"Copy that, Mikey," Nick replied.

The track loader's massive blade struck the front surface of yet another old RV, and whatever else Nick might have said was lost in the squeal and shriek of twisted metal.

When he was out from underneath the double-wide, Billy ran across an open stretch of Slab toward a trailer where a short wall had been built around a picnic/patio area with what looked like found bricks and desert stones all piled up around a base of old tires. There were fucking tires everywhere on the Slab, used to mark "property" lines, driveways, picnic spots—anything that might need marking. Sometimes on a summer's day all you could smell was old rubber cooking in the desert sun.

He leapt the wall and crouched behind it, his Glock out, looking back toward the double-wide and the trailer from which someone had fired on him. He held the gun sideways, even though Ken had repeatedly warned him against it, because it just looked so awesome in *The Matrix*. Ken claimed that it might be fine for one shot but accuracy would suffer if he had to fire multiple shots at that angle. Maybe yes, Billy thought, maybe no. But Ken wasn't here now.

There's something hinky about that trailer, he thought. There hadn't been any gunfire in the immediate vicinity, so it was almost like whoever was inside there—and he was sure no one had come out yet—was waiting for him, or for a uniform, since he didn't even think they'd have been able to get a good look at him in the dark. And if they fire at any uniform that comes around, he reasoned, that must mean they're up to something. He wondered if there was a way to get a better look inside that trailer without getting his head blown off.

For now, though—as long as no one popped out from the vehicle he had his back to—he was relatively safe behind this wall, shadowed by the big RV from the moonlight and the flames that licked ever higher into the sky a slab or two over. He'd just stay here for a bit, catch his breath, and shoot anyone who showed himself.

Lucy Alvarez was running out of patience. She knew where those guys were, still hiding inside the trailer she'd seen them enter hours ago. One had come out, and she'd nailed him. Maybe he was dead, maybe just wounded, but she'd put the hurt on him and that was good. But it left three to go, and that was not good. The whole freaking world was falling apart, it sounded like. Flames brightened the night, guns were going off everywhere, and occasional crashes like the world's biggest demolition derby sounded over everything else. Earlier she had thought there was no way she'd

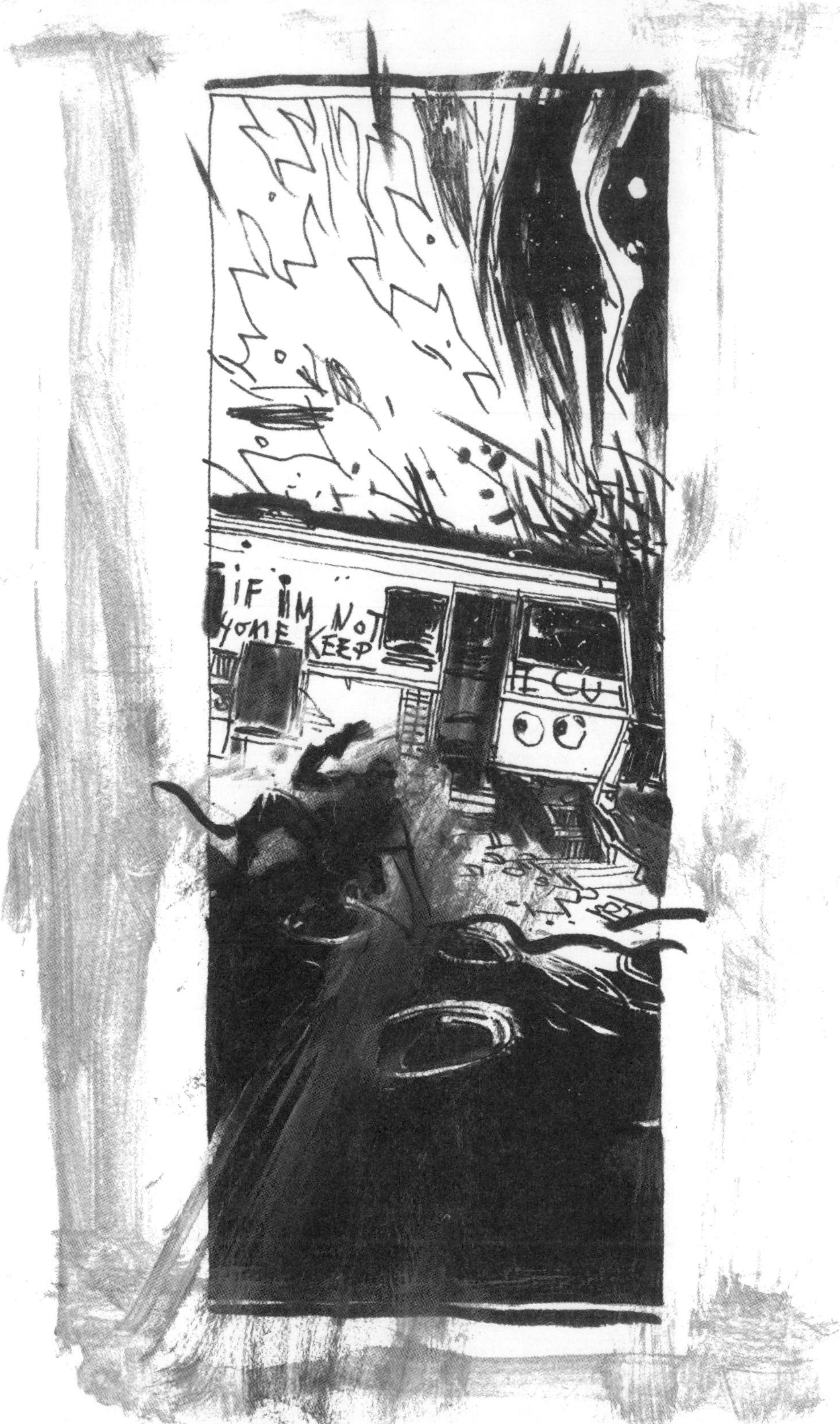
IF IM NOT
HOME KEEP
I CU

get her revenge and not have to pay the price in jail time, or maybe even the death penalty. But the way things sounded up on the Slab, on this night, of all nights, she stood a good chance of being able to murder four men in cold blood and just walk away from it all.

But she had to drive them out of that trailer, or go into it herself. That latter option held limited appeal. If she had more bullets—or if she knew how many bullets she had, or even how to find out—she could just start shooting into the walls of the trailer, figuring that her shots would penetrate its thin skin and either cause some damage or chase them out.

On the other hand, maybe creating the impression that she could do that would serve just as well, she thought. There was that one window facing off this way, after all. She hadn't seen anyone at the window for a while, but if the intent was terror, then that might not matter. The biggest drawback she could think of was that shooting through the window might pinpoint her own location for them—because she had to shoot uphill, a shot through the window would likely go above everybody's head and into, or through, the ceiling. From that they'd know about where she was hiding, and with more people and more ammo they might be able to finally finish their ungodly hunt.

Hell with it, she thought. It was a chance worth taking. She took careful aim, blew out her breath, held steady, and squeezed the trigger firmly. As before, the gun sounded very loud to her, even though the night was full of gunshots and the general din from the Slab. But the bullet sailed true, shattering the small window in this end of the trailer. She heard a shouted curse, but there was no immediate visible response.

A moment later, she heard a gunshot, loud, from the direction of the trailer. But she didn't see a muzzle blast, just a bright flash of light inside, through the window.

She was lowering the weapon when the door burst open and men piled out, crouching to minimize the targets they presented, and carrying guns of their own. As quickly as she could, she raised the rifle and fired again, but her shot went high. She pulled the trigger once more. It clicked on an empty chamber.

"There she is!" one of them shouted. Suddenly the air around her was alive with the buzz and whine of bullets, thudding into the dirt and chopping bits of brush. She dropped the rifle and ran, back down the slope, the way she had come from. She had no goal in mind, just away, anywhere away from them until she could regroup and arm herself again.

It didn't take them long to realize what she was doing and to give chase. A moment later, she could hear them crashing through the brush, coming toward her. She didn't know if they had flashlights, or simply followed her by moonlight or by the sounds she made. They were back there, that was all that mattered.

After running blindly for a few minutes, she realized that there was someplace she could go, someone on the Slab who would offer shelter and probably had a gun of his own. A friend of her brothers.

Eddie Trujillo would help her.

When the bullet shattered the glass window of Rock's trailer and ripped up through the roof, Kerry had just polished off the last of Rock's beers and was about to stand up to throw the bottle out the door, in the general direction in which he'd last seen Vic Bradford trying to crawl toward the loving arms of his wife.

But he dropped back into his seat as glass sprayed and metal tore. "That's her," he said. "Got to be."

"All the gunfire around here tonight, it could be anyone," Terrance countered.

"No one else would target us," Kerry said. "Let's go put an end to this."

"You go," Rock said. "I don't want it anymore. None of it. Go ahead, just don't come back. I don't want to see you as long as I live, Kerry."

"I can arrange that," Kerry said. He snatched up his rifle, knowing there was already a round in the chamber, and squeezed the trigger. The slug tore through Rock's throat and blew out the back of his neck with a spray of blood. Rock dropped facedown on the trailer's formerly immaculate floor, and made gurgling noises. But Kerry didn't hang around to listen to him die, much as he'd have liked to.

"Get going," he said to Terrance. "We've got to kill that bitch."

By the time Ken Butler reached the first of the slabs, there was almost nothing left of it.

The earth moving machines had flattened every dwelling that had stood there, fifteen or sixteen of them, Ken thought. Rubble was strewn over the concrete surface, but the smaller machines scooted this way and that, scraping up the smoldering mounds and shoving it off the slab into the desert brush beyond.

The two bigger track loaders idled at the edge of the slab, their headlights shining toward the second one. Most of the shotgun-toting guards stood behind the machines, guns trained across the narrow dirt space toward the welcoming committee that waited for them.

The majority of the Slab's residents were out now. Many wept openly, women and men alike. Others, men mostly, and most of those elderly, in their late sixties or seventies, held guns: hunting rifles and small handguns, .22s and the like, that were no match for the military quality of the shotguns that faced them. Their bullets would likely not even penetrate the flak jackets their opponents wore. But they lined up at the edge of the second slab, a human wall, bravely facing the smaller but better-equipped force that had already felled a number of them. Ken had seen some of the bodies, and even now, as he watched, saw the bulk of a man who could only be Jim Trainor, the Slab's fattest male resident, scooped up with the remains of someone's home and pushed off the concrete.

Dogs, at least a dozen of them, barked at the noisy machines, but even they had learned to keep their distance. Some of them sat and scratched or whimpered, noses in the dirt and tails up, for their lost owners. A kid who couldn't have been more than eleven stood with a couple of the dogs, fumbling with a rifle nearly as big as he was.

Ken forced his way through to the front of the line and called across to Haynes's goons. "You men have got to stand down!" he shouted. "I'm the law here and I'm tellin' you to put down those weapons and shut off those vehicles!"

One of the goons took a half-step forward. He was a burly guy with upper arms the size of one of Ken's thighs. Even the shotgun looked small in his hands. "Can't do it, Lieutenant!" he called. "Mr. Haynes owns the land. He has a paper from his attorney saying he's got a legal right to evict trespassers from it."

"Not by committing murder," Ken replied. "There's no law says you can do that."

"Every shot we've fired has been in self-defense," the goon called. "And in defense of our employer's private property!"

"We'll let the courts decide that," Ken said. "But in the meantime, I want you men to put down those weapons."

The goon looked at him across the dirt divide, as if from the other side of a bottomless chasm, without a bridge in sight. Finally, he shrugged and turned back to the drivers sitting in the big machines. He cocked a thumb toward the second slab, and the operators put their loaders into gear and started forward.

Ken fought back a moment of panic. He couldn't tell these people not to defend their homes. But they had little or no chance against those well-trained men with their modern weapons and giant equipment. And to throw away their lives for a few hundred square feet of land they didn't even own, instead of just picking up their few possessions and moving elsewhere, seemed the height of lunacy to him. Looking at the faces that surrounded him, he saw their determination displayed in every crease and wrinkle of sun-leathered skin. These were people who faced the desert every day, who summered in hundred-and-ten degree heat that would melt softer, more civilized folks, who lived life on their own terms instead of society's.

There was a bloodbath coming, and nothing he could do would stop it.

At least, nothing he could do alone. What was it Penny had said as he'd left? Something about not trying to do everything by himself. That was the way he had lived his whole life, certainly since Shannon had died, and maybe even before that.

He pushed his way back out through the throng of people willing to stand together against their common enemy, and broke into a run once he was free of them.

Halfway across the second slab, on his way back to Hal Shipp's RV, he spotted Billy Cobb crouched behind a low wall, his Glock held out sideways, elbow locked. He looked like an idiot, and if he fired the gun that way, he'd be as likely to snap his elbow as hit his target. Looking at him, Ken's run slowed to a walk and the fury ebbed back into him like a rising tide.

He closed to within a few feet without Billy noticing. "Billy," he said.

Billy's head swiveled toward him. "Ken, am I glad to see you! This whole place has gone nuts. I've been tryin' to do what I can, but someone in a trailer over there took some shots at me."

Ken kept walking, closing the gap. He wasn't even thinking clearly now, just feeling, remembering the terror that Mindy Sesno had felt in her final moments and the rage that had filled him back at her house.

"You killed her," he said, his voice low and menacing.

Billy gave him back a look of newborn innocence that just infuriated him all the more. "What are you talking about, Ken? Who's been killed?"

"Mindy," Ken said, and now he finally stopped his forward advance, just on the other side of the low wall from the deputy. Close enough to smell Billy, the acrid tang of his sweat, tainted by fear.

"No," he insisted. "I didn't do any such—"

"Yes," Ken said, and Billy stopped arguing. He stood, bringing the gun to waist height, not with as much subtlety as he probably thought.

Ken gave him no chance to use it. He let his left hand take the weight of his shotgun and jabbed with his right, his fist driving into Billy's gut as if trying to reach right through the deputy. Billy made a whooshing sound as the wind blew out of him. Ken dropped the shotgun on the pavement then, and followed up with a left jab to Billy's jaw. The wedding ring he still wore, Shannon's gift to him, caught flesh and tore it, spraying blood.

Billy rocked back against the trailer behind him, shook his head and brought his pistol up again. Ken reached forward and caught Billy's gun hand and pulled it toward him, yanking Billy off balance. With the gun safely pointed past him Ken gripped the weapon beneath the barrel and twisted up. Billy grabbed Ken's throat with his left hand, trying to choke him, but Ken's pressure on his right hand brought tears to the younger man's eyes and he let go of the gun before his fingers broke. Ken threw the gun to the ground and punched Billy again, staggering him and breaking his grip on Ken's neck.

Billy fell back against the trailer again. But this time he'd planned it, and when he came back at Ken he scooped up one of the bricks from the loosely-constructed wall and slammed it into Ken's chest. Ken fell back a couple of steps. Billy took advantage of the chance to swing the brick in a roundhouse aimed at Ken's head. Ken dodged it, though, and when Billy's brick-laden fist whistled past him, he followed up with a hard right hook to Billy's chin. He felt bone give under his fist; Billy spat blood and teeth, but brought the brick back for another try. He was slowing, though, and Ken sidestepped easily, attacking Billy's chin and jaw again with a left uppercut and another right hook. Billy's head bounced off the trailer once more, and this time he staggered drunkenly as he tried to regain his balance.

Ken didn't let up. Feet apart for stability, he pounded Billy again and again. His deputy's face was cut in half a dozen places; blood flowed from his mouth and nose, his right eye swelled toward shut, a flap of skin on his cheek revealed white bone underneath when he moved his head.

Billy flailed back, but his blows carried less and less force. He connected with Ken's ear and once with Ken's stomach, but Ken was able to shake off both punches without trouble. He continued hammering on Billy, his own fists getting numb from the pounding.

Finally, Billy fell forward, against Ken's chest, knocking over the low wall between them. Ken closed his hands on the man's throat, meaning to strangle the life from him just as he'd done to Mindy. He watched, almost as if he was dissociated from the act, outside his own body, as Billy's face reddened, eyes starting to bulge from his skull. The drumming of the deputy's fists against his back and ribs grew weaker.

And then he sensed, rather than heard, the aircraft coming.

Eddie Trujillo punched the arm of his couch. "Man, I can't believe you shot at a cop!" he complained loudly. "Are there any more of 'em out there?"

Diego stood at the edge of the window, risking the occasional peek outside. "I haven't seen any since that one ran away," he said.

"If he'd come in here we'd all be in some deep shit," Eddie said.

"If he'd come in here we'd have shot him," Jorge replied. "But what do you got to worry about, Eddie? If you got some dope or something in here, I don't think the cops would give a shit considerin' what all else is breakin' loose outside."

"Ain't dope I'm worried about," Eddie said. His face held a kind of knowing smile, and Diego realized that he'd been keeping secrets, even from them.

"What, then?" he asked. "What are you hiding, dude? What are you into?"

"Hey, you think I live up here cause I got to?" Eddie asked them. "I like it here. It's quiet, peaceful, there's no law to speak of. And I got a solid customer base."

"For what?" Diego wanted to know. "Solar panels?"

Eddie just sat back smiling, and held a hand up to his ear as if listening to something far away. Diego listened to, but all he could hear was the intermittent pop pop of gunfire.

Then it dawned on him, leaving him feeling like an idiot for being so blind. "Guns? You deal guns?"

"Not a lot," Eddie confessed. "Just enough to pay the bills, you know?" He rose from the couch and went to the table in the old camper's dining area, which had been made by laying a piece of a door over a long wooden crate. Pulling aside the door, Eddie opened the hinged lid and reached into the crate's depths. When he brought his hands out, they were filled with something Diego had only seen in movies.

"The fuck is that?" he asked.

"Is that loaded?" Jorge demanded.

"All that shooting going on outside, it will be in a second," Eddie replied calmly. The way he held the thing, gingerly but with confidence and a touch of pride, reminded Diego of the way some people held their babies. He reached back in and brought out a belt of ammo, huge bullets, to Diego. Maybe .50 cal. "Heckler & Koch," he said. "HK21." It looked to Diego like some kind of futuristic space gun. All the usual parts were there, in a kind of olive drab color that made it look intended for military use: stock, trigger, barrel, sights. But it came with additional knobs and buttons and attachments, and a bipod hung down from the slotted barrel. "Hundred round belt," Eddie went on. "Available only to military and law enforcement customers. In this country, anyway."

"That's not legal, is it?" Diego asked him. He moved over to the crate and looked in. There must have been a dozen guns in their, mostly flat black steel, mean-looking weapons such as nothing he'd ever seen.

"Whatever you done that got you so scared you're hiding out at my place, shooting at cops, is that legal, Diego? Didn't you guys maybe break a teensy little law somewhere along the line?"

"Yeah," Jorge said, "but—"

"Shut up," Diego snapped. "None of us needs to know any more about what the others done, okay? I think maybe that's best all the way around."

"Yeah, okay," Jorge agreed.

Eddie flopped back down on his couch, but he kept the HK21 in his hands. "Anything you say, man. It's all okay by me."

Ken didn't want to go back into the home that Hal and Virginia Shipp shared. When he'd touched Virginia, he had flashed back to the vision he'd seen earlier, the lined, aged hands on a shovel's handle, digging up a grave to find the skull that had found its way to the fire pit on the Slab. But this time, he knew that the hands belonged to Virginia, and he, through her eyes, looked up to see Hal holding the flashlight in shaky hands, causing the light's circle of illumination to wobble this way and that. If they had dug up the skull and secretly planted it on the Slab, then they had some guilty knowledge of the victim's death, he surmised. It was hard to believe of either of them— both gentle people, as far as he knew. But then, he had never known them well.

The worst part was that Ken could, to some degree, feel what Virginia felt at that gruesome moment—his muscles ached with hers as she pushed the shovel's blade into the earth with arms and shoulders, then lifted a weary foot that wanted nothing more than to be propped up and massaged and pressed down on the back of the blade with it, forcing the shovel in deeper still, then turned the blade, heavy with dirt, and strained the muscles of back and ribs to spill it outside the hole. Beyond the physical, he had a sense of her emotional state. And he knew, as she did, that this body was just one of many.

He even understood her motivation. Hal Shipp had not committed these murders alone. He'd had help, he had been part of a group. But now the group was out there again, without Hal—certainly too old, too wracked with dementia, to be trusted with firearms even by killers—and another victim would be in danger. By putting the skull in a place where it would surely be discovered, Virginia hoped to spur an investigation that would reveal the killers and save a life.

Except it hadn't quite worked that way, Ken feared. Either he hadn't been a good enough cop, or she hadn't planted quite enough evidence. Because that investigation had fallen by the wayside while the rest of the Slab went insane, and now many people had died. All while Ken made no progress at all in finding out anything about the killers.

Well, now he had a clue. He had Hal Shipp, whose mind was sharp enough, thanks to the magic, to rat out his friends. He wasn't sure how well Hal's testimony would hold up in court, though, when the defense could call just about everyone Hal came into contact with on a daily basis to testify to his dementia. But a price had to be paid. Wrongs had been done. He despised the crimes in which Hal been complicit, and through the bond they shared, he felt that Hal genuinely regretted what he'd done—and more to the point, could barely remember it, most times. In prison, his Alzheimer's would doubtless degenerate fast, and did it do any good to lock up someone who had no understanding of why he was there?

Still, Ken knew what his duty was. Soon as they had some time, he'd do it. He'd arrest Hal Shipp, and the others involved, whose faces he had seen through Hal's eyes.

So stepping back into their RV and facing them, burdened with the terrible knowledge he had, was something he would have avoided doing if at all possible. But he remembered what Penny had told him, the thing he'd remembered before, when he ran into Billy and was interrupted by his own murderous urges. Don't try to do everything by yourself, she had said. Words to that effect, anyway. He had realized before, back at the space between the slabs, the war zone between residents and locals, that he couldn't bring this conflict to a close by himself.

Now, there was an even greater threat brewing, and once again, it wasn't one he could counter alone. He needed Hal and Penny if he hoped to have a chance against it. He had left Billy in the dirt, bloodied and battered, but not dead, and run, full tilt, for the Shipp residence. As he ran he could hear the thunder of guns and the roar of the machines and the screams of the wounded.

And over it all the whine of the jet's engines as it came closer and closer.

When he reached Hal's place he didn't knock or shout, just yanked the door open and burst in, half-tripping over the top step to land on his hands and knees just inside the door. Penny let out a shriek and fired the Glock and the shot went high, missing Ken because of his trip but punching a hole through the flimsy aluminum door.

"Oh my God," she said when she realized what she'd done. "Oh my God, Ken, I'm so sorry!"

He pushed himself to his feet, walked to her, and took the gun from her, holstering it. "It's okay, Penny," he said. "No harm done." The damage to the RV didn't count, since he had a feeling that before too much longer the Slab would be empty of trailers and RVs and shacks. And maybe people. "But I need to borrow Hal again, Virginia."

The two of them sat on the couch, looking like they never planned to let go of one another again. Ken saw her fingers tense on his arm at his statement. "It's important."

She forced a smile. "Will you bring him back when you're done with him?"

She was joking, he knew. Cops told lies all the time, little ones and sometimes big ones. But scrupulous honesty seemed crucial now. Hal might not live through what was still to come tonight. If he did live, Ken would have to lock him up. "I don't know," he said. "Maybe."

"All right, then," she said, relinquishing her husband's scrawny arm. "You be careful, Harold. That's all I ask."

Penny looked at Ken with an even expression on her face. "Me too?"

"You too. I think outside is better than in here. Out on the Slab."

She rose and trailed Ken and Hal out of the RV. "There's a jet coming," he said as soon as they were outside. He didn't know why but somehow it felt like what he had in mind would work better under the open sky. There were stars overhead but the smoke had grown so thick it blotted out most of them. And the jet, of course, wouldn't be apparent until it was too late.

"What kind of a jet?" Penny asked.

"I don't know," Ken said. "Military. From the Marine base in Yuma, I guess. But they're not gunning for the Impact Area. They're coming for the Slab."

"You know this how?" Hal asked him.

"I just feel it," Ken admitted. "It's not much to go on."

"It's good enough for me," Hal said. He reached out and took one of Ken's hands. "I think we should all feel it."

"Yeah," Ken agreed. "That's what I was thinking." He took Penny's hand in his left, and saw her clasp Hal's with her own left.

Touching either one of them, the magic was intensified, an almost physical sensation of hyper-intense power and energy and awareness. But standing together in a ring, each touching the others, that feeling was magnified exponentially. The world fell away.

And they stood together, completely revealed to one another in a way none of them had ever known.

Ken knew that Penny was premenstrual, starting to feel swollen and uncomfortable. He knew what she'd been doing on the gunnery range; knew of her relatively recent but passionate commitment to environmentalism; knew of her Gulf War experiences; knew everyone she'd ever slept with or flirted with; knew who her best friend had been in the third grade. And he knew just as much about Hal—he was suddenly aware of the Dove Hunts and Hal's part in them, and who else had been involved; of the full extent of Hal's dementia; of Hal's postwar ambitions that had not been realized; and of his gradual acceptance of his lot—what Virginia called, when they argued, his giving up on his own life. And he knew that Hal had become convinced that she was right, that he had gone beyond resigning himself to the fact that he would never achieve the things he wanted, but he couldn't bring himself to come around to her way of thinking, which was that success needn't be measured in financial terms. He and Virginia had a close, precious bond. They had raised a son, dead now, but a loving child in life. They had shared the decades. That should have been enough—Hal knew it should—but he couldn't make it be. He couldn't make himself not feel like a failure because he'd never held the big executive job or made the big killing he'd wanted.

For their part, he knew that he was just as wide open to them as they were to him, and through their eyes he could see himself—the widower who had moved to the middle of nowhere rather than stay put and face his ghosts, the shy man who didn't like to meet new people and would as soon stay inside his house with a book as go into

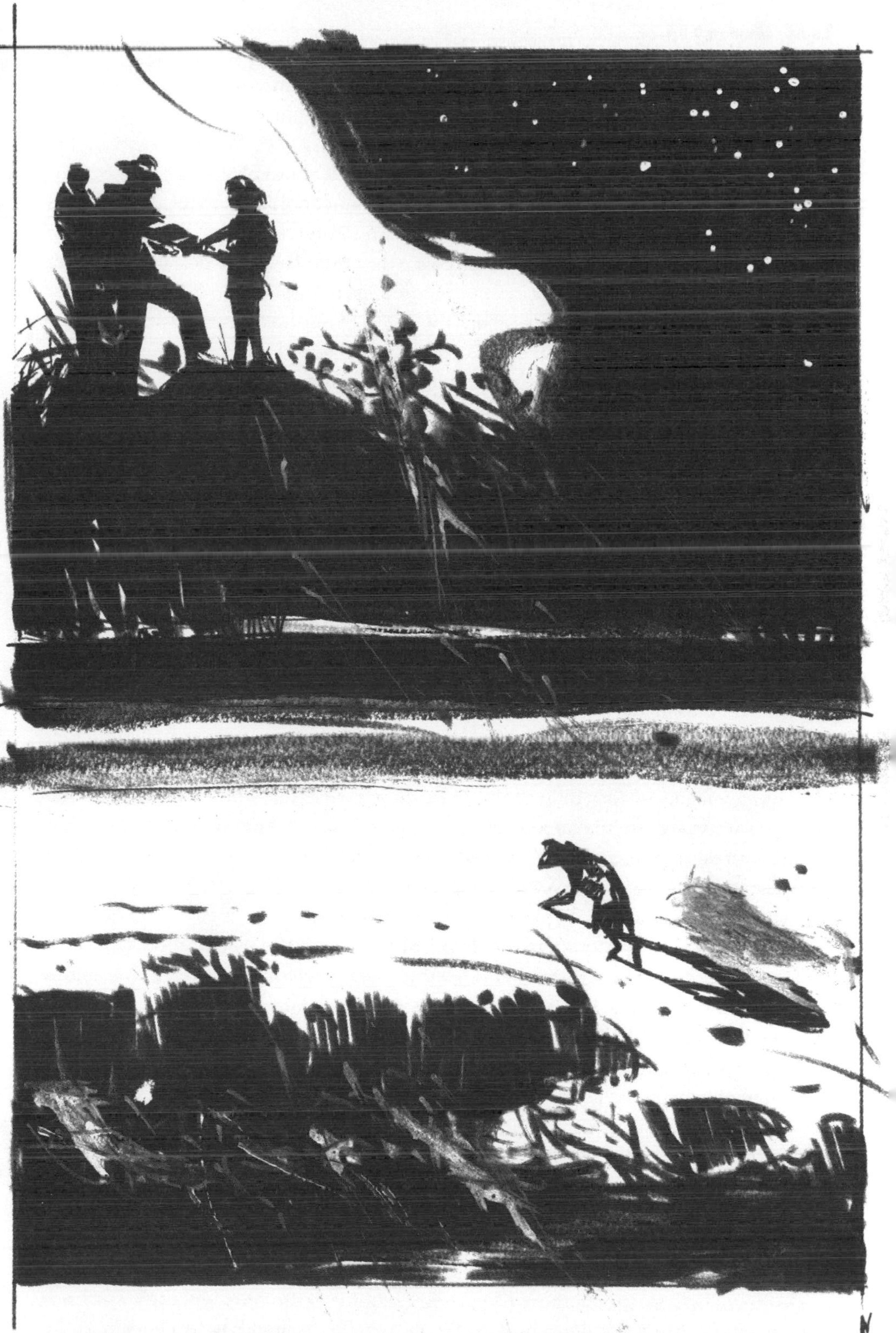

the world, the angry man who knew that Billy Cobb had murdered Mindy Sesno and knew that Billy Cobb had made love to Mindy Sesno but didn't know which fact enraged him more.

None of it made him like himself very much. But there was something he saw, reflected through Penny and Hal, some core of admiration for him that surprised Ken. They knew his innermost secrets, but they liked and respected him anyway. He was, they felt, a man who lived up to his promises, who worked hard to do the right thing, who didn't shirk from duty or decisions, who tried his best to tell the truth. He guessed he had always known those things about himself too, but was surprised at the weight other people ascribed to them. For his own part, he had a hard time looking past the elation he'd felt at having Billy's throat in his hands, just a few minutes ago.

"We need to look beyond us," Ken said, finally realizing that they could spend a lifetime standing here gazing into each other's hearts and minds, but that he'd gathered them for a reason. He supposed speech was probably unnecessary, but still felt more comfortable speaking out loud than somehow mentally projecting his thoughts. He felt, rather than heard, the assent of the other two.

Far above the Slab, still at some distance but gaining ground rapidly, was a Marine Corps jet with two men inside it. Ken, Penny, and Hal reached for the aircraft, with their minds, and touched the minds of the two Marines aboard. But those minds were foul and confused, dark holes where human thoughts should be, tangled knots of tendrils and ganglions and sparking synapses instead of functioning brains. Ken felt himself recoil from the contact.

"We don't need them anyhow," Hal said. His meaning was clear to Ken. The men in the jet were just tools, carrying out a task. There were ways to prevent their goal from being achieved that didn't involve dealing with them, and Ken thought they were probably beyond human reasoning anyway. He wasn't entirely sure what Hal had in mind, though…which meant that Hal wasn't either.

"Seat of the pants," Penny said. Shorthand, but good enough.

"Right," Hal agreed.

No further words passed between them. They hadn't let go of one another's hands, and they wouldn't. The jet was almost overhead and there was no time for hesitation or debate. They concentrated, the three of them, on doing something that not only had none of them ever done, but something they'd never even conceived of.

They had no way to know if it would work.

Or could work.

The air crackled with something like electricity. The noise of the Slab, the running gun battle, the screams and shouts, the din of big motors, was all gone. They could hear nothing over the electrical static in their ears, as if the blue glow that surrounded them somehow muffled the rest of the world.

When they saw the blue glow, Ken/Penny/Hal realized, for the first time, that they might succeed.

As they gripped one another's hands and focused on the blue glow, it grew. From their position it ballooned outward, as big as a trailer. A building. A single slab. Its shape was plainly dome-like, now, getting wider than it was high, but still growing in every direction.

And growing.

Enveloping the whole Slab, finally, before it was done. Because, while they didn't know why, they knew that the Slab had to be protected. And the jet meant to do the Slab harm. Not the aircraft itself, and not the people in it, and not even, really, the one who had ordered them to do this, but the force behind that one, they understood. That power—Ken wasn't even sure it could be called an entity, but maybe—wanted a bomb to fall on the Slab, wanted the concrete to be turned to rubble and the blood of hundreds to spill down the hole it made.

But the blue glow turned into a blue dome and the blue dome covered the Slab, from the concrete guard station to the most distant shack, and everyone who was on the Slab, shooting or hiding or writhing in pain, was contained within the dome. And still it grew, blossoming into the sky like a fast-growing agave or the overnight shoot of a mushroom. And still the Hornet came, its pilots sightless, no longer in control of their own senses, performing the motions that were expected of them.

Over the Slab, they released the GBU-12.

But the blue glow pressed up against the bottom of the jet, holding the bomb against it, holding the Hornet in place above the Slab. The airplane's engines strained, to no avail.

The bomb detonated.

No matter where they were on the Slab, no matter what they were doing, everyone heard the explosion, and they looked up to see what resembled a massive skyrocket. Streaks of flame and burning steel shot out from the Hornet, sliding down the outer skin of the blue dome in every direction. Within the dome, though, they couldn't feel the heat or the concussive wave the blast generated. They lowered guns, they crawled out from underneath trailers, they stepped outside and stared at the sky, at the glowing blue shield, at the fiery yellow and red tracings dripping down its transparent surface like molten lightning.

Without conscious thought, the three broke the contact necessary to maintain the glowing dome and it winked from existence as if it had never been there. But where the bits of flaming wreckage had come to rest, fires caught in the tinder-dry brush at the edges of the Slab, smoke rising into the dark sky from a couple dozen new spots in addition to the fires that already burned. After a few glorious moments of silence, the gunfire continued.

"That was cool," Penny said, a broad smile on her face. She laughed. "Really cool."

"Yeah," Ken agreed. "But we're not done yet."

"Not even close," Hal said. "They're shooting each other again."

"I know," Penny said. "But hey, you remember what I said before? About us making love? Umm, never mind. I just don't see it getting any better than that."

She's right, Ken thought. That's what it was like. He had felt a closeness with these two that he hadn't had since Shannon had died. It was like making love, like having someone there all the time who knew your moods and your mind. Who knew but didn't judge, only accepted. And when the two of you were together, moving together, inside each other, well, there was, he had thought, no other feeling like it in the world.

Now he knew that he'd been wrong. He could have that feeling, without sex, without romance, just by reaching out and touching these two people again.

And how easy it would be to do that instead of taking care of what needed doing.

"Let's go," he said. "We've got to cover some ground."

They all knew, he was sure, what their destination was. The place from which all this madness stemmed.

They had to trespass again, on the aerial gunnery range.

They had to get back into that cave.

It took Billy a few minutes, after Ken stopped strangling him and ran off, to gather the strength to stand up. Ken would be coming back to finish what he'd started, he figured. And if it wasn't tonight, it would be some other day. He had no idea how Ken knew it was him, but he did and that was really what mattered. Billy needed to get himself gone, and he needed to do it fast.

But there was no way he was going to try to go out through the roaring gun battle that he could hear taking place between him and where he'd left the Crown Vic. He'd already been shot at, beaten up, and choked tonight, and whatever that explosion in the sky had been, he wanted nothing to do with. The whole point of leaving was to avoid more physical damage, not to tempt it. Instead, he figured he'd just get off the Slab at the closest possible point and work his way cross-country to the car, dodging, he hoped, the worst of the flying lead.

Rubbing the raw flesh of his neck, he hurried around a couple of homes, keeping well clear of the one from which he'd been fired on earlier. When he came around the last one, he saw a wall of flames encircling the Slab—this portion of it, at least. The flames were only five or six feet deep and maybe that high, but from where he stood, he couldn't see any breaks in the wall big enough to slip through. And walking through fire didn't fit in at all well with the whole damage-avoidance idea. He swore. Sometimes it seemed like the whole world was conspiring against a man, he thought. Figuring he'd just have to find another way out, Billy Cobb turned and headed back into the Slab, for what he hoped would be the last time.

They ran straight toward Ken's Bronco, even though that route took them right through the worst of the gunfire. Somehow, though, they knew they had nothing to fear from that—anything powerful enough to hurt them on this particular night would be much more dangerous than mere bullets. Ken was surprised at the pace that Hal kept up, but realized that they were all drawing strength from the magic. He should have been exhausted too, for that matter, and Penny, as far as he could tell, had been going nonstop for hours. By rights they all ought to have been dead on their feet.

Around them as they dashed across the Slab, they saw residents using their own homes as bunkers, firing around corners or from beneath shelters made of tires, lawn furniture, and stones. Muzzle flashes lit the night periodically, while flames from the burning desert beyond lent a hellish illumination to the scene. The men working for Haynes fired back from the cover of their armored machines.

But even as they heard the gunfire and the metallic clanking of spent cartridges hitting the concrete and saw the bursts of flame and the bodies littering the earth, they were removed in some way from it all, as if it happened on the other side of a screen. As if, Ken thought for a moment, it happened in some other reality that only pressed against theirs but didn't bleed through.

In this way, observing the ongoing battle without participating in it, they made it to the Bronco. Ken slid in behind the wheel and the other two took their now-customary positions, Hal riding shotgun while Penny straddled the rear bench, leaning forward between the two men.

"It's in the cave, isn't it?" she asked as soon as the vehicle was in motion.

"What I'm thinking," Ken agreed.

"Seems it's got to be," Hal said.

"I never wanted to go back in that freaking cave."

"You're not alone there, Penny," Ken said. "But it looks like we have to."

"Yeah, I know. Just saying I don't like it, that's all."

"Don't have to like it," Hal said. "Nobody's asking us to like any of this."

Ken drove the Bronco up the dirt road that led away from the Slab and paralleled the Coachella Canal. At the first siphon he came to—the only points where the road crossed the canal—he went across and onto the road that followed the line of warning signs the Marines had put up at the border of their bombing range.

"You've lived with this whole magic thing since the second World War?" Penny asked Hal. "And never told anybody?"

"I tried to tell a couple of people, in the beginning," Hal admitted. "But I couldn't even explain it. Hell, I could barely believe it myself."

"I know what you mean," she said. "When it was happening, I never really doubted it. But the next day, it was like, no, that didn't happen. There's some other explanation."

"It happened," Ken assured them both. "It all happened. It's still happening."

"Has it ever lasted this long, for you?" Penny wondered. "I mean, it's been, like, three days or something."

"Always just been a day or so, far as I can remember," Hal said. "Of course, half the time I can't remember what my thumbs are for, so don't pay too much mind to me."

"Your memory's just fine now, you nut."

"Now, yeah. Either of you given any thought to what's going to happen to us whenever it wears off? We've been running around like maniacs, not eating, not sleeping, working ourselves too hard. I know my body isn't up to this kind of punishment any more. Yours might be, Penny—don't know as I've seen a body in shape like yours outside of a magazine in twenty years or more. But I've got a bad feeling that when the magic is gone we're all going to be hurting something fierce."

Ken glanced over at him. Hal was right—he'd been acting like a thirty-year old man, but he still looked every bit as old as he had a few days ago, before they had touched. Ken tried to keep himself in reasonable condition, and he might be just sore and aching for six months or so after this extended workout. But Hal...well, he didn't quite see how Hal would survive it.

"Who's to say it's going to wear off?" Penny asked. "I mean, it's already broken all the rules, right? If there were rules in the first place. It's never lasted more than a day before, but now it's all Sears Diehards. We've never shared it with anyone but now it's stronger if we're together. I don't know about you guys, but I've never been able to do anything like that...whatever that was, protective bubble or whatever that we put over the Slab back there. That's all new."

"I think we're all just guessing," Ken said. "Assuming it's going to wear off, because...well, if it doesn't, what does that make us? Some kind of gods or something?"

"That might be going a little far," Hal said. "But something other than human, that's for sure."

"Maybe we're some kind of mutation. A new generation of human, a new subspecies, I don't know...metahuman."

"And maybe they'll write comic books about us, Penny," Ken said. "Dress us up in tights and give us red capes." He turned up the jeep road that led into the Chocolates. Into the gunnery range. He left he headlights on, even though they were now trespassing on military land. This was not a road he'd be willing to drive in the dark, especially in a hurry. And he had a feeling the folks over in Yuma would have other things on their mind tonight, like trying to figure out what had happened to their airplane. "I'm thinking we need to just play it by ear. Don't try to parse it out because we don't know enough about it anyway. We got so many questions we don't know the answers to that we don't even know what all the questions are, or who to ask. I'm for just letting things play out, and we'll see where we go from there."

"Yeah, okay," Penny agreed. "I guess that makes sense. I'm the kind of person who likes to know where I'm going, that's all. But—"

"I know what kind of person you are," Hal interrupted.

"I guess you do," she said with a low laugh. "I guess you both do. And vice versa. And by the way, I can't believe how long it's been since you got laid."

Hal turned around in his seat and looked at her, one eyebrow riding up high on his forehead. Ken caught a glimpse of the glare he gave Penny as he turned the Bronco's wheel to the right. "You are talking about Ken, right, Penny?" Hal asked.

Penny laughed again, full-throated and loud this time. "Yes, I am," she confirmed. "You stud."

The image of Mindy Sesno flashed across Ken's mind again. He'd pinned a lot of hopes on Mindy, without ever doing anything to make those hopes become reality. Well, that wouldn't happen again. Penny was right. He'd been denying himself for too long, and once this all was over with—if he could still stand on his own legs and get out of the house—he'd find himself someone, first thing.

The key phrase in that was the "once this was all over" part, he knew. Survival was implied, but not guaranteed.

Having taken the rudimentary dirt road as far as they could, Ken braked the Bronco and killed the engine. "Here we are, boy and girl," he said. "The rest of it's on foot."

A cold wind whistled through the valley, kicking up billows of sand, rustling the brittlebush and the branches of mesquite and paloverde. As they approached the cave entrance again, Penny couldn't shake a profound sensation of dread. It had been bad enough last time, when they'd gone in looking for Mick's body and found that it had disappeared. And then she'd had that vision or whatever Hal had called it, of the gray man and the ancient Cahuilla Indians who had lived here thousands of years ago.

But when she shone her light on the gaping maw, her blood froze and she stopped where she stood, unable to persuade her legs to take another step. The mushrooms had spread and now choked the entrance, leaking like pus from a torn blister onto the sand outside. Some of them were nearly a foot tall, and they all shared the same sickly-pale white flesh etched with seams of red.

Hal seemed to understand her hesitation. He stopped at her shoulder, carrying the Mini-Mag from Ken's belt. "You can do this," he said. "You've done worse."

"Yeah," Penny agreed, surprised that she was even able to speak. "Only I can't remember when, just now."

"That's because I'm lying to you," Hal said. "If you've encountered anything worse than what we're likely to face in there, I doubt you'd be standing here today."

She noticed that Ken had stopped just inside the mouth of the cave, practically standing in the mushrooms, and looked back at them. He'd mounted a light on his handgun. "You coming, or not?" he asked. "Don't have all night here."

"That we know of," Penny said under her breath. "No telling how long we have. We could lose all the magic any second."

Hal laid a hand on her arm, in a gesture she understood was meant to be reassuring. "Best reason there is to go in and get it done with," he said. "Then we can go back to our regular lives, maybe."

"But do we really want to?" she asked him. "I mean, isn't it better when the magic is here?"

"Could be," Hal said. "But you can't count on it. It's like pinning all your hopes on a dream."

"Maybe that's what I'm good at."

"I've seen inside you, Penny. What you're good at is suppressing your own needs to serve what you consider the greater good. You keep trying to save the world but you haven't even taken the time to learn to enjoy living in it. Well, now you've got to save the world again, or a piece of it anyway. Maybe after you're done, you'll give it a rest and look out for yourself for a change."

"Yeah, I guess so," she said. "You're pretty smart for an old guy, you know?" She tossed him a smile and then followed Ken into the cave, wincing inwardly as her feet crushed the mushrooms. They really had spread dramatically; dotting the walls and floor of the cave as far as her light's beam could show. The fungi creeped her out, and she knew that its rapid growth was well beyond anything that could be natural. But Hal was right—what they needed to do could only be done inside the cave.

Of course, before they could do it, they'd have to figure out what it was.

Penny steeled herself for anything as she walked through the sudden, bizarre growth. She'd read about "sick houses," places in which mold or fungi of some kind had taken root behind the walls, poisoning the air and causing all sorts of illnesses. No options here, though…she didn't have a MOPP suit, like she had been issued in the Gulf in case of chemical warfare. She didn't even know if it would make a difference if she took shallow breaths or deep ones. She settled for trying to breathe only through her nose, on the theory that the spores released as they crushed mushrooms underfoot would be filtered better that way. The smell in the cave was rich and pungent, now, instead of the dry, stale air it had contained on her first two visits. She knew that when she smelled something she was, in fact, taking minute particles of that substance into her body, and the idea that any of these unclean, unholy mushrooms were entering her in any way repulsed her.

Still she kept on, following Ken with his gun-light, and leading Hal. The cave, familiar by now, was horrifyingly changed by the new growth. The sensation of stepping through the unbroken tide of mushrooms ankle-high or taller was not unlike wading through surf, but a surf of something thicker than mere water. Penny almost gagged at the image, and forced herself to focus on the upper sections of wall, where the mushrooms had not yet reached.

As they neared the bend where the writing on the wall started—where she had left Mick's body, then discovered it missing and new mushrooms growing in its place when she had brought Ken and Hal back—Penny realized that her hands were trembling uncontrollably, the light from her flashlight jumping and flitting around the cave's walls like Tinker Bell on speed. She knew that would just be the beginning of the journey—that whatever they were here to see or do might start there, with the ancient writings, but that their path would lead them much deeper into the earth than that point. Nevertheless, that was the part she was most nervous about, that one stretch of cave where people had stopped to leave messages to whoever might come later, across the span of centuries.

And then, there it was. Ken rounded the bend and disappeared in that section, and Penny suddenly felt an urge to catch up to him, not to let him out of her sight, particularly here, in this part of the cave. "Ken, wait!" she called.

"What?" his voice came back. She felt reassured by that. He hadn't fallen off the face of the planet or stepped through a rift in the space-time continuum. He had just turned a blind corner, and she'd see him when she had rounded it too.

But it wasn't Ken she saw when she came around the bend into that fateful stretch. It was Mick.

"Hi, Pen," he said.

Penny screamed until her chest ached, then took a few gasping breaths, refilling her lungs, and screamed again.

Behind her, Hal crowded in, playing his little flash over Mick's form. Her own light had fallen to the ground, illuminating only the sea of mushrooms. Up ahead, Ken had turned back, and his light was partially obscured by Mick's form, blocking the cave passage.

Mick sounded like Mick, and the shape was certainly Mick's. But the Mick she had known—the Mick she had killed—had been a flesh-and-blood Mick. She still had some of his blood on her shirt.

This Mick, though, had pale, white skin mottled with red dots and veined with tiny red threads. This Mick was made of mushroom-stuff.

Billy's head began to throb as he wandered the Slab. Smoke from the fires filled his lungs, the crackle of the flames and the flashes of muzzle bursts stung his eyes. He'd had a plan, before—not that long ago, he thought—but he couldn't remember what it might have been. He blinked a couple of times and looked at his surroundings as if he'd never seen them before—old trailers, broken down school buses, camper shells, scattered seemingly at random about a desert landscape as if they'd just fallen from the sky. Walls made of bald tires. Hubcaps nailed to yucca stalks. Flat concrete slabs with dirt between them, and in the dirt, seashells catching the firelight, gleaming.

The dirt.

Billy's mind emptied, his focus narrowed. He had a plan again. He didn't know where it had come from—not from within him—but he knew it was important. He ran to the dirt stretch between two concrete slabs, dropped to his knees, and started to dig, furiously, using only his hands as tools.

Across the Slab, others did the same thing. Men who had been shooting their rifles, like Darren Cook, instead shoved the barrels of those guns into the earth, makeshift shovels to break the ground. Others came out from hiding, like Virginia Shipp, and worked at the concrete with bare fingers that quickly bloodied, trying to pry up sections of it. Carter Haynes threw himself down, and Gray Boonton, and Nick Postak, and Mikey Zee. All digging, barehanded or with whatever was within easy reach. Lettie Bosworth tore frantically at the concrete, the flesh of her fingers shredding to the bone and bone splintering to the marrow. Jorge and Diego Alvarez left Eddie Trujillo's trailer to paw at the dirt outside. Vic Bradford, barely conscious, moved his hands weakly against the cement slab.

They all did this because they knew there was something beneath, something calling to them. And it needed to get out.

Penny's screams reverberated throughout the cave, hurting Hal's ears—like his physical strength and endurance, and his mental focus and concentration, his senses had been heightened to the point that his glasses were nearly unnecessary, and his hearing was much more acute.

So Penny's unending scream was shattering.

Hal stepped forward, rounding the corner and putting a hand out to touch her shoulder, hoping to reassure her, to quiet her. But as he did, his light caught the strange shape, so human-looking but yet clearly not human, that stood before her.

That spoke to her.

And somehow, Ken had walked right past it, as if it had only materialized when Penny showed up. At the sound of Penny's screams, Ken had turned, and now he held his gun and light on the thing as he looked past it at Penny, questioningly, as if wondering whether or not to shoot.

Hal heard a hitching in Penny's voice as she tried to bring her terror under control. The mushroom man hadn't made a move toward her, had only uttered two words. Maybe it wasn't malevolent at all.

But with a hand on Penny's back, Hal could feel her quaking in mortal dread. She was scared of it, at any rate. He was too, for that matter, but maybe not scared down to his bones like she must have been. She tried to bull her way past it, but it turned, blocking the way. She pulled back from contact with it.

"Did you miss me, Penny?" the unnatural thing asked her. "I've missed you."

Its tone was familiar, even intimate. Hal couldn't help thinking that Penny and this person—or the person this thing represented—had been lovers. Or nearly so, anyway. Based on what Penny had told them, Mick had wanted to be, and the Mick-simulacrum was apparently still thinking along those lines.

"You're not even...even here," Penny said, voice quavering. "You're dead. I...I killed you."

"Yes," the thing said. Hal noted that when it opened its mouth, there was just more of the mushroom-stuff inside. It was a Muppet's mouth, with no oral cavity, no throat. No legitimate way for it to be speaking. "But the difference between us is that I know how to forgive."

Ken fired his handgun then, three times. The bullets tore through the mushroom man with almost no resistance, knocking chunks of him into the air—and releasing more spores, Hal found himself thinking—then flew down the cave, one nearly hitting

Hal. Behind him, they hit the cave's wall and ricocheted around, kicking up chips of rock and dirt.

"Better not shoot in here," Hal said.

The mushroom man wasn't even phased. "Your friends don't like me," it said. "But we have unfinished business, don't we?"

"N…no…" Penny said. "You're dead. We have…"

"Penny, I don't think you understand. We have unfinished business. We need to talk some things over." Its voice was calm, as if it had never been shot. And as Hal watched, the sections that Ken's bullets had torn off it filled in, the mushroom-stuff growing back almost instantly.

"No," Ken said. His voice was firm, commanding. "Penny, just walk past it. We don't have time to argue with it—damn thing's most likely all in our heads anyway. Some sort of mass hallucination. A peyote dream. Air in here must be filled with hallucinogens, right?"

"Penny," the thing said, as if Ken and Hal weren't even here. "A few minutes to talk. Five minutes. I think you owe me that much, right?"

"I don't…"

"No, Penny," Hal warned. "You can't give in to it."

"But he's right," she argued. "I killed him. Maybe I can explain why."

"Penny—" Ken began. She cut him off.

"You guys go on ahead. There's no time to debate. I'll take three minutes with him and join you."

"No," Ken said.

"Three minutes." She sounded every bit as determined as Ken did.

"Not a second more," Hal said. "We'll be back. And you're right, there isn't time to fool around."

"You heard them," Penny said. She crossed her arms across her chest, and looked to Hal as if she were braced for anything the fungus-Mick might have in mind for her. "You have three minutes, starting now. You have anything you want to say to me, start talking."

Hal squeezed past Penny and pressed himself nearly flat against the cave wall so he could get past the mushroom man. When he reached Mick, both started walking, looking back over their shoulders the whole time. The mushroom man spoke to Penny in low tones, but he didn't seem to be making any physical overtures toward her.

A minute later the cave crooked again and Penny was out of sight.

"That's…" Hal began, but he didn't know how to end his sentence.

"Damn strange," Ken offered.

Hal chuckled, amused by the understatement in spite of the circumstance. Ken wasn't a religious person, he knew, and neither was Penny. He wasn't particularly devout himself, but he believed in something greater than themselves. Some kind of God with a capital G. A Creator. And he knew that whatever they were facing here in this cave, it was on the other side. So it had to be defeated, and there could be no reason for them to be here, imbued with what they called the magic, except to do that job. They had all been rescued, during their respective wars, by the magic, and brought to this place. There had to be some kind of intelligence operating behind that. "Yes, it is that."

"Didn't even see it when I walked through that stretch. Like it was part of the mushrooms or something, and then it separated out from them after I'd gone by. Like it knew Penny was coming."

"I'm sure it did."

"Sorry about almost shooting you."

"Don't worry about that," Hal said. "You probably thought the thing would stop your slugs a little better. Or slow them down, at least."

"That's what I thought. I'm sure I hit it."

"You did," Hal said. "I saw the impacts. They just didn't do any damage. At least, not long-term."

"What I thought." Ken continued walking for a moment. "Life sure is funny, ain't it?"

"Stranger than most of us could possibly imagine," Hal agreed. They continued on, into the depths of the cave, past writing that grew older and older. Like descending into the Grand Canyon, he felt as if they were walking past a visual record of the planet itself. "Do me a favor?"

"What's that?" Ken asked.

"You see anyone you've killed show up in here, don't stop to chat."

"You've got my word on that," Ken said. "No problem at all."

Lucy ran, breathless and exhausted, as fast as she could manage. When she approached the area she thought Eddie's trailer was in, she began to feel heartened. Eddie would hide her. Eddie would be an ally—the first one she'd had since all this started. She could still hear the crashing of brush and thumping of feet behind her, but she allowed herself a moment of optimism.

Which was when the bullet slammed into her left shoulder, spinning her half around and slamming her down into a creosote bush as surely as if someone had pushed her. Stiff branches clawed at her, cutting her exposed flesh, snagging her clothing and loose, wild hair.

Damn it, she thought. So close…

She started trying to regain her balance, to extricate herself from the greasewood, but she was too tangled up. Then she felt a strong hand on her, tugging her by the wounded shoulder. The pain was unbearable.

The touch was worse.

She saw the curly guy looking at her, smiling. The one she believed was Kerry Williams. He pulled her free of the bush and then let her go. Her legs gave out beneath her and she dropped to her knees.

"You've run us a merry chase, bitch," he said. "A merry Goddamn chase."

Lucy was breathing hard, through her mouth, trying to push the pain in her shoulder into a separate compartment of her mind where it wouldn't interfere with thinking, with trying to find a way out of this.

"There has never been a Dove I have so looked forward to seeing dead," the man went on. "You have no idea of the pleasure you're about to cause me."

He began to lower his gun to her head. With nothing to lose, she tried a desperate ploy.

The knife she'd taken from Ray Dixon was still tucked between her belt and waistband, at the small of her back. With her right hand, she grabbed for it and lashed out. The blade drew a fine red line across his thigh. He screamed and wobbled on his feet, and she slashed up as she pushed herself to her own full height. This time, the knife caught his right hand, the one groping for the gun's trigger. He screamed again.

Behind him, the other guy, the fat one, angled for position. He looked like he wanted to shoot her but didn't dare, for fear of hitting Williams.

She didn't bother to watch any longer, but ran. Behind her, she heard loud swearing and then the sounds of pursuit.

A minute later, she plowed through the flaming brush that had been left behind when whatever it was had exploded and dripped down the weird blue bubble, and into the little clearing where Eddie had parked his trailer, next to the upside-down wreck of a Chevy Impala that always signposted his place for her, and what she saw stopped her cold.

Her brothers, Jorge and Diego, pawing at the dirt like animals. Their hands were bleeding; the ground before them was soaked with blood, wet and black in the firelight. She gave a little, wordless shout, but they didn't even look up.

"What are you doing?!" she demanded. She grabbed Diego's shoulders, bent down to get in front of his face. "Diego! Jorge! It's me, Lucia!"

Diego shook her off, swatted at her like an insect.

"Don't do no good," Eddie said. Now she saw him, sitting on the step of his own trailer and watching the whole scene. There was a massive gun cradled in his arms. "They're like, loco or some shit. It's fucked up, man."

"Can't you do anything?"

"They don't listen, Lucy," Eddie told her.

She ran to him. "Eddie, there's these guys chasing me. Trying to kill me."

He smiled, as if she were telling a joke. "Seems like everybody's tryin' to kill somebody. Except your brothers—I think they already did their killing for this week."

Before she could continue, though, two more figures came through the flames. Kerry and Terrance. Kerry's walk was a half-stagger, as his right leg couldn't support his weight. They looked at Diego and Jorge, digging like crazy people, at Eddie, and finally at Lucy. Both men looked awful, exhausted, filthy, half-mad. Kerry was splattered with blood. Probably, she thought, a lot like me.

But Kerry's grizzled face was split in a sinister grin, as if finding Lucy again had made everything she'd put him through worth it. "You," he said weakly. "You cut me."

"Those the guys?" Eddie asked quietly.

"What's left of them," Lucy replied. She snatched the big gun from his hands. "Give me that."

Kerry barked out a laugh, looking at her struggling to lift the big weapon with a wounded shoulder. But she made the effort, lifting the thing to her waist and tugging the trigger.

The first burst was a quick three shots that completely missed her targets—loud but not significant enough to be heard by many people over the Slab's apocalyptic soundtrack. She squeezed again, holding down the trigger this time, and the thunder started.

A line of slugs cut across Kerry like stitches. Then Terrance, same thing, even as he tried to raise his own rifle. Both men fell—Kerry nearly torn in half—and still Lucy fired, bullet after bullet after bullet chewing flesh and shattering bone and spurting blood, giant brass shell casings hitting the ground around her.

Finally, the gun fell silent. Eddie looked at her. Even her brothers had stopped digging for the moment and stared at her. Eddie was still sitting on the trailer's step, his posture casual, a faint smile playing about his lips and eyes.

"Guess they won't bother you any more," he said.

Diego and Jorge went back to digging.

Ken hated the idea of leaving Penny alone with that thing, that abomination. But she was right, they needed to keep going, and if she couldn't get past it—or if taking three minutes to converse with it would let her do so safely—then he guessed she'd made the right decision. He and Hal needed to hurry on. He couldn't have said why, but he knew that time was becoming an issue—that no matter how much he'd come to like Penny in the last hours, her survival wasn't as important as their task here, the sense of urgency he felt. The three minutes had come and gone and he didn't know if she was following yet, but he wasn't turning around to find out.

He practically ran now, and Hal kept pace right behind him. The cave's floor slanted more and more, and the path seemed to lead almost straight west. His assumption was that it would end more or less directly underneath the Slab. He still didn't know what waited for them down there, but one thing was certain.

It wasn't good.

As he ran, he began to wonder what Hal brought to the table. He'd always handled problems himself. He had Billy Cobb at the substation, but that was only because the Imperial County Sheriff insisted on it. If it had been up to him he'd have run the station solo, taking calls when he could. The way he did everything else in life. If you didn't depend on other people they couldn't let you down. They couldn't abandon you if they weren't there to begin with. Maybe, he thought, I should just tell Hal to go back, to stay with Penny. Keep them out of my way while I check things out.

But Penny's voice came to him as clearly as if he'd had a telephone held against his ear. "You can't do everything by yourself, Ken," she had said. She was right. He knew that. Which meant that this was just the cave—no, not the cave, but whatever was inside the cave—trying to trick him. To split them up.

And that's when he understood.

Jeff Mariotte

It had made that person from the mushrooms in order to slow Penny down. Because they were strongest when they were together. Two of them were strong, three were, they had agreed, practically godlike.

So it had already won, and they didn't even know what the fight was yet. If it took three of them to beat it—and why else had the magic spared three of them, directed their lives, brought them through the years to this one specific place and time, if not because it did—and there were only two, then they'd already lost. Going back for Penny was out of the question; they'd lose too much time, and time was definitely the other factor.

All those years, all those lives—Shannon's life, Mindy's life, and so many more— to bring them here. And they'd blown it.

He stopped and let Hal catch up. He almost didn't feel like going any farther.

"We fucked up," Ken said. "We shouldn't have let Penny stay back there."

"Yeah," Hal said. "I've been thinking the same thing."

"What are we gonna do?"

Hal reached out and touched Ken, and Ken felt the power surge through him again, recharging him. His mood elevated with his strength.

"We go on," Hal said. "We go down there and we stop it."

"We don't even know what it is," Ken protested, knowing even as he did that he was going to give in.

"Doesn't matter," Hal said. "What matters is that we try. We don't back down from the fight. We'll know it when we see it."

"You're right," Ken said. "I sure wish Penny was here, though."

"That makes two of us," Hal said. "Probably three of us. But that choice has been made, so we've got to go on without her."

He started walking down the sloping cave floor again, and Ken followed. The mushrooms weren't so thick anymore, just an occasional one here and there, as if they weren't needed down here like they were closer to the surface. The cave's floor and walls were solid stone, floor smoothed with the passage of feet over the centuries, walls, devoid of pictures or writing now, nearly as rough as if they'd been hewn from the earth with stone axes. No timbers supported the ceiling—this had the feel of a tunnel built by human hands, though Ken was sure it wasn't—but somehow the cave felt strong and secure just the same. Ken had no idea how deep they'd gone, but it felt like they were completely cut off from the rest of the world.

Finally, they reached the end.

The cave widened into a small chamber, a couple of dozen feet in diameter, almost perfectly round. The roof was lost in the darkness overhead. There were pictographs on the walls, as illegible to Ken as if they'd been Chinese or Arabic, though he suspected Penny would have been able to read them if she'd been here.

In the middle of the room stood a small, round rock structure, looking much like the opening to an Anasazi kiva. A slab had been laid on top of its low rock walls, its surface completely covered with the same kind of pictorial language that appeared on the main walls of the cave. The slab must have weighed a ton or more, a solid piece of granite, smoothed and rounded and carefully fit to cover the top of the rock construction.

From the cracks between the rocks, mushrooms grew. As Ken watched, they seethed through the cracks, tiny tendrils at first, growing heads that expanded as they reached away from the rocks. Ken put a hand out, caught Hal's arm, held him back.

"I don't like this at all," he said.

"I'm sure we're not supposed to."

They were still standing that way, flesh touching flesh, when the stone slab rocked and tipped back, sliding to the ground with a crash.

Something emerged from underneath.

Ken was predisposed to see him as the gray man, from Penny's vision. Through whatever it was that linked them, Ken could see him from Hal's perspective, and knew that to Hal, he looked like an enormous insect, vaguely cockroach-like but pale, as befitted something that never saw the sun—a huge white carapace over an insect's thorax and abdomen, six twitching legs, long antennae on stalks protruding from its small, glistening head, clicking as it came out from underneath its rock.

And now, looking at it, Ken understood. He knew that Hal did, too. Penny's impression had been correct—the thing was, more or less, a personification of evil. Not *the* personification, because evil was everywhere, in everyone, and around all the time. But a bad thing, nonetheless.

The knowledge raced through his mind like a movie, as he imagined it must have done for Penny when she'd been reading farther up the cave, earlier. He saw what must have been the same scene she did, on the shores of the ancient lake, water lapping at the very plateau on which they stood. Long, long ago, thousands of years ago, this presence had set upon the Cahuilla Indians, turning them against each other. They had lost many—the bodies scattered around, skulls stacked in morbid piles like cannonballs, transgressors writhing, impaled on massive stakes—testified to that.

But they had learned to fight back, had somehow tapped into magic of their own, and had eventually beaten the thing. Penny had described that, too—shoving the gray man into a hole and sealing it with a slab of rock.

Here, the internal movie went dark for a long time. Maybe the thing had been comatose, maybe they'd actually killed it. Impossible to tell. But eventually, there was light again, and life—as portrayed, in this movie, by water. Only this water was foul, poisoned, filled with chemicals that made it unhealthy for man and beast alike. Which made it, as it soaked into the water table and then down, and down, through the layers of rock and dirt and the very crust of the earth, perfect sustenance for the gray man. He tasted that water, and found it sweet.

And wanted more.

And began to hunger and thirst and look for a way out.

But after all those centuries of death or near-death, it needed more than just the few drops of water that made their way this far down. It needed blood. It needed death and destruction, fire and fear. These things gave it strength. So it reached out. It found what it needed, as living things will.

If it's alive, Ken thought, it can be killed. He raised his weapon and unloaded it, one shot after another booming in the enclosed space, deafening. Bullets tore through the gray man and pinged from stone walls behind him, tearing off chunks but not seeming to injure him. When the gun was empty, Ken threw it aside.

"Ken, don't," Hal said, grabbing his arm. Ken shook off the older man's grip and charged the gray man. He swung a fist at the thing's head and connected. It felt solid enough under his hand, but there was no response, no flinch, no indication that it felt any pain. Its eyes were blank, just more gray tissue in its monochromatic self. Ken hit it again, two shots to the gut. Finally—not as if it was hurt, but as if swatting an annoying insect—the gray man swung an arm at Ken that hit with the force of a falling tree, sweeping him back across the little chamber.

"You tried," Hal told him, helping him back to his feet.

"And I'm not done," Ken said. But before he could take another step toward his opponent, the tendrils of mushrooms that grew from the pit reached for Ken and Hal, snaking around their legs, up their torsos, and more of the mushrooms sprouted from the hole itself, following the gray man like ducklings after their mother. The gray man stalked the chamber, stretching and enjoying newfound freedom of mobility, and the mushrooms reached for the ceiling, filling nearly every square inch of space in the room except where the gray man paced. Shoots twined around Ken and Hal, twisting up in front of their faces, tendrils worming into their noses and mouths, cutting off air. Ken gagged on the pulpy mass of it as it filled his mouth, tried to bite but couldn't even bring his teeth together. It snaked obscenely down his throat.

Ken felt the world start to go black, feeling like the gray man must have when he'd been forced into the hole in the first place. His head swam, he felt dizzy and weak-kneed. The sad realization came to him that if the gray man got out today, he'd find a very different world—one in which the planet's population had multiplied to a barely sustainable level, a world that was on the edge of insanity to begin with, with powerful weapons and equally powerful hatreds. A world, in other words, ideally suited to the gray man's nature. He—or whatever it was he represented—would flourish in a world like this one.

And there was nothing he could do to stop it. He couldn't fill his lungs, his limbs weighed a thousand pounds each, his vision was going. At least, he thought, if I have to go now, I'm going at the side of a good man. A man who's done bad things but made himself stop, who has done everything in his power to atone.

But Hal gripped his right hand. Ken felt the other man's skin, warm against his own, and some of Hal's power and positive mental focus seeped into him.

We have to try, Hal thought.

Ken was at a loss. If Hal wanted to try something, he was game, but he sure didn't know what it might be. He couldn't speak but he thought a response back to Hal. Yeah.

Mushrooms and evil are the same in one way, Hal sent.

What's that?

They hate the light.

Penny gave Mick, or the thing that looked like him, his three minutes. And like Mick would, it used them talking. About nothing in particular, as far as she was concerned—betrayal and disappointment, mostly. Enough to make Penny believe it really was Mick, dead but not dead, in some way, because anyone else would have shut up and tried something, or at least engaged in conversation instead of monologue.

She didn't care. She spent the time looking at the second hand sweep the face of her watch. At three minutes, she said, "Time's up."

"You can't go down there, Penny," it said. "I can't let you."

"You've never been able to stop me from doing what I needed to do," Penny replied. "You think being dead's going to change that?"

"I can stop you—"

"You can't stop dick."

She started past it, and it grabbed her. But Mick-shaped or not, magically animated as it was, it was still mushroom-stuff. She took its arms and yanked, shredding them in her grip. They began to grow back and she swung an arm as hard as she could, knocking its head flying. Blinded, it crashed into the wall. Its head started to grow back, too, but by then Penny was running, pushing as fast through the mushroom jungle as she was able.

And the Mick-thing was rooted.

She didn't stop, didn't slow. Eventually the mushrooms were no longer a factor and she raced through the dark, the cave just tall enough and wide enough to let her reach something approximating a reasonable speed. She didn't seem to need the flashlight any more; she could see in the dark almost as well as if she'd had it anyway, and her vision became more and more clear as she got deeper and deeper into the cave.

By the time she reached the end of the cave, Hal and Ken were almost completely engulfed in massive mushroom stalks. She couldn't see through the thicket, but she felt the presence of the gray man within, growing stronger and more confident with each passing second, while Ken and Hal weakened. She was struck by a wave of gloom, a certainty that they'd all been too late to do any good, to keep the gray man down in his pit.

But then she noticed that Hal had begun to glow.

This wasn't the blue glow they'd all manifested back at the Slab, to protect it from the bomb. It was a yellow glow, strengthening as she watched toward pure white light. Just looking at it gave her hope.

She hacked with her hands at the mushroom trees that were, even now, beginning to writhe toward her. They wanted to trap her, to hold her back, but Penny wouldn't be trapped. She kicked and hit and forced her way through the growth, until she got close enough to the two men. A massive mushroom trunk, as big around as an oak tree, slammed into her and knocked her to her knees.

As she went down, she reached out and closed her hand around Ken's left hand. And Ken, she saw, held Hal's hand in his right.

They were together again.

She felt Hal's words ring in her head like an echo, even though he'd thought them, she knew, several minutes before.

They hate the light.

She focused on the light, basked in it, felt it bathe her like pure, cleansing water.

And where Hal was, the light grew. More intense, more brilliant…as if the sun itself had come into this forsaken place.

Even as the realization struck her, a pillar of pure sunlight blasted through the rock, through the earth, through the sky above. As if Hal were its conduit, the pillar illuminated him and then obscured him, too bright to look at, too intense to see through, but it came from above and it enveloped Hal and it shot out through his right hand, which he extended through the forest of mushroom stalks and toward the gray man. And the light cut through the mushrooms, which withered as it touched them.

The gray man tried to hide from it. Panicking, he ducked behind the slab of stone he had shoved off his own place of internment.

But the pillar of sunlight would not be denied. It glowed through the slab as surely as it shone through the earth above them, as surely as it passed through the Slab, on the surface, where even now men and women died to feed the gray man's terrible hunger.

Hal had grown too hot—Ken had to let go of him, and he and Penny backed off, their hands still clasped together. It was as if Hal channeled the sun itself into the chamber. Now he had both hands raised toward the gray man, directing the streaming sunlight through himself.

Where the light touched the gray man, he sizzled.

Where it burned him, he screamed.

Where it cleansed him, he shrank.

The magic worked through them, through Penny and Ken and Hal, and the magic was stronger than the gray man, because he lost shape, lost form, lost mass. As he did, so did the mushrooms, collapsing in on themselves, shrinking, finally vanishing altogether.

But not the gray man.

The gray man shrank and burned and popped, collapsing in a small heap on the chamber's clean stone floor. But he retained some mass, some presence, even under the incredible onslaught Hal directed at him.

Penny watched Hal and realized that he was changing, too—dissipating, as though the effort of blasting sunlight at the gray man was using him up.

That's just what was happening, she understood suddenly. Whatever Hal discharged at the gray man didn't come just from some external source, but from within him. It was Hal, in a very real way—his own essence.

Finally, the stream of light dried up, like the trickle of the Colorado River as it, dammed and diverted and hoarded, tried to make its way to the Gulf of California. As it faded, so did Hal, burning more brightly than ever for a moment, then blinking out altogether.

She stood with Ken, hands clasped tightly as if they'd never let go. She didn't know what to say, didn't know if words could begin to describe how she felt about what had happened here. Awe, she thought, overused but apt nonetheless. She had witnessed something glorious, maybe miraculous, as selfless an act of sacrifice as she'd ever imagined.

But the price had been high. Hal was gone, used up. With the light gone, the room had been plunged back into darkness, only the light mounted onto Ken's gun illuminating the cavern's interior. But he played the light over the floor where Hal had been, where now there was only a faint scorch mark.

Finally, Ken broke the silence. "He's just...gone," he said. Sorrow was evident in his trembling voice.

"Yeah," Penny agreed. "Whatever it was he did there, it took him with it."

"It wasn't just him," Ken replied. "It was all three of us. He started before you got here, but he couldn't really get it going until you joined us. Then the power flowed through the three of us and he was able to...I don't know, to pull down the sun's own power, or whatever that was. If you hadn't made it, Hal and I'd both be dead by now, I expect." He spat onto the cave floor.

"Maybe," she said.

"Anyway, it's gone now."

"What is?"

"The magic," Ken clarified. "I'm pretty sure. I can't feel it any more. Do you?"

She reached out and touched his hand. Warm flesh. A tingle, but not an electric shock. Something different. Maybe more real.

Human contact.

"You're right," she said. "There's nothing there. Well," she amended with a smile. "Not 'nothing.'"

"Yeah," he said. "Just not the kind of magic we're used to."

As Penny's eyes began to re-acclimate to the darkness, she remembered the gray man, or what little was left of him. He wasn't much more than two feet long, now, curled on the floor, still smoldering at the edges. "What about that?" she asked. "Do we just leave it there?"

Ken shrugged. "Maybe back in the hole?"

Penny felt a chill run down her spine. "You want to touch it?" she asked him.

"Don't reckon it's going to make much difference now," he said. "Not like we've never touched evil in our lives." He went over to the ugly gray mass, picked it up with one hand, and tossed it without ceremony back into the hole it had come from. Then he beamed his light at the slab of rock that had covered the hole.

"That was over it," he said. "That rock."

"I've seen it before. It must weigh a ton," Penny said. "No way we'll be able to move it."

Ken shrugged again. "Won't know until we try, will we?" he asked.

Penny supposed he was right. She came around to the back of the pit, where the massive piece of rock leaned against the hole's low wall, like a lid from a well. She squatted—lift with your knees, she remembered, not your back—and got a grip on the slab's right side. Ken did the same on her left. But before they started straining to lift it, he touched her cheek. The gesture was somehow innocent and intimate at the same time, just a brush as if to move a stray hair. But there was a buzz just the same; she felt it to her toes.

And when they lifted the rock, it moved in their hands as easily as if it had been hollow, or made of wood instead of stone. They positioned it carefully over the top of the pit and let it rest there.

"Guess maybe it wasn't a hundred percent gone after all," Ken observed. "Maybe it never is. Or maybe we've been looking at it all wrong, thinking it comes from outside us. Maybe it's been in us all along."

"You could be right," Penny said. "Good thing, either way, or we'd never have lifted that slab. But…if it was over him in the first place, then did we really do any good by putting it back?"

Ken rubbed at the stubble that had grown up over his chin and cheeks these last couple of days. "I don't know what this place is," he said. "I don't know if it's real, or some kind of symbolic construct, or maybe all in our own fevered brains. I know what we've agreed the gray man represents—Hal saw him as a kind of bloodless white cockroach, by the way—and if he is what we think he is, then there's no getting rid of him altogether anyway. Best we can do is put him back in his hole and hope it's a good long while before he gathers the strength to make another try."

"Well, it's done, then," Penny said. "And I miss Hal like crazy already. I bet Virginia does too. Can we get the hell out of this place?"

"Sure," Ken replied. "I'm kind of anxious to see the sun again myself."

At the Slab, the gunfight petered out, almost as if those shooting had come to a gradual realization of their own actions. People put down their weapons and began to look about, instead, for first aid supplies, for bandages and disinfectants and tape. Fires still burned all around the Slab, but sirens were audible now in the distance, coming closer. Some began to believe that help was on the way, that they'd get through this night.

But across the Slab, with bizarre suddenness, others collapsed and died on the spot. Billy Cobb, Carter Haynes, Virginia Shipp, Nick Postak, Jorge and Diego Alvarez, Heather and Royal Justice, Gray Boonton, Darren Cook, Mikey Zee, Lettie Bosworth, almost a dozen more. Away from the Slab, the same thing happened to others, including one Colonel Franklin Wardlaw, USMC, who had left his office in Yuma and gone looking for a shovel. The life blew out of them with no warning and no apparent reason. Lucy Alvarez and Eddie Trujillo watched Lucy's brothers stop digging and look up briefly, startled expressions flitting across their faces, and then their muscles went slack and they slumped onto the blood-soaked earth they'd been digging in.

Years later, living in Los Angeles, Lucia Alvarez wrote an account of the whole experience in a journal, which she shared with no one, and she described the moment. "It was almost like they had been inhabited by something—that whatever was making them dig was a presence inside them that had forced out everything that I knew, everything that made them my brothers. And then, it went away, suddenly and completely. When it did, there was nothing left, no life essence, and while Diego and Jorge had both been dead for some time, their bodies had been compelled to go on until that moment.

"It wasn't until later that day that I learned from my mother that my father had run from the house at about the same time my brothers began to dig—that he had jumped into a truck and sped away. Still later, we learned that he had been driving south on the 111. Probably heading for the Slab, I thought, and still believe. Probably to join in the digging. But he died behind the wheel, and the truck slammed into an oncoming eighteen-wheeler on the highway. Fortunately, he was gone well before the impact.

"That was the last day we stayed in the Imperial Valley, me and my mother and grandfather Oscar. The last day we've seen it. Mama died, this last summer, which is when I decided I really needed to write this all down. She never wanted to go back, and neither do I. I haven't missed it for a moment."

Ken led the way with his gun-mounted light, through the cave that was now empty of mushrooms—a fact which added to its overall unnatural quality, since there was no other life, no spiders or insects or worms, no coyote scat or bat guano. It was a Hollywood version of a desert cave, an unreal place. He had to wonder if it would even be here tomorrow, or had been here a week ago, before Penny had arrived and needed to find it.

He was torn by a dozen conflicting emotions, to the point that he couldn't even get his own internal bearings. What had they really done, if anything? How did you define Hal—accessory to mass murder, or savior of the world? Both? And how much did the gray man contribute to those murders, if anything? How responsible was he for the madness that had overtaken the Slab during the night, and how much of that was just simple human nature?

"Trouble with seeing what we've seen," he said as they neared the cave's mouth, "is that we didn't really get any questions answered. But before, we didn't even know the questions were there. Now they're just about all we've got."

"I know what you mean," Penny said. "My mind is reeling with them."

"Same here."

Casually, she wrapped her fingers around his. No surge of power, but it felt fine just the same. "But we have plenty of time to puzzle them out, right?"

"Here's hoping," Ken replied.

"Listen, Ken, I…I'm gonna need someplace to stay for a little while. At least until I figure out what I'm going to do now, where I'm going, you know? Think there's any room at your place? I'm a quiet sleeper and I don't take up much space."

The suggestion took Ken by surprise, but it wasn't an unpleasant prospect. And he hadn't had another soul in the house for longer than he could even remember—the price of being handy was that you didn't need plumbers and electricians coming around when things went wrong. "I reckon that'd be okay," he said, after what he hoped wasn't too much hesitation. "It's not much but it's cheaper than the Motel 6."

As they came out of the cave, the desert seemed to spring to new life around them. The sun crested the hills to the east, its slanting rays throwing coronas of light around the tops of the fuzzy chollas, limning the branches of mesquite trees against shaded ground, painting the slopes across the valley with warm yellow light. With it came an explosion of sound and motion; the zigzag flight of bats angling toward shelter, the joyful swoop and noisy chirp of wren and starling and shrike, the gentle susurrus of a breeze that rattled creosote bush and smoke tree and the broad, daggered leaves of agave.

The desert awoke like this every morning, Ken knew, but he didn't. He felt like a bear emerging groggily from his den after a long hibernation, blinking against the forgotten brightness of day. Something had changed during his absence from this earth; everything had changed. The magic was gone—most likely, he believed, for good. But neither that, nor Hal's death—or transformation, if that's what it was—left the hole in his heart that he found himself expecting they might have. Instead, when he reached around inside himself he came away with a new sense of something very right, an unfamiliar sensation of comfortable fullness there. He glanced at Penny, a triangle of sunlight on her cheek bisected by a strand of brown hair, a curious half-smile playing about her lips as if she were still deciding whether she liked a flavor she'd never tried before. Then she caught him looking and the smile blossomed until her face rivaled the morning sun for sheer radiance.

Her hand felt good in his, her strong fingers holding on as if he were something precious that might blow away in a strong wind. He had no idea where they went from here. He didn't even have a name for the alien sensations he felt. He was half afraid that if he searched for one, the feelings would go away, back into whatever deep internal cavern from which they'd been lured. It wasn't magic, though, he knew that. The one word that came to mind didn't seem quite right, but he thought he'd take it anyway.

The word was peace.

It would do for a start.

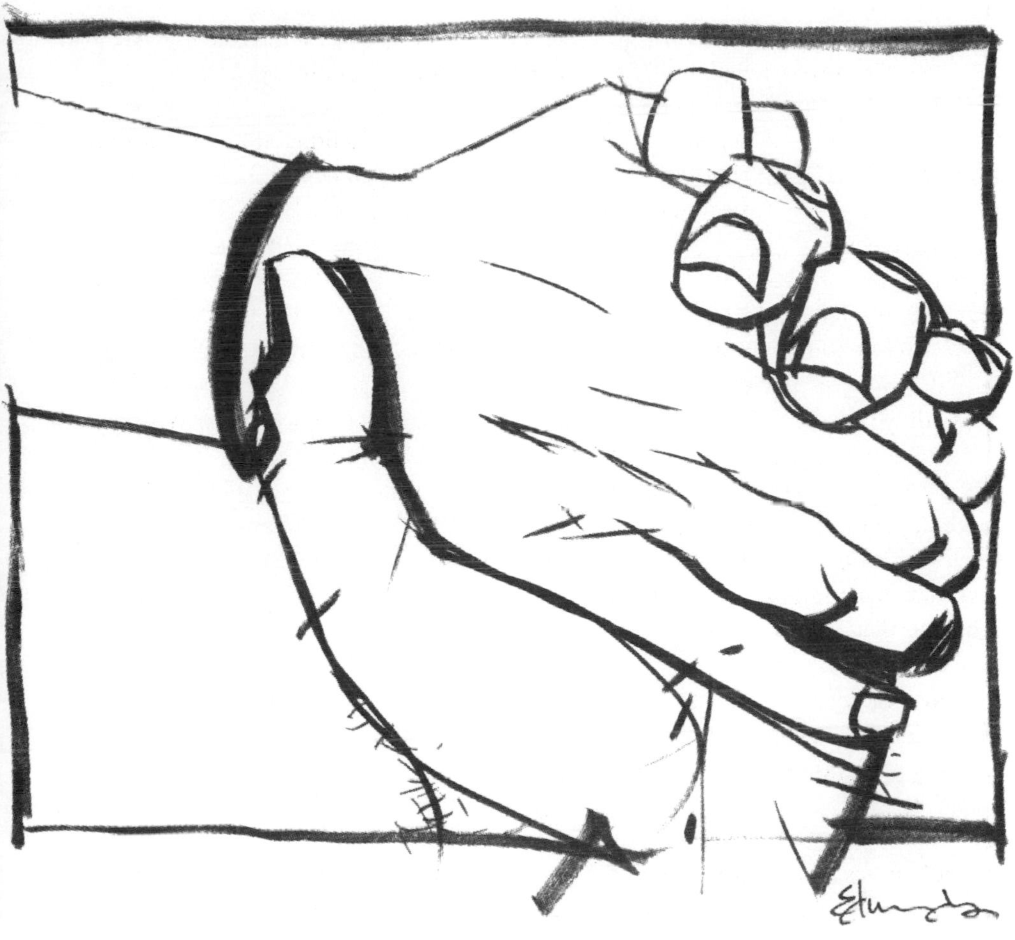

The End

Author's Note

This is, obviously, a work of fiction, and I've used my auctorial license to rearrange geography as needed to suit my story.

That said, the reader should know that the basic settings used here are very real. The Salton Sea is where I put it, with most of those communities—except Salton Estates, which more accurately resembles a place called Salton City, on the other side of the Salton—are where I put them. Moreover, the amazing history of the Salton Sea, the accidental ocean, two hundred and some feet below sea level, is as I've presented it here—except, since this is a novel and not a work of history, there's really a lot more to it than I have detailed.

The Slab is real, too, and basically where I placed it, between the Chocolate Mountains and the Salton. But it's really called Slab City, and, like life itself, is wilder and both more bizarre and more vital than could possibly be represented in a single novel. People like Linda, the Slab City hostess, and Leonard Knight, folk artist and the driving force behind Salvation Mountain, are larger than life themselves, and would have overwhelmed this story if I'd tried to include them. Slab City can be visited online at www.slabcity.org, through photos by the author at www.jeffmariotte.com/slab.htm, or better yet, the reader can get in a car and go see it in person. It's not an experience soon to be forgotten.

Long time desert rat Jeff Mariotte is kept too busy by other obligations—editing comics and books, owning (with Maryelizabeth and Terry) specialty bookstore Mysterious Galaxy, writing constantly, including many books set in the universe of *Buffy the Vampire Slayer* and *Angel*, and comic books that include the Stoker and International Horror Guild Award-nominated series *Desperadoes*, being a husband and father—to spend nearly as much time out there as he'd like. But his home in San Diego isn't too far away from desert, and it's full of books and comics and music and toys and animals and laughter, so he likes it. To find out more, visit www.jeffmariotte.com.

IDW™

www.idwpublishing.com

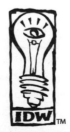